CLOUD ORCHID PUBLISHING

CLOUD ORCHID PUBLISHING

Check out our entire Catalog of Titles

http://www.CloudOrchidPublishing.com

Also available on Amazon

SUCCUMB TO DARKNESS
1st Edition
by
Cloud Orchid Publishing
http://www.CloudOrchidPublishing.com

Novel by
Lauren A. R. Masterson

Cover Design by R. Taylor

Chapter One

Evanangela hid her face in her hands as her wings disintegrated. The feathers turned from their glorious silver splendor to grey, then to black, then to ash; the flames consuming them as she fell. Her eyes changed from colorless, to cobalt, then to cherry. Her teeth grew and sharpened until they were serrated and hung low like ivory thorns.

The fallen angel clutched her chest as her inner light went out and was replaced with cold darkness. She screamed as her heart blackened and the clear holy blood darkened. Red tears flowed down her cheeks, leaving her veins empty. When her virgin feet touched the Earth, she slumped into a heap. Her leg muscles were weak, as she was used to flying, never having walked. The solid ground was foreign compared to the shifting clouds and winds she was used to frolicking through. Her bare hands skimmed the cool grass. She flinched at the sensation, her mind racing to process all the new feelings that flooded her body.

Evanangela turned and saw the setting sun. "My last sunset. How I wish I could fly once more and burn in it."

She watched in quiet remorse as the sun disappeared below the treetops. A breeze rustled her tunic gown. She shivered. The warm feathery weight of her wings had always insulated her against the wind. Now, she felt naked, her body light and exposed. Evanangela reached back and brushed her empty shoulder blades. They were solid and smooth.

My beautiful wings! I know it to be true that Dieu[1] is righteous and just, but this is simply too much!

She sank to her knees, bowing her head as she cried, but no tears came. Her eyes burned from the lack of release and her face was flushed. Evanangela sat back on her heels. The sky was dark now, and she could see the bare plains as she never had from above. Silver mists in the shape of humans floated about through the grass. Had Evanangela still been an angel, she would have ushered these lost souls to peace. But her new dead heart could not hear their pleas.

---

1 God

1

"Mon Seigneur Dieu,[2] why have you forsaken these souls? Are they damned as I have been?" She watched the mists writhe and shift until she was startled by the sound of footsteps.

A shiver ran down her spine. The scent of living flesh was near and her veins contracted with desire. Evanangela clutched the long grass, willing herself to stay and erase the thoughts of killing. Her heart burned to release tears, but her eyes could find none. The sticky residue of her bloody tears was drying in streaks down her cheeks; making her look like a fearsome banshee or forest demon. The human's footsteps thundered as he approached. Evanangela cringed, her skull ached from the noise.

The fool! He is tramping so loud, all of France must be able to hear him blundering through these fields!

Reason slowly dripped away as her breathing became shallow. His scent was on the wind, faint, but it rolled over her tongue, igniting her instinct to hunt. She traced the sound, her body tense, ready to strike once the traveler was in range. The hunger took over, driving her muscles to spring. Evanangela ran, without stealth or grace, and tackled the lost traveler. Her crimson eyes were bright with the madness of the feed as she threw her jaws open, exposing the glinting fangs.

"Oh, Seigneur Dieu, sauvez-moi!"[3] He covered his eyes, trembling and screaming.

Evanangela froze. The fire in her eyes extinguished and she released her grip. "Seigneur." She whispered.

The man took advantage of her confusion and pushed Evanangela away. She sat there, staring at nothing while the traveler ran back down the dirt path, taking his tantalizing scent with him. The desire for blood escaped to the back of her mind, for now.

"A demon! Dieu, save us from the demon!" The traveler's cries were becoming faint as he reached a farmer's fence line.

What am I to do? To live this half-life I must kill, to kill is to die, and to die is never to return to whom I once was.

Evanangela grabbed her hair, shaking her head and prostrating herself on the grass, screaming. "Why must it be this way?"

---

2 My Lord God
3 Oh Lord God, save me!

"...le bête été la bas!"[4] It was the traveler again; his footsteps were becoming louder as he approached.

His scent wafted toward Evanangela on the cool night breeze. She swallowed; her mouth dry as she tasted the air. The thirst for blood cleared her mind of all else. She crouched in the tall grass and listened. Her skin bristled with anticipation. The frantic footfalls of the traveler were drawing near again, but there was another lighter pair as well. Evanangela strained her ears.

"Oui, je sais. J'ai entendu la bête hurler de l'église."[5]

This voice was new. Evanangela held her breath. A familiar thought struck her, flooding her with shame.

A church? No, not a priest! He cannot see me this way!

"Vite! Avant de partir!"[6]

The traveler's voice was closer now, as was the priest. Evanangela could hear the swish of his robes in the grass.

Damn him!

She could not allow a priest to see her this way, scuffling about like a beast on the hunt. What would Seigneur think? Evanangela scanned her surroundings, open fields; nowhere to hide and forever to run. The traveler and the priest came into view. She poised to flee, but something crossed her path, flitting before her eyes. It slowed and she recognized it to be a vampiress. Her luminous skin was far too pale and well-kept for a villager. The gleam in her eyes was otherworldly. The motion of her elegant limbs far too quick and precise for a mere mortal.

The vampiress crouched before Evanangela in the grass and cocked her head to one side, her platinum blonde hair sliding from behind her ear, like a spray of fallen stars. "Salut."[7]

Evanangela wrinkled her nose. Beneath the expensive perfume of a noblewoman was the stench of death. It was true what Michael had said about these foul cursed creatures – they roamed in packs like wild dogs. Always tied to one another; find one, and you'll find a whole nest

---

4 The beast is over there!
5 Yes, I know. I heard the beast scream from the church.
6 Hurry! Before it leaves!
7 Hello.

of them nearby; vermin. Her dead heart clenched as another wave of shame overtook her, making her gasp.

Why Michael? Why Dieu? Why would you damn me to be this twisted thing? To become what you despise?

"What is a cursed thing like you doing here where there are priests about?" Her acid tongue flicked the insult at the vampiress to ease the pain of her inner turmoil.

"Can you hear yourself?" The vampiress laughed. She twisted a lock of Evanangela's hair between her fingers, but Evanangela flinched away. "What a smug little mortal you must have been."

"At least I know my place!" Evanangela hissed. "And soon, that priest will send us both to deliverance."

The vampiress laughed, tossing her hair. She stood up and brushed the grass from her skirts. "How very silly! You think a mortal priest can harm me? Still, you are right. It would be unwise to stay here."

Evanangela twitched as the priest's muttering became louder. He was chanting a psalm. What had once brought Evanangela comfort now burned her ears, making them ring.

"I came to see what all the screaming was about, and wanted to see if there would be some left for me." She raked her eyes over Evanangela. "And yet, you have no stains. Have you not fed?"

The humming was growing louder and the psalm was making Evanangela's head ache. The vampiress cringed at the sound, her body swaying as if she could not bear to stand still.

Evanangela plucked at the grass, her eyes downcast. Her senses warred as the human scent wafted in the air, growing stronger by the minute. "I was the one screaming."

The vampiress raised an eyebrow, then flinched. Evanangela could hear the loud swishing as the priest ran through the grass with the traveler close behind. She grabbed Evanangela's hand. Her grip was firm and her skin was cold, sending shivers down her spine.

"Time to go!"

Evanangela looked over her shoulder, the scenery blurring as they ran faster than any human. The priest pulled a gold crucifix from his robes. It glinted in the moonlight. She shuddered, the sight of the

4

cross sent a wave of animalistic terror and rage through her mind. The vampiress jerked to a stop. Evanangela faltered and caught herself by grabbing hold of her shoulder. She saw a strange tattoo behind the vampiress' ear; a sword with briars twined round the blade.

A large black and purple carriage stood before them. Enormous black war horses stamped the ground as they stood at attention. Great purple plumes adorned their black bridles. A footman jumped down from the back of the carriage and opened the door, holding out his hand. The vampiress took it, and turned to Evanangela.

"Well, aren't you coming?"

She gaped at the carriage, shaking her head. "What is all this? Where are we?"

The vampiress shrugged and let go of the footman's hand. "Does it matter? You clearly do not have a place to call home. Why else would a newly born be flailing about screaming in a field?" She tapped her chin. "It is a mystery, why your sire would leave you in such an odd place."

"A sire?" Evanangela darted her eyes about. She could no longer hear the priest, but the mortal scent of the footman danced about her nostrils. She licked her fangs. Their serrated edges snapped her back and she covered her mouth with her hand.

"Get in!" The vampiress rolled her eyes and snatched up Evanangela's hand, shoving her at the footman. "Verseau is expecting me to bring news of the Mors, and instead I have found a new toy for him."

Evanangela squeaked as she was bundled into the carriage and the vampiress got in beside her. The footman shut the door and the heavy clop of the horses' hooves punctuated the rattle of the carriage as they drove over the dirt road, pitted by dried mud.

"What are you *wearing?*" The vampiress plucked the sleeve of Evanangela's robe. It had been singed from the fall.

"It is all I have." Evanangela hugged herself. She noticed the smell of burnt fabric and feathers. Her eyes widened and she looked away out the window, hoping the vampiress would not suspect what she truly was.

"Were you tossed into a fire? Is that what happened to you?" The vampiress hissed and shook her head. "Those wretched peasants! They

5

always make a holiday out of finding a vampire whenever they can. I suppose they dressed you in those ridiculous rags as part of their game. No matter, we'll get you properly dressed."

The groan of iron gates opening startled Evanangela. She straightened up and gasped when she saw the looming château[8] from out the window. A long stretch of fine cobble road melted into a flat stone boulevard. Dark trees with luminous flowers flanked the road, leading the eye to the yawning doorway of ancient oak, varnished to perfection.

"Finally!" Àmichemin snapped as the carriage door flew open and she took the footman's hand.

Evanangela followed her. The footman bowed his head as her unshod feet touched the cold stone. She shivered. Her mind reeled at all the new sensations bombarding her – the hardness of the stone, the scent of the night flowers mingling with that of mortal blood. Her thoughts were shattered when the vampiress pushed Evanangela toward the doors.

"Now, just pretend you know what you're doing, or else I'll be endlessly badgered for bringing you here."

"Where exactly is here?" Evanangela studied the crest carved in the heavy doors, a stag and briars.

"Ç'est Le Château d'Astucieux[9] and it has been the home of the Nacre[10] Court for many generations." The vampiress gave a dramatic sweep with her hand.

Evanangela gasped. "Do you mean to tell me that a vampire lord lives here?"

"Yes, and a grand vampire lord he is." The vampiress knocked on the doors. "Our Seigneur rules this court and the neighboring lands. You will be meeting him very soon."

Evanangela balked at that. She was being led straight into a vampire nest. She looked over her shoulder down the avenue again. It was impossible to see the past the tree line in the dead of night. But a château meant there had to be a nearby village. What a misfortune to have a vampire for their lord!

---

8 castle
9 This is the Castle of Clever
10 Mother of Pearl

"And the villagers *approve* of a vampire lord?"

Àmichemin laughed a deep throaty laugh. "Oh you *are* funny! Goodness no! Those idiot pests haven't the faintest idea." Her demeanor grew stony and her gaze cut through Evanangela. "And it shall always stay that way. Lest they come to kill us."

The doors swung open without a breath of noise, revealing a cavernous hall. Inside was lit by indigo candles mounted on the walls with cobalt flames licking their blackened wicks. Centuries of cleaning had polished the stone walls so they were unnaturally bright and smooth.

An attendant bowed near one of the doors. "Mademoiselle Àmichemin, et Mademoiselle-?"[11]

"Evanangela." She muttered, not taking her eyes off the drapery that hung from the walls. Long tapestries depicting moonlit picnics and hunting wildlife in the forest were hung from the vaulted ceiling and nearly touched the stone floor.

The scent of his living flesh ignited the animalistic fire in her once again. Evanangela turned her gaze on the attendant. Her muscles coiled as she took a sharp inhale. Àmichemin squeezed her hand hard enough to make the bones bend. Evanangela winced, her thoughts returning from the haze. Àmichemin released her grip.

"We do *not* hunt the attendants." The playful lilt of her voice was replaced with a low growl.

Evanangela nodded, darting her eyes to the floor. "I'm sorry."

He nodded. "Je m'excuse, Mademoiselle Evanangela, les autres sont dans le salon."[12] The attendant closed the heavy doors. Music from a harpsicord wafted into the hallway.

"Merci, garçon."[13] Àmichemin responded as she led Evanangela further into the château.

Her head was on a swivel as they walked. There were portraits of what must have been the original owners of the château and their families. The people in the paintings became paler further down the hall. Soft rosy faces became replaced with severe alabaster. Tiny points between their lips revealed they were not human.

11 Miss Halfway, and Miss-?
12 My apologies, Miss Evanangela, the others are in the salon."
13 Thank you, server.

"Lovely, aren't they? Almost as old as the château itself." Àmichemin gestured to one of the portraits.

She nodded as she studied a tapestry depicting a woman riding a black stag surrounded by red roses and briars. All the beauty of the château at once seemed ghoulish. The unnerving portraits were a foul reminder of what human greed could lead to. She glared at Àmichemin. "But have you no shame, living in such splendor as a damned creature? Lords are meant to be anointed by Dieu. *You* are an affront to Dieu!"

Àmichemin whirled about and grabbed Evanangela by the shoulders. Her nails dug into Evanangela's skin and the air in the hall at once seemed cold as a winter's morn. "Do not speak to me as if you were a sharp-tongued nun! I *saved* you from those beastly villagers. *You* are a damned creature, as we all are. All of France is ruled by us. Do not forget your place. Lest I remind you by tossing you out at sunrise and allow your twisted prayers to fall on deaf ears as you burn!"

"Mademoiselle Àmichemin, you had us worried!"

Evanangela froze as a figure approached from the end of the hall. Àmichemin released Evanangela and turned to face the man; she gave a shallow curtsy. He was handsome and well-dressed, his red jacket showcased polished gold buttons. His eyes drew Evanangela in, his hawk-like gaze snaring her like prey. A smile crept across his face, revealing blood-tinged fangs.

Something stirred within her as she beheld his beautiful visage. Though she was staring at the leader in a den of the damned, her dead heart clenched and her hands shook. She found herself frozen to the spot and all at once she felt the foolish desire for him to touch her. Evanangela clenched her hands at her sides and swallowed as she fought not to grin like a fool.

"Bonjour Mademoiselle, qui êtes-vous?"[14] His yellow-green eyes flitted to Evanangela's mouth.

Power emanated from him and his presence was overwhelming up close. She bowed her head, hoping he would not see the nervous trembling in her limbs. "My name is Evanangela."

"Enchanté."[15]

---

14 Hello Miss, who are you?
15 Lovely to meet you.

8

He bent his head to kiss her hand, and in doing so grazed her skin with his fangs. His scent wafted up to her. It was faint, but had a rich musk that had her licking the roof of her mouth. The blood had made him temporarily alive once more; the most devious trick of vampires.

"Mademoiselle Evanangela, I am Seigneur Verseau."[16]

Her veins were cramping and she felt dizzy, but she managed a smile and a rough bobbed curtsy. "Merci, Seigneur Verseau."

"What news from the Mors, Àmichemin?"

She shrugged and flipped her hair over her shoulder. "Dreadful news. The plague has already reached the Low Country. The plan to bring in outside mortals would require far further travel; ships possibly."

Verseau scoffed. "That won't do."

Àmichemin pulled a rolled parchment from her dress pocket. It was bore the black and gold wax seal of the court she had visited. She slapped it into Verseau's hand. "Here is the latest report, though it won't tell you much different."

He sighed and handed it back to Àmichemin. "Hold onto this for me, won't you? We can discuss this later." He turned his gaze to Evanangela and smiled wide, flashing his fangs as he spoke.

"Please tell me, Àmichemin, will this ebony star be gracing us with her ashen company for long?"

Àmichemin relaxed. "That is actually what I need to discuss with you. I found her a little too near to the churchyard." Verseau winced, but Àmichemin continued. "She was just born when I found her. And the peasants seem to have burned her."

Verseau tutted his tongue. "That won't do. And she stinks of a pyre. Get her properly dressed."

Voices echoed from down the hall; giggling and boisterous chatter. Evanangela could see figures milling about and talking to one another. They too wore fashionable clothing and hairstyles. Their jewels sparkled in the candlelight and their hair was piled high in complex braids or ringlets of curls. Only Àmichemin wore her hair down and it on its own was a sight to behold.

---

16 Lord Aquarius

Evanangela touched her short auburn locks. They had been permanently shorn before her fall. Adding to the great punishment for her deep vanity. Her hands flew back down to her sides as shame flooded her once more and her tears burned, begging for release. She pushed back the pain.

I must not cry! I must bear it. This is my penance.

He nodded and placed his hand on Evanangela's cheek, startling her from her thoughts. His palm was soft, but his nails tickled her skin as he petted her. "May I?"

"I beg your pardon?" Her nerves made her heart flutter, causing her to gasp as it clenched like a hard knot. Her veins contracted, reminding her that they were empty.

Verseau hooked his finger under her top lip and forced her jaw open, revealing her fangs. Evanangela froze, unsure of whether to feel insulted or flattered.

He frowned, let go of her mouth, and looked up at Àmichemin. "She hasn't a healthy gleam to her teeth."

Àmichemin put her hand on Evanangela's shoulder and traced a finger down the side of Evanangela's face. "When I found her, she seemed apprehensive."

"I understand. A churchyard is not the most appetizing place to hunt." Verseau nodded. He looked back down at Evanangela; his expression a mix of amusement and curiosity.

She fidgeted with the cool bloodless sapphire blush of a vampire vixen. "I-I just wasn't given the chance."

"What a lovely little creature." He whispered and patted Evanangela's hand. The warm weight of his hand should have disgusted her, but it was instead an odd comfort. "Ma chérie, allow me to arrange a private feeding for you so you need not feel uncomfortable." His eyes gleamed as he allowed her hand to slip from his grasp.

Evanangela squeezed her hands to stop their shaking. "That is very generous of you, Seigneur, however, I would not want such an important entity as yourself to waste your time having to look after me."

He put his arm around her waist. "Nonsense! I would enjoy dining with you. Jacques!"

Another attendant appeared by his side, startling Evanangela. He wore the same silver grey as the door attendant with the same crest pinned to his lapel; however, his pin was gold instead of iron.

Verseau nodded. "Jacques, arrange a feed for Mademoiselle Evanangela in the study."

He bowed, "Oui, Seigneur," and then disappeared back down the hall.

"Excuse-moi, s'il vous plaît[17], Mademoiselle Àmichemin." He kissed her hand, lingering as he scraped his fangs.

His arm snaked behind Evanangela's shoulders and drew her into his side. "I shall attend to our guest. I apologize for keeping you. Indulge yourself. La Valse Noire[18] is underway. There should be plenty left for you."

Àmichemin withdrew her hand with a smirk on her face. "Merci, Verseau, it has been a pleasure speaking with you as always. May I have a moment with Evanangela before I depart?"

Verseau released Evanangela, sidestepped, and gave a shallow bow. Àmichemin took Evanangela's hand and led her out of earshot. "I'm impressed! I have never seen him act this way." Àmichemin looked to ensure Verseau was out of sight and too far to hear. "He usually dislikes those recently turned. It seems he has taken notice of you."

Evanangela raised her eyebrows. She looked down the hall, then back at Àmichemin. "Are you saying that Seigneur Verseau was flirting with me?"

She laughed. "I daresay he is! I must go now before I miss the feed. Now, enough with this nun nonsense. Act like the vampire you are and you shall be in safe hands. He is le Seigneur. *He* holds your very life in his hands. Be grateful." Àmichemin kissed Evanangela on both cheeks, then ran into the ballroom; her heels clicking on the marble floor.

---

17 Excuse me, please
18 The Black Waltz

Chapter Two

Evanangela walked back into the main hall and saw Verseau waiting. She returned to his side. Without Àmichemin, his presence felt magnified, powerful and thrilling. Her words whispered through her mind. *Il est le Seigneur.[1] He holds your very life in his hands. Be grateful.* Her desire to burn in the sunrise only an hour before felt hollow and foolish. She was meant to serve her penance, and to do that she must live, and to live meant she must ingratiate herself to a vampire and his court.

At least he is handsome!

She stuffed down the lusty thought and approached Verseau, doing her best to copy the curtsy Àmichemin had done at the doorway.

He offered the crook of his arm. "So, how is it that you met Mademoiselle Àmichemin so shortly after being born?"

"On particularly *flighty* terms." She swallowed hard as her starved veins clenched. The scent of human flesh all around taunted her. She took his arm.

"I see." Verseau had a glint in his eyes, his nostrils flared for a moment and then relaxed. He led her away from the music to the study.

Oh, but you do not see.

He opened the door, revealing a middle-aged man reading a book in one of the high-backed indigo chairs. A fire was crackling merrily in the grate, offering a bit of warmth to the otherwise cold room. The heady scent of his flesh smacked Evanangela full in the face. At once, her muscles coiled and her skin bristled. The pain in Evanangela's chest was unbearable as her empty veins urged her forward. She clutched her chest to steady herself.

Verseau slipped his arm across her lower back. "I understand, ma chérie, the first feed is the most difficult." He whispered. "You must learn that a mortal is no different than the boar at banquet."

_____
1 He is the Lord.

13

Her eyes darted from the man to Verseau. Evanangela had never sat at a banquet, never feasted on flesh. Angels never had want of food or drink. The new sensations and desires overwhelmed her, warring with her previous nature. This innocent mortal sat blithely in his chair, licking his thumb to turn the page of his book. Like a deer serenely drinking from a stream, unaware of the hunter waiting in the brush.

"Go on, I will be here." He gave her a small push.

Evanangela nodded and let her eyes rest on the man again. His skin seemed to glow, his black hair had a healthy sheen, and his eyes were fixated on his book. Her breathing quickened as she neared her prey. She should have allowed herself to be destroyed by the priest in the churchyard, rather than to indulge bestial instincts and live as a damned creature. And yet, she had been brought here to this magnificent place, and her body was screaming at her to live.

The man turned and lowered his book. "Is someone-?"

She lunged, knocking him from the chair down to the floor. The book flung across the room and landed open with the pages curled and bent. It was so simple to allow her body to take over. Her mind screamed as she committed the atrocity, balking at the mortal sin. And yet, her body did not falter, did not stop.

"Lovely." Verseau murmured.

The man's eyes bulged as his scream was snuffed out. She sunk her fangs into his neck before his frightened stare could fill her heart with remorse. Warm blood exploded into her mouth, sliding over her dry tongue. It was ecstasy. She sucked and laid open his quivering vein. Blood dripped down her mouth and chin, staining her teeth scarlet. Her eyes glazed over as she became intoxicated. The blood flowed over his dying skin and pooled onto the floor. She lapped it like a cat, hungry for every drop. Her hazy mind cleared and she stared at the scene on her hands and knees. She was covered in blood and the film of death was fast spinning over the man's eyes.

I have taken a life! I have destroyed an innocent human life! After eons of giving guidance and love to these mortals, I have betrayed my purpose!

Her hands shook and blood tears slipped down her cheeks, quenching the burn to cry at last. She took a long shuddering breath.

My former purpose. Her mind hissed. *I am a vampire now. There is no turning back.*

The cold horror ebbed away, leaving her body feeling as if it were baptized by ice and blood. Her grace had been washed away. Now her soul was just as black as the other vampires of the court. Something brushed her shoulder and she became aware that Verseau was kneeling at her side.

"Well done! Impressive that you were able to knock him over." He inspected the body and smiled at Evanangela.

She suppressed the growl that was rising in her throat. Her instincts pushed her to guard the kill, but something about Verseau made her bow her head and acquiesce. Once again, she remembered Àmichemin's instructions. "Merci, Seigneur Verseau. It was you who gave me the strength."

Verseau crouched down over the dying man. Again, Evanangela fought the urge to drive him away.

He inclined his head toward the man, his eyes on her. "May I?"

Evanangela moved back from the body and watched with a wary eye as he sucked on the open wound. His clothes were not stained as hers were, as he was careful and did not allow the blood to run down his chin as she had; but Verseau's lips were bright with blood. He licked them clean.

"You are able to share." He wiped his mouth with a handkerchief from his pocket. "You shall do fine living here among us. It is rude to brood over one's feed." The glint returned to Verseau's eye. "You have a stain. May I remove it for you?"

She nodded. "If you insist."

Verseau leaned into her, the body still on the floor. The air between them felt charged as if before a summer storm. He placed his hand behind her head and kissed her stained lips. Something jolted within her as their lips met. The closest she could relate to the sensation was when she would feel the static in the clouds that would build and snap from lightning. Her body had been warmed by the blood, but now she felt a deeper heat coursing through her veins. Verseau pulled away and held her gaze. It forced her to stare at him as his hand was still entangled in her glossy hair.

"I have never met a new shade that has tempted me so." The quick rise and fall of his chest revealed his excitement. "You truly are extraordinary. I understand why Àmichemin brought you here." He untangled his hand.

Evanangela tilted her head and looked up at him from under her lashes. "You are much too kind with your words."

He shook his head. "You don't understand, when a vampire is turned, they are beasts at first. Mindless creatures that rampage and kill until at last, the sense seeps back into their mind. But that is followed by the snap. They realize the horror of what they have done and either throw themselves at the danger of the sun or lofty mortals because they cannot live with what they have done, or they lose their humanity completely and kill without remorse or care. It takes many years, sometimes decades to mold a new vampire into a being suitable for court. And yet, you were turned, burned, and retain such dignity and grace. Like that of the ancient ones."

Verseau's voice trailed off and he pulled her by the hair with both hands. She was startled, but as he kissed her, she wound her arms around his neck and ran her fingers against the grain of his black hair. The curls were silky as she combed her fingers through them. His soft lips made her hunger for more. They drew apart again, their eyes locked on one another.

"Seigneur, I have never felt love before." She stroked his cheek.

He hid his surprise by pressing his nose against the crown of her hair and sniffed. The hot breath fluffing her hair and sending gooseflesh rippling down her neck.

"Mademoiselle, how could such a fleur noir[2] such as yourself not ensnare a single heart?" His voice was low and rumbled. "Even those trapped in a nunnery live with the stirrings of past love."

Evanangela looked away. *I do not belong here. I do not deserve such kindness, even from damned creatures. There is not meant to be joy in penance, save for the joy of redemption! And even that I am barred from!*

"I was not permitted to love. Not in this way." Her voice wobbled as she whispered. "Such a thing had not occurred to me until now."

---

2 Black flower

Verseau withdrew from her, loosening his hold. "I am sorry that I have upset you."

Evanangela bit back tears. Her mind was overwhelmed and his presence was intoxicating, "Please, hold me, Seigneur."

She raised herself up and their kisses grew rougher. Her fangs pierced his lip and she licked the dark blood that flowed out. It was sweet and rich, far more tantalizing than the ambrosia she had sipped in her past life. He put his arms around her waist and she draped her arms around his neck. Verseau began to lower Evanangela to the floor. She flinched when she hit something soft. It was the man they had fed on.

Evanangela recoiled, cringing. "What will happen to him?" She stared at the man as Verseau let go of her.

He chuckled, helping her to her feet. "Oh, Mademoiselle, you are darling! He's dead. Jacques will remove him."

A chill went through Evanangela, cutting through the haze of her base desires. The blood on her hands was already starting to dry. *What have I done?!*

In all the centuries of her existence, she had never harmed a living thing. In a single moment, she had killed; drained the life from a mortal. If her fall had not damned her, she truly was damned now. A whimper caught in her throat.

Verseau realized her discomfort and offered her his arm. "Let us talk no more of this. Would it please you to join the waltz now? I believe the feed is over."

She nodded and took it, allowing him to pull her to her feet. "Are you all right? I hope you didn't drink too much. That will make you drunk and possibly succumb to a deep slumber before you are ready for the night to end. Though, I can't imagine how one would accomplish such a feat after just being born."

"No, I just feel a little-" she was cut off by Verseau tugging at what was left of her robe. "Seigneur! What are you doing?"

He wrenched the soiled fabric from her body and she tried to hide her nudity with her hands. His eyes raked over her form, but he turned away and hefted a bundle from the nearby couch.

17

"We must get you dressed. First impressions are *everything*. The court must see you with me to solidify your place here."

Before Evanangela could protest, he dropped the fabric over her head, blotting out the room for a moment before he pulled the dress into place. He tightened the laces and the sash and it hung loose on her slight frame.

"There is not time for all the fuss of underthings, but it shall do for a quick waltz." He gave her a reassuring grin and offered his arm again. "Shall we?"

Evanangela allowed him to lead her out of the room, but she turned to gaze over her shoulder at the dead man one last time before they slipped back into the hall. His expression was one of shock, his eyes wide and his mouth hung open. She took a deep breath and faced forward again.

Vampires now filled the hall, flitting about and whispering behind fans. They were a rainbow of decadence drifting in and out of rooms. The hems of their gowns fluttered as they walked. All wore sumptuous clothing; the latest fashions. Though only Verseau wore gold and red. Many of the vampires dressed in rich jewel tones or airy pastels, their outfits timed with bright colors and twinkling gems. Their gazes followed Evanangela as she floated down the hall with Verseau.

She looked down at her dress. It was a deep lapis lazuli blue trimmed with powder blue lace and ruffles. The seemingly random whims of fashion were a phenomenon Evanangela did not understand. As an angel, she had worn the same soft robes all of her existence. The intricate designs and combinations fascinated her. Evanangela looked up at Verseau. His smiling face seemed unbothered by the curious and petulant stares of his court.

Does he find me attractive? Is this form of dress considered beautiful here?

The coppery blood at the back of her throat soured as the painful thought struck her. The weight of her wings was gone. They had made her beautiful, as she had been graced with silver wings; rare among angels. The heavy gown that swathed her was a poor replacement. It could never be as lovely as her shining wings reflecting the sun's rays at daybreak.

Her morose thoughts were broken as music hit her like a wall of sound. The band was playing a tune unlike anything she had heard before. It was rather loud and the vampires and vampiresses were dancing wildly with excited expressions on their now rosy faces. Verseau swept her onto the dance floor. They whirled about, making her head spin from all the noise and color. The room was filled with a heady miasma of fresh blood with the permanent undertone of decay. Bouquets of flowers were placed in vases lining the room, but as a vampire, Evanangela was able to detect the rot despite the floral perfume.

"You are a divine dancer." He said as he drew her closer.

Evanangela looked back at Verseau. "Seigneur, I don't understand why a vampire of your-"

Verseau put his finger over her lips. The warm weight of it made her heart flutter, though this time, her heart was full of blood and it sent a pleasing rush through her veins.

"Ma chérie, what is there to understand? You must learn to enjoy the things handed to you and not waste time pondering them."

She nodded and glanced at the vampires that danced close by. Cool, unimpressed faces swirled around the room. Their faces were bright and hale as mortals, but they would flash their fangs as they talked or laughed, revealing their true nature. When a couple would get close, she could see their eyes filled with fire as they stared at her. Evanangela felt the shreds of confidence Verseau had given her earlier slip away.

She turned her gaze back to him. "Seigneur Verseau, who are all these vampires?"

"They reside here with me. They are my court." He dipped her, then raised her back up. "This is the Nacre Court of France. Courts are exclusive and all the new vampires must be accepted by the leader of a court in order to join."

Evanangela tilted her head as Verseau twirled her. "And how would I be accepted into this court?"

He grinned and drew her close, pressing his body against hers. "You already are. I forbid you to choose a different court."

There was a playful gleam in his eye as he said this, and Evanangela struggled to hide her shock. She broke from his embrace and gave a deep curtsy. "Seigneur, I-"

Verseau cupped her chin and pulled her to her feet. "Ma bijou[3], as my new favorite, you bow to no one."

Again, he wrapped Evanangela in his strong embrace and kissed her, a small peck on the lips. The dancing halted and the vampires watched. Low growls peppered the court. Fear snared Evanangela, wondering if they would attack. When Verseau let go, he gazed over the court. The music started again, and the others continued dancing, avoiding his eye.

He looked back at Evanangela; his frosty demeanor gone. "Please, join me in my apartments tonight. Tomorrow, preparations will be made for you."

Àmichemin appeared, almost out of nowhere, at Verseau's side. She too had fed, her cheeks rosy and her skin luminous. But her face was arranged in an annoyed scowl. "Verseau, may I speak with you, pour un moment?"[4]

Verseau shrugged and took Evanangela's hand. The court curtsied and bowed, which Verseau returned. Àmichemin and Verseau left the dance floor and strode down the hall with Evanangela in tow. The indigo candles on the walls had not gotten any shorter or dripped any wax.

"I shall only be a moment." Verseau whispered as he indicated for her to sit on an ebony chair against the wall near the doorway. She arranged herself on the seat, unease settling like a stone in her chest. He opened the door for Àmichemin, then closed it behind them.

"Mademoiselle Àmichemin, what seems to be bothering you?"

Evanangela could hear them through the door, but kept her eyes forward toward the end of the hall, not wanting to appear as if she were eavesdropping. More vampires were flitting in and out of the ballroom. Their laughter and chatter drowning out the music.

"Verseau! Have you no tact? This is an infant vampiress and you parade her about like some vixen! Well, I won't stand for it. The court is on edge as it is. Shuffling the ranks and rubbing a new favorite in their faces will only make it worse. Tomorrow, you can make the arrangements for her, but tonight she sleeps in my apartments. There is much she needs to learn and those lessons won't be taught by you and your endless indulgences!"

---

3 My jewel
4 For a moment?

She was stunned. How could Àmichemin use such a tone with Seigneur Verseau like that? Speaking to Dieu out of turn had cast other angels from the eternal kingdom. She cringed, waiting for Verseau to slap her for her insolence.

The merriment in Verseau's voice was still apparent. "Ma chère, Àmichemin, did you not have a good feed tonight?"

"Don't ignore this, Verseau." Àmichemin sounded irritated. "I believe it would be best for you to dismiss the court before they turn to ash and leave Evanangela to me. The night is fading away."

Evanangela straightened her back, staring down at the rug as the doorknob turned. She dropped her gaze into her lap, fidgeting her hands. Verseau held open the door for Àmichemin, who walked over to Evanangela and stroked her hair like a pet.

"M'Àmichemin, you do know how to get the lifeless blood flowing." Verseau winked. "I cannot wait for another of your delightful talks."

Àmichemin rolled her eyes as Verseau disappeared into the dance. She bent down to address Evanangela. "I'm sorry if he frightened you," she patted her hand, "tonight you must sleep with me in my coffin. There is enough room."

She led Evanangela up the stone stairs to yet another candlelit hallway lined with closed doors. These candles were black with burgundy flames licking their wicks.

"Àmichemin, what are all these candles for?" Evanangela asked, staring at the bewitched flame.

"You needn't worry about that. Just be sure to never touch them." Àmichemin opened a door that was in the middle of the hall. It was black, save for a plum oval inlay. The doorknob was a large polished amethyst.

She ignored Evanangela's confusion as she escorted her into a beautiful sitting room. There were deep plum armchairs made with ebony wood and a soft black couch. A fire burned bright in the grate. The violet flames matched the furniture.

Evanangela gasped in awe at the finery around her. "Is this your room?"

"That's just my sitting room. This is my bedroom." Àmichemin opened another door.

Velvet curtains trimmed with gold fringe and tassels were drawn tight with amethyst pins over the western wall, blocking the windows. There was a vanity with no mirror, an armoire that scraped the ceiling, and a canopy bed fit for a queen. An elegant "A" was inlayed with amethyst on the headboard. But there were no pillows atop the bed. Instead, there was a black coffin with gold leafing perched on the violet sheets.

"We're sleeping in there?" Evanangela asked in horror as she pointed at the coffin. She was used to sleeping out in the open on drifting clouds - the gentle breezes caressing her skin and the prayers of humanity whispering on the wind.

Àmichemin rolled her eyes. "Yes, and you better stop fussing because if you don't get in you will die."

She plunked her jewelry onto her vanity and began removing her clothes, letting them drop onto the floor. The fabrics tumbled into a heap. Àmichemin seemed unbothered to be nude in front of Evanangela as she opened the armoire and pulled out two lace nightdresses. Evanangela took off the gown Verseau had given her, and accepted the nightgown.

"Where should I put my clothes?" She held her clothes in one hand, the nightgown in the other, staring at Àmichemin's heap on the floor.

"Oh, anywhere. The attendants will take them to be laundered." Àmichemin clambered into the coffin.

Evanangela pulled the nightgown on, adding her clothes to the pile. She bit her lip, staring at the coffin. It looked like a gaping maw, waiting to swallow her up. "Can't I just-?"

Àmichemin sat up. "Get in!"

She nodded and climbed onto the bed. The coverlet was soft and cool beneath her legs. Evanangela crawled into the coffin and Àmichemin slammed down the lid, plunging them into darkness. She felt an arm drape over her. Evanangela scooted closer toward Àmichemin and was enveloped in a warm embrace. Before she could ask how Àmichemin could bear to be in such a small dark space, a sleep like death crept over her, ceasing all further thought.

Chapter Three

Evanangela stretched, yawning, and saw that the lid was already removed. The coffin, which had seemed so frightening before, was now just a piece of furniture that she stepped out of without a second thought. The violet fire crackled merrily in the grate; an affront to nature. Evanangela swiveled her head to the western wall, the drapes hung open to reveal three arrow slit windows. A velvety black sky dotted with winking stars greeted her instead of the bright cheery sun.

She swung her legs over the side of the bed, stepping out onto the cold marble floor, and walked over to Àmichemin, who was painting her nails a deep plum purple at the vanity. Colored varnish was an expensive commodity from the East. Evanangela found the opulence, and the smell, distasteful.

"I was about to wake you up." Àmichemin dipped the brush into the varnish and colored her pinky nail. "You don't want to sleep all through the night without a feed."

"Why did you chastise Seigneur Verseau last night? Aren't you afraid he will send you away from court in disgrace?" Her veins contracted as she moved about. Evanangela shivered, the blood lust hitting her brain as her body urged her to feed.

Àmichemin snickered and went back to her meticulous work. "Really now. Why on earth would Verseau have the gall to banish me? I rule the château more than he does. He is incapable of organizing an anthill, let alone the entire court." She held up her hand, examining her work.

She leaned against Àmichemin's vanity chair. "So, Seigneur Verseau is not angry with you?"

"Angry?" He was downright amused!" Àmichemin set down the brush and picked up a powder puff. "Believe me, Verseau would eat his foot before he would get rid of me." She began patting her face with the puff.

There was no mirror on the vanity. Evanangela wondered at how she crafted such a perfect face without being able to see herself. She turned away from the bare wood. The longing to see her own reflection and at last see her transformation weighed on her mind.

"Àmichemin, why were you so concerned about Seigneur Verseau's invitation last night?" She toyed with one of the baubles sitting on the vanity. It was a gold ring adorned with a large purple spinel surrounded by diamonds. It sparkled as she twisted it.

Àmichemin's grip on the puff tightened and Evanangela set the ring back onto the vanity. She closed her eyes, then opened them again. "I won't have that bastard taking advantage of you. For some reason you seem naïve, even more so than a newborn vampiress should be."

She unclenched the puff and went back to dabbing her face with it. Little clouds of perfumed powder swirled about her. "No, I will not have an infant like you exploited. You still have much to learn, and he should know better."

Àmichemin finished her makeup and opened the armoire. She looked back at Evanangela, giving her a bright smile. "Let us leave these thoughts while we have the fun of dressing you. I think this will do nicely."

The dress she pulled out had a sweetheart neckline and was decorated with onyx buttons. There was black lace from the elbows all the way to the wrists. The violet fabric below the lace gleamed in the candlelight.

Evanangela sat, pulling at her nails while Àmichemin brushed her auburn hair. "I thought you had said you did *not* want Seigneur Verseau treating me like a vixen? Surely, I-"

"No, in this outfit you look like a proper vampiress." Àmichemin snapped. She looped Evanangela's hair and added jeweled pins in to secure the knots. "It is unfortunate that your hair was so cruelly shorn. We will make do."

She blushed a cool sapphire again. "Do you think Seigneur Verseau will like it?"

Àmichemin smirked and looked over Evanangela once more. "We shall see, won't we?"

She led Evanangela out into the hall and down to the salon. The court was milling about in the main hall. When they descended the stairs, they were met with whispers and side glances.

"La Valse Noire must not yet have started." Àmichemin's cool breath tickled the inside of Evanangela's ear.

Jacques appeared at their side, startling Evanangela. A few vixens giggled behind their black fans. Their skirts rustled as she fidgeted, whispering to one another. Àmichemin gave them a biting glare under her lashes. They slinked away, clacking their fans shut and shooting glares over their shoulders.

"Seigneur Verseau has requested your presences dans La Chambre du Lapin Noir,[1] Mademoiselles." Jacques led them to a black door with gold inlay and knocked. "Seigneur, les Mademoiselles sont ici maintenant."[2]

The door swung open, revealing Verseau with an amiable grin plastered on his face. When he saw Evanangela, his grin softened with a thin veil of desire.

"Ma bijou, how wonderful to finally see you again." He purred as he took Evanangela's hand and scraped his fangs over her wrist. Àmichemin rolled her eyes.

Evanangela shivered as the fangs brushed her empty veins. "It is a pleasure to see you as well, Seigneur."

When Àmichemin could bear no more of their pleasantries, she grabbed Evanangela's hand and jerked her away from Verseau. "I believe we have business to attend to, and the Feed and the sun will not wait."

Verseau nodded, wrapping his arm around Àmichemin's waist. "Of course, ma chère douleur."[3] He gave her side a pinch.

Àmichemin smirked. With his arm still around her, Verseau took Evanangela's hand with his free hand. "Voici!"[4]

---

1 The Room of the Black Rabbit
2 Lord, the Misses are here now.
3 My dear pain.
4 Here it is!

They walked further down the hall, past several apartments. He let go of them both, and opened the door with a flourish, revealing a stunning drawing room. Everything was a rich shade of azure. Evanangela inspected the room, two plush sitting chairs before a glass table and a tapestry of a river. She opened yet another door, and found herself delivered into a room with powder blue wallpaper, marble floor, and two of arrow slit windows bordered by blue velvet curtains.

Verseau watched her. "Is it pleasing to you, ma chérie?"

Evanangela nodded. She could see every detail of the garden outside the court. The moon was high and it made the white cobblestones outside glow. Ivy and morning glories were growing up the side of the château adjacent to her room. A line of trees blocked her view of the main road. How splendid it must look in the morning when the first rays of sunlight spilled through the windows! If only she were able to see it. She looked up, and saw sparkling crushed gold covering the ceiling like hundreds of tiny stars.

"The attendants were up nearly all afternoon polishing." Verseau gestured toward the bed. "I had this room specially made for you."

There on the silk four-poster bed was a wenge wood coffin. She traced the lapis lazuli inlay. It was carved with the crest of roses and a stag.

"I-I don't know what to say." Evanangela ran her fingers along the edges of the coffin.

"You don't have to say anything." Verseau put his arm around her, and gave her waist a squeeze. He smirked and touched the coffin as well, brushing his fingers over her hand.

"Well, I have something to say." Àmichemin rolled her eyes again. "Why not get back to the feed before there is none left?"

"N'importe quoi[5], ma chère Àmichemin!" Verseau laughed, drawing Evanangela away from the bed and offered Àmichemin the crook of his arm. "There is always plenty!"

Vixens were spilling out of doorways and corners all down the hall as the three walked past. Each one showed playful, hungry eyes over painted or feathered fans at Verseau. These looks hardened as they beheld Evanangela on his arm.

---

5 Nonsense

Once they reached the ballroom, Evanangela wondered if it was some sort of holiday. Outside the windows, she could see carriages lined with gold and onyx queued up near the château's entrance. All around the walls purple candles burned, giving off the sharp scent of crushed pine needles. An attendant was playing a charming ditty at an ornate harpsicord. The doors to the ballroom were closed, and a line of attendants stood before them.

Evanangela dropped her head from looking at the décor, and her eyes rested on the opposite wall, which was made of mirror glass. Her heels clicked on the marble as she neared the mirror. At last, she could see her transformation! Before she could get close enough, Verseau grabbed her wrist.

"Now, now, ma chère, you mustn't wander off before feeding." He led her back onto the dance floor, taking her hands into position for the waltz. "It may take me hours to find you again." Verseau's eyes held a teasing fire.

She felt as if she could melt under those eyes. She sighed, leaning into Verseau's strong frame.

A young man approached and tapped Verseau on the shoulder. "May I, Seigneur?"

Verseau raised an eyebrow and smiled without showing his fangs. The man was mortal, his scent overwhelmed Evanangela as Verseau stepped away. She curtsied. He took her hand, and together they danced in slow circles about the room.

"You're lovely, Mademoiselle." The mortal tightened his arm around her waist.

She could feel his beating heart as his body pressed closer to hers, beckoning her to bite. Over the mortal's shoulder she saw Verseau flirting with a ruddy brunette. Evanangela looked around and saw many vampires were dancing or conversing with mortals. The smell of living flesh hung in a miasma. Screams erupted as the music changed and blood spattered on the ground.

The man dancing with Evanangela gasped, his face blanched. He drew her closer in horror. "What is going on?" He attempted to shield her with his body from the grotesque scene. Her lips brushed against his neck as he bumped into her. The skin was warm and she could smell the living blood that thrummed just below the surface. Blood lust ignited, and her body trembled with anticipation. She poised to lunge, her fangs exposed, when she caught a glimpse of her reflection in the mirror wall.

"Sweet Dieu! You are one of them!" The man screamed, pushing her away.

Evanangela stopped and let him go. He sprinted for the door, but was tackled by another vampire. She stared into the mirror. There were reflections of mortals dying, mortals screaming, but no reflections of their attackers. Evanangela found her own reflection invisible as well. She put her hands on the cool, flat surface of the glass wall, but then jerked her hands away. They were burned by the silver in the glass. She rubbed them together, unable to tear her gaze away. Her lack of reflection taunted her. Dieu had warned her the punishment would be fitting, but this was unbearable.

Her breathing became rapid and her chest tightened. *There must be something wrong with my eyes! I am dreaming this!*

She tore herself away from the wall and ran toward the doors. A vampire lunged to make prey of her, but then saw she was not mortal and let her pass with a sneer. The attendants opened the doors, allowing her through, and shut them quick to prevent mortals from escaping. She bolted down the hall, her heels scraping and clicking on the marble floor. The vixens glared after her, their skin was alive and fresh beneath their makeup, and their lips were dyed red with blood. Her lungs burned as her dead veins constricted her chest. She sank down on a cushioned bench, holding her head.

Evanangela cried out, her veins screamed in hunger as her heart clenched. The muscles began hardening as the small amount of blood left from the night before was absorbed and began to congeal. Evanangela grabbed her chest as her heart pressed against her sternum. Her veins tightened, trying to pump the last drops to her heart. She panted, her nails digging into her flesh. The smell of blood all around urged her to move, to hunt. She shrieked in pain as her mind and body fought.

A pair of vixens descended upon her, grabbing at her arms, when Verseau smacked them aside. They swallowed their hisses, curtsied, and scuttled off down the hall.

"Evanangela, you need to get back to the feed! You have not yet had a full feed cycle. You could die!" Verseau snatched Evanangela's hand and tried to lead her back to the ballroom.

She yanked her hand away. "Verseau, I cannot live in this form! How can any of us live on if we can only see ourselves through the eyes of others? How can I live if I cannot see myself?"

Verseau watched as more vampires exited the ballroom. His eyes scanning the crowd for a mortal.

"How am I to know if I am beautiful, or I am wretched? How am I to truly know?" Evanangela wailed. "Dieu stripped me! Stripped me of everything I hold dear!"

A pair of vixens sat nearby, giggling at Evanangela's outburst. They whispered to one another as they jeered over the tops of their fans.

"Damn." Verseau muttered and grabbed one of the nearby vixens. "Have you fed?"

"Oui, mon Seigneur!" The vixen dropped her fan, her eyes bright with excitement.

The other vixen sulked, pouting as she fluttered her fan to hide her embarrassment. Evanangela took a deep breath to try and soothe her agony, as she had no blood for tears.

"Excellent." Verseau sunk his fangs into her neck, bringing forth a rush of blood.

She moaned and tilted her neck to do the same to Verseau. He pushed the vixen toward Evanangela. "You must feed before the sun rises, or you won't survive the night, ma chérie."

The vixen screamed and tried to push Evanangela away. "Non! Please, mon Seigneur Verseau! Don't make me blood-share with her! I don't want to share with this brat!"

"But Verseau, what will happen to her?" Evanangela struggled as the scent of blood was heavy in her nose, but she could not shake the empty mirror from her mind.

Verseau tightened his grip and the vixen squirmed. "She will be fine." He forced the vixen's neck under Evanangela's chin again. "Now drink!"

She obeyed and sucked at the vein. The blood had begun to drip down the vixen's neck and onto the floor from her struggle. She screamed and writhed under Evanangela's lips, but Verseau held her down. The warm blood surged over Evanangela's tongue and down her throat. Her heart swelled and became heavy again, ceasing to strain against her sternum like an angry fist. The veins relaxed as they were engorged with blood and her muscles uncoiled. Her eyes rolled into the back of her head as pleasure rippled through her body. It was different than the mortal man she had taken in the study the previous night. The blood was more intense and alive as she drank. Not even the gift of flight brought as much excitement and feeling as the blood rushing through her choked veins. Shards of memories that were not her own flickered through her mind, like specks of dust drifting in the sunlight.

"Enough, ma chérie." Verseau pulled the vixen away.

Evanangela opened her eyes, bewildered as the strange new feelings coursed through her. Her body felt more alive than it had during her days in the sky. She slid her fingers up and down her arm, eliciting gooseflesh and shivers. The vixen huffed, fixing her rumpled dress and pressed her gloved hand against her neck to stem the flow. She glared at Evanangela, then gave a curt curtsy to Verseau, and trotted off.

Verseau stroked Evanangela's cheek. "How are you feeling, ma bijou?"

She pressed his hand against her cheek, holding it there. Her body burned with the desire to be touched all over. And yet, she also wanted something more. She leaned toward Verseau, unsure as she gazed into his eyes.

"Ah, ma chérie choupinette[6] how I wish to give in to you. But it is not to be this night. Your distress caused an uproar during the Feed and I must placate the court. It's best if you get back to your apartments before Àmichemin scolds us both."

He escorted Evanangela down the hall. Satiated vixens were draped on furniture, or heading to their small lodgings. Evanangela wound herself around Verseau's arm, delighting in the feeling of his embroidered jacket sleeve rubbing against her bare forearms.

He opened the door and gestured inside. "Here we are. How time flies when I am with you."

Evanangela stood in the doorway, waiting for something, anything, to happen. The blood buzzed in her mind, her heart racing as she stared up at him. She clasped her hands over her bodice, her fingers toying with one of the decorative buttons.

---

6 My dear sweetie

"You've finally had a full feed cycle and your body is still adjusting. You need to rest, especially after all you have experienced. I shall give you a parting gift if you promise to go sleep." Verseau winked, then bent down and kissed her.

Something sparked as their lips met, just as it had the night before. Evanangela felt the blood in her veins turn to fire. Her body was hot, and the strange sensations coursed through her, begging for more. She wound her arms around his neck, pulling him in for a deeper kiss. Verseau steadied himself against the doorframe, then pulled away.

"Sleep well." He whispered, then dashed down the hall.

Evanangela touched her fingers to her lips. They tingled and she could feel the living blood charging beneath the delicate skin. She turned, facing the grand room. It seemed too large and cold. Evanangela wrapped her arms around herself, wishing she could chase Verseau down the hall for one more kiss.

The sky was still inky black, the night full and ready to be discovered. Evanangela's shoulders shook as she heaved a sigh and shut the door. The powder blue sitting room was just as she had left it, the azure flames winking in the fireplace. All at once, her body felt heavy, as if the blood weighed her down. She dropped into one of the chairs and stared into the fire.

Verseau must find me attractive. I must still be beautiful if he has claimed me as his new favorite. Evanangela stroked and poked her face with the tips of her fingers, trying to find any difference in her visage. *And yet, how can I know? What if I am grotesque and vampires find that to be beautiful? What if I am a mockery, a toy for them to deceive?*

She had seen such places where humans cajoled unfortunate humans; the ugly and the malformed. "Circuses" they were called, as the voices on the wind had told her. The holy fire during her fall had burned her body, burned away her wings. Was it possible that the fire had burned her face as well? She shivered at the thought.

The fire was bright, but it did not bring her warmth. She moved through to her bedroom, closing the door behind her. The massive wenge wood coffin waited on the bed. Evanangela stripped off her clothes, struggling with the laces of the dress. At last, she shimmied out of the outfit, and climbed onto the bed.

Her limbs were tired, but not in an unpleasant way. Sleep beckoned, and Evanangela pushed the lid of the coffin open, and climbed inside.

31

She pulled the lid closed and snuggled into the cushions. Her heart slowed and she could feel the warm blood nourishing her body. Her eyes became heavy as her unnatural heartbeat slowed and lulled her into a deathlike sleep.

Chapter Four

The next evening, a knock woke Evanangela in the darkness of her coffin. She pushed the lid open and the waiting attendant bowed and left. Rubbing the old makeup from her eyes, she crawled out. Evanangela pulled the pins out of her hair and shook it loose. Tendrils of auburn hair framed her face and curled outward. It was in need of a good brushing.

She opened her armoire and found herself faced with the sumptuous wardrobe Verseau had given her. One of the dresses stood out, a black silk with a white ruffled skirt. On the bust was an embroidered white rose. The neckline was high on her collarbones. She laced up the back and tied the pretty black sash into a bow. Evanangela was searching through her shoes, when Àmichemin burst into the room wearing a flowing violet gauze dress. She straightened up, but her smile melted when she saw the expression on Àmichemin's face.

"Where did you get that dress?" She sounded almost frightened.

Evanangela trembled. "It was with the rest of my clothes." She sat down on her vanity stool. Her shoes in her hands. Verseau's attentions had emboldened her, and now, she wanted to impress him with such a grand ensemble.

Àmichemin shook her head. "I think it would be better if you wore something else." Her eyes shifted between Evanangela and the armoire.

"If I'm not meant to wear it, then it shouldn't be in this wardrobe." She was surprised by her own impertinence.

She sighed and rolled her eyes. "If you insist upon wearing it, you may as well look the part."

Evanangela wondered at what Àmichemin meant as she came toward her. She shivered as she turned to her vanity, remembering there was no mirror. It pained her not to know what she looked like, whether or not her makeup was pleasing. She pushed aside her discomfort.

"I'm sure Verseau will enjoy seeing you in this dress." Àmichemin mused. "I hope you know what you're getting yourself into." She brushed Evanangela's hair.

She opened a jar of face cream and sniffed. "What would I be getting myself into?" It smelled of lilacs. She had loved it when their scent had wafted up into the clouds in the spring before she had turned.

Àmichemin tied black ribbons across the crown of Evanangela's hair. Her curls were coppery whisps draped down her neck.

She laughed at the question. "To put it bluntly, you will be getting into Verseau's breeches."

Evanangela felt the cool sapphire blush fill her cheeks and Àmichemin smirked. "I-I don't know what you're talking about!" Evanangela pouted.

"I won't let him take advantage of you. *Unless you want him to.*" Her voice purred in Evanangela's ear.

Will Verseau find me beautiful in this dress? Evanangela stroked the ribbon around her neck and turned to face Àmichemin. "Why do you think Seigneur Verseau has taken such a liking to me?"

Àmichemin started doing Evanangela's makeup. The rouge helped to hide her sapphire blush. "I've been asking myself the same question. It takes quite the vampiress to capture his attention." She patted the powder puff on Evanangela's face.

Evanangela dropped her gaze. "Àmichemin, was my face burned in the fire? How have I been changed?"

She put down the makeup and ran her finger along Evanangela's jawline. "What on earth gave you that horrid idea? You are *beautiful* ma chère. Even in a charred burial gown, Verseau could not resist your charms!"

Her heart fluttered as the flattery nourished her vain ego. It quenched her thirst deeper than the blood had. "Truly, Àmichemin? I'm still beautiful?"

Àmichemin smiled, showing her fangs. "You're a lovely creature, Evanangela. Your eyes are especially alluring. The color of shared blood and so full of naïveté and wonder."

34

The words were a balm, healing the loss of her wings and her divinity. She craved more, but feared further prodding would annoy Àmichemin.

She draped a pearl necklace around Evanangela's throat. The cool beads sliding over her skin.

"It's clear you are no vixen. I was in the area conducting my own business when I felt your presence shortly after you were born. It was strong, and yet delicate. That's why I left my carriage and came searching for you."

The guilt struck through Evanangela again as she remembered the fear of the traveler in the churchyard. "What would happen if I did not feed tonight?"

Àmichemin froze. "Why would you ask such a thing?"

"I do not feel the urge," Evanangela sighed, trying to appear nonchalant, "it all seems so ghastly and brutal."

"That is not an option." her voice was firm. "You *must* feed."

Evanangela tilted her eyes up. "What would happen?"

She shook her head. "While vampires can hibernate as a last resort, the process for entering that suspended animation is painful and takes many hours. One would not expect to awaken for several years at the very least. And one would wake a ravenous, withered corpse of a creature."

"And…for one night?" Evanangela clutched her chest, the fear curled around it.

Àmichemin looked away. "A vampire can survive a few nights without feeding. But it is agony. Your dead veins will feel as if they are aflame. Your heart will become a heated stone in your chest, burning and weighing you down. The thirst will consume you. Most burn up in the sun while blindly seeking prey."

Her hands flew to her mouth, stifling her gasp. Such a hideous way to suffer and possibly die. Evanangela nodded. "I will feed. I'm sorry. I understand."

Àmichemin smoothed Evanangela's hair. "Of course, you will. Verseau would never allow such a thing to happen to you. And neither would I."

35

She bowed her head. A cool sapphire blush bloomed in her cheeks as she realized how quickly Àmichemin and Verseau had endeared themselves to her. *To think, even monsters can be kind.*

"Oh, this ribbon is twisted." Àmichemin undid the black ribbon on the pearls around Evanangela's neck. She froze, then brushed her finger behind Evanangela's ear. "What is this?"

Evanangela shivered as felt Àmichemin's fingers press on her delicate skin. "What is what?"

Àmichemin dropped the necklace. "You have wings twined around the blade instead of briars in your tattoo." She whispered. "The mark of all vampires is the same, save for yours."

Fear flooded Evanangela's brain like a broken damn. It was a shock that Dieu had left the mark of the angels upon her, even after the change. She hoped with all her might that Àmichemin could not sense her fear.

"Evanangela, did you notice-" Àmichemin stopped touching the tattoo and cocked her head to the side, "Evanangela...Evan-angel-a."

She clutched her hands in her lap, trying to still her trembling. *Please don't realize what my name means! Pretend you never saw my mark!*

Àmichemin swallowed hard as she bent to retrieve the fallen jewelry. She redid it around Evanangela's neck and smoothed a lock of hair. "Well, I guess I will have to continue unraveling you, *Evanangela.* Very slowly, I shall unravel your secret." She kissed the top of her head.

Evanangela stood, shaking. Àmichemin watched her with a soft smile and heavy-lidded eyes. Her hands trembled as she struggled to put on her shoes keeping her gaze to the floor. The moment replayed over and over in her mind. The kiss Àmichemin had given her was the strangest piece of all.

What must she think? She seems amused more than anything. These are ruthless murdering creatures. I should be on my guard, and yet, she acts fond of me, like a pet.

"Ready?" Àmichemin put her hand on the doorknob.

She hesitated, squeezing her hands as she searched Àmichemin's face. Not a trace of anger or betrayal, she was her usual, mischievous self.

Evanangela took a deep breath and nodded. Together they descended the stairs to the ballroom.

Once they reached the landing, Evanangela's senses were bombarded and gave her brain little room to think on the earlier incident. Her nostrils were filled with the fresh scent of mortals, and her ears pricked at the chatter of vixens gossiping, and vampires and vampiresses chatting. The rich decorum dazzled her. All the while, Evanangela fidgeted her hands, as her anxiety clenched her heart.

Evanangela looked down at her shoes. "Àmichemin, I-"

She smiled. "Let's enjoy the night."

Àmichemin could reveal me to them if she chose, and yet, she does not. Evanangela recalled the sweet kiss Àmichemin had placed atop her head. *Perhaps, it does not matter? I am one of them. I feed on blood and flee from the sun now. What else could there be?*

As they passed through the maze of halls, the vixens stared at Evanangela in shock. Their infuriated gazes followed her over the top of their fans as they whispered to one another. Àmichemin's haughty gaze remained unchanged as they passed through the court. Vampires and vampiresses recoiled and gasped at Evanangela as she strode past, pointing at her dress.

To survive this court, I must be one of them. Àmichemin found me out so easily. Any of them also could. And they are not fond of me. What would they do to me if they knew?

Evanangela mustered her courage. She kept her head high as she passed the annoyed vixens, and even sent them a glare not unlike one of Àmichemin's. Her bravado swiped away their glares, forcing them to edge away and look elsewhere. The whispers continued, but a distance had grown around her.

"You are becoming quite the vampiress." Àmichemin was amused by Evanangela's newfound confidence.

She nodded, smiling and revealing her fangs. "I'm pleased you find me so."

They descended the second stairs to the ballroom. Their skirts whispered and their heels clicked on the stone steps. The handrails were polished from thousands of evenings of hands caressing them up and down. Verseau appeared at the bottom and pretended as if he had been waiting there the entire time. Tonight, he was dressed in a deep plum, the gold accents winked in the candlelight. When he turned and saw Evanangela walking toward him, his eyes widened.

"Mademoiselle, I did not expect you to wear that gown!"

She lowered her eyelashes as she had seen the vixens execute in their shameless flirting. "Do you not like it?"

Verseau's throat bobbed as he swallowed. "Yes. It looks absolutely *saccharine* on you."

Evanangela giggled, causing him to clear his throat and dart his eyes away as a sapphire blush appeared on his cheeks.

He turned his gaze back to hers and took her arm. "Would you care to join me?"

She nodded and lowered her eyelashes again after noticing a pair of vixens staring at her. Evanangela flashed her fangs and leaned in closer to Verseau. The vixens scoffed, indignation burning on their faces as they flicked their fans. Verseau offered Àmichemin his other arm, which she took with an elegant toss of her hair. It shone like burnished white gold.

"You can admire her later. I'm starving." Àmichemin threw her free arm in the air with a theatrical flourish.

He laughed. A few vampires and vampiresses near the doors bowed and curtsied as the three made their entrance. Àmichemin flicked her hair as they strode through, her gaze already on the prowl.

"Ah, Mademoiselle, I would be a fool to keep you waiting." Verseau nodded to Àmichemin, who glided away into the dance.

He turned to Evanangela. "Enjoy yourself, ma fleur." He kissed her hand and also melted into the crowd.

Evanangela took small steps into the dance, alone. "Merci, mon cher." She whispered to herself.

A tall young mortal bowed before her. His large hand swallowed hers up as she allowed him to sweep her into the dance, distracting her thoughts with the basic hunger for blood. Her dance partner was taller and lankier than Verseau. His eyes were dark, almost black, and they too held a hunger in them.

"You are quite lovely, Mademoiselle." He squeezed her waist, his fingers lingering as they dug into her dress.

Evanangela's eyes narrowed as she discretely pulled away from his grasp, making it into a twirl. "Merci, monsieur."

"Did you come with an escort, or may I be your escort home from this sumptuous party?" There was a nasty grin on his lips.

She smirked, careful to hide her fangs. *Lust. Poor fool.*

"I do not need an escort. You see, I live here." She nodded to where Verseau was chatting with a young woman, walking his fingers up her neck as she tittered behind a fan. "I belong to the Seigneur."

The poor mortal seemed confused. "Seigneur? But, no one lives here. This château has sat empty for generations, making it the perfect playground for nobles such as ourselves."

"Oh no, monsieur," she laughed, exposing her fangs, "we are very much alive."

His face paled as Evanangela flashed her fangs at him, delighting in his lost bravado. Before the mortal could scream, the music reached the crescendo, and the vampires started making their kills. Evanangela pounced. He was caught off balance, and there was a sharp metallic sound as his skull hit the marble floor. She ripped his throat open with her serrated fangs, and lapped like a greedy cat. Evanangela gave soft moans as she sucked the rich, coppery blood from his neck, the warm liquid rushing over her tongue and filling her withered heart.

A nearby vampire was also drinking his fill, but he held his victim upright, as one might hold a lover. He too seemed to be enjoying his feed. Their eyes met for a moment. A hot jolt went through Evanangela before he looked away.

Just as she was reaching an ecstasy from the rush of warm blood filling her veins, Verseau swooped upon her, as if he could sense her pleasure from afar. Evanangela was startled and nearly spit the blood from her mouth.

"Ma chérie, voulez-vous joindrez moi dans ma chambre?"[1] His eyes were bright with excitement, his face animated as his gaze pierced her.

---

1 My dear, will you join me in my room tonight?

Evanangela nodded. A droplet of blood trickled from her lip, tickling her chin.

"You have a stain, ma chérie." Verseau whispered.

"Si vous devez."[2] She whispered back as she felt her lips parted by his.

They kissed, and this time, the court ignored them, too engrossed in the feed. Evanangela pressed closer to Verseau, daring herself to test the complacency of the vampires around her, to test her place. They did not look up. Vixens were engrossed in seeking heated company, while mated pairs were dancing about the ballroom. Evanangela looked up at Verseau, pleased with her small victory.

Verseau pulled away. "Allons-y, ma fleur!"[3]

He led Evanangela up the maze of stairs and hallways to his secluded apartments. The music from the ballroom was dim, and the echo of their footsteps overshadowed the dying screams of mortals. He unlocked the ruby-handled door and slammed it shut behind them, then grabbed Evanangela, pulling her into a deep kiss.

"Verseau!" She moaned as he sunk his hand into her tresses, and leaned her head to the side so he could smell her hair. His warm breath tickled her neck, sending gooseflesh down her spine as she giggled.

"The blood makes you truly come alive, ma chérie!" He trailed his fangs down her neck.

She dug her hands into Verseau's jacket as she pressed herself against him. Her body craved to be close to his. Evanangela whispered into his ear. "Oh, mon cher, je vous veux!"[4]

His mood changed, and his eyes snapped open wide, his hands were hovering over the laces of her dress. He pulled away, shaking his head. "I'm sorry, ma fleur."

Evanangela latched onto his jacket. "Qu'est-ce qu'il y a?"[5] She tried to catch his eye, but he looked away.

---

2 If you must.
3 Let's go, my flower!
4 I want you!
5 What's the matter?

Verseau dropped his gaze to the floor and he sunk onto a nearby couch. He deflated; the cheeky gleam gone from his eyes. Even the room seemed smaller and colder as he turned away from her.

She followed him. "Seigneur Verseau, what is the matter? Avez vous malade?"[6] She sat next to him, and he put his head in his hands.

He shook his head. She put her hands on his shoulders, but he flinched and waved her away. "Ne touches moi, s'il vous plaît."[7]

Evanangela froze, her heart in her throat. Her breath quickened as tears threatened the corners of her eyes. All at once, her small victory in the ballroom seemed so petty. His affections were like water running through her fingers. She didn't know how to keep it.

"Jacques!" Verseau shouted, startling Evanangela.

The attendant entered the room, and made a swift bow to Verseau. "Oui, Seigneur?"

Verseau looked up, and sighed. "Please send for Dame...Dame-? Just any one of them will do!" He jumped up from the couch and turned heel. "I really don't care at the moment!"

Jacques bowed. "Tout de suite, Seigneur."[8] He exited the room.

A few moments after Jacques left, a knock sounded at the door. "Entrez!" Verseau shouted, grinding his teeth.

She watched in horror as a simpering vixen came in, flashing her blood-stained fangs from behind her black painted fan. "Seigneur, you sent for me?"

Evanangela looked away, her eyes downcast, swallowing the hot tears. Her face burned as she blushed scarlet. The vixen sashayed up to Verseau, draping herself onto his shoulder. Her eyes flicked to Evanangela, dancing with mockery and delight.

"Un moment,"[9] Verseau muttered, dismissing the vixen's comment, "I wish to speak with ma petite Mademoiselle first."

---

6 Are you sick?
7 Please don't touch me.
8 Right away, Lord.
9 Just a moment,

The vixen withdrew, settling onto the couch and fanned herself. Evanangela refused to look at Verseau. She bit her lip to keep it from trembling.

"Ma chérie, please understand," he tried to put his hand under her chin, but she moved away, "go to Àmichemin. I cannot bear to look upon you tonight. I fear for what I might do."

Evanangela stood and curtsied. "As you wish, mon Seigneur."

She strode to the door. Her limbs trembled with hot indignation as she passed the smug vixen. She clenched her hands, resisting the urge to attack. Once she exited, the door shut behind her. The hall was mercifully empty. She sank to the floor, her back against the wall as she heard the sound of Verseau claiming the vixen in a frenzy of blood-sharing. Their moans cut through Evanangela. Her tears dripped down her cheeks and onto the floor, leaving scarlet petals of sorrow.

Àmichemin rounded the corner, her eyes bright as she licked blood off her lips. She flinched when she spotted Evanangela, and rushed to her side. Her heels a staccato on the marble floor.

She scooped her up, her arms about her shoulders. "What are you doing out here?"

Evanangela shook her head, wiping the red tears on the backs of her hands. She swallowed her sobs, attempting to explain. Àmichemin embraced her, stroking her hair.

"Please tell me." Àmichemin whispered.

Evanangela took a deep breath and hiccupped. "Seigneur Verseau took me to his ah-apart-ments. And then he-he sent. He sent for one of those horrid vixens! And then, he said, he said, h-he could not bear to look at m-mm-me-ee!"

"Don't you worry, tomorrow night we shall talk to him. Go to your apartments and wash your face. You'll feel better." Àmichemin patted Evanangela's head.

She hugged Àmichemin tight and took a few deep breaths. "Oh, please! Don't make me sleep all alone in that wretched thing he gave me!"

Àmichemin pried Evanangela off her. "You can sleep with me tonight." She smoothed her hair and wiped away the tears dripping down Evanangela's cheeks with a handkerchief scented with lilacs and lavender.

"Merci." She whispered as she pushed herself to her feet. Her breath caught as she sniffled.

Evanangela's makeup was ruined and there were stains on her dress. Only a few attendants saw her as they strode down the hall. Most of the court were either still in the ballroom dancing, or were enjoying themselves in their apartments. Evanangela was grateful to be spared further humiliation. The vixen's triumphant smirk burned in her mind as Àmichemin guided her down the hall to her apartments.

"Why would Seigneur Verseau do this to me?" Evanangela shook her head. "I thought-"

Àmichemin took Evanangela's hand and squeezed it as they walked. "Ma chérie, Verseau is a calculating master of this château, however, when it comes to matters of the heart, he is ruled by his emotions."

She let her gaze drop to the floor. Her eyes followed the swirls of the natural marble as they walked. Àmichemin opened the door to her apartments, and guided her inside.

"Jacques!" Àmichemin shouted, startling Evanangela.

A polite knock sounded at the door. "Entrez vous!" She called out.

Verseau's attendant opened the door, and bowed before crossing the threshold. "Bonsoire Mademoiselles. How may I assist you?"

Àmichemin waved her hand. "We need a wash basin. Make sure it is warm."

Jacques bowed again. "Right away, Mademoiselles."

The door shut with a soft click and his footsteps retreated down the hall. Àmichemin slumped onto her couch and let out a long sigh. "Tomorrow, I shall drink until the sun kisses my coffin."

Evanangela was about to ask what she meant, when Jacques returned. He set a beautiful porcelain water pitcher and basin onto the vanity. An unblemished white linen was draped over his arm.

"Go on," Àmichemin waved her hand at Evanangela.

She curtsied, "Merci."

Jacques poured the water into her cupped hands over the basin and she scrubbed the blood tears from her face. Rose petals floated in the water, giving a fresh scent and soothed her skin and her mind. Remnants of her makeup clouded the water until she felt clean and refreshed. Jacques handed her the linen, which was still warm.

"Merci, Jacques." Evanangela curtsied.

Àmichemin clucked her tongue and Jacques gave her a sympathetic smile.

"Non, you do not curtsy to the *garçon!* Gracious, those vixens will eat you alive!"

A blush bloomed across Evanangela's cheeks, hot with embarrassment. Jacques gathered up the crockery and the towel, and bowed.

"Bonne nuit, Mademoiselles," he left the room in long graceful strides.

Evanangela sank onto the couch next to Àmichemin. All the excitement and crying had worn her out. "Is it so terrible to treat the attendants with kindness?"

Àmichemin shook her head. "Of course not. But there is a difference between kindness and rank. A curtsy or a bow shows respect to those ranked above you. You do not dip your head for those beneath you."

The human invention of servitude had always been distasteful to Evanangela. It had pained her heart to see humans treating each other worse than cattle. She had wished Dieu would intervene in the face of such cruelty, but it seemed floods and famines had not swayed the stone hearts of mortals.

"They are not mistreated and standing in your rank does not hurt them." Àmichemin was growing weary and annoyed. "But looking foolish *will* hurt you."

She leaned her head back and stared up at the ceiling. The gold molding glinted in the firelight. She turned her gaze to the purple flames, watching them dance and flicker. They sat together in silence, both lost in their own thoughts. Evanangela draped her hand over her eyes and

44

tried to pushed aside the visions of Verseau calling for the vixen. Her heart fluttered.

Why does it pain me so to see him cavort with another? I feel such longing for him; such powerful feelings. The sweetness I felt for Gabriel pales in comparison. It's enough to drive one mad.

Àmichemin reached over and took Evanangela's hand, startling her. "You must forgive Verseau. It is his nature, and his duty as the Seigneur. This is France, and the men of the court find power in the women they keep."

Evanangela's face crumpled in disgust. "I thought you said *you* were the one who is actually in charge?"

"I am!" Àmichemin laughed and squeezed Evanangela's hand before letting go and draping herself on the end of the couch. "As I said, the men of the court find power in *the women they keep.*"

She sat up and leaned toward Àmichemin. "Then why do you let him cavort about as he does? Why let him take me as his new plaything?"

"Men are fickle and need their distractions from time to time." Àmichemin reached out her hand and toyed with Evanangela's hair. "Besides, who said you were only *his* plaything?"

Her eyes grew wide as Àmichemin smiled up at her, a mischievous gleam in her gaze.

"Besides, it is not as if Verseau and I are fresh sweethearts. I have been the *companion* of *many* vampire lords." Àmichemin's voice grew low, sending shivers down Evanangela's spine.

"There were others before Verseau?"

Àmichemin nodded. "Many in fact. He is newly turned and newly appointed in terms of the past vampire lords' reigns. I have seen them come and go. I must say, Verseau is one of *my* favorites."

Evanangela took Àmichemin's hand and squeezed it. "So, you are an ancient being as-!"

Both of them flinched at the statement as Evanangela stopped herself. She darted her eyes away as Àmichemin tightened her grip.

"...as the ancient ones. Verseau told me of them."

Àmichemin's eyebrows rose, then her expression returned to its natural coy state. "Ah, the ancient ones, yes. Of course. What has he told you of them?"

Evanangela shrugged, relieved to have changed the subject. "That I remind him of them. That the newly born are beasts and take many years to acclimate, but I did not."

"So it seems," Àmichemin nodded, "I have noticed that peculiarity as well. But to answer your question, yes, I am an 'ancient one'. Therefore, many of the court's rules do not apply to me. I do as I like."

She poked Evanangela's cheek. "That does not mean you are entitled to do the same. You may share company in my presence, but you do not share my rank."

Evanangela bowed her head. "Oui, bien sûr!¹⁰"

The sky was lightening from a rich indigo to streaks of dove grey, heralding the sunrise. Àmichemin sighed and hoisted herself from the couch.

"So it seems it is time for bed." She turned to Evanangela, offering her hand.

They dropped their clothing onto the floor, and jewelry onto the furniture for the attendants to gather up later. It seemed almost like magic that they all appeared back in their boxes and on their shelves the next moonrise.

Evanangela snuggled into the coffin as Àmichemin slid in beside her. The warmth of their bodies was a comfort. As the darkness enveloped them, Àmichemin put her arms around Evanangela.

"No more sad thoughts." She whispered. "Don't think about the court. Only think of the joy of your feed tonight. Block everything else out, and tomorrow we shall deal with them together."

Evanangela nodded and Àmichemin squeezed her. The deathlike sleep took them, blotting out their worries.

---

10 Of course!

Chapter Five

The following nightfall, a pretty little knock came on Àmichemin's coffin. Evanangela woke with a start and felt the pain of the previous night flood her heart and mind. Àmichemin slid out of her coffin with silent grace and dismissed the waiting attendant. She then peered over the lip at Evanangela's hunched figure inside.

"Aren't you going to get up and get dressed?"

She shook her head and squeezed her eyes shut. The shame boiled in her stomach, making her heart clench. Evanangela took a deep breath to stave off the burning of her empty veins.

"Now, now, what did we talk about last night? You're a full-fledged vampiress now and you must solidify your rank. The vixens taunt you as they do in the hopes to lower your rank and therefore, potentially raise their own. As Verseau's current favorite, you are an untouchable."

Evanangela jolted and sat up. "Untouchable?"

"Well, of course. Are you a witless vixen who flits behind her shabby black fan? No. You're like me. And we are the only two vampiresses who have real power in this court."

"Power? What power?" Evanangela leaned against the lip of the coffin. She finally met Àmichemin's gaze.

"Why, the power to influence the court, of course. The only power greater than that is to rule the court itself." Àmichemin shrugged.

Evanangela blushed a cool sapphire across her cheeks. "You mean I *used* to have influence. After Seigneur Verseau rejected me, I'm sure things will come crashing down."

Àmichemin laughed. "Oh, you silly naïve thing! You have plenty of influence, especially with your sway over Verseau!"

"I'm more powerful than Seigneur Verseau?" Evanangela questioned.

"Now, let's not get ahead of ourselves." Àmichemin raised an eyebrow. "You simply have sway, which means you can influence him. But Verseau is still the ruler of this court."

Evanangela nodded and shifted in the coffin. The silk cushions whispered against her skin. They had grown cold and she shivered.

Àmichemin patted her hand, stepped off the bed, and strode toward the vanity. "Now, hurry up and get dressed. We haven't much time."

"But we always have time to lounge before the feed. Has something happened?" Evanangela crept out of the coffin.

"Pas de tout.[1]" Àmichemin ran a brush through her platinum locks. "But we must catch Verseau off guard."

She stopped rummaging through the wardrobe and stared back at Àmichemin; her fingers draped over a burgundy gown. "Catch him off guard? Whatever for?"

Àmichemin sighed as she set her brush down and picked at the stays of her corset, tightening it further. "This is best suited as a private affair. No need to parade your emotions before the court."

"I see." Evanangela darted her eyes about the floor, then went back to selecting a dress. "What shall I say to him?"

Her heart clenched thinking of the look he had given her, the pain and hunger in his eyes. She clutched a velvet gown to her chest, willing the sharp throbbing to pass. Tears would not come, as her veins were empty. Her eyes burned as she stared up at the ceiling, her fingers digging into the fabric.

"I'm sure it will come to you in the moment." Àmichemin slipped a violet velvet dress on. It slinked along her corset, showcasing her slight curves.

Evanangela's body was numb as she dressed, her hands moving over buttons and clasping jewelry without thinking. Inside, her mind was aflame, her imagination blazing with suppositions of what Verseau might say. And yet, all her supposed responses seemed to fall flat, or were laced with desperation that made her cringe.

"You look beautiful, quit sulking." Àmichemin lifted Evanangela's chin, then took her arm. "Now, let's be off."

---

1 Not at all.

They passed the grand staircase, and trotted down toward Verseau's apartments. Jacques was standing guard again; his expression bored and unreadable. He bowed and opened the door, allowing Àmichemin to pass. Evanangela hesitated, but Àmichemin grabbed her wrist and dragged her inside.

Verseau looked up from the window he had been gazing out of. The stars were bright, as the sky was clear. One of the garden magnolia trees seemed to glow in the moonlight. When he saw Àmichemin, his face lit up with a playful smile. He rose from the plush chair he had been lounging in. When Evanangela stepped out from behind Àmichemin, his smile disappeared.

"Àmichemin, I don't believe I sent for you." Verseau's voice was strained, his words measured. He darted his eyes away.

"Well then, please explain why you sent for a vixen last night." Àmichemin crossed her arms. She sent him a scathing glare.

He flinched, but maintained his cool demeanor. "Ma chérie, Àmichemin, I-"

Evanangela ran up to Verseau and knelt before him. She prostrated herself, touched her lips to his shoes. "Mon Seigneur, why have you done this? What have I done to displease you?"

Verseau gazed into her eyes, then petted her auburn hair. "Ma charmante[2], charmante petite Mademoiselle," he lifted Evanangela to her feet, "you have done nothing wrong. Except steal mon coeur."[3]

"I don't understand." Evanangela shook her head as she looked up at him. Her auburn curls bounced around her face.

He leaned down and kissed her trembling lips. She melted into him, reassured by the feeling of his closeness and his faint scent. When he drew away, her blush had deepened to a rich blue. "Ma chérie, I would have felt utterly evil last night if I had taken something as magnificent as you."

"But you said you could not bear to look at me." She darted her eyes away.

Verseau nodded, cupping her chin in his hand, forcing her to gaze into his sharp yellow-green eyes; like that of a raptor's. "I said that

2 My charming
3 My heart

49

because if I looked upon your radiant beauty, I would not have been able to control myself."

Àmichemin slinked toward them. "Well, well, Verseau, behaving yourself for once?"

He smiled his famous delectable grin, and held Evanangela closer. "When don't I mind my manners, ma chère douleur?"

Àmichemin rolled her eyes, but there was a smile on her face. Verseau turned his gaze back to Evanangela.

"I did not mean to cause you such distress, ma fleur," he kissed her hair, "you are my favorite and that cannot be easily shaken. As such, I intend to savor you."

His words sent gooseflesh racing down Evanangela's arms and spine. She darted her eyes away, embarrassed by the feelings that gripped her. Verseau chuckled at her discomfort and pulled her into a close embrace. Àmichemin sighed and shifted her weight to one of her hips, shaking her head.

"You are as insufferable as ever," she smiled, revealing her fangs, "always insisted on pomp and drama."

Verseau twirled his hand in the air and laughed. "Bien sûr, ma chère," he took Àmichemin's arm, "Come now, the feed will not wait."

Together, the trio descended the stairs down to the ballroom. A chill ran through Evanangela as they neared the vixens. She could feel their piercing gaze. But instead of chattering and glaring, they stood silent as she passed by. The only motion was the vixens slowly fanning themselves. One of them took a step forward and gave a polite curtsy; catching Evanangela off guard. Àmichemin smiled, and Evanangela returned it.

"Ma chérie, you feel tense. We must hurry and get you to the feed." Verseau murmured.

Evanangela leaned her head on Verseau's shoulder as they set foot in the ballroom. A chilling tune was being plucked and whispered from the musicians' instruments. It sounded like polished stones tumbling in a glittering moonlit river.

Verseau kissed the crown of her hair. Evanangela leaned back so she could look up into his eyes. He smiled, revealing his ivory fangs.

"Go on, ma fleur. Pick someone out. I will be waiting for you."

Evanangela set off into the dance in search of a victim. As she danced, she watched Àmichemin separate from Verseau. After only a few strides across the ballroom, Àmichemin caught the attentions of a young man. He slipped his arm about her waist, and together they settled into a window seat that overlooked the gardens. Evanangela followed, curious.

The young man gazed into Àmichemin's violet eyes. "I cannot tell the difference between your eyes and the night sky. Both are filled with sparkling stars."

She smiled and gave him a kiss. The young man pulled back; his lips shiny with what looked like a thin coat of ice. The music reached a feverish pitch, and Àmichemin sunk her fangs into his startled form. She sucked greedily and Evanangela watched in fascination. It went on and on, her face latched onto his neck. His skin paled as she drained him.

When he was limp, Àmichemin let him drop into the window seat. He looked almost peaceful, but his neck revealed the secret of his death with black crusted blood and crystalline frost around the puncture wounds.

Àmichemin looked up at Evanangela, suddenly noticing her placid presence. "Did you need something, ma chérie?"

She shook her head. Àmichemin left him propped in the window seat. Her lips were stained red with fresh blood. "Better get your own feed then. He's dry."

The dance beckoned; the frenzy had yet to start. Evanangela circled the edges of the dance floor, waiting for a poor mortal. At last, an older man placed his hand on her shoulder. The scent of living flesh hung about him, heavy and rich. There was a deeper quality to his essence. That of an older mortal, rather than the heavily perfumed freshness of youth. She curtsied, and he returned it with a bow.

"Would you care to dance, Mademoiselle?" He extended his hand.

Evanangela nodded, feeling tipsy on the smell of his blood. "I would love to."

He swept her onto the dance floor, meandering in slow circles about the others. The fragrance of blood was becoming stronger. Other vampires were taking their chance and making their kills. She allowed the dance to continue, savoring her prey. He had a good-natured round face and a mole on the side of his cheek. His hands were soft and doughy as he held her, twirling her about the dance.

A sudden movement caught Evanangela's eye. She looked over the mortal's shoulder and saw a vixen approaching. Her yellow gown fluttered as she marched. It was rude to interfere with a feed. Evanangela glared at her, but the vixen continued to advance.

"Is something the matter, ma chérie?" He turned, spotting the vixen. He raised his eyebrows. "Is this a friend of yours?"

Evanangela bared her fangs at the vixen, stopping her cold in her tracks. The man screamed as she dove into his neck, the blood spurting forth from the force of her fury. She maintained eye contact with the vixen, a cruel hunter putting a lesser predator in its place. The vixen hissed and turned away.

She closed her eyes, allowing the deep rippling pleasure to take hold as the blood rushed down her throat, bringing her veins to life. The mortal batted at her, his soft hands clawing at her gown. She pinned him to the floor, surprising herself with her own strength as she nearly snapped his wrists. The warmth spread through her body like liquid fire. The blood at his neck burbled as she moaned into it. The pressure snuffed out his screams, leaving him gaping like a fish.

Once her veins were swollen, Evanangela scanned the court. More vampires were making short work of their prey, or acting with just as much voracity as she had. Her eyes rested on Àmichemin. She was leaning against the windows, watching her. As Evanangela stood up, Àmichemin opened her arms. Evanangela rushed to her and threw her arms around her neck.

"Ma chérie, ma petite chérie." She murmured as Evanangela buried her face in her hair. "Are you even sure of what you are asking?"

Evanangela shook her head, inhaling the soft perfume, now magnified by the living blood coursing through Àmichemin's veins. "I do not. But I want it all the same."

Together, they dashed up to Àmichemin's apartments; their hands linked tight. The clacking of their heels and their bubbly giggles echoed in the hall. She threw the doors open and they sat on the violet coverlet. At once, Evanangela was showered with kisses. Àmichemin pulled

Evanangela into her lap and kissed her on the mouth. Her hair spilled like bright white stars onto Evanangela's shoulder as she kissed her neck. Evanangela tilted her head in invitation, and Àmichemin sunk her fangs, bringing forth the fresh blood.

The sensation overwhelmed Evanangela. She squealed as the ivory daggers plunged into her flesh; the pain dazed her. After having glutted on mortal blood, the feeling of Àmichemin's tender lips sucking at her vein was as if a tight valve had been released. Pleasure washed through her as she surrendered to the rush of the blood leaving her body, making her feel light, and yet filled with sparkling sensations. Evanangela trembled as Àmichemin licked up the blood.

"Don't be afraid, ma petite fleur. Tu es avec moi."[4]

She took Evanangela's head into her hands, and brought her face to her neck. Evanangela bit Àmichemin, and allowed the blood to surge into her mouth. A sharp hiss escaped Àmichemin's lips and she wove her hands into Evanangela's hair, holding her firm. Now, Evanangela was able to enjoy the taste, rather than the frantic panic she had been in when Verseau had thrust the vixen under her nose. Vampiric blood had a richer quality than mortal blood. Fragments of memory and thought flew through her mind, too fast to examine. Her mind became overwhelmed as she lapped the wound.

Àmichemin then disengaged Evanangela and kissed her full on the mouth, licking the blood off her lips. She grinned as Evanangela licked her own lips, still tasting the blood and the kiss. Evanangela's grip tightened, and Àmichemin undid the laces of her dress.

Evanangela mimicked this and soon both dresses were thrown to the floor. She shivered with anticipation. The enchanted fireplace had made the room quite warm and Àmichemin's blood ignited her body with a thrill even bolder than when she had first kissed Verseau. Àmichemin sunk her fangs into Evanangela's corset and ripped it down the front through the ribbon ties, and flung it over the side of the bed.

She grabbed Àmichemin's corset and ripped it with her bare hands, tossing it aside. Àmichemin sunk her fangs into Evanangela's left breast and drew blood. Evanangela hissed at the combined pain and pleasure. Àmichemin then dipped her fingers into the wound, smearing the blood onto her fingertips and held them up. Evanangela licked her fingers clean, and kissed the wound on Àmichemin's neck; inhaling her wintery scent.

4 You are with me.

53

Àmichemin threw Evanangela onto her back on the bed and reared up on her knees over her body. Àmichemin came down upon her with hands gripping her breasts and fangs buried in her neck. Evanangela arched her back and screamed again. Her auburn hair sprayed as she flung her head and Àmichemin held fast to her. Evanangela then grabbed a fistful of Àmichemin's soft hair and yanked her head to the side laying her neck bare without disengaging her. She reopened the wound on Àmichemin's neck and sucked. Àmichemin moaned into Evanangela's neck and pressed herself against her. Evanangela rose up to meet her, clinging to her hair. She felt as if the heat between them would set them afire, utterly consumed by pleasure. The two vampiresses were so frenzied that they did not hear Jacques come in.

"Mademoiselles, I don't mean to interrupt, but Seigneur Verseau has summoned you both." He kept his gaze on the floor.

Àmichemin removed her fangs from Evanangela and licked the blood off her lips. Her voice was a low, rumbling purr. "Merci. We shall be there shortly."

Evanangela released her and looked up at Jacques, her mouth half open and a blush rising on her cheeks. Her mind swirled as the mortal and vampiric blood rushed through her veins. Jacques bowed, then left the room. She sat up and watched as Àmichemin wiped the blood from her mouth with the back of her hand and slid off the bed.

"Àmichemin, I do so enjoy the feeds." She giggled and took a deep shuddering breath to try and clear the sweet haze that made her brain slosh in her skull.

"I know you do." Àmichemin crooned, "but Seigneur has summoned us. We must get dressed."

The ruined dresses were scattered on the floor and their undergarments were spattered with blood. Their wounds had begun to crust over, and Evanangela was careful as she pulled a new gown over her head. Àmichemin slipped into a floral gown the color of lilacs. She snatched a necklace from the floor and clasped it about her throat.

"Come now, we mustn't keep him waiting."

Chapter Six

Evanangela took her hand and they trotted down the hall. Jacques was waiting for them, and opened the door, bowing as they crossed the threshold.

"Seigneur?" Àmichemin curtsied, and Evanangela followed suit.

Verseau rose from his chair and nodded to them both a playful grin spread on his face as his eyes raked over their fresh wounds. "Enjoying the spoils of the feed I see. I feel I must spoil your fun with some news."

Àmichemin straightened up, her playful air evaporated into her cool demeanor. Evanangela froze.

"It seems the news your brought from the Mors is more urgent than expected." Verseau sighed as he plucked the rolled parchment Àmichemin had given him the night Evanangela had been brought to the château.

"Are they calling a meeting of the council?" Àmichemin took the missive and read it for herself.

Verseau shook his head. "Not yet, however, this problem has officially spread to even the far corners of Europe." He plucked a grubby parchment from his desk. "There is word the plague has reached as far as the Ottoman Empire. If this is true, then the situation has become dire and we may have to consider more stringent solutions."

Àmichemin pressed her lips together into a thin line. She nodded and handed the rolled parchment back. "I have lived through plagues, including the terror of the sweating sickness that nearly destroyed all of England. Their fetid traders brought it here, wreaking havoc in the villages. We must proceed with caution. The court is already on edge with the current restrictions."

Evanangela tilted her head. "Restrictions? But the court is filled with such dazzling opulence-?"

Verseau shook his head. "That may be true, but material wealth is simply a means to an end for us. True wealth in the courts is blood. All vampires are rationed to only one kill per night and no one is allowed to leave without express permission to prevent hunting in the villages. The court will not take to more of their freedoms and privileges of rank being stripped from them."

Àmichemin turned her gaze to Evanangela. "Our gold is useless if there is no blood for us to buy."

Evanangela swallowed hard, the blood that coated the back of her throat tasted even sweeter and more precious. She had seen true hunger in the mortals she had watched over. How famine drove families to destroy one another over a crust of bread. The brutal violence that could break in a starved vampire court was a terror she could not imagine.

"I do not mean to sour your evening, but this is a matter we will need to address sooner rather than later. We must protect ourselves against the potential rumors of the court when this news breaks."

Àmichemin nodded. "I shall see to it that careless whispers are quashed. The season is mild and I can reach the Mors again in haste if required."

Verseau took her hands in his and brought her knuckles to his lips. "Merci ma cher coeur. I can always count on you."

He turned to Evanangela and took her by the shoulders, giving her arms a gentle squeeze. "Do not let fear consume you, ma fleur noire. I give you this knowledge to protect you. The court is a dangerous place, and outside the château walls, it is even moreso."

She nodded and Verseau smiled at last. "I'm afraid I have nothing for you this night, mes chéries."

Àmichemin curtsied and Evanangela followed suit. She took Àmichemin's hand as Verseau turned back to his desk, his head bowed. Jacques opened the door, ushering them out into the hall.

"Go directly to your apartments and speak to no one, not even the attendants what you have heard." Àmichemin squeezed Evanangela's hand. "Tomorrow, we must appear as if nothing is amiss."

Evanangela nodded. "I understand."

They parted ways, Àmichemin heading to her own apartments. Her door banged shut, echoing in the empty hall. Sunrise was drawing near. Evanangela trotted to her own apartments. Finally, she would have to sleep alone.

The following nightfall, Evanangela was startled awake by the brisk knock of a attendant. The lid of her coffin slid open, allowing the soft light from her room to pour in.

"Merci garçon," she murmured as she gathered her wits.

The previous evening came to her in pieces. She shivered as she recalled Àmichemin's hands and fangs upon her. She slid her fingertips up and down her neck. The wounds had healed as she slept. Verseau's warning stopped her cold. She squeezed her hands together, trying to push away the sudden panic.

We must appear as if nothing is amiss.

Evanangela took a deep breath and pushed the thoughts away. In any case, what was she, a newly formed vampire, to do with such news? She was as useless as the heaps of gold sitting in Verseau's coffers. The air was cold that night, and sent a shiver through her naked body. Her hands gripped the lip of the coffin as she pushed herself up and out. Her eyes fell on the intricate details of the wood.

She traced the lapis lazuli inlay of her coffin, remembering how Verseau had smiled when he had gifted it to her. The stone was cool under her fingertips. The azure fire in the grate made the room cozy and warm, despite the color resembling ice. Though the floor was cold under her unshod feet. She opened her armoire and pulled out clothes for the evening. There was a knock at the door while she was lacing up her dress.

"Entrez." She muttered.

Àmichemin strode into the bedroom. She looked over Evanangela's outfit, then lifted the ivory brush from the vanity, and started brushing Evanangela's hair. "Did you really think you were going to run off to the feed without me?"

She smiled and shook her head. The rhythmic brushing was soothing. She loved the drag of the bristles against her scalp and the gentle pull of her hair. While in heaven, she had taken for granted the small pleasures and gestures of affection mortals shared with one another. Though simple things like having her hair brushed lacked the intensity of the feed or blood-sharing, it held a charming and comforting quality of its own. Àmichemin smiled back, and continued brushing, piling it into an elegant knot.

Evanangela played with a crystal hairpin. "Àmichemin, Verseau gave me these sumptuous apartments, and yet, he still will not see me privately as he does with you. I don't understand what he wants from me."

"As I told you, he is taking his time with you. Which still surprises me, but Verseau is also prone to whimsy. As for the apartments, Verseau merely enjoys spoiling his favorites." Àmichemin took the hairpin, and placed it into the updo.

Evanangela felt jealousy stab her heart as Àmichemin turned to go. "Does Verseau have any other favorites aside from you and I?"

Àmichemin turned back around. "Don't be silly! Who could he possibly favor? Those wretched vixens and their petty gossip? Never. None of those chiennes[1] compare to us."

She followed Àmichemin out of her apartments. Upon reaching the main hall, they found themselves surrounded by smug vixens simpering behind their shabby black fans. She recognized one vixen to be the same Verseau had called on that awful night. Evanangela straightened her shoulders and shifted her gaze straight ahead, ignoring the quirk of her eyebrow. As they strode past, the tinkling laughter of another vixen stopped Evanangela in her tracks. She turned and saw the vixen pointing at her and giggling.

The news from the previous evening flooded her mind once more. *The court is set to starve and yet these fools cling to their petty games!*

Evanangela felt her body taking over as she dashed across the room. In the next moment, she held the vixen by the throat, her feet dangling inches off the floor.

"Do I look amused?" Evanangela snarled. The other vixens edged away.

The offending vixen struggled as Evanangela tightened her grip. "Non, Mademoiselle!"

"Then why are you laughing?" Evanangela squeezed harder. "Do you laugh when Seigneur is not amused?"

---

1 bitches

The vixen managed to shake her head as her mouth opened and closed in vain. Evanangela opened her hand, releasing her into a terrified heap on the floor. Her heels scraped the marble as she scampered to get up.

"Then take note of when I'm amused." Evanangela growled. She scanned her gaze over the other vixens. "All of you!"

Àmichemin hovered behind Evanangela. "Verseau is waiting."

Evanangela nodded and together they continued down the hall. Her odd rage slipped away, though she could still hear bits and pieces of the vixens whispering.

She put her hand on Evanangela's shoulder. "I'm proud of you. It is necessary to remind them of their place. Lest they try to take it from you."

The memory of the vixen trying to steal her feed during La Valse Noire surfaced in Evanangela's mind. She nodded, and Àmichemin flicked her hair over her shoulder in a starry spray. Verseau was waiting for them at the bottom of the stairs, as always. His fangs exposed as he smiled up at them.

"Ah, les étoiles qui tombons du ciel pour accordant mes vœux!"[2] He spread his arms wide to embrace them.

Àmichemin rolled her eyes and scoffed, but did not hide her smile as she allowed Verseau to wind his arm about her waist. Evanangela stepped forward. Her hands shook as she studied his face. All the solemn gravity from the previous evening was gone. His mischievous grin back in place. He opened his arms again and wriggled his fingers.

"Ici, ma petite."

Evanangela felt the excitement rise, squeezing her dead heart as his arm drew her in. Her hope was ignited once more that he would finally sweep her away to his apartments after the feed. She smiled up at him, her nervous energy turning to excitement. Verseau steered them toward the ballroom, all heads turning as the trio entered.

Àmichemin slipped away, eager to find prey. Evanangela lingered, enjoying the weight of Verseau's arm about her body. He turned to her, a glint in his eyes.

---

2 Ah, the stars fall from the heavens to grant my wishes!

59

"Go on, ma petite. Find someone *delicious.*"

She was rooted to the spot as he pecked her on the cheek, then strode off toward a group of giggling mortal women. Evanangela was startled when she felt a tap on her shoulder. She turned and found herself facing a mortal with bright blue eyes and blonde hair. All at once, a rush of emotions washed over her.

Could it be? Has he come to take me home? Or perhaps, he is here to test me?

Her joy erupted as she squeezed his hand, longing to throw her arms around him. "Gabriel!"

The mortal was about to kiss her hand and jerked his head up. "Yes? How did you know my name?"

Evanangela's breath caught and her eyes widened. He smelled of mortal blood and flesh, not sunshine and summer breeze. *Of course, it is not your Gabriel! How could it be? You must be more careful.*

"Oh, you just remind me of an old friend." Evanangela gave her best smile, though it twitched at the corner as her nerves got the best of her. "Shall we dance?"

Gabriel nodded and together they waltzed. None of the vixens dared to come near her, not this time. But Evanangela could feel their frigid glares like barbs upon her back. She ignored them, choosing to dance wilder with the mortal instead; her dress billowing and swishing as she twirled.

"You dance with such grace, Mademoiselle!" Gabriel grinned as he spun Evanangela.

She giggled, allowing herself to be pulled close again. "Ah, but grace is precisely what I lost that allowed me to live here."

He quirked an eyebrow at her strange comment. "I'm certain grace is something we cannot lose, only *misplace* when we don't have our priorities in order."

Evanangela froze for a moment. She scanned his face. His eyes were the crystal blue of a summer sky. Just like the Gabriel she had once been fond of, back before she knew the carnal calling of love. She found herself faltering, supposing it could indeed be *him.*

"I-I suppose-"

"Forgive me, Mademoiselle," he turned her, falling back into the dance, "perhaps it is I who has misplaced his priorities."

The longer the dance went on, the more Evanangela was certain she could not suck this man dry. The screams of dying mortals erupted around them, and she felt the telltale throbbing in her veins, and the angry pounding of her empty heart pushing her to attack. And yet, she could not.

Gabriel tipped her chin up to study her face. "Ma chérie, you look flushed. May I escort you home?"

Her mind was on fire, as those were the words she longed to hear spill from his lips. She knew it was not her Gabriel, come to take her back home to the eternal kingdom. It was some poor mortal served up on a golden platter for her to feast upon.

Evanangela shook her head, her gaze riveted on his face. His *angelic* face. "Oh, mon cher Gabriel, if only our paths had not crossed. Not like this. Run away before they kill you!"

He caught Evanangela as she fell into a faint. Her body crumpled into his arms, his hand cradling her head to prevent it from snapping back. He held her close to his chest, at last, aware of the carnage that surrounded them. "Mademoiselle! Réveillez-vous! Réveillez-vous, maintenant![3] We must leave this place!"

Verseau appeared at his side in an instant. His fiery gaze bore into Gabriel, freezing him on the spot. "What have you done to ma petite fleur noire?"

"I-I have not-! I would never harm such a delicate creature, Seigneur!" Gabriel balked. "She fainted, and everyone is attacking one another! We must get her to safety!"

His jaw tightened when he saw how even in her unconscious state, Evanangela's hands tightly gripped Gabriel's sleeves. He growled and shook his head. "Come with me. Vite! Vite!"

Gabriel nodded, cradling Evanangela in his arms. He followed Verseau toward the doors. Blood spattered all around them as the vampires made their kills, glutting on fresh blood. The attendants allowed them passage, opening the doors to the hallway. Gabriel flinched when the doors closed behind him. Their shoes echoed off the marble as they

---

3 Wake up! Wake up, now!"

61

moved further from the blood-curdling screams of the dying and the hissing of the vampires.

"Through here," Verseau called as he strode toward Evanangela's apartments.

He obeyed, holding Evanangela tight as he trotted after Verseau. He threw open the doors to the apartments, revealing the dazzling glass room. Gabriel gasped at the sight. The azure flames crackled in the grate, defying nature. A shiver ran down his spine as Verseau stopped next to a bed that housed a stunning gilded coffin.

"Place her here." Verseau nodded.

He looked down at Evanangela, slacking his arms to allow her head to roll back. Her lips parted, exposing her gleaming fangs. His face contorted in horror. "A vampire!"

Verseau rolled his eyes. "Yes! Now put her to bed, you foolish human!"

Gabriel looked up at the coffin again. It was obvious she was well cared for. Her room was afforded the same luxury as a noble or a high mistress. He looked down at her again. She had spared him the fate so many others had suffered in the ballroom. The least he could do was spare her from the sun. He approached the bed, the soft blankets brushing against his breeches as he leaned over the coffin, settling Evanangela into the over-stuffed cushions. Verseau slid the heavy lid closed.

Verseau grabbed the mortal by the front of his jacket. "Listen well, I don't know what whimsy has taken hold of my beloved, but she spared you. As an outsider, you cannot be trusted, least of which, avec ma fleur."

"What will happen to me?" His voice trembled.

"Jacques!" Verseau bellowed.

The door flew open and Jacques strode into the room, performing a smart bow before looking Gabriel up and down. "Oui, mon Seigneur?"

Verseau lifted the mortal to his feet, and pushed him toward Jacques. "See to it ma chérie's new pet is kept out of trouble until moonrise."

Jacques nodded and turned to face the door. "Guards!"

Two men in chainmail with swords at their hips burst into the room. Jacques waved his hand. "Seigneur has asked us to escort our new *guest* to secure lodgings."

The guards saluted Verseau. "Oui, Seigneur!"

Jacques held up his hand as one of the guards advanced. "No need to be rough." He turned and nodded to Gabriel with a stern glare. "I'm sure our *guest* will oblige."

"Oui, absolutement!" His voice cracked, the fear plain on his face.

The party exited the apartments. Gabriel turned back with one last frightened gaze at Verseau before the guard shut the door.

The air rushed from Verseau all at once and he leaned heavily on Evanangela's coffin. "Ah, ma petite. It seems your past has come to haunt you. Or is it something else?"

He traced the carvings on the wood, his longing tinged with melancholy. "How I had hoped this night to make you mine."

The following nightfall, Evanangela woke in a daze. Her head was swimming and there was a fire in her chest, pumping through every empty vein. She screamed aloud in searing pain.

"She's awake!" Àmichemin cheered.

Evanangela whipped her head around, trying to find the mortal. "Gabriel? Gabriel!"

"Oh no, not this again," Àmichemin smoothed Evanangela's tussled hair and took out a wineskin, "come, ma chère, take a few sips for me."

She managed to swallow a mouthful of the blood that poured from the wineskin. She panted, choking as she tried to catch her breath. The vision of Gabriel burned bright in her mind. She knew there was no escaping La Valse Noire, and yet she clung to her small hope.

"Gabriel! I want to see him!" Her voice was hoarse, strained with fear.

Àmichemin gritted her teeth. "Would you bring that stupid mortal into the room? Maybe she'll stop screaming if it's in here."

"Jacques!" Verseau barked.

63

Another voice floated above her. "Oui, Seigneur?"

"Fetch that stupid mortal, Gabriel. He's under guard in my study." Verseau snapped, exasperated.

"Tout de suite, Seigneur." Jacques' voice was clear and monotone as ever. His footsteps disappeared as he left the room.

After a few moments, Evanangela tried to sit up in the coffin, but her head was heavy and her mind sluggish. There was whispering, then another set of footsteps were coming toward her. Then a face peered over the side of the coffin.

She reached up. "Oh, Gabriel!"

"Petite princesse, il faut que tu boire mon sang.⁴" Gabriel offered his arm. "Voici."

The pungent scent of mortal flesh hit Evanangela's nostrils like water to a desert traveler. The warm skin was pressed against her lips. She grabbed hold and pierced it with her clean fangs. There was a sharp intake of breath as the blood gushed over her dry tongue. She shuddered as her veins filled with the warm living liquid. Within moments, her mind cleared. The pain in her chest subsided and her heart was swollen and beating.

"She's all right!" Àmichemin pulled Evanangela upright, crushing her in a frantic embrace. "Damn you, Evanangela! Damn your beautiful black soul to hell!"

Evanangela wiped away the red tears that had fallen onto her dress once Àmichemin let go. She saw Verseau and Gabriel standing nearby, looking relieved. Gabriel was wrapping his arm in a linen bandage. Evanangela struggled to pull herself from the coffin, her limbs still shaky from missing the previous night's feed.

She stumbled as her feet hit the floor. Both Gabriel and Verseau moved to catch her, but Verseau was quicker. He gathered Evanangela into his arms and sent Gabriel a scathing glare.

"Careful now, ma petite." He crooned as he petted her hair.

Evanangela embraced him, leaning her head on his shoulder. Relief washed over her. "Mon Seigneur, j'avais peur de ne pas te revoir!"⁵

---

4 Little princess, you must drink my blood.
5 I thought I might never see you again!

Verseau held her tight. "You silly, silly girl! You gave us all such a fright!"

"Thankfully, you did not cause a scene at the feed. Everyone was too busy with the frenzy to notice." Àmichemin brushed aside a lock of Evanangela's hair and kissed her cheek as Verseau held her, "Honestly, must you really start collecting pets already?"

She tipped her gaze up to Verseau. "Do you have mortal pets, Seigneur?"

Àmichemin laughed and he sent her a chastising glare.

Verseau released his grip on Evanangela, allowing her to stand on her own. "Non, pas du tout.[6] Now tell me, ma chérie, pourquoi veux-vous ce mortel?[7]"

She dropped her gaze to the floor. "Il me rappelle un vieil ami."[8]

"A friend?" Relief spread on Verseau's face. "That's all?"

"C'est tout.[9]" Evanangela took Verseau's hand and curtsied deep. "Seigneur, may I keep him under the court's protection as my personal attendant, s'il vous plaît?"

Verseau's jaw tightened, but Àmichemin sent him a quick glare and he darted his eyes away. Àmichemin crossed her arms, her chastising scowl gave way to an amused smile. He sighed and kissed Evanangela on the forehead.

"If it makes you happy, ma petite, then the answer is yes." Verseau turned to Gabriel, "However, he will be kept under guard until he can be trusted. He is an outsider. Just because you chose him does not mean he will protect us."

"You have saved me from a monstrous fate," he knelt before Verseau and bowed his head, "I am in your debt. I swear upon my own life that no harm shall come to you."

Verseau turned to Àmichemin. She nodded, and Verseau motioned for Gabriel to rise. "The guard will remain. You are an outsider and it is protocol."

6 Absolutely not.
7 My darling, why do you want this mortal?
8 He reminds me of an old friend.
9 That's all.

"I understand, Seigneur." He turned to Evanangela and kissed her hand, "Princesse, j'accepte votre aimable offre.[10]"

Evanangela drew her hand away. "Et merci beaucoup pour sauve moi, Monsieur-[11]"

He bowed. "Ç'est 'garçon' maintenant, ma princesse."

Verseau gave Evanangela a deep kiss, then looked up at Àmichemin. "See to it that she's properly dressed and down at the feed as quickly as possible." He then strode out into the hall, shutting the door behind him.

"Neh! Neh! Àmichemin faites ceci, faites cela!"[12] Àmichemin rolled her eyes once Verseau had left.

"Why did he leave so abruptly?" Evanangela asked as Àmichemin opened the armoire and started pulling out clothes.

"He will be fine." Àmichemin was about to pull out Evanangela's underthings when she noticed Gabriel was still standing near the bed.

"Jacques, please give the garçon his attendant badge and see to it he is kept out of sight."

"Of course, Mademoiselle," Jacques bowed and tilted his head to Gabriel.

Àmichemin waved her hand. "You are dismissed."

Jacques gave another swift bow, motioned for Gabriel to follow, and left the two vampiresses to dress. Àmichemin turned back to the wardrobe, sifting through clothes. Evanangela fidgeted, looking back at the door. She had surprised herself at her newfound boldness.

Is this what Àmichemin was talking about? Is this what it means to become a fully grown vampire?

As she pondered this, she recalled the warnings from Verseau and Àmichemin that if she did not feed that she could die. Her heart tightened as she remembered that since she could not bear to feed on Gabriel that she had not fed the night before.

"Àmichemin, what happened after the feed last night?"

---

10 Princess, I accept your kind offer.
11 And thank you very much for saving me, Sir-
12 Do this, do that!

"You didn't feed and fainted, clutching that mortal. Verseau eventually pried you off him, and had you put into your coffin before the sun came up. Verseau sent the mortal away before waking you, worried that seeing him again would be upsetting." Àmichemin flicked her hair, annoyed.

She nodded, playing with a hairbrush, her fingers sliding over the coarse bristles. "Is Verseau angry with me for keeping him as an attendant?"

Àmichemin shrugged. "It will pass. Verseau can become jealous, but it is typically short-lived." She leaned her hand on her hip and turned her gaze to Evanangela. "Why did you keep him?"

Evanangela sat down at the vanity, brushing her hair. "Àmichemin, can I tell you something. Can I trust you to keep a secret?"

"Ma petite, you can tell me anything." Àmichemin said as she sat down next to Evanangela and brushed her own silvery hair.

She squeezed the brush in her hand to keep her voice from trembling. "Àmichemin, that mortal was familiar to me. He is almost identical to the Gabriel I loved before I was turned."

Àmichemin finished brushing her hair and began putting on her stockings. "Don't go chasing the past by having a triste with that mortal. Verseau will not stand for it. It will bring your ruin."

"No, it's not like that," Evanangela took a deep breath, "our love was not one of bestial desires. You see, avant d'être un vampire, j'étais une ange."[13]

She stared at her, frozen with her shoes in hand. "A what?"

"Une ange. I was never mortal. I lived in the clouds as a being of light and air." Evanangela looked away. Her breath hitched as her nerves threatened to close her throat. "Gabriel was as well. It startles me how much this mortal resembles him. It is a comfort to see his face. He reminds me of home, nothing more."

Àmichemin shook her head, her eyes glazed over in faraway in thought. "That explains the tattoo-"

"Hmm?" Startled by her response, Evanangela turned her gaze back to Àmichemin.

---

13 Before I was a vampire, I was an angel.

She reached under Evanangela's hair and traced the tattoo again. "I knew there was something not quite right about you. This tattoo explains it all!" She let go, allowing the hair to fall back into place.

"Please, Àmichemin, please don't tell anyone!" Evanangela begged, trying to grab Àmichemin's hand.

"I had suspected, what with your name and the wings twined in your marking. But I had thought it far too absurd! What would an angel be doing walking as a creature of the night?" She babbled, waving her hands, almost tossing the shoes she held.

"Àmichemin, I didn't mean to upset you. I just wanted to explain. Please, forget what I've said." Evanangela trembled.

"Jamais![14]" Àmichemin shouted, throwing her shoes across the room. "How could you ask me to forget such a thing? Evanangela, don't you understand? This is where your power comes from! This is why you are more than just a petty vixen. You are the same as the ancients; those from the tales of old. They too had fallen from grace. And now, we are their dark legacy."

Evanangela twisted her hands in her lap. The fear was boiling in her belly. "Then, you shall not reveal me to the court?"

Àmichemin swept her into a deep embrace. "Jamias, ma petite. You are far too precious. You and I are the only ancients in this court. It is possible you may be what we need to save us from ruin."

She kissed Evanangela on the forehead, then smoothed her hair. Evanangela let out a shuddering breath, and wiped away the tears that threatened to fall. "Merci, Àmichemin. I am finally home."

---

14 Never!

68

Chapter Seven

Evanangela trotted after Àmichemin out of the apartments. Her thoughts receded when they were met with the pompous court once more. The lively chatter of the gossiping vixens died down as she and Àmichemin glided past. Once they reached the main hall before the ballroom, Verseau appeared and watched them descend the staircase. His smile widened once they reached the landing.

"Mes Mademoiselles, vous avez l'air absolument morbide ce soir."[1]

Àmichemin gave a cool smile with a hint of sapphire dusting her cheeks. "Merci, mon Seigneur."

They took Verseau's arms, allowing him to lead them into La Valse Noire. Evanangela relished the comfort of his closeness, the power that exuded from him as the vampires made way. She held her head high, satisfied by the obedience of the court. Àmichemin was first to disappear into the dance, but not before sending Verseau a sultry smile over her shoulder. He growled under his breath, his grip on Evanangela's waist tightening.

"Go on, ma petite," he whispered, kissing her hair before slipping away.

Evanangela stood near the dance floor, feeling shy as vampires claimed their mortals for the night. She shuddered as she recalled seeing Gabriel's face in the dance. The partners spun about, twirling and trotting. Evanangela took a deep breath, her mind quieted from the blood Verseau and Gabriel had given her earlier. But it was not enough, only a few mouthfuls. She needed to feed, lest she feel the pain of empty veins again.

The sway of dancers revealed a knot of mortals who had not yet been chosen. Evanangela found it easy to lock eyes with a rather tall and slender mortal. His coppery hair shone against the flicker of the candles. Evanangela curtsied to him, holding her gaze.

---

1 My ladies, you are absolutely morbid this evening.

"Bonjour Mademoiselle, I don't believe we have met." He bowed to her.

She shivered as the mortal kissed her hand. "Monsieur, it is a pleasure to meet you."

They began dancing, and Evanangela's skin rippled as she envisioned tearing into his soft neck and tasting his blood. With Gabriel, horror had spread through her mind at the very thought of harming him. Whereas this mortal felt like all the others; he was simply her next meal and nothing more. Such a thought should have weighted her with guilt, but all she felt was delightful anticipation as she stroked the roof of her mouth with her tongue.

A low moan escaped her lips and she covered her mouth with her hand. "Je regrettes,[2] Monsieur, I-"

The mortal removed Evanangela's hand and kissed it again. He reached up and caressed her cheek. "Mademoiselle, you have nothing to apologize for besides being la plus jolie fleur de cette cour."[3]

He dipped his head and closed his eyes to kiss her. She giggled, leaned her head toward him, and put her lips to his ear. "Monsieur, je te veux."[4]

Evanangela tilted her head to the side, smiling and exposing her fangs. The mortal's eyes widened. Before he could scream, she sunk into his warm skin and pierced his neck. Her fangs tore at his flesh and she delighted in seeing the red burst forth. Evanangela's tongue was drenched in his sweet blood and her body was smoldering with pleasure. She wrapped her arms around his strong body and pressed against him as his blood filled her, warmed her.

Oh, if this is death then I never, never want to live ever again!

She licked the trickling blood off the mortal's neck and drew it into her mouth. Once the wound crusted over with black, she released the body and let it fall to the floor. Her lips were stained crimson. A warm hand rested upon her shoulder. She turned and came face to face with yet another mortal man.

"Mademoiselle, is your escort ill?"

---

2 I'm sorry

3 The most beautiful flower in this court.

4 I want you.

70

Evanangela giggled, blood trickling down her chin. "Oh, he's fine. He's just *dead*."

The mortal gasped, yanking his hand away as if touching hot coals. Another vampire took the gasping mortal from behind. Blood dribbled onto his lace collar as the vampire dug deep into his neck. Evanangela watched, fascinated as the mortal's eyes rolled up into his head and he gurgled his last breath. Apart from her shock with Gabriel, she felt no connection with the mortals in the ballroom. Up in heaven looking down on them, their problems had seemed so real and her heart had ached to help them with more than just grace and forgiveness. Now, on earth, she felt disconnected and numb. Their desires seemed far pettier and emptier up close. She wondered if the other angels had felt the same as she did now.

The attendants began corralling the vampires and cleaning up the kills. Evanangela had had yet to see what happens to the bodies after a feed. Teams of attendants dragged the bodies into carts, wheeling them out of the ballroom, and out of the château. Gabriel was not among the cleanup crew, and Evanangela felt nothing as she looked about at the scattered corpses. To her, they seemed nothing more than discarded party favors that disappeared one by one.

Evanangela retreated to a window seat. The attendants were shooing vampires away from the cooling heaps. She turned her attention out to the garden. White blossoms silently wafted down from the black tree branches and kissed the glassy surface of the moonlit pond in the courtyard. The ripples whispered around the petals. Evanangela sighed, leaning against the woodwork of the window seat, wondering why no one ever went out there. Verseau appeared at her side, Àmichemin not far behind.

"Verseau, what is happening? Why is the feed being cut short?" Evanangela's gaze bounced between them.

The vampires muttered in small knots, just as confused by the sudden end to the festivities. The tension grew, further alarming Evanangela. She took Àmichemin's hand, who squeezed it in turn.

He sighed and steered her toward the front of the ballroom. "We needed to catch her unaware. There is to be justice tonight."

Before another blossom drifted down, loud voices echoed off the high walls and the vaulted ceiling. Startled, Evanangela froze as a vixen ran into the ballroom like a deer. Her black bouffant was coming

71

undone, leaving worn, scraggly locks of hair drooping over her face. She had no makeup on and her eyes were bloodshot. Her cobalt irises were speckled with blood, and her bosom was stained with red tears. As she banged her hip on one of the tables, her corset flapped open, revealing her luminescent skin in a haphazard attempt at a hasty redressing. The veins in her chest almost seemed to glow a faint scarlet. She had fed recently.

Guards followed her, like a pack of wolves stalking cornered prey. They moved without hurry, but their right hands remained on their sword pommels, at the ready. More guards stood at the closed doors. Attendants stood at attention before the windows, their demeanor aloof and cold.

As she bumped into the yew table, the red velvet tablecloth wrinkled, puckering the fabric around a few candles. Their wax had melted into the cloth, fusing them to the table setting. One cracked and fell onto the table, revealing the unburned wick like a broken spine. The vixen jerked her neck from side to side, a spray of black hair flowing about her in waves, further ruining the bouffant.

There was a booming knock on the ballroom doors. The guards opened them, and several vampires charged through. The vixen let out a piercing scream and yanked down one of the long red velvet banners that hung from the ceiling. A pine bough crashed down beside her, the red ribbon and loose needles fluttered to the floor.

"No! No! Let me go, you don't understand!" She begged as two vampires seized her by the arms. She threw her head back and wailed.

"I will be the judge of that. Bind her!" Verseau's booming voice echoed in the ballroom.

Evanangela tore her gaze away from the frantic vixen. She had never seen Verseau so infuriated. They roughly deposited her on the stage at the back of the hall. The musicians gathered there for the feeds, but the stage was empty now. It seemed so vast with just the vixen. The vampires tied her wrists to the candleholders on the walls.

"Mercy! Mercy! I beg you!" She screamed as she writhed and struggled like a snake against the ropes holding her.

"No mercy for traitors. Bring it in. I don't want it trying to hide in the halls." Verseau turned to Àmichemin and his voice dropped back to its soft comforting lilt; the voice Evanangela knew best. "Ma chérie, please sit with Evanangela. I'm sure all the commotion has frightened her."

Àmichemin glided over to the window seat, her long plum dress rippling around her feet as her hips swayed in her eerie saunter. As she sat down next to Evanangela, Àmichemin gracefully threw her neck in a half-arc, sending her lovely platinum hair spraying like a halo of stars. She reached over and took Evanangela's trembling hands into hers.

Verseau marched toward the vixen. Red tears streamed down her face in bloody rivulets. "Please don't harm Henri! He didn't know!"

A full procession of the court followed him. All were solemn, but none guarded their hot glares from the vixen as they took their seats around the long yew tables. The vixen shrieked until her throat rasped the awful broken wail of a banshee. At the end of the procession, two vampires dragged a mortal. His face was beaten and swollen, but that did not compare to the damage on his neck. It was bruised black and blue with whorls of purple and red. Dried blood crusted around a series of holes.

"Oh, mon cher Henri! What have they done to you? How dare you!" The vixen strained against the chains, but she could not break them. Her matted hair was wet with tears, and stuck to the corner of her mouth. The vampires forced the man to kneel before her.

"You have been caught with this human filth! You thought it wise to cavort with a peasant? You did this while we hide from the rampant hunts in the name of Dieu? While we ration our feeds because of the blood shortage? And endure increased isolation to the point that we have not left Le Château d'Astucieux on progress to La Maison de Printemps[5] in over twenty years? Your selfishness could kill us all!" Verseau's voice thundered, echoing through the ballroom.

A shock ran through Evanangela. It had not occurred to her that the shortage had brought on isolation. The court had always appeared lavish. She looked out the window again, recalling her wonderment that no one ever went out onto the lawns or left the château. Evanangela turned back to the cruel scene. Her mind buzzing with questions.

The vixen shook her head. Her voice was hoarse as she begged. "Please, I was going to change him-!"

5House of Springtime

Verseau growled and his eyes narrowed. "A lowly vixen such as yourself *change* a mortal? A mortal *peasant* of all things? You think you have the authority to raise an underling on your own volition? The court is suffering from the downsized La Valse Noire as it is!"

Nods and murmurs rippled through the court. Disdain oozed from them as they glared at the vixen. Several clacked their fans in disgust.

"What about that spoiled chienne you and Àmichemin brought to court? We are starving after all, *mon Seigneur*." The vixen spat at his feet.

"Tais toi! Votre insolence est stupéfiante!"[6] Verseau slapped her hard across the face. The loud crack of his hand echoed in the ballroom. "You think you are bold to spite the name of ma fleur noire? We'll see how bold you are when your precious human is drained!"

"No! Please just release him! He didn't know!" The vixen screamed, more tears dripping down her chin and dotting the floor. All the bravado in her voice was gone.

"We'll release him back to his precious village after he's dry. We can't risk the chance you already turned him." Verseau sneered at the mortal as the two vampires hauled him to his feet. He hissed in his face.

The vixen bowed her head, begging and clenching her hands. "No! I didn't turn him, je promets! Ç'est vrais! Ç'est vrais!"[7]

Verseau snapped his fingers. "Drain the human."

Two vampires took positions on either side of his neck and sank their fangs deep into his throat. The human could not scream from the pressure of their sucking. Soon, the veins in his forehead stuck out, ropy and twisted. He tried to thrash in their grip, but the vampires held tight, until he slumped. They let him fall to the ground like so much trash.

"Slit its throat. The humans will think it was robbers." Verseau waved his hand. Two attendants stepped forward and began dragging the body from the ballroom.

"Please let me bury him. Don't just throw him out on the street." The vixen begged, her body shuddering with sobs. Her hysterical pleas were met with cold silence from the court.

---

6 Shut your mouth! Your insolence is astounding!
7 I promise! It's true! It's true!

The two vampires now stood on either side of Verseau. One spoke in a calm measured tone, but his voice held the bite of contempt. He sneered down at her. "You know the high law of the court. You are never to associate with a mortal without the court's permission. Mortals that know of the court's location are never allowed to leave. You have broken *both* of these high laws. The punishment for breaking a high law is to be burned."

Verseau bared his fangs at the vixen. Evanangela shivered. She had never seen such fury in him.

"Parce que vous n'avez pas enfreint une seule loi, vous avez enfreint deux lois, vous brûlerez donc deux fois."[8] Verseau nodded.

"No! Banish me! Drain me! Anything but that!" The vixen screamed, her eyes wide and wild. She recoiled into the wall.

Verseau tilted his head. "Use the cobalt candles. No need to waste noir candles on a lowly vixen. The sun will finish her off."

Three more of the court approached her with the enchanted cobalt candles. The vixen writhed against the chains. "Mon Seigneur, I beg you! No, please! Henri! Henri!"

Evanangela now discovered why they never dripped or burned any lower; and why Àmichemin had told her never to touch them. The vampires tipped the candles upside-down over the vixen's head. The flames dripped onto the crown of her hair like liquid fire. She ignited into azure flames. Her keening wail pealed through the ballroom, setting Evanangela's teeth on edge. The vampires stepped back and watched her burn.

Àmichemin held Evanangela, her grip gentle, but firm. "You must watch, ma petite. This is the way of the court."

Horror gripped Evanangela's heart as she watched the vixen scream and writhe on the floor in agony, the blue flames consuming her body. Verseau's face was stony, his gaze locked on the vixen. A new, even more horrible realization ignited Evanangela's fear.

"Àmichemin, why was I spared this horrible fate when I asked to keep Gabriel?"

---

8 Because you didn't break just one law, you broke two laws, you will thusly burn twice.

She turned; her face stamped with bored amusement. "Your *Gabriel* was fated to die here in the château. You also asked *permission* for him to be your attendant. You did not to turn him into a member of the court. You did not leave the château and cavort with an outside mortal that could relay information to the villages, and therefore, put the court at risk. *You* have done nothing wrong. This chienne has endangered us all with her selfish nonsense."

Evanangela nodded, relief washing over her. She understood now by what Àmichemin had meant before – she had power. Her power protected her from such a frightening fate like that of the vixen, but only so long as she stayed within the boundaries of the court's rule, and within Verseau's favor. Should she reach too high, she too could burn.

"You are all dismissed. Unless, you want to burn with the wretch." Verseau took both Àmichemin and Evanangela's arms. His voice was harsh and his grip was firm.

"Come my darlings, the sun shall soon be upon us." The soft lilt was back, the bitterness gone. He led them away from the ruined corpse with the court gliding behind them.

Chapter Eight

Evanangela woke to the sound of heavy knocking. She turned in the darkness of the coffin and felt Àmichemin stirring herself awake. Àmichemin reached up and pushed the lid open. She stretched and yawned. Evanangela leaned over the lip of the coffin and saw Gabriel looking down at her. A second attendant stood behind him.

He moved away from the bed and lowered his gaze to the floor. "Réveillez-vous, Mademoiselles. Ç'est la nuit et le flux commence."[1]

"Merci, Gabriel." Evanangela stifled another yawn.

"Merci, *garçon*." Àmichemin corrected with biting annoyance.

She shrugged, then stepped out onto the bed. "Ç'est le même."[2]

Àmichemin slapped Evanangela hard across the face. Her body shook as she growled. "Jamais! Ne me parle jamais comme ça!"[3]

Evanangela shrieked, clutching her cheek. She backed away from Àmichemin, trembling and bowing her head. "Je regrettes, m'amie! Ne frappes pas moi encore, s'il vous plaît!"[4]

Àmichemin gathered her wits, and her face fell. "Non, je suis désolé, ma chère."[5] She drew Evanangela into an embrace. The odd rage was gone, and Àmichemin's familiar stillness comforted her.

"Let's just go to the feed." She whispered as Àmichemin released her.

"Oui." Àmichemin nodded and busied herself finding her brush.

Evanangela was still shaken by Àmichemin's outburst. She held her hands to hide their shaking as they walked down the hall toward

---

1 Wake up, ladies. It is night and the feed is starting.
2 It is the same.
3 Never! Never speak to me like that!
4 I'm sorry, my friend! Please don't hit me again!
5 No, I am sorry, my dear.

the feed. Both she and Verseau had seemed on edge since the vixen's execution. He had left at Àmichemin's door the night before without so much as a "bonne nuit"; marching off to his own apartments in stony silence.

Verseau was standing at the bottom of the stairs. Joy surged through Evanangela when she met his gaze, the tension forgotten. Her mind craved his comfort above all else. She galloped down the stairs to meet him.

He opened his arms in a smooth arc as she folded into his chest. His voice was warm and playful once more. "Ah, ma petite, how are you this evening?"

She looked up into his eyes, her cheeks bright blue with the bloodless blush. "Absolutely lovely now that you're here."

"Ah, but I am always here." Verseau smiled as he escorted Evanangela and Àmichemin into the ballroom. The dance had already begun and the miasma of mortal scent washed over them.

Àmichemin disappeared into the dance, snaring a mortal at once. She did not look back as her dress swished through the rainbow of dancers. Verseau, however, did not release Evanangela. He pulled her onto the dance floor, twirling her.

"Forgive me, ma petite fleur," he whispered in her ear, "I know last night was particularly frightening for you. But it is important you see how I protect this court, and you, as Seigneur. We can never be too careful, lest the peasants riot and attack us again."

Evanangela's mind whirred as Verseau dipped her, then swung her back into his embrace as the waltz became more frenzied. She remembered how frightened the villager priest had been upon discovering her. "Riots? Why would the peasants riot and act against us?"

Verseau opened his mouth to speak, but a mortal tapped him on the shoulder. He turned his head, locking eyes with the mortal.

"May I cut in, Seigneur?" He bowed his head, then smiled at Evanangela.

Her eyes darted between them. Verseau nodded, slipping her hand into the mortal's grasp. "Bien sûr, take good care of ma petite."

He disappeared into the dance to find his own victim. The mortal's hands drew about her waist and took her hand, leading her into the waltz, much slower than Verseau. She met his gaze, the hunger welling up in her heart as she stared into his eyes.

The mortal's lips spread into a salacious grin. "What a fool to give you up. I don't think I'll let you go after this dance."

"Pardonnez?" Evanangela titled her head, her thoughts hazy with blood lust.

He laughed as he swung her into a twirl. "You certainly are beautiful, Mademoiselle. I should like to explore your beauty after this dance. I'm sure you know of a quiet corner we could-"

Evanangela giggled, a cool sapphire blush rising in her cheeks. She slid her hand down from his shoulder to his chest. "You are perfectly ridiculous! You shan't live to the end of this dance. But you shall know me."

The mortal loosened his grip, confusion replacing his cocky grin. She dug her nails into his jacket and thrust her fangs into his throat, strangling his screams. His fear heightened her excitement as she tightened her grip. Evanangela's eyes rolled into the back of her head as she suckled his severed vein. The warm blood was rivulets of ecstasy over her tongue, igniting her mind to wish for Verseau's strong arms to drag her to his coffin for the night. She lapped at the mortal's neck, imagining she was blood-sharing with Verseau.

A crash jolted Evanangela from her feed. She jerked her head up, blood trickling down her chin. She swallowed, her eyes swiveling to find the disturbance. A pair of vampires were mauling one another, their clean fangs exposed as they grabbed at each other, trying to gain leverage to slash with their gruesome teeth. They looked like vipers, hissing and darting.

Mortals began screaming, bull-rushing the doors. The attendants rushed to shut the ballroom doors, but a few escaped. The remaining mortals began banging on the doors, shoving each other out of the way. The cacophony drowned out the music, until Evanangela realized the music had stopped all together; the musicians joining the frenzy. More vampires and vixens descended upon the crowd, turning La Valse Noire from a graceful waltz of death into a gruesome hunt. A hand grabbed Evanangela, pulling her to her feet. She whirled about, hissing, coming face to face with Verseau. The terror on his face ripped away the warmth and comfort of her feed. The blood was heavy like lead, weighing her down.

"Que se passe-t-il, Seigneur?[6]" Evanangela pressed tight against him.

Verseau wrapped his arms around her. Àmichemin approached them, putting her hand on his shoulder. "Maintenant!"

He nodded, pulling Evanangela off his jacket, and took her by the hand. Together, they ran from the bloodbath at the main doors. Verseau pulled one of the black candles from the wall sconce, and a crack in the wall appeared. Àmichemin dug her fingers into the crevice and wrenched the wall open, revealing a staircase. They darted inside, Àmichemin closing up the wall behind them. It was a dark, dank space and there was the scuttling of rats.

"Que se passe-t-il?" Evanangela repeated, gasping for breath as they charged up the stairs.

They were met with another wall, which Verseau pushed open, spilling them out into the west end of the hall. It was empty, save for an attendant or two darting past toward the ballroom. Àmichemin led the way to Verseau's apartments. Jacques was standing at attention at the door as always, though his face was pinched with worry. He bowed and opened the door, allowing the trio to barrel inside. He came in, closing the door behind him.

"Will you be taking refuge here, Seigneur, or shall I ready the carriage?" His voice shook.

Verseau shook his head. "We will stay here. It is too risky to leave the château. Bar the doors."

Àmichemin flopped onto the couch, her limbs splayed as her chest fluttered. Her eyes were wide as she stared up at the ceiling. Evanangela sank onto a burgundy cushion, her body folding under her. She held her hand over her chest, willing her breath to slow.

"Where did you get those mortals from?" Àmichemin gasped, rolling her eyes up to Verseau. The alarm in her gaze cut through Evanangela, magnifying her fear.

He shrugged, allowing his body to drop into his reading chair. Verseau rubbed his face with a handkerchief, then balled it into his fist

_____
6 What is happening, Lord?

and held it against his forehead as he caught his breath. "The Mors Ivoire[7] Court sent them. They are lower vassal mortals. Our contracts for more sensible class mortals have long since run dry, so to speak."

Evanangela slowed her breathing, her ears thundering from the living blood rushing about her system. "Contracts? The court has contracts for mortals from other courts?"

"Where did you think the mortals came from?" Àmichemin slid herself into a more dignified position on the couch. Her demeanor had calmed, but her body was still stiff and agitated.

The thought had never occurred to Evanangela. She sat, pondering her past feeds, going over the details of the mortals in her mind. They did seem of more standing than mere peasants, like those she had met in the churchyard. Their clothes were made with fine fabrics and expensive dyes. Their necks, wrists, and fingers often crusted in jewelry.

"But why would other courts give us their mortals?" She had seen the selfish ways of the court and was unconvinced other vampire courts would be any different.

Verseau rubbed his forehead, his eyes closed. "Because of a past blood debt. When a court has a blood shortage, they reach out to their fellow courts for help. When a court is rich in abundant mortal population, it is their duty to share the surplus. And as such, the cycle goes."

Evanangela contemplated this. She recalled the empty churchyard, though most mortals do not venture out at night, it was eerie how empty the roads had been as Àmichemin had led her to the château. Another thought struck her.

"Àmichemin, why were you outside the night of my fall?"

She flinched and sat up from the couch, caught off guard by the question. "You mean the night of your birth? It is as Verseau said, I was returning from negotiating the contract with The Mors Ivoire Court. It was a long journey, and I was restless from so many nights cooped up in a carriage with a donor attendant. So, I got out for a little old-fashioned hunting and found you instead."

Verseau leaned back in the chair, his face grim. "Soon, we shall all be beggars in the night draining peasants."

---

7 Ivory Bit

"Don't say such vile things." Àmichemin flopped onto her side. Her panic had dissipated, returning back to her bored and haughty demeanor.

Jacques cleared his throat, startling the trio. "Seigneur, mes Mademoiselles, the sun approaches."

"Ah, yes, yes." Verseau grumbled. "I suppose tonight shall be rather crowded."

He loosened his cravat and flung his jacket onto the floor. Verseau let the air rush from his lungs, making a low whistle between his lips as his anxiety subsided. He made quick work of his shirt, revealing his naked chest. His bare cedar brown skin sent a scarlet blush burning into Evanangela's cheeks. She longed to run her fingers through his gleaming black hair.

"Ah, ma petite Mademoiselle," Verseau chuckled as his eyes met hers, "I fear we do not have time for such delightful things this night. Come."

Evanangela took his outstretched hand. He made short work of the clasps at her back, her dress sliding down, puddling at her feet. Àmichemin threw off her own dress. She drew her bright hair to the side as Verseau's patient fingers unlaced her corset. He snuck a kiss on the back of her neck before leading them to his bed. The enormous black coffin was waiting.

"Ah Verseau, only you would turn a night of terror into such a pleasing pile of flesh." Àmichemin teased as she climbed into the coffin after him.

He drew his arm around her, cradling her head onto his shoulder. Àmichemin smiled as he placed a gentle kiss on her forehead. He then lifted his free hand up, beckoning Evanangela. "Come, ma petite."

She obeyed, lowering herself into the coffin. It was warm, as both Àmichemin and Verseau had both managed to feed before the wild frenzy. She snuggled against him, her head on his chest. The soothing rhythm of his heartbeat slowing her amorous thoughts to simple comfort. The lid of the coffin slid closed. Her thoughts slipping into the darkness of sleep.

Evanangela woke warm and snuggled between Verseau and Àmichemin. She considered lounging for the evening, but the horror of the previous night broke through her comfortable thoughts. Her hand flew up to her mouth as she gasped.

Verseau sat up, yawning and exposing his clean fangs. "What is it, ma chérie?"

"What's going on?" Àmichemin grumbled as she sat up and ran her hands through her hair.

"I'm sorry," Evanangela shook her head, willing her panic to dissolve, "I know I should be used to it by now, but the feed last night-" she trailed off, shivering.

Àmichemin kissed her forehead, and then Verseau took Evanangela into his arms. "Fear not, ma petite. I foresaw such a thing happening. Tonight, the courts are coming to the château to discuss the crisis." He stroked her hair.

"Crisis?" Evanangela's eyes widened. The terror from the previous night hit her all over again. "But, Seigneur, if there is a crisis, then why has the court been living so lavishly? You had said there was a shortage, and yet, we are all fattened with blood, dancing as if each night were a festival!"

"Sweet Evanangela, La Valse Noire is *not* lavish." Àmichemin laughed as she stepped out of the coffin. "Merely a construct to keep the social order from falling apart. No, there were once days when we would be drunk on blood while lounging on heaps of cooling flesh. It took all Verseau's influence to convince the court to adhere to the one victim per vampire rule in order to stave off the shortage for as long as we have."

Verseau nodded, lifting Evanangela up out of the coffin. His firm grasp soothed her, grounding her fears. She found her feet, fidgeting her toes on the cold black stone floor. He climbed out and stood beside her.

"The Seigneur of old had dealt with the Days of Terror when a shortage caused the court to leave the château to hunt in the villages like savage beasts. I cannot have that stain upon my legacy as well."

Àmichemin plucked a long black velvet robe from the nearby wardrobe and put it on. She pulled a second one out and tossed it to Evanangela. Her abruptness startled Evanangela; Àmichemin was not one to be rushed.

"Come, we must prepare. The Council shall be arriving soon." Àmichemin took Evanangela's hand.

He nodded. "Yes. Be sure Evanangela is suitably dressed. She will have a seat at the summit." He walked alongside Àmichemin, seeing them out.

The hall was quiet, save for attendants scurrying to and fro. Àmichemin led Evanangela to her apartments. They were just as dazzling as before. The rich gold rugs were warm under her bare feet. Àmichemin set to work sorting through the enormous wardrobe.

"How can there be a shortage of mortals if there are so many attendants about the château?" Evanangela mused as Àmichemin tossed her stockings and other underthings.

She pulled a heavy black silk gown trimmed with violet lace and ribbon from the wardrobe. "The attendants are not "mortals" in that sense. They and their families have served us here at the château for many generations. On the agreement we do not attack them and their families, they protect us from the villagers and the sun. They are also protected from famine and plague here in the château."

Evanangela nodded. She had thought little of how easy it would be for an attendant to open a coffin in the height of day, sentencing a vampire to death. And yet, she had always felt utterly safe. "I see. So, then the villagers have reduced numbers for La Valse Noire?"

"No, we only hunt villagers as a last resort." Àmichemin shook her head. "We prefer to prey on the merchants, vassals, and lesser mortal nobles. They are easily fooled into thinking they have been invited to a lavish ball. The mortals we dine on each night have more *flexible* morals and allow their desires to cloud their judgement. The villagers are simple, suspicious creatures; clinging to their faith above all else. They know what we are and would not come to the château willingly."

Chapter Nine

Once dressed, the two exited out into the hall. It was eerily quiet. Verseau met them at the corner, offering both his elbows to them.

"Where is everyone?" Evanangela took Verseau's left arm as they descended the stairs.

Àmichemin took Verseau's right arm. "They are all locked away in their quarters. The feeds will be brought to them. We need clear heads and no distractions for the summit."

Evanangela nodded. The doors to the ballroom opened, revealing a long black table with a gold runner along its entire length; the stag leaping over the briars emblem was embroidered in red on the runner's ends. There were vampires already seated at the table. Some mingled, standing in small clusters, while others stood peering out the windows into the garden. Their outfits were much different than those of the court. Their jewelry sparkled in the candlelight, creating sprays of rainbows about the room.

"Announcing Seigneur Verseau and his Mademoiselles, Àmichemin and Evanangela." One of the attendants hailed into the hall.

All the vampires bowed. The scraping of chairs was the only sound as everyone took their seats. Verseau sat at the head of the table, Evanangela on his left, Àmichemin on his right. She kept her gaze on the table before her, nervous of all the vampires that swiveled their gaze to Verseau. Unlike the vampires and vixens of the court, these were officials of their own courts. Their fashions varied wildly, showcasing the latest trends of their territories. Seigneurs and envoys trained in ruling, not simply vassals of power and pleasure.

Verseau cleared his throat. "As you all know, there is a blood shortage in the Nacre Court. The Mors Ivoire Court has been generous in providing mortals to make up for the shortage. However, this is only a temporary solution and will not last. It has come to my attention that the Nacre Court is not alone in this blood shortage, as in recent years the Black Death has swept over much of France and our neighboring countries. This shortage will soon affect us all."

One of the vampires nodded. "It is true, the humans cannot breed fast enough to replenish their numbers. The remaining suitable mortals must be left as stock. We have two options left – we must find a safe way to prey on the lesser mortals, or our courts will be forced into hibernation."

"Yes, we must avoid the hunts of old at all costs. The Year of the Blood Moon led to the times of Great Terror, and the Nacre Court, and other courts, being reduced due to the lesser mortal uprisings. Such a blemish tarnishes our great history. Repeating such a travesty is not an option."

The vampire knocked his hand on the table. "Agreed. We are better than our past. The hunts of old were barbaric, wasteful, and dangerous."

Àmichemin tucked a lock of hair behind her ear. "It seems that our current means of feeding for the summit may be a solution. Currently, we have individual mortals being sent to the apartments of the members of our court. Perhaps, the same could be done with the villagers. However, there is the problem with procuring them in the first place."

The vampires mused, their voices blending together. Evanangela fidgeted her hands in her lap. It seemed odd to speak of human lives the same as sheep or cattle. Though it had become easier, and even enjoyable, for her to participate in the feed, it still nagged at her heart that these humans were led blindly to their deaths each night.

Another vampire knocked on the table. "We know the villagers are wary of our courts. We cannot fool them with invitations. However, they often find their way to death through the gallows in their own courts. Perhaps, we could capitalize on their crimes and take the prisoners for ourselves?"

Several of the vampires grimaced. "Common thieves and bandits? How revolting!"

"Indeed." Verseau sneered. "While the prospect of feeding on slovenly criminals is ghastly, perhaps we can take advantage of their little system – steer the more appetizing mortals into the ranks for the gallows so to speak."

The first vampire gestured. "And how would we do that? While our courts preside over these villages, we do not have a hand in their local justice proceedings."

Verseau shook his head. "We would need to install our vassals into their justice systems. But that takes time; time we do not have."

Again, the vampires muttered and talked amongst themselves. Their voices blended together in a buzz. Evanangela looked up at Amichemin. Her chin was squared, her eyes darting over the other vampires. She was absorbed in the conversation, her eyes calculating. Evanangela looked away, settling her gaze on the braided table runner.

Why did Verseau ask me to be a part of this summit? Surely, he did not think I had anything intelligent or helpful to add?

She looked up at him. His face was passive, save for the taut line of his jaw that gave away his foreboding thoughts. He turned his gaze to Evanangela, and his eyes softened for a moment before returning to their stony scheming.

Another vampire knocked on the table. "There is human trade – the humans sell one another to be attendants. However, this would involve outright stealing cargo ships and would certainly result in a direct attack upon our courts."

The vampires went round and round, seeking new solutions and refuting them due to the mounting risks. Evanangela soon grew tired and bored. The summit seemed no closer to solving the shortage than when it had started. She dared to gaze up at the moon out the windows. It was peaceful and beautiful in its cold, sterile way. She suppressed a sigh and returned her attention to the circular discussion.

Verseau knocked on the table. "We ask for your courts to consider possible solutions. We hope to remedy this shortage before it becomes an emergency. In the meantime, we are grateful to our neighbors, the Mors Ivoire Court, and hope that all your treaties are kind and generous as well."

Amichemin bowed her head. Evanangela followed suit. "We are grateful for you coming to the summit to discuss this grave matter. We hope you enjoy your accommodations this night, before returning home. Your feeds are waiting in your guest chambers."

The vampires rose, the scraping of chairs echoing in the ballroom. Evanangela stood, and Verseau took her hand. He scraped his clean fangs along her wrist, sending shivers through her body. She bit her lip to stifle a sigh.

"Ah, ma petite, I know that was not entertaining, but I hope you learned much." He drew his arm around her.

She nodded. "Oui, Seigneur. I did not realize that the court had such organization with the other courts."

Àmichemin laughed. "This certainly was an uneventful summit. I remember those in the past when voices were raised and fists pounded. Verseau has certainly had a pleasing impact on how things are run."

"Such high tempers do not bode well for proper discussion." He nodded. "Living blood can leave the mind hazy and prone to volatile emotions. I have had your feeds sent to my chambers. Forgive me, I would love to have a different end to our delightful close quarters from the previous evening."

Evanangela tilted her head. "A different end, Seigneur?"

"He means he prefers us to be a quivering pile of blood-satiated flesh, rather than the huddled terror of last night." Àmichemin laughed.

Evanangela blushed, the cool sapphire dusting her cheeks and nose. She darted her gaze about to see if any of the officials had overheard. Their nonplussed faces swirled around her as she fought to formulate an appropriate response. "Oh! I-I didn't realize-"

Verseau tilted her chin to gaze into her eyes. "Ma fleur, you do not have to participate if you do not wish to. Though, I'm sure it will be hard for you to resist once your veins are warm and your heart is pounding."

Àmichemin slapped him on the shoulder. "You and your teasing!"

Jacques bowed and opened the apartment door for the trio. "Your guests await, mon Seigneur et mes Mademoiselles."

In the sumptuous sitting room, three mortals were waiting. Two were sitting on the couch, deep in conversation, while the third was standing, staring into the fireplace. The doors to the bedroom were closed, hiding the enormous black coffin. Evanangela's nostrils flared as the delicious scent of blood spiked her brain.

Verseau gave a short bow. "Ah, mes amis, merci vous pour attendez."[1]

---

1 "Ah, my friends, thank you for waiting for us."

The older man nodded from the couch. "Merci, mon Seigneur. We are honored by your private invitation."

Àmichemin strode up to the younger man standing before the fire. "Nonsense, the pleasure is ours."

Evanangela felt the hunger twinge her shriveled heart as she watched Àmichemin press her body against the bewildered young man. Verseau extended his hand to the older lady sitting on the couch. She blushed, and accepted, outstretching her gloved hand. He drew her to her feet, his eyes playful as they scanned her up and down. Evanangela locked eyes with the old man. He looked about, flustered.

"This is not a proper audience! Mon Seigneur, what have you called us here for? Please, I-"

"Shhh," Evanangela sat next to the older gentleman, her body turning to liquid as she slinked toward him, "there is nothing to fear."

Her gaze captivated him, silencing his protests. His mouth was agape as his mind struggled to keep up. She sniffed his skin, wrapping her arms around him. His body stiffened, but he did not push her away. Evanangela tickled his neck with her fangs, earning a delightful shudder and a gentle waft of scent from the man.

Evanangela's ears pricked as she heard the sharp intake of breath. Verseau had taken his victim. She moaned as she pierced the older gentleman's neck with her fangs. The familiar hot rush of blood pooled over her tongue, easing the tension in her chest. She closed her eyes as she drank deep. Her veins swelled, and her heart began to thump, sending waves of pleasure racing across her skin.

She felt a hand on her shoulder as her tongue lapped at the wound, the blood trickling down her chin. Evanangela tilted her head up, and saw Verseau standing over her. His lips were stained with blood, his eyes bright with desire.

"Go on, ma petite. Finish your feed." He crooned as his hands stroked her shoulders through the heavy gown.

His deft fingers began unlacing Evanangela's stays as she drank greedy gulps of blood. Her sighs and groans became heavier and more insistent as the gown loosened, revealing her luminous skin. Evanangela let the old gentleman fall back onto the couch, his head lolling. Verseau leaned against her back, his hot breath tickling her ear.

"Are you ready, ma fleur?" He whispered.

Evanangela nodded. Verseau lifted her up off the couch. She squeezed his hand. Àmichemin stood nearby, her mortal dead and discarded on the floor. She cuddled up to Verseau's side, a drop of blood trickling from the corner of her lip.

"Ah, ma chère douler, you have a stain." He licked the blood from her lip, then kissed her hard while digging his fingers into Evanangela's flesh.

Àmichemin sighed, returning his kiss. Her arms wound around his neck; her body pressed against Evanangela. He broke the kiss, pulling them toward the doorway. Àmichemin swung the door open, giggling as they made their way toward the enormous bed.

Verseau picked up Evanangela with grace and ease, and plunked her into the coffin. The sumptuous cushioning cradled her limbs. Verseau climbed in after her, and offered Àmichemin his hand. She took it, stepping into the coffin, and lowered herself to sit inside. She raked her fingers through Verseau's hair. The faint scent tickled Evanangela's nose, making her heart pound. He cupped Àmichemin's chin in his hand, tilting her head to expose her neck. Gooseflesh rippled across her body as he brought his lips closer.

"You are always such a tease!" Àmichemin purred as Verseau grazed his lips over her throat.

His tongue traced the vein in her neck, eliciting gooseflesh racing across her skin. "And you are always in such a hurry."

Àmichemin's mouth fell open as Verseau's fangs pierced her skin. She cradled his head as he lapped at the vein. His hands slid past her neck and wound into her hair. The shimmering locks snared in his dark hands, like stars in the night sky. Evanangela's face was hot as the living blood sent a true blush into her cheeks. She held her hands over her beating heart, the humming vibrating her body. Thin streams of blood dribbled from the puncture wounds on Àmichemin's neck. She shivered, watching the two pet one another. Verseau dipped his fingers into the wound, and dragged them over Àmichemin's waiting tongue.

"Mon Seigneur, I-" Evanangela darted her eyes away, embarrassed at the question she was about to ask.

Verseau turned, drawing his fingers out of Àmichemin's mouth. "Forgive me, ma petite, are you feeling neglected?"

Evanangela's eyes widened as Verseau pulled her closer. She could feel the heat of their bodies. Their faint scents brought to life by the blood heightened her excitement and her nervous hesitation. Àmichemin leaned forward, and tucked a lock of hair behind Evanangela's ear.

"There is plenty to go around." Her breath tickled as she whispered. It sent shivers through Evanangela's body.

Verseau smirked, revealing his bloodstained fangs. "Ah yes. I have been waiting for ma petite Mademoiselle to finally *come around*."

Chapter Ten

Evanangela felt like prey, cornered as they pulled her in. Instead of fear, she felt hot excitement grip her heart. Àmichemin traced her fingernail over the vein on Evanangela's neck, while Verseau pulled her into his lap. His body was hard beneath hers, his thick frame swallowing her up as Àmichemin hovered over her.

"Relax, ma fleur." Verseau kissed her hair.

Àmichemin sunk her fangs into Evanangela's neck. The sharp pain was quickly overcome by the intoxicating rush as the blood was sucked from her. As an angel, she had never known the earthly pleasures of the flesh. Now she understood why great humans had fallen to their base emotions. The wild night she had blood-shared with Àmichemin was a whirlwind; her memories of which made up of rushed feelings and heavy scents. This was slower and sweeter.

Her vision was traded for hazy ecstasy as her body went limp. Àmichemin's warm lips pulled away from the puncture wounds, her slick tongue lapping at the oozing blood. There was an odd coldness, as if a winter breeze played across her neck. Verseau pressed his lips against Evanangela's, drawing her into a deep kiss. The wave of comfort and joy consumed her mind.

She gasped for breath as Verseau released her. Evanangela opened her eyes and saw him staring back. The hunger in them urged her forward, her body aching for more. He tilted his head.

"Oui, ma petite, venez à moi."[1] Verseau guided her head toward his neck.

Evanangela allowed instinct to take over. Her mouth found the vein. She grazed her fangs over it, extricating a deep groan from Verseau. Àmichemin giggled. Evanangela allowed her fangs to pierce the skin, letting the hot blood rush forth. Her eyes fluttered as it bathed her tongue. It was sweeter and richer than mortal blood, but was different from Àmichemin's. She had tasted of deep mulled wine and

---

1 Yes, my little, come to me.

snow. Verseau tasted rougher and richer, like roasted boar and ale with the warmth and comfort of the hearth. She swallowed and lapped at the wound. Shards of memories and thought raced through her. They were quick, like a fleeting thought at the corner of one's mind. Evanangela pulled back, licking the blood from her lips.

Àmichemin was kissing Verseau deeply, her hands busy undoing the buttons of his shirt. He tossed the garment off, letting it fall to the floor. His scent wafted up, and Evanangela tasted it as she dragged her tongue along the roof of her mouth. Àmichemin relinquished her kiss, allowing Verseau to draw back. Àmichemin turned, and he began unlacing her dress, the ribbons whispering against the fabric. It joined the shirt on the floor.

Feeling emboldened, Evanangela moved forward, and Àmichemin took her into her arms. Verseau leaned over Evanangela, kissing Àmichemin once more. His hands petted Evanangela's soft flesh as she was cradled against Àmichemin's body. They soon became a tangle of limbs. Àmichemin's hands were wound around Verseau's neck as he continued to run his large hands over Evanangela's petite frame. Evanangela was unsure of what to do with herself, as she was pinned between them. Their bodies were hot against hers, adding to her excitement.

Àmichemin broke away from the kiss once more. She lowered her head, allowing her chin to rest on the crown of Evanangela's hair. Verseau leaned down and sunk his fangs into the wounds Àmichemin had left, reopening the puncture and allowing the blood to flow. Verseau lapped at the vein, sending a frenzy of shivers through Evanangela's body. Her hands flew up, her nails digging into his back and she held onto him. Àmichemin's grip tightened, holding Evanangela snug against her body.

Verseau released Evanangela. His throat bobbed as he swallowed. Àmichemin nipped Evanangela's ear, her hands petting Evanangela's chest as Verseau leaned forward again, ensnaring her in a kiss. All her sensations were heightened. Their scents, the smell of blood, the glide of their skin, all of it was driving her wild. Evanangela returned his kiss, her arms still wound around him. She slid them up into his hair, her fingers toying with his short black curls. He moaned into her mouth. A shuddering sigh caught in Evanangela's throat. He released her and leaned back. She allowed her hands to slip away from him, settling into her lap as he leaned against the side of the coffin.

"Ah, mes chéries, the sun will cut our decadent feed short. The night has left us."

Evanangela's lip quivered as she turned. The first dovetails of dawn were creeping up the horizon through the arrow slit windows. Àmichemin leaned over Evanangela's shoulder, and kissed her cheek.

"Not to worry. There will be many, *many* other nights."

Verseau nodded, grinning as he raked his hand through his hair. "Ç'est vrais, we have eternity to enjoy one another. So long as the sun does not catch us. To bed mes chéries."

Àmichemin gave her a small push. Evanangela leaned over the edge of the coffin as Verseau slid down so he was on his back. He opened his arms, and wriggled his fingers.

"Venez à moi." He crooned.

Evanangela curled into him, nestling herself against his side and rested her head on his shoulder. He wound his arm around her. His firm muscles gripped her body, sending a pleasant shiver down her spine. He waved his free hand at Àmichemin.

"Yes, yes," she laughed, sliding herself down into his embrace.

Verseau sighed, then kissed each of them in turn. "Bonne nuit à vous deux."[2]

She snuggled into Verseau, and Àmichemin threw her arm across his chest and over Evanangela's side. His warm weight was a comfort as the lid of the coffin slid shut. Evanangela could hear the click of Jacques' shoes receding as the familiar darkness enveloped her.

Something jostled Evanangela awake. She sat up, stretching and yawning. Her hand brushed against something cool and soft. She opened her eyes and saw that she had bumped Àmichemin who was sitting up in the coffin, running her hand through her hair.

"Je regrettes," Evanangela muttered as she withdrew the offending appendage.

---

2 Goodnight to you both.

Àmichemin shook her head and yawned. "Ç'est d'accord." She looked down at Verseau's sleeping form and poked his face. "Réveillez-vous, vous cul douler."[3]

Verseau's fangs gleamed as he yawned and sat up. He grinned at Àmichemin. "Is that any way to wake your Seigneur?"

She snorted and shoved him. Verseau laughed. His eyes softened as his gaze fell on Evanangela. "Ah, ma petite. Did you enjoy yourself last night?"

Evanangela darted her eyes away as a cool sapphire blush revealed the truth. Such base pleasures were beyond her heavenly past, but now, she craved them the way the wolf craves the hunt. The previous evening had left her eager for more. Verseau laughed and petted the crown of her hair.

"Take it all in, ma chère, relive it if you wish at the feed tonight." Verseau slid out of the coffin and looked back down at both of them. "The first frenzy is always the most *overwhelming*."

Àmichemin traced her finger down Evanangela's cheek, then drew in close. Her cool breath tickled Evangela's skin. "He is right. Think on it. Relish in being chosen for such an intimate dance."

She drew away. Evanangela's lips tingled with anticipation, wishing Àmichemin had kissed her. She did not dare correct Verseau about her first frenzy having been with Àmichemin. Evanangela swallowed and took Verseau's hand as he helped lift her out of the coffin. Verseau pulled out two black robes from his wardrobe and handed them over.

"Vite, mes fleurs. The feed will be starting soon."

Evanangela followed Àmichemin into the hall down to her apartments. It was quiet with no vampires chatting, no vixens leaning and fluttering fans. Àmichemin closed the door, sealing them off from the barren hallway. The blue flames crackled merrily in the grate. Evanangela lowered herself onto the over-stuffed footrest. She kept her gaze on the azure fire.

"Àmichemin, if there is to be a feed tonight, where is the court? Surely not everyone is in the ballroom already?"

---

3 Wake up, you pain in the ass.

She sat on the powder blue couch, draping herself over the armrest. "Non, ma petite. All feeds shall take place in our apartments. Verseau has requested we feed in his chambers, lest he become lonely."

Evanangela straightened her shoulders. "How long shall we be locked away like this?"

Àmichemin made a rude noise with her mouth and slumped further into the couch. "We have always been *locked away*. It just seems less like a prison with all the *distractions*."

It was true. They had not left the château since her night in the churchyard. Evanangela wondered if that was what fueled the petty squabbles – being locked away in a château, even one so grand as this, for decades, or possibly even centuries. Suddenly, the expanse of eternity seemed to be stifling. Evanangela took a deep breath to stave off the growing malaise of dark thoughts.

"So, now you see why Verseau was so eager to have you." Àmichemin sat up, her bare feet silent. "Novelty is the highest luxury of the Nacre Court."

The sumptuous wardrobe did not excite Evanangela as it had only a few nights before. She allowed Àmichemin to dress her. The details of her outfit left her mind once they slipped back out into the hall and hurried to Verseau's apartments. Evanangela's skin rippled with gooseflesh as the silence pressed in on her. The only sound was the click of their shoes and the muffled voices of vampires behind the closed doors of their own chambers. She was glad for Verseau's smiling face and the merry scarlet flames in the grate.

A trio of mortals greeted them, just as the evening before. Evanangela allowed Àmichemin and Verseau to select the two dapper young men who sported the latest fashions. Leaving the more eccentric fop for her to take. Their floral perfumes, and the fop's over-powdered face and wig irritated Evanangela's nose. It masked the rich scent of blood and living flesh, like a roasted goose marinated in too strong of herbs. She sighed, seating herself on the couch where the fop was artfully lounging.

"Bonsoire, Mademoiselle," he purred, his eyes scanning her velvet dress, "it is simply a crime for a dazzling creature such as yourself to be in such a dour mood."

Evanangela sighed, then stifled a cough in her throat as the perfumed powder agitated her senses. "Some things simply cannot be helped."

She looked up, watching as Verseau and Àmichemin chatted with the boisterous boys. They were savoring the hunt, which further annoyed Evanangela. Her body quivered with the desire to strike. She decided to mirror her prey to amuse herself, leaning back into the couch, and gazing at him from heavy-lidded eyes.

The fop took Evanangela's silence as intense interest as he chattered on about the fashion he was wearing and the perfume he had selected for the evening. He blathered on about the silk trade and his quest for the perfect dye from the East. Her ears were pricked, listening for the smallest hint that Verseau and Àmichemin were making their move. His words floated in the air, petty useless things about his various escapades at masked balls and wild parties.

Verseau leaned forward, as if to confide in his prey. Evanangela heard the intake of breath. She lunged forward, nearly toppling the couch as she drove her fangs into the fop's neck. Àmichemin had her prey pinned against the wall, his limbs flailing and bumping as she sucked him dry. The only sound in the room was the knocks and bumps of their victims' fruitless attempts at escape.

The blood gushed over Evanangela's tongue, spraying down her throat from the force of her attack. She drank deep, seeking to wash away the acrid taste of powder. His wig tumbled to the floor in a heap, like a lost pet. Evanangela was quick to drain her prey, leaving his limp corpse pressed into the cushions. She sat up, licking her lips as the hot blood began circulating through her dead veins. The warmth spread through her limbs, easing her mind at last. Verseau and Àmichemin were still devouring their mortals. Their moans and whimpers of pleasure muffled by the throats of their prey.

Evanangela watched, cold detachment spreading through her as quickly as the warm blood. The excitement of the feed seemed to have vanished now that she knew there was no art in snaring her prey on the dance floor. They simply waited in the apartments, like fattened hens in the coop. The pleasurable rush and coppery taste of blood was still tantalizing. She licked a droplet from the corner of her lip. But the thrill was gone. She lifted herself from the couch, stepping past Verseau, and climbed into the black coffin. Waiting for the death sleep to take her.

Life at the château became hollow as the nights began to blur together. Soon, Evanangela and Àmichemin did not bother leaving Verseau's apartments. They cycled through voracious nights heated with blood-sharing, warm nights of the closeness of shared comfort and conversation, to cold nights of exhausted boredom. Evanangela found herself craving to fling the door open and run through the empty halls. But the realization that there was simply nowhere to run to, left her languid on the low black couch, her eyes unfocused as she stared up at the ceiling.

Verseau sat down on the couch next to Evanangela. He leaned over her, brushing a lock of hair behind her ear. "Ma petite, you have been a heap of misery these past few nights. Please, tell me-"

Jacques cleared his throat. Verseau bristled as he pulled away, seething at being interrupted. Jacques bowed and nodded. "Seigneur, I regret to inform you that two members of the court have been apprehended trying to leave the château. They have been confined to their chambers. One of the attendants that worked to secure them is gravely injured."

A sharp hiss escaped Verseau's throat as he squeezed his eyes shut and shook his head. "As if we need another mouth to feed."

Àmichemin leaned against the mantle, her eyes downcast. "Perhaps an exchange is in order."

He nodded. "Yes. It is a crime to harm an attendant. They safeguard our lives. To disrespect them is to disrespect and endanger the safety of the court. I shall preside over the turning."

Evanangela shivered. "You're going to turn the attendant into a vampire?"

"Yes," Àmichemin sighed, "it is a fitting punishment for the vampire that harmed them. They shall lose their place in the court, and the attendant shall be *elevated,* so to speak."

The memory of her dying body and burning wings shot through Evanangela. She wrapped her arms around herself. *Perhaps it is different, and less painful, for a human.*

"We shall reopen La Valse Noire tomorrow night." Verseau stood, his gaze sharp as Jacques drank in his every word. "But *only* for tomorrow night. I see that we must still have distractions, lest these attempted

99

escapes keep happening. The waltz will give the court something to look forward to every few weeks."

"As you wish, Seigneur." Jacques bowed and led the way out into the hall.

Chapter Eleven

The hall echoed with the bellows and shrieks of vampires taking their feeds. Verseau's jaw was tight as he strode past the barred door. They were brought to a small room that served as an infirmary. Fresh blood ignited Evanangela's senses as they entered. The pitiful moans of the injured attendant, and her long nights of boredom, heightened her desire to hunt.

Verseau approached the bed. The young man was pale, and his uniform was soaked with his blood. His young wife stood at his bedside, along with the chief mortal doctor. He shook his head, and stepped away, allowing Verseau to take the attendant's hand.

"Do you have any children?" His voice was pained, his eyes warm and kind.

The woman shook her head as she dabbed her tear-stained cheeks with a soggy handkerchief. "Non, mon Seigneur. Pas des enfants."[1]

Verseau nodded. His jaw relaxed a fraction. "And you are his wife? You wish to join him and remain his wife?"

She nodded. "Oui, mon Seigneur! I would follow mon cher Philippe even in death!"

"You understand what this means?" Verseau tilted his head, his tone grave. "You shall be turned and enter the court."

The woman's eyes grew wide. She looked at her husband, then took his hand and looked back at Verseau. "Oui, mon Seigneur."

He nodded. "Then, we begin."

Evanangela watched as Àmichemin stepped forward and gently restrained the woman. She did not resist, only looked up at Àmichemin, her gaze resolute. Verseau pierced the injured attendant's neck, only drinking for a moment before using his fangs to open a vein on his own

---

1 No, my Lord. No children.

101

forearm. He held it over the attendant's lips, and lifted the man's head so he could drink easier.

The woman did not struggle in Àmichemin's arms. She never took her eyes off her husband as Àmichemin suckled from her neck. The woman paled as her blood was drained, her limbs shaking. Àmichemin then disengaged and did the same as Verseau, presenting her arm to the woman.

"Drink, and join your husband."

She grabbed Àmichemin's arm and latched on with a voracity that startled even Àmichemin. Evanangela was shocked at how ready she was to receive the damned communion. The woman dug her fingers into Àmichemin's flesh. She then hissed, pushing the woman away and clutching her arm.

"That's enough!"

The woman slumped to the floor, her bewildered eyes darting about the room. Her skin had taken on a strange grey ashen quality and her eyes were fever bright. Verseau stood over the bed, clutching his own arm. The doctor sprang into action, providing clean linen bandages for them both.

Evanangela balked as the injured attendant sat up. His eyes were glazed over. Then, he began to scream. Evanangela clapped her hands over her ears as the attendant and his wife howled. They clawed at their chests as ropy veins pushed against the skin. Their bodies writhed in pain as they gasped and frothed at the mouth. The mortal doctor stepped forward, giving each attendant a soil bucket. They purged. The scent of fouled blood and rot erupting from their mouths along with their entrails. Verseau was still, standing by the bed, watching. As suddenly as it had started, they stopped. Their eyes had changed, becoming bright and colorless, their skin had paled, and their mortal scents were gone. Their eyes darkened again, changing to unnatural colors that marked them as vampires.

Verseau helped the attendant out of bed. His wife scrambled up from the floor, rushing to embrace her husband. Their limbs quivered, and their breaths were quick and labored.

"There is not much time. You both must feed." Verseau nodded to them both, then strode out of the infirmary.

Jacques trotted out after him, leading the way to the guilty vampires' apartments. Àmichemin walked a pace behind the newly turned vampire husband and wife, ensuring they did not stray. Evanangela replayed the turning over and over in her mind. While they had suffered, their agony had been nothing compared to her burning and the twisting of her bright soul. Their bodies did not burn, but were emptied and scraped clean of all else but vampiric blood. She clenched her hands into fists.

Perhaps they are right. Man truly is dipped in sin. So few are truly worthy of the kingdom of Heaven, and yet, Dieu forgives and lets them in.

She pushed aside her hateful thoughts as they returned to the barred door. It was quiet. The two attendants posted at the door bowed, undid the locks, and opened the door. Jacques took his place next to the other attendants as the group of vampires entered the apartments.

Two slain mortals lay bleeding on the rug. It seemed the guilty party had fed, and gone straight to sleep. Verseau shoved the lid off the coffin, letting it fall to the floor with a booming thud. He seized each vampire by the hair, tossing them both onto the floor.

"Mon Seigneur! Pardonnez-moi! Pardonnez-moi!"[2]

Verseau hissed in the pathetic begging vampire's face and wrenched his arms behind his back. "How *dare* you defile my court!"

The other vampire looked up at Verseau in shock. Àmichemin nudged the two newly-turned vampires forward. Their bewilderment gave way to raw hunger as they approached. Verseau yanked the vampire's head to the side, exposing his neck. The veins were plump with living blood. Àmichemin did the same, dragging the frightened vampire off the floor, and exposing his neck as well.

"Feed, and take your place as my newest subjects." Verseau ordered.

They shrieked and writhed as the newly-turned husband and wife attacked. Their throats bobbed as they suckled the rich blood. Gasps escaped their noses as they rushed to drain the courtiers.

Verseau's muscles strained the fabric of his coat as he held the guilty vampire in place. His voice was cold. "Drain him."

---

2 My Lord! Forgive me! Forgive me!

It seemed to go on forever. Evanangela wondered at every swallow. Blood dribbled from the corners of their mouths, and down their chins. She felt the hunger and thrill for the hunt rise in her brain once more.

Àmichemin nodded to Evanangela as she held the dying vampire in place. "It will be over soon."

Before long, the two vampires pulled away. Their lips bright crimson with spilled blood. Verseau tossed the dead vampire onto the pile of mortal corpses. Àmichemin did the same.

He stepped past the newly-turned, bellowing out into the hall. "Jacques! Have this mess cleaned up and prepare these apartments for my new subjects!"

Jacques and the two attendants scurried in. The husband and wife glanced about, overwhelmed by the flurry of activity. Verseau gave Evanangela a small push as Àmichemin followed them out the door. It closed, leaving them in the empty hall. Evanangela wondered at the swiftness of Verseau's judgement. He had not wasted a moment, or at any point faltered with indecision. A cruel thought crept into her mind.

"Mon Seigneur, what will happen to the dead vampires?"

Verseau looked down at her as he ushered them back into his apartments. "They will be disposed of."

His words had a finality that made Evanangela afraid to ask any further questions. She sat down on the black footstool, staring into the fire. Her mind wandered to the rest of the court, wondering at how each of them could fall from Verseau's grace in a single moment. Àmichemin flopped onto the couch and let out a long sigh, interrupting Evanangela's morose thoughts.

"I'm sorry you had to see that, ma fleur." The familiar softness had returned to Verseau's voice, tinged with exhaustion. "But this is how order is kept in the court. A Seigneur is only as powerful as his ability to enforce. To hesitate is to show weakness."

Àmichemin did not move from the depths of the couch. "It is also well-known that while the attendants are our attendants, it is never allowed for a vampire to assume they are *beneath* us. They hold our lives in their hands."

Evanangela nodded. Her mind replayed the visions, the screams, the blood. She thought of the darkness that enveloped her before each morning. The soft slide of the coffin lid as it closed above her. Their actions seemed so insensible. She could not fathom lifting a hand against an attendant and live eternity in fear that her soothing darkness would be pierced with the golden light of dawn, and then know the true embrace of death.

Verseau knelt beside her, wrapping his arms about her as she shivered. "Never fear, ma petite. So long as the order is kept, all shall be well."

So long as the order is kept, all shall be well.

The words rattled in Evanangela's mind as the attendants ushered mortals into Verseau's apartments. It was true, here in the château there was order. They were awakened each night once the last streak of the sunset was gone, and the attendants brought the mortals for each night's feed like clockwork. And yet, the tension was growing. His increasing silence and coldness as he spent his nights deep in thought with Àmichemin draped over his lap, or lounging on the couch by his side. The anxious quiet was only broken by the frenzied footsteps and mad screams of an escaped vampire in the halls.

Evanangela began counting the nights until La Valse Noire. She knew the rest of the court was anxiously awaiting the waltz as well. Only Àmichemin seemed unbothered by it all. But then, nothing seemed to bother her. Evanangela shivered as Àmichemin slid onto the couch, pulling Evanangela into her lap. It startled her how easy it was for Àmichemin to lift her like a small pet. She toyed with Evanangela's auburn locks, twisting them round her fingers.

"Sulking makes for a dull night." She sighed. "And we both know Verseau is not going to help lighten the mood. Dance for us, ma chérie."

Verseau shook his head, annoyed. "Pardonnez-moi, finding a solution for the blood shortage is *hardly* entertaining for me, you know."

Àmichemin pouted as she traced her fingers up and down Evanangela's waist. "Wracking your brain every minute of every night isn't going to help either."

"And what would you propose?" He growled, staring into the fire.

She tried to scoot further away on the couch, not wanting to be in the middle of an argument, but Àmichemin held firm. "Why not escape somewhere? At least for a little while? The château is *so* boring!"

"Ma chère douleur, that is not an *actual* solution to our problems. Merely, a distraction." Verseau rubbed his eyes and sighed.

Evanangela slipped away, snuggling into the nest of cushions she had built on the floor before the fireplace. It was her tiny oasis, as she had become nervous of his annoyed outbursts, especially when Àmichemin would tease him into a fit. Their constant close quarters was wearing their patience thin.

"Ma chérie, I know this is your first time being confined, but truly, it's not so awful." Àmichemin purred as she fidgeted on the couch.

She drew herself up. "This isn't the first time the court has been confined?"

"No. Though they are behaving as if it were." Verseau rolled his eyes.

"The court was slaughtered in the peasant revolts in the reign of the previous Seigneur." Àmichemin ran a languid hand down Verseau's sleeve. "The few that were left went into hiding, and hibernated until enough generations had passed for the peasants to forget and deem the château abandoned. That was when-"

"That's enough Àmichemin!" He growled; his glare fierce.

She pouted, but for once did not chastise him for his outburst. Àmichemin turned away and settled her hands into her lap. Evanangela leaned back into the cushions, unsure of what to do with herself. The tension in the room buzzed, and the silence rang in her ears.

He shook his head. "I did what needed to be done. At least, that's what I believed. Now, I feel as if history shall repeat itself, and I will have done no better."

Àmichemin curled herself round Verseau, her long willowy arms holding him tight. "Hush. The court would have devolved into beasts by now, and the mortals wiped out, had it not been for you. The court is spoiled and abhors new restrictions. They will become complacent eventually. The first few years are always the most difficult."

"*Years?!*" Evanangela froze. The blood from her feed thundered in her ears, her heart hammering in her chest. She gasped, clutching the lip of her corset, overwhelmed by her sudden panic. While she too had lived eternity as an immortal in the heavens, she had never been confined. It had been difficult enough to adjust to sleeping in a coffin, but the idea of spending all her waking hours trapped sent her mind spiraling.

Verseau slid from the couch and embraced Evanangela. His body was warm from the new blood. Her breath caught in her throat as she wound her arms around his middle.

"I know this is frightening for you." He whispered in her ear. "But Àmichemin is right – being confined is not as awful as it seems. We're here together. Some members of the court are locked away completely alone."

He drew away, settling onto one of the cushions and pulled Evanangela into his lap. The living blood had brought his scent to life, and it comforted her as she relished in his closeness. Àmichemin joined them, lounging against Verseau's shoulder.

"That's terrible! Why must they all be locked away? To be isolated without anyone to talk to-" Evanangela trailed off. In heaven, she had the company of the other angels and Dieu. She shivered as she imagined what her life at court would be like without Verseau and Àmichemin at her side; of being completely alone. She could not bear such a thought.

Verseau stroked Evanangela's hair. "Ah, ma fleur noire, it's for their own good. They are not like you; so sweet and pliant. They would be fighting, possibly killing one another, if they were not properly separated."

Evanangela snuggled against his chest. She inhaled his scent, heightened by the fresh blood coursing through his veins. It was rich and dark, like the wet earth and electric air during a summer storm. "But then, why do you and Àmichemin not fight?"

Àmichemin nipped at Verseau's ear, making him smile. "*Real* consorts don't fight."

"There are mated pairs locked up together," he traced his finger down one of the plump veins on Evanangela's neck, "A true pairing has forged mutual respect and found a balance of power. The lower ends of my court have yet to mature into such a state."

Evanangela toyed with one of the buttons on his tunic. "But I'm newly-turned compared to the rest of your court."

Verseau tilted her chin up. His face once again had the warm and playful expression she knew. "*You* are not like the rest of the court.

107

Amichemin and I have molded you, and you have been most pliant and willing."

He closed his eyes and brought his lips to Evanangela's. She pressed against him, eager for warmth and reassurance. Verseau tipped her back until she slid into the pile of cushions. Her body sank into the soft pillows, the different fabrics and tassels tickling her skin. He knelt over her, Amichemin leaning on his back, over his shoulder. A shyness crept over Evanangela as she saw the two vampires hovering over her. She curled in on herself, peeking from under her sleeves. Verseau's face lit up with fresh excitement. He growled as Amichemin slunk into the cushions. His gaze fiery as she kissed his neck.

Evanangela reached up, winding her arms around Verseau's neck as he leaned down to kiss her again. His body pressed against hers as he relaxed into the cushions. Amichemin lay on her side, her arm holding her head up as she watched. Verseau's lips were velvet as he kissed Evanangela. She tasted their softness, and melted as he scraped his teeth over her lips. He drew away, sitting back on his haunches as Evanangela looked up at him, her eyes filled with anticipation and longing.

Amichemin shifted her weight, cradling Evanangela's face with her hand. She leaned down and kissed Evanangela. Her scent was also heightened from the new blood. Amichemin smelled of lavender and winter wind. Evanangela ran her hands through her silky hair. It was fine as spun silk and ran through her fingers like cool water.

"Mes fleurs, you are divine." Verseau sighed as he too petted Amichemin's hair.

They lay together, in a heap before the fire. Amichemin drew lazy circles on Evanangela's back with her thin, deft fingers. Verseau had Jacques fetch Amichemin's favorite brush from her apartments, and started gliding it through her starry locks. Evanangela felt cozy, though her longing had not quite cooled. She watched the flames in the grate dance; the simple comforts banishing her anxiety.

Chapter Twelve

Evanangela flicked through the dresses in her wardrobe. The château was buzzing with excitement. La Valse Noire was to commence at long last. Gabriel had woken her that nightfall; a refreshing sight after being only attended by Jacques for so long. As always, he was tailed by one of the more senior attendants to ensure he followed protocol.

Verseau had ordered them the previous night to sleep in their own coffins, wanting to add anticipation to the long-awaited celebration. She jumped when Àmichemin trotted into her apartments; a silk orchid dress swished about her. She draped herself over Evanangela's shoulder and pecked a kiss on her cheek.

"Ma chérie, vites, vites! The feed shall be starting soon!" Àmichemin spun away and flopped onto the couch. Her hair fanned out onto the cushions, creating a halo about her head.

She sighed as she rifled through her dresses again. "I don't know what I should wear. I know Verseau will expect-"

Àmichemin rolled her eyes and rose from the couch. "Honestly, at this point you could wear an attendant's shift and Verseau would be ecstatic. Here, let me see."

Evanangela watched as Àmichemin plucked dresses, murmuring as she played with the fabrics. Finally, she snatched up a cerulean gown. The shortened length would reveal her ankles, and was rather scandalous. Evanangela blushed, her cheeks sapphire.

"A-are you sure? This one?" She held the dress up to herself.

"Oh, you simply *must!* Everyone will be wearing something salacious after being cooped up for so long." Àmichemin winked and flicked her dress, revealing a slit on the side that revealed her leg and the frill of her petticoats.

Evanangela darted her eyes away, her empty veins constricting as excitement knotted in her dead heart. Her sapphire blush embarrassed her further. "Oh. I see."

Àmichemin helped Evanangela dress quickly, tying her hair back into an elegant knot with a sparkling hairpin. One lone curl hung at the base of her neck, tickling her skin as she moved. Her nerves replaced her excitement from Àmichemin's touch. Even attending her first waltz had not been as intimidating. There was no way of knowing when the next waltz would be. The anxious energy worked itself into a knot in her stomach.

"Très jolie,"[1] Àmichemin nodded as she admired her handiwork, "now let's be off!"

The noise of the hall hit Evanangela like a stone to the chest when they finally exited her apartments. Once more, the hall was dripping with vampires and vixens draped on the couches and walls. All eyes swiveled to Evanangela and Àmichemin as they sauntered toward the ballroom.

Their awe seeped into Evanangela, stilling her nerves. The old confidence rose in her as she pressed her shoulders back, her chin up. Her lidded eyes scanned the court. Their respect was still there, though it was tempered with something more. Jealousy perhaps? She slipped her hand into Àmichemin's, the daring move earning her hard stares and whispers behind fans.

Verseau was waiting for them at the bottom of the stairs, looking dashing in a jacket the color of a bloody sunset adorned with gold embellishments. It was as if they had been frozen in time, and now they were picking up right where they had left off. He smiled up at them, his clean fangs gleaming. Evanangela took a deep breath to still her excitement. Her heart fluttered and she bit back the pain of her empty veins.

"Truly a vision, ce soir."[2] He purred as Evanangela took his arm. "I did not expect to see so *much* of you."

Evanangela blushed again, darting her eyes away. Àmichemin laughed. "The whole court is watching. Of course, we must give them something to see."

They entered the ballroom together, their shoes clicking on the floor. The music was boisterous, and the dance was fervent. The hot scent of blood was dizzying. Evanangela clutched her chest as her heart tightened with the excitement of the hunt.

1 Very pretty,
2 tonight

110

"Go on, pick someone." Verseau's breath tickling as he whispered in her ear.

Àmichemin frolicked into the dance, her dress sparkling as the candlelight reflected off the tiny jewels stitched onto the gossamer overlayer of fabric. Evanangela took a shuddering breath and slipped away from Verseau. Her gaze swiveled to find an unclaimed mortal.

A knot of young men were chatting near the windows. Their scent overwhelmed Evanangela. Her mind felt hazy, as if from drink. After being locked away with only three mortals each night, a whole room full of them was intoxicating. She squeezed her hands into fists, her nails digging into the soft flesh to keep herself from outright pouncing.

One of the men turned and spotted Evanangela. He laughed and nodded to his companions. They exchanged sly glances before he left them, approaching Evanangela with a confident smirk.

"Bonsoire, Mademoiselle. You must be the Lady of the House, such a *fine* ensemble." He bowed and took her hand.

Evanangela giggled, allowing him to kiss her hand. "As the Seigneur's consort, I am entitled to such bawdy attire, non?"

His grin was wolfish as he pulled her onto his arm. "Shall we dance?"

"Bien sûr." She inhaled his scent as they melted into the waltz. Her hands held him tight as they spun with the others.

"You seem flushed, Mademoiselle," he let his eyes roll up and down from her chest to her face.

Evanangela inched her face closer to his, her veins screaming as his rich musk rolled into her nose and over her tongue. "It has been quite some time since we *celebrated*."

He leaned closer, his nose a hair breadth from hers. "That sounds tantalizing, ma chérie. But we have all night. Let's not rush things and enjoy the evening as it unfolds."

A scream pierced the joyful music. Evanangela turned and saw two vixens draining a mortal. Their fangs tearing his neck to ribbons as they devoured him like beasts. All at once, the vampires pounced. The music continued on, adding to the frenzy of screams and growls.

Evanangela felt the mortal pull away from her, but she snatched his arms, her nails cutting into the stiff fabric of his jacket.

"What is happening?" He screamed as he tried to wrest himself away, his bravado gone, and his eyes wide with terror.

She snarled, baring her fangs, and threw herself onto the mortal, sending them both crashing to the floor. The impact rendered him unconscious, allowing Evanangela to feed without resistance. Evanangela lapped at his vein, the blood pouring over her tongue and dribbling down her chin. She moaned into his neck, the pleasure surging as it coursed through her veins, making them plump and lush once more. Her heart fluttered as it filled and softened.

The ecstasy of her kill was ripped away as she heard the screeching of vampires fighting. She drew back from the corpse, swallowing the last of the blood. A group of vampires were ripping at a mortal's body and sniping at one another. There were mortals banging on the main doors. They were locked fast against their efforts. A crash sounded, startling everyone into silence.

"Stop them!" Verseau bellowed as attendants and guards rushed into the ballroom.

One of the windows was broken; something heavy had been thrown through it. Mortals were jumping through the jagged glass, leaping onto the lawns below. One landed poorly; the sickening crunch of broken bones overtaken by his screams. The attendants sounded the alarm, and guards rushed out of the château and into the garden.

Àmichemin appeared by her side, startling Evanangela. She put her hand on Evanangela's shoulder, a comforting grace amidst the chaos. Evanangela took her hand and Àmichemin helped her to her feet. A vampire rushed past to tackle one of the straggler mortals, the air ruffling their hair and gowns. Evanangela squeezed Àmichemin's hands. A strange fear crept up her spine.

"What will happen if they escape?"

She shook her head, her eyes fixed on the window. "We will be killed."

The room was spinning. Evanangela's legs buckled under her, but Àmichemin held her firm, holding her upright. Together, they watched the guards try to corral the mortals. At first, they were able to bind them, so as to capture them alive for another feed. But as the other mortals saw what was happening, they evaded the guards' attempts, and were struck down with the heavy halberds. In the blood-soaked ballroom, Verseau stood, frozen as he watched the slaughter unfold. His jaw was tight as his gaze remained unbroken and fists shook at his sides. Evanangela gasped in horror as the mortals were rendered to pulpy carnage.

This is what we are. They die so we may live. We are monsters!

Hot tears rolled down her cheeks, staining her skin with the fresh blood. Àmichemin hugged her, pulling her away from the windows. "Do not look, ma chérie. Ne regardez pas."[3]

Vampires whispered, the tension rising as they realized the severity of the breach. They clustered about the windows, the attendants and guards pushing them aside. Verseau finally broke his vigil and strode toward Àmichemin and Evanangela.

"Venez avec moi."[4] His voice was low and hard.

They followed him out of the ballroom while the other vampires milled about, nervous and unsure of what to do with themselves. All the mortals were gone, either dead or being chased down on the lawn. The excitement of the evening had gone out like a snuffed flame. Evanangela felt heavy with the blood filling her veins. It roared in her ears. Her heart thundered in her chest, making it difficult to catch her breath.

Àmichemin seemed calm, but her eyes were wide. Verseau led them to his apartments where Jacques was waiting. He bowed and shut the doors behind them.

"What are your orders, mon Seigneur?"

Verseau clenched his teeth, his words a seething hiss. "We are to take the court on progress to La Maison de Printemps."

Àmichemin put her hand on Verseau's shoulder. "Mon cher, I hardly think-"

He shrugged her off. "It was *your* suggestion, non? That we all *get away for a while?* Well, your little distraction has now become our only solution."

Evanangela pressed herself against the wall. She could not escape, as Jacques blocked the door. Even if she got that far, it was sure to be

---

3 Don't look.
4 Come with me.

chaos out in the hall. She took a deep breath to steady her frazzled nerves, hoping Verseau would not take notice. Àmichemin stepped away from Verseau, but she did not flop onto the couch as she usually did. Instead, she also seemed flustered. A rarity that further frightened Evanangela.

"We must anticipate the possibility that the guards will not catch them all. An attack on the château is almost certain. And we are in no position to defend ourselves with the court so fragmented."

Jacques bowed. "I will begin the preparations at once, mon Seigneur."

He exited the room, his footsteps fading down the hall. She turned her gaze back to Verseau. The anger drained from him, leaving him looking defeated and exhausted. He crumpled onto the couch, his face in his hand.

"I am sorry, mes chères coeurs." He shook his head. "I have failed the court. I am not fit to be addressed as 'Seigneur'."

Àmichemin sank onto the couch, drawing her arms around him. She ran her fingers through his hair. The urgency and empathetic nature of her embrace made Evanangela even more disconcerted. Never had she seen this softer side of Àmichemin. Evanangela was frozen in place, her mind screaming, unable to speak.

"You could not have foreseen that such a thing would happen." Àmichemin pressed herself against Verseau, her body seeking to snuff out his self-loathing. She kissed his cheek.

"We can only hope that the "holiday progress" will buy us some time to create a *real* solution." He kept his gaze on the floor.

They sat together, Verseau bristling and Àmichemin trying to comfort him. Evanangela hugged herself, her nails digging into her arms as panic overwhelmed her mind and froze her body. She tore her eyes away; a cold thought snared her like claws digging into her heart.

I do not belong here. I had thought I was a true consort to Verseau, and yet, I cannot bring myself to soothe him when he is like this. I tremble in fear and wait for him to comfort me instead.

More tears rolled down her cheeks in bloody rivulets. Her body shook as she fought to move, to fling herself at his feet. Instead, she slid down onto the floor, folding into herself, her knees to her chest. She shut her eyes, wishing to shut out the pitiful scene. Evanangela was startled when the apartment door swung open again. Jacques stepped back into the sitting room and bowed.

"Mon Seigneur, mes Mademoiselles, the sun shall soon be upon us."

Verseau nodded. A sharp exhale was his only response as he rose from the couch. Jacques bowed again. Evanangela finally found her body moving, her desire to hearten Verseau overriding her fear. She crept toward him. His gaze was still lowered. Àmichemin remained on the couch, her hands clutched at her chest.

Evanangela took Verseau's hand and squeezed. He lifted his chin, meeting her gaze. Verseau turned and seemed to finally notice Àmichemin. He reached out his other hand to her. She placed hers in his, and rose from the couch.

Together, they climbed into his enormous coffin. Their limbs heavy with exhaustion. Verseau held Evanangela and Àmichemin tightly to him, their bodies snuggled into his sides. At last, his body relaxed, the tension leaving his limbs. Evanangela could hear his heartbeat slow. He kissed each of them on the forehead.

"I would be lost without you, mes petites." He whispered as the coffin lid slid closed over them and Jacques' footsteps receded.

Àmichemin snuggled into his chest. "No more sad thoughts, mon cher."

"We shall always be at your side." Evanangela shifted her head and kissed Verseau on his jawline.

Chapter Thirteen

The court reveled as they prepared to go on progress. It had been so long since the court had left the château that the frightening escape was forgotten. All were swept up in the excitement of going on holiday. Evanangela watched as the attendants packed her belongings. Gabriel oversaw the details, ensuring all her essentials would arrive at La Maison de Printemps, ready for use.

"Princesse, your feed should be arriving soon." Gabriel bowed. "Is there anything else you require?"

She tilted her head as she thought, wondering over the items she had requested to be packed. "Non, merci."

His gaze lingered on her for a moment, earning him sniping glares from the other attendants. Evanangela lounged on the couch in her black robe. The sweet spring air fluttered into her room due to the large window that was propped open, as the bustling activity stirred up the attendants' mortal scent, overwhelming Evanangela. She felt drunk as she fluttered her gold fan, her eyes sloshing in her skull.

A polite knock at the door was muffled from the clatter of packing trunks of clothing and odd things. Gabriel answered, revealing a bemused mortal escorted by yet another attendant.

"Monsieur Dupuis has arrived for Mademoiselle." The attendant drawled.

Gabriel nodded and bowed, gesturing for the mortal to enter. Evanangela shifted her weight onto her elbow to look up at the mortal, a pose not unlike Àmichemin was often found in. The mortal's affable smile disappeared when he saw Evanangela draped in nothing but a dressing gown.

"Ah! Pardonnez-moi, Mademoiselle! I-I did not realize you were-"

She stood from the couch, the dressing gown billowing about her ankles. It hung loose on her petite frame. She clacked her fan closed and tapped the mortal on the chest with it.

"There is nothing to apologize for, Monsieur." Evanangela purred. His scent was heavy with male musk and the floral scent of a recently applied perfume. She drank it into her nostrils and sighed.

He took a step back and turned toward the door where Gabriel was posted; blocking his escape. "Perhaps, Mademoiselle has had a bit too much aperitif? I should take my leave until-"

"I did not ask you to leave." Evanangela took another step toward him and placed her hands upon his chest. His nervousness mingled with mild excitement, making his scent grow stronger. She tilted her chin and whispered in his ear. "Though, you will be punished for accusing a lady of being a boorish drunk."

He blanched as Evanangela hissed, revealing her fangs. She dove into his neck before he could scream. Her arms held him tight as she sucked his flayed vein. The blood flowed down her throat, easing the tantalizing desire to hunt she had been suppressing while the attendants packed. Her eyelashes fluttered as the warm pleasure overwhelmed her senses. He went limp in her arms as his pulse slowed. Evanangela lapped up the last of his living blood, then let his body fall to the floor with a dull thud.

"Enlève ça, s'il vous plaît."[1] She flicked her fan at the discarded corpse.

One of the attendants stopped packing and grabbed the dead mortal by the ankles. Gabriel opened the door, allowing the attendant to drag it out into the hall. He bowed as Àmichemin entered. Her eyes were bright and her skin was rosy from a fresh feed.

Gabriel closed the door as she pranced into the room. "Presenting, Mademoiselle Àmichemin!"

"Bonsoire," Àmichemin purred, "My, we aren't even bothering to dress for dinner now?"

Evanangela sank back onto the couch and fanned herself. The heat of the living blood made her mind and limbs sluggish with comfort and pleasure. "It seems too much of a bother with all the packing."

Àmichemin folded herself onto the couch, her body warm against Evanangela. "Are you excited? This will be your first progress. It has been many years since the court last left the château."

---

1 Remove this, please

"What does it mean to 'go on progress'? I thought we were going on holiday to La Maison de Printemps?" Evanangela shifted, giving Àmichemin more space to stretch her legs.

"La Maison de Printemps is in the southern countryside of the Nacre Court territory. It will be several days journey. We ride via carriage, and if it is safe to do so, stop at small shelters along the way." Àmichemin toyed with the hem of Evanangela's robe.

She leaned her back against the armrest. "Is that not dangerous? Taking the court out into the open where the peasants could attack us?"

Àmichemin shook her head. "We travel with a retinue of guards. No one would dare an attack. Besides, now is the perfect time to move the court. The spring planting is underway – the peasants will be too busy to track our movements."

Evanangela tapped her fan against her chin. "If the peasants are preoccupied, why move the court at all? Surely the château is a stronghold?"

"That it is. But in that case, they could starve us out if they don't breach the guard. Le Château d'Astucieux was built to be a pleasure palace, not a fortress. As you saw with the disaster at La Valse Noire, while the large windows of the château display the court's power and wealth, they offer little protection."

Àmichemin tugged on Evanangela's robe, loosening the stays. "Enough of this boring talk of strategy-"

Evanangela pulled her robe closed, her pink cheeks growing red. "Àmichemin! The attendants-!"

She made a rude sound with her mouth and leaned over Evanangela. "You are such a timid creature behind closed doors. Though, that is part of what makes you so enticing."

Her protests were cut short as Àmichemin dipped her head, her bright starry hair sliding down like a curtain as she kissed Evanangela. She slid her body over Evanangela, pinning her into the couch.

Àmichemin trailed her kisses down Evanangela's jaw, to her neck where she grazed her fangs over one of the engorged veins. Evanangela shivered under her, her robe falling open, exposing her naked flesh. The bump and clatter of the attendants packing continued on, masking the sound of their shaking moans and tight gasps.

Evanangela yelped when Àmichemin pierced her neck, gently lapping as the blood spilled forth. Àmichemin drew away, then kissed Evanangela again, allowing her to taste the warm coppery delight of her own rich vampiric blood.

"Presenting Seigneur Verseau!"

Gabriel's herald cut through the hazy air, snapping Evanangela and Àmichemin to attention. Evanangela's flustered hands tried to close her robe, and Àmichemin attempted to straighten her mussed locks. Blood trickled down Evanangela's neck. She pressed her hand against the wound.

"Having fun without me?" Verseau pouted.

Àmichemin leaned back into the couch, her lips stained dark with shared blood. "Very much so. Until you interrupted." She smirked.

Evanangela withered with embarrassment. "My sincerest apologies, Verseau."

Àmichemin bopped her with one of the couch pillows. "You're *sorry?* Well, I suppose I shan't do that again!"

She gasped in horror. "Non, non! I only meant-"

Verseau laughed and wedged himself onto the couch between them. "Mes petites are endless entertainment for me!"

He too had recently fed, his scent adding to the dizzying perfume that hovered about the room. Evanangela leaned against his shoulder, drinking him in. Àmichemin quirked an eyebrow, then grinned and draped herself over his other shoulder.

"Have you come to *entertain* us before the long journey?" Àmichemin purred.

She sat up. "You mean, we won't be riding together?"

Àmichemin laughed. "Don't be absurd! A carriage would not be able to hold the three of us and all three of our coffins. It would simply be too much!"

"I see." Evanangela dropped her gaze, the excitement of the holiday drying up as she realized she would be trapped alone in a carriage for hours on end.

Verseau stroked her cheek. "Ah, ma petite, not to worry. There shall be stops along the way where we can *refresh* ourselves. It's only for a few days' time."

Evanangela nodded, placated with his soothing words. "I'm honestly surprised the court so readily agreed to go on holiday. I would think they would be more concerned with the shortage-"

"They are easily distracted. A complacent court is an obedient court." Verseau squeezed Evanangela's hand. "Besides, that is part of the plan. Taking the court on a frivolous distraction gives us more time to smooth over this crisis and prepare for the possibility of *other* solutions."

Àmichemin leaned back into the couch and slid her legs onto his lap. He began idly stroking her ankles, wrinkling her stockings. "Staying here will only escalate things. It's clear the court is devoid of patience or sense at this point."

He nodded. "The guards have informed me that, unfortunately, two of the mortals did indeed escape from La Valse Noire. The guard we leave behind will prepare the château against the inevitable attack. Putting up those measures with the court here would only alarm them further and cause more chaos."

He drew his other arm around Evanangela's shoulders, pressing her against his hard frame. Àmichemin was lounging with her eyes closed, enjoying his ministrations. Evanangela snuggled into his shoulder, her mind replaying the mortals jumping out the broken window. She wondered if they had informed the priest she had met on the night of her fall. If he would be one of the mortals to attack the château.

"There's no sense in worrying over what has already come to pass." Verseau interrupted her thoughts. "We must prepare. That's all we can do. Though the peasants are numerous, we do have fear on our side."

He jumped. "Zut alors![2] I nearly forgot." Verseau untangled his hand from Àmichemin's quicksilver tresses. "Ma petite, you have not yet learned boire à petites gorgées du sang."[3]

Evanangela raised her eyebrows, but before she could respond, Verseau turned and waved his hand. "Garçon, ici!"

---

2 Exclamation of shock
3 Sip blood

Gabriel dutifully strode up to the couch and bowed. "Oui, mon Seigneur?"

Verseau fluttered his hand. "Kneel. Oui, bien, bien." He turned to Evanangela. "Sit forward, ma petite."

She did as instructed, hovering over Gabriel's bowed frame. He kept his gaze lowered. Verseau slid his hands about Gabriel's neck, guiding him into position.

"It is good that you have already fed, so you have your wits about you." He mused. "Now then, you will not have a full feeding until we have our stops along the journey. To ensure your sanity, you must learn boire à petites gorgées du sang – only fill the mouth. That is all."

Evanangela froze. She had never fed off the attendants, as she was sure it was forbidden. Her hands shook. "Verseau, I-"

Àmichemin placed a comforting hand on her shoulder. "It's all right, this is what the attendants are for on long journeys. They safeguard us. A mouthful of blood is nothing for them, but so much more for us. Your pet shall be fine."

She leaned forward again. Gabriel did not move, not even a tremble. Evanangela could feel the warmth of his skin as her lips grazed his neck. His scent was overwhelming, the deep musk combined with the subtle fragrance of lilies. She allowed her fangs to sink into his neck, a quick entry, fearing prolonging it would be more painful. The blood rushed into her mouth.

"Now, swallow and lick the bite." Verseau crooned.

She did as she was bid. Her saliva was coated red with new blood. Other than the smear she left; the wounds were gone. She covered her mouth with her hand, startled at the small marvel.

"Are you hurt?" Evanangela tried to catch his eye.

Gabriel shook his head and stood up. He took out a handkerchief from his pocket and wiped his neck, "Non, princesse. I am fine."

Àmichemin flicked her hand. "See, it's fine."

He smiled, further reassuring her. Evanangela darted her eyes away as she licked the blood from her lips. Gabriel lowered his gaze again as Verseau fussed over her.

He pulled a black handkerchief from his pocket. "Here, ma petite fleur noire."

Evanangela dabbed her mouth with the handkerchief. It was embroidered with blue roses and was steeped in Verseau's scent.

"Pour vous, ma petite." Verseau whispered.

She clutched the handkerchief to her chest. It was the first true gift she had ever received. "Vraiment?[4] Pour moi?"

He nodded. "Oui, for those nights when you are lonely."

"Merci beaucoup, mon Seigneur!" Evanangela kissed Verseau on the cheek, a fierce blush darkening her face.

Verseau waved his hand at Gabriel as he chuckled at Evanangela. He bowed again and resumed packing. Gabriel lifted a large trunk and carried it out into the hall. Evanangela saw that he was no worse for wear, he did not seem weakened or even dizzy. She sniffed the handkerchief again and snuggled into Verseau's chest as he began playing with Amichemin's hair once more.

---

4 Truly?

Chapter Fourteen

Dark figures in heavy cloaks filed out the doors of the château. Dozens of black carriages lined the circular avenue, attached to teams of black horses standing at attention. The scent of apple blossoms wafted through the air as a breeze toyed with the hems of skirts and horses' manes. A church bell tolled in the distance, declaring the witching hour.

Verseau escorted Àmichemin and Evanangela down the path. The hood of his cloak lay against his back, revealing his gleaming eyes reflecting what little light there was in the gloom. Evanangela and Àmichemin had their hoods drawn over their heads, obscuring their faces. He led Àmichemin to a carriage that bore a large "A" in twinkling amethysts on the door.

"May the night keep you, and the silver winds bear you." Verseau let go of Evanangela's hand as he drew Àmichemin into his arms for a fervent kiss. Àmichemin clung to him, her shaking hands uncharacteristic of her typical bravado. Evanangela looked away, not wanting to intrude on their intimate moment.

"A bientôt,[1] ma chérie." Verseau whispered.

Evanangela turned and watched as Àmichemin climbed into the carriage; the attendant waiting nearby as Verseau acted as her footman. The attendant closed the carriage door. Verseau pressed his hand on the glass, and Àmichemin did the same from the inside. He tore himself away and took a deep shuddering breath, turning to Evanangela.

"Are you ready, ma petite?"

She nodded. Verseau took her arm, and led her to a similar carriage. This one had an "E" done in lapis lazuli. The attendant opened the door, revealing powder blue cushions and cobalt curtains. Verseau took Evanangela's hands in both of his.

"I know this will be frightening for you, so I arranged for your little pet to accompany you for the journey." He darted his eyes away.

---

1 Until we meet again,

"It is your first progress, and the solitude can be difficult. I know he brings you comfort."

Evanangela slipped her hands from his grasp and wound them round his neck. "Mon Seigneur, mon Verseau, it is *you* my heart aches for."

He smiled and kissed her. She could feel a slight tremble in his body as his lips met hers. Verseau petted her cheek as he pulled away. "Then wish upon the stars for me each night we are apart, ma chère coeur."

Just as he had done with Àmichemin, Verseau helped Evanangela climb into the carriage. Inside, Gabriel sat in the back-facing seat. He nodded in lieu of a bow.

"Bonsoire, Mademoiselle." He whispered.

Evanangela settled herself into the front-facing seat. Verseau lingered in the doorway. She leaned down and kissed him one last time.

"Tu me manques déjà mon amour."[2] Evanangela's voice hitched, though tears did not fall.

Verseau nodded and jumped down from the carriage. The attendant outside closed the door. Evanangela scrambled to place her hand on the glass, but Verseau was already walking away to his own carriage.

"Pardonnez-moi, princesse," Gabriel's voice startled her, "fear not. You will see the Seigneur again in two days' time."

She bit her lip, her serrated fangs grinding into the soft flesh. "*Two days?*"

His eyes widened as she shuddered, hiding her face in her black handkerchief from Verseau. "Non, princesse, ne pleurez pas."[3] Gabriel patted her hand. "The time will pass by quicker than you know. And I shall be here to entertain you."

Evanangela nodded. She wiped away one last red tear that threatened to roll down her cheek. "Merci, Gabriel."

They sat in the carriage, waiting for the last of the court. Evanangela gazed out the window at the courtyard. She had not seen it since the

---

2 I miss you already, my love.
3 No, princess, don't cry.

night Àmichemin had brought her to the château. There was a large fountain depicting rabbits and deer galloping alongside a faun with an enormous rack of antlers, rather than the typical goat's horns. Water sprung from his panpipes and the mouths of the deer.

A thumping on the ceiling of the carriage startled Evanangela from her thoughts. Then the carriage lurched forward. Gabriel caught her before she slid from her seat.

"Careful, princesse!" He held onto Evanangela's arm as she righted herself.

Evanangela leaned back in her seat and smoothed her skirts. "I'm all right. Thank you."

The carriage followed the gentle curve of the boulevard leading out to the main road. Guards stood on either side of the gates inside the property. They bowed their heads as Àmichemin's carriage passed through. The road opened into the sprawling estate of lawn, gardens, and manicured trees. In the distance, she could see clusters of buildings behind the property stone wall.

"Those are the homes of the attendants – Le Village du Sang."[4] Gabriel explained. "There are a limited number of apartments inside the château, but those are only meant for attendants such as myself or Jacques who attend to Seigneur, or Mademoiselle Àmichemin, or you, princesse."

Evanangela could see the roofs of the little houses, and curling smoke from the chimneys. "So, even the attendants do not leave the château?"

Gabriel shook his head. "Non, princesse. There is no need, other than the attendants whose sole duty is to go to the village market for supplies. But that is rare. The château is self-sufficient. Leaving exposes the attendants to crime and disease from the peasants."

"Do they not feel like prisoners?" Evanangela turned away from the window.

He smiled. "No more than you feel imprisoned." Gabriel gestured. "There is disease, famine, poverty, theft, and even murder in the villages. Why would the attendants want to leave the safety and abundance of the château and subject themselves to such horrors?"

---

4 The Village of Blood

127

She fidgeted her hands, twisting her handkerchief in her lap. "Is it not a horror to watch us murder night after night?"

Gabriel tilted his head. "It is still something I have difficulty witnessing." He darted his eyes away. "Though, the attendants have explained it is no different than watching a beast feed upon prey. Like the mighty wolf upon the deer."

"That is how it feels," Evanangela nodded, "I feel as if some beast inside me hungers for the hunt."

He turned his gaze upon her again. "I have witnessed humans capable of truly monstrous things. And though your existence is considered an unholy abomination, there is also order and even beauty in it. There is no light without the darkness. In that darkness, your kind has created this community of safety and prosperity for humans. It is a marvel."

Evanangela looked out the window. "Yes, but at the expense of other mortals."

"There is no gain without sacrifice." Gabriel shifted in his seat. "And yet, even that sacrifice is not taken in greed or contempt, rather simple necessity."

She mulled his words. It was true, despite the court's petty nature, they did not take more than they needed. They did not destroy and waste life as mortals did on the battlefield. All was life in exchange for life. Evanangela let her eyes drift over the scenery as the manicured lawns gave way to the fields of wild grasses and stands of ancient gnarled trees. Buildings dotted the hills, little thatched abodes. The further they rode, the closer the clusters of cottages became until they passed the outskirts of a sprawling village.

The faint outline of a steeple speared the sky. Evanangela's heart tightened as she recognized it to be the same churchyard she had been born in. She wondered what might have become of her had Àmichemin not stumbled upon her that night. Most likely burnt up in the sun while wandering lost, had the peasants not killed her first. She shivered.

"Have you a chill, princesse?" Gabriel pulled her away from the dark suppositions. "There is a fur-lined blanket here in the seat trunk should you need it."

Evanangela shook her head. "Non, merci. I'm quite all right."

It did not take long for the carriage to rumble past the village. The tightness in her chest eased, and Evanangela watched as the landscape opened up again into acres and acres of farmland and grazing. To her surprise, the sky was beginning to lighten by small degrees. Gabriel busied himself with a latch on the floor of the carriage.

"The sun shall rise soon, princesse," he opened the hinge, revealing the floor had been secured to the lid of her coffin, "best prepare and put yourself to bed."

She nodded. She unlatched the cumbersome cloak and handed it to Gabriel. He folded it onto the seat next to him. Evanangela slipped off her shoes, handing these over as well. It would not be as comfortable remaining in her corset and dress, but there was not room for her to undress and then redress the following night. An inconvenience Àmichemin had warned her of.

Gabriel helped Evanangela lower herself into the coffin. Once she had snuggled into the deep, plush cushioning, he gave her a warm smile.

"Sleep well. Bonne nuit, princesse."

He closed the lid, allowing the darkness to swallow her up. Evanangela pulled the handkerchief from her sleeve and held it up to her nose. It smelled of Verseau. At that moment, she felt a sharp longing, wishing she also had one that smelled of Àmichemin. Her bittersweet comfort soon gave way to the sway of the carriage quieting her mind. She felt the stillness of the death-sleep creep over her body, and all was dark.

Evanangela woke. She could feel the coolness of the night hovering about her coffin and pressed her hand against the lid. Panic filled her mind when she found it heavy. Her eyes snapped open in alarm. She pressed with both hands, forcing the lid. Someone helped her to open it the rest of the way. Gabriel's face swam into focus as her panicked breathing slowed.

"Bonne nuit, princesse," he soothed, offering his hand, "you are safe."

She took his hand, and pushed her hunger aside, as the mortal scent curled into her nose, and hoisted herself into her seat. Gabriel closed the latch, hiding the coffin under the floor.

"Would Mademoiselle like her shoes and cloak?" He offered.

Evanangela shook her head, drawing her stocking-clad feet under her skirts. "Non, merci."

The window revealed they were traveling through a wooded area. It was even darker than the night at the château, as the trees blotted out even the light of the moon and stars. Little lanterns hung on the carriages for the drivers and horses to see.

"Are you hungry, princesse?"

She faced Gabriel again. The gnawing hunger tore through her as she raked her eyes over his mortal frame. She swallowed down the raw feeling. "Oui, j'ai faime."[5]

He bowed his head. "Would you prefer my neck or my arm, princesse?"

Evanangela took a shuddering breath. "I-I am afraid I will hurt you."

Gabriel shook his head. "N'important. You shall not hurt me. Seigneur explained that as long as you only take one mouthful that I shall be unharmed. More than that, and you shall lose your senses."

She leaned forward. "Then, we only need a mouthful to survive?" Horror raced across her skin. "All this time, we have been murdering these mortals simply for the pleasure of gluttony?"

He took her shaking hands in his own and squeezed them. "Non, princesse! This is a tactic your kind uses during travel, or when blood is scarce. You will wither into a ravenous wraith if you feed this way for more than a few days. Do not torment yourself with such thoughts."

Evanangela nodded. Soothed by the explanation.

"Drink, ma princesse." Gabriel offered his arm.

She lifted his wrist to her lips and slid up near the crook of his elbow. She could feel the living pulse as her fangs scraped the skin. They punctured, filling her mouth with blood. The richness of the blood made her dizzy, but she held onto the fragment of rational thought and swallowed, licking the wound to seal it. Evanangela pushed his hand away. She held her hand over her chest as her withered heart screamed for more. The small trickle of blood had ignited her senses, not quelled them.

---

5 Yes, I'm hungry.

Gabriel wiped his arm with a simple white handkerchief. She looked away. Each thud of her dead heart sent fire through her empty veins. Evanangela searched her mind for a distraction.

"Why did Verseau not heal himself and Àmichemin?" Her voice was low as she concentrated on her breathing. "When they turned those wounded attendants, why did they not heal themselves?"

He shrugged. "I suppose the healing does not work on your own kind, Mademoiselle. I am not entirely sure."

Evanangela nodded, annoyed with his lack of knowledge. She pursed her lips. "Pardonnez-moi, you had said you could...*entertain* me while we travel?"

Gabriel nodded, realizing her discomfort. "Oui, princesse, my apologies! Would you care for a tale?"

"Oui, something long and wonderful." Evanangela curled against the side of the carriage, her feet tucked under her skirts.

He turned, unlatching his seat, and pulled a fur-lined blanket from the compartment. "Ici, ma princesse."

"Merci," Evanangela took the blanket, wrapping it about herself. Though she was not chilled, it did provide soft comfort and a mild distraction from her pain.

"Then, I shall tell you a tale of my home." He settled back into his seat.

Gabriel took a deep breath, and relaxed his shoulders. "I come from a land quite far from the Nacre Court. I recently made my home in a neighboring land, which is how I found myself at your little fête.[6] A select few had been invited to the château, and as lesser nobles with small land holdings, it seemed the perfect offer for improving our prospects."

Greed. Evanangela felt an odd twinge considering the motivations of the mortals who doomed themselves to the nightly Valse Noire. Their desire for connections to grow their wealth or their status. For lust and other base pleasures. It was always the same.

He nodded. "Yes, greed is what brought us to the lion's den, so to speak. Nobles are never satisfied with their titles and wealth; they must always have more."

---

6 party

Surely, that does not justify such a bloody end. She mused to herself. Dieu had taught her to always forgive and to have an open heart. But seeing mortals up close and experiencing their decisions herself oft made her question what exactly it was that they deserved.

Gabriel continued. "In any case, I found myself there, hopeful to improve the circumstances of my family. Already, I was making better connections for us through life at court, and an invitation to such a wealthy and high-standing Seigneur would only bring further benefit. I do not know the purpose behind the desire for more the others had that night. However, mine are certainly far less self-indulgent."

His voice was tinged with a deep grief as he continued. Evanangela squeezed her hands in her lap, wanting to reassure him, but not wanting to interrupt his story.

"My father sent me away after disowning my fair sister. She was the prettiest lass in the land. Beauty unrivaled, but she had found scorn with our father. Immediately after, he regretted this harsh punishment, but there was no turning back. After some time had passed, he wished me to find and watch over her. To see if she had repented her ways and could be brought back home in good grace."

A strange chill crept up Evanangela's spine. She fidgeted, scratching the tattoo behind her ear, then clenched her hands in her lap under the blanket.

"As you may have guessed, it was my thin hope that my sister had somehow found herself in such a grand château, or that I might find someone there who knew her." Gabriel suddenly tore his gaze from Evanangela, and peeked out the window.

"Did you find her?" She darted her eyes down to her lap. "Were you able to locate your sister?"

Gabriel turned his gaze back to Evanangela and smiled. "Yes, I did."

Chapter Fifteen

He took Evanangela's shaking hand as he helped lift her from the coffin. Her skin clung to her bones and her veins were blue ropes snarled over her hands and arms. The air was chilly. She shivered as she clambered into her seat. It had been three nights of single swallows, and now there was hardly anything left to hold her together.

"Ici, ma princesse," Gabriel held out the fur blanket, "the spring frost is upon us tonight."

She nodded, accepting the warm wrap. Her breathing was ragged as her heart clenched, a fierce stone in her chest. "Merci…Gabriel."

His face fell when he heard her raspy voice. He leaned forward, extending his arm. "Drink, ma princesse."

Evanangela stared at his wrist. She could see the living pulse quivering beneath the skin. The warm musky scent of blood radiated from his naked flesh. Evanangela hissed, recoiling.

"Non, s'il vous plaît, non!"

Gabriel flinched at her strange behavior. Her held out his wrist again. "Princesse, you must drink. I can see this pains you-"

"I cannot!" Evanangela gasped. Her eyes burned with unshed tears. Without blood, she could not even cry. "I cannot, Gabriel! It is too painful. I will surely drain you, mon cher Gabriel!"

He shook his head, inching closer. "I trust you, princesse. I know you have no desire to harm me."

Evanangela waved her hand, trying to fend him off. The smell of mortal flesh swirled in her nostrils, igniting her brain. The desire to hunt roared in her ears. She bit her lip, shaking her head.

"Get away from me!"

Gabriel knelt on the floor of the carriage and took Evanangela's hand. "Forgive my impertinence, Mademoiselle, but I must insist."

She looked down at him. His beatific smile and angelic upturned face met her gaze with sincerity. Horror wrenched her heart as she realized he was like a sheep at the slaughter, trapped with her in the carriage with nowhere to run.

"It will be all right, princesse. Je promets."[1] He squeezed her hand.

Evanangela drew a long, rattling breath. His scent was overwhelming. Gabriel reached up, offering her his arm. Evanangela cradled his arm; her hands looked more like white, bony spiders. She bent down and grazed the vein in the crook of his elbow with her fangs. His skin quivered. The blood rushed up as she bit down. For a moment, her mind went quiet. The warm coppery blood gushed over her tongue, and her body sang with joy. But a small voice in her mind screamed at her, and she swallowed the blood. Her tongue slathered the wound, and she jerked herself back, pressing against the carriage cushions as hard as she could.

Gabriel wiped his arm with a linen. He was still sitting on the carriage floor, looking up at her, and smiled. "See? I knew you would not harm me."

"Please, get away from me." Evanangela begged. She dug her fingernails into her palms to keep from crying and wasting the precious blood.

He clambered back into his seat. "There now, princesse. I will stay here, as you wish."

It's not enough!

Her mind was spinning as her veins screamed. The tiny trickle of blood that awakened her heart was not enough! Every breath was a struggle. Every heartbeat felt like a hammer on an anvil.

"Would you like another story, princesse?"

Gabriel's voice was far away. Evanangela pressed her fingers to her forehead. Her head was pounding. The jostling of the carriage sent liquid fire through her body as it vibrated through the seat, the floor, and the walls. She wrapped the blanket tighter around her. The air was frigid, threatening to freeze and split her paper skin.

"Princesse, comment allez vous?"[2]

_____
1 I promise.
2 How are you?

She shook her head, refusing to look at him. "Pas du tous."[3]

The sounds were all too much. The squeak of the carriage wheels, the crunch of the horses' shoes, all of it raged in Evanangela's skull. She bowed her head, swallowing her sobs.

"I am not sure how to help. Seigneur only told me how to feed you." Gabriel's soft voice was monstrously loud in the tight carriage space. "Would going back into your coffin help, princesse? Would that offer you some comfort?"

Evanangela shook her head. "I-I don't know."

Gabriel opened the latch. "Would you like to try and see? I can open it again immediately if you like."

She took a deep breath and nodded. The luxurious coffin swallowed her up as she folded her fragile body into the cushioned space. Gabriel lowered the lid, careful not to let it drop. The darkness enveloped Evanangela, but it was not like when the death-sleep would come at dawn. She was awake, and able to feel how stifling and small the space truly was. Her eyes tried to focus, but there was only pitch darkness. A scream tore from her throat. Her hands beat on the lid. It was ripped open, moonlight pouring in. Gabriel snatched Evanangela up out of the coffin, and held her in his arms.

"Forgive me, princesse." He whispered as he embraced her. "I had no idea you were so frightened of the dark."

Evanangela hugged him back. She gulped the air to keep the tears at bay. Her heart felt as if it might leap up her throat it was beating so fast. Her fear overtook her instinct to hunt, allowing her a moment of respite from the searing pain. After a few moments, Gabriel loosened his arms.

"Would you like me to stop, Mademoiselle?"

She swallowed, trying to piece together her frantic thoughts. "Quoi?"[4]

The carriage lurched, causing Gabriel to tighten his grip once more. Evanangela melted into his embrace. It felt warm and familiar. Her mind quieted as her body wore itself out.

---

3 Not at all.
4 What?

The carriage jostled and Evanangela's eyes popped open. The silk interior of the coffin was warm. She tried to piece together where she was. She remembered sitting in Gabriel's arms, but that was all. The shock of the exhaustion and comfort must have worn her down. She supposed Gabriel had slid her into the coffin soon after she had fallen asleep.

She pressed her hand against the heavy lid. A thread of orange sunlight came through before the lid was slammed down.

"Not yet nightfall, princesse." Gabriel tapped the coffin lid.

Evanangela snuggled back into the soft fabric. "Where are we, Gabriel?"

His voice was muffled by the coffin. "About two hours-time to La Maison de Printemps. By then it will be dark, princesse. Sleep now. You need your rest."

The sleep enveloped Evanangela, and all was quiet. Her hair rustled as the fresh air taunted her eyes open once more.

"On est là?"[5] She sat up and stared at the slender crescent moon and the winking stars from the windows. The sky was velvety black.

"Oui, vous etez arrivez[6], ma princesse. Voici La Maison de Printemps." Gabriel took her hand and escorted her from the carriage.

Other attendants were doing the same with Verseau and Àmichemin. A parade of carriages behind them carried the rest of the court. A sweet scent hung in the air. Evanangela's veins contracted. The mouthfuls of blood had been nothing on her journey. Her skin felt tight and her heart squeezed in her chest. The other vampires looked just as ragged; their skin pulled tight over their skulls and bodies; their eyes sunken.

"Beautiful, isn't it?" Verseau grinned as he interrupted her painful thoughts. He escorted Evanangela up toward the brick manor. Gabriel bowed as they strode past.

She looked up at Verseau and noticed how the hollows of his cheeks had deepened. His skin was ashen, and his eyes had a fierce fire behind them, like that of a raptor on the hunt.

---

5 We're here?
6 Yes, you have arrived

Àmichemin took her place next to Verseau, but did not take his hand. "It's hard to believe the court still owns this place."

Evanangela darted her eyes over Àmichemin's frame. Her arms had always been slender, but now they were just bones wrapped in skin. Evanangela could see the slow beats of her empty heart against her ribs in her sunken chest.

Verseau opened the iron gate with a large key and guided the vampiresses through. "The last to actually reside here was the Duchess Printemps, Eloise, and her children." His face darkened. "Court life did not suit her."

Àmichemin rolled her eyes, but remained silent.

He patted Evanangela's hand. "Fear not, this is a calm abode. There are no human villages within a day's ride from here. Some vampires are just less *sociable* than others."

She nodded. Her opal-inlay boots clicked against the flagstones as they walked toward the entrance. Behind them, Gabriel and the other attendants carried the coffins and trunks.

"How long are we staying for, Seigneur?" Evanangela peered up at the dusty tapestries.

"Only a few nights, ma choupinette. Too long and the vixens would be at it!" Verseau laughed at his own joke, but there was a serious undertone in his jest.

The sticky, heavy miasma of human scent engulfed Evanangela, instilling the urge to hunt. Verseau laughed at her stooped posture. "There's nothing yet to hunt! Patience ma chère coeur, we are all hungry."

She straightened and forced a smile, the cool vixen blush rushing to her cheeks. Verseau either did not see, or ignored it as he said nothing more.

Once inside the maison, it was clear why Verseau had picked it for the outing. It was a large space, plenty of small apartments for the vampires and the attendants, but unlike the château, there were only arrow slit windows, and these were covered by moldering tapestries. There was no grand ballroom; no space for festivities. So long as the front gate was barred, an attack would be utter folly.

The trio made their way up the stairs toward the upper apartments. All the décor was green and gold. Verseau led them all the way to the back of the maison, and flung open the door at the end of the hall with a flourish. Inside was a tidy room, a ruby-red fire already crackling in the grate. Jacques bowed as Verseau led them inside.

"Bonsoir, mon Seigneur, mes Mademoiselles." Jacques turned back to the trunk he was unpacking.

Gabriel appeared from a side door, carrying odds and ends into the room. He bowed as well, and assisted Jacques with putting the clothes and baubles away.

Verseau led them to the couch. It creaked as he sat down. Evanangela found that the cushions were a bit musty, but soft and comfortable. Àmichemin flopped down onto the couch, sending a puff of dusty air floating about them. Verseau cleared his throat, then draped his arm over Àmichemin.

"It needs a bit of airing out, but it will do." He chatted as he toyed with Àmichemin's hair.

Evanangela nestled herself into Verseau's side, leaning her head onto his shoulder. "The change of scenery is welcome."

Àmichemin waved her hand. "The château can be such a grand *stifling* place."

Verseau nodded. "It will be good for the court – distract them, calm their nerves. We may even have a few small outings into the back garden."

"There is a garden?" Visions of the château garden wafted through her mind – the moonlit magnolias, the dark apple trees with their effervescent blossoms, the deep calm ponds.

He leaned and kissed her on the forehead. "Yes, a charming rustic space. Gnarled old apple trees centuries old, tall grass, daisies and sunflowers, that sort of thing."

Evanangela closed her eyes, imagining such a place. There had been snippets of time where she had gazed from the heavens upon the humans below. Farmers tending to their fields, and travelers making their way down winding roads. How she wished she could feel the golden warmth of the sun on her face sitting in such a garden.

Àmichemin snorted. "Such a garden is a waste of moonlight. Eloise was an odd one."

They soaked in the comfort of each other's company as they lounged before the fire. Evanangela fought to tamp down her hunger. Being near to Verseau was much stronger than her craving for blood, but she could not help but hear the noisy begging of her body.

Jacques bowed, startling them from their stupor. "Mon Seigneur, mes Mademoiselles, the merchants of Montpellier are waiting."

Verseau sat up, prompting Evanangela and Àmichemin to straighten themselves. He waved his hand. "Send them in."

Two young men and an older woman entered as Jacques opened the door. They spilled into the room. The young men seemed nervous and excited, but the older woman raked her eyes over the disarray of trunks and unpacked belongings. She pinned her gaze on Verseau.

"Mon Seigneur, it is an honor to have an audience with you in person." She curtsied, and the two men bowed.

Evanangela could not hear the woman's speech. Her nose caught the sweet aroma of living blood, and all other senses were blotted out. She gasped for breath as her dead heart squeezed in her chest. Her veins contracted terribly, making her body feel as if it were afire. She darted her eyes and saw Àmichemin gazing with the same intensity at the trio.

Verseau stood from the couch, receiving the merchants as a typical lord might. He steered the woman away from the two men, clearly their senior. Her demeanor remained frosty as he attempted to flirt.

How are they not afraid? We look like living skeletons!

Evanangela's eyes darted from Verseau to Àmichemin. Their eyes were alit, as if by fire. She looked again at the mortals. Their eyes seemed glazed over, as if in a stupor.

That must be it! She took a sharp breath, inhaling the scent of rot they were all exuding from so many days without living blood to nourish their dead bodies. *An unnatural hypnotism to trick the eye and the mind! How else would they agree to stand here and not run out screaming at the mere sight of us?*

Àmichemin then rose from the couch and approached one of the nervous men. She giggled as his eyes widened upon her approach.

"Bonsoire, Mademoiselle!" He chirped, bowing, "We were not expecting-"

She slinked up to him, silencing his words with her long, deft finger upon his lips. "Nor was I expecting you. Yet, here we are."

Her breathy tone made his knees wobble. Evanangela rushed to stand, impatient with the desire to feed. The rich smell of blood was impossible to ignore. She licked her lips, tasting the air. The remaining man froze, his face slipping into unease as she strode toward him.

"Bonjour, Mademoiselle," he bowed lowed, "we have traveled far, and it is an honor to-"

"Tais toi." Evanangela growled.

Verseau and Àmichemin whipped their heads around, shocked at Evanangela's base behavior. Àmichemin gave a nervous giggle. "Ah! Pardonnez! She is simply weary from traveling."

Evanangela snapped to attention, realizing her misstep. She gave a shallow curtsy. "Oui, pardonnez-moi. I am not used to traveling, and it has been a long journey."

The merchant nodded, bewildered by the quick exchange. "Ç'est d'accord, ç'est d'accord."

Àmichemin turned back to her merchant, her body inching closer to his. Verseau was whispering something into the woman's ear. Evanangela stood at attention, allowing the mortal to prattle on about his journey and how he is quite used to traveling and something or other about how to make it less strenuous for a fine lady such as herself.

"How kind of you," Evanangela took a deep breath to steel herself, only to draw in his intoxicating scent, "how very *kind*."

A soft hiss cut through the air. Evanangela at last let her mouth drop open, revealing her fangs. His yelp was extinguished as she sunk into his soft neck. Her nails cut into the homespun fabric of his traveling tunic as she held him upright against her. The blood poured into her mouth and down her throat. His body was hard, muscled from physical labor and hard travels. Her nails dug into his taut flesh. Warmth spread through her body, and her eyes rolled back in pleasure. Evanangela sucked hard, forcing the blood to rush faster. It sprayed onto her tongue as his face contorted from the pain. She moaned into his neck, creating a strange burbling humming sound as blood dribbled down her chin.

The mortal was dry much quicker than the victims of her previous feeds as the extreme hunger had decimated her patience. Evanangela still suckled at the empty wound, her mind lost to the rippling waves of gratification that overwhelmed her senses. Then, there was the soothing weight of a hand on her shoulder, and a pleasing voice tickling her ear.

"Ç'est finis,[7] ma petite," Verseau purred, "you can let go now."

Evanangela obeyed and released her grip, allowing the mortal to drop to the floor. Her senses returned, as if the room had finally come into focus after being blurry and muffled for so long. Verseau wrapped his arms about her, drawing her into a warm embrace. His scent had come alive with the living blood coursing through his veins. Evanangela snuggled into him. His flesh was beginning to plump once more; his garish bony features softening.

"There now, isn't that better?" Verseau chuckled as he led them back to the couch.

Jacques and Gabriel appeared from the side door. They set to work dragging the bodies out into the hall. Àmichemin draped herself onto the couch, nestling against Evanangela. Verseau petted them both. His eyes sparkled as he looked down at the both of them.

"Ah, may this holiday never end." He crooned.

---

7 It's over,

Chapter Sixteen

The fire crackled merrily as they lounged on the couch. All was quiet, a welcome comfort from the bored screams of the mad vampires at the château. The tranquility soaked into Evanangela's body and mind, just as the blood into her veins. Her heartbeat was quiet, plump and satisfied. She slid her hand onto Àmichemin's breast and could feel the same slow, content heartbeat. Àmichemin sighed and petted Evanangela's hand.

Evanangela opened her eyes and gazed into the fire. The flames were not as crystalline as those at the château. They too had a rough and rustic quality like the maison. She rolled her eyes up to Verseau.

"Shall we visit the garden, mon Seigneur?"

"Hmm?" He stirred from his stupor. "Non, pas maintenant, ma chère. Perhaps tomorrow."

Àmichemin drew Evanangela closer and rested her chin atop the crown of her hair. "We have had a long night already. Let's just enjoy one another."

She acquiesced and burrowed deeper into Àmichemin's embrace. Thoughts of the maddening hours in the carriage dripped away as she drank in the presence of the two creatures she craved more than even blood. She squeezed their hands, feeling their realness. Peace washed over her as her mind was at last reassured.

Before long, Evanangela found herself half-awake, swaying as a strong presence was guiding her.

"You dozed off, ma fleur noire," Verseau's deep voice reverberated in Evanangela's groggy mind, "Come now, it's time for bed."

Àmichemin was bumping along next to her. Evanangela took Àmichemin's hand as they crawled into Verseau's enormous coffin. He stood beside it, waiting for them to get comfortable.

"A sight more beautiful than all the art in France." Verseau murmured as he stared down at them.

Àmichemin held up her hand, gesturing for him. "Join us, s'il vous plaît."

He took her hand, and climbed in. "Of course, ma chère douleur. Here I am."

They were a mess of twined limbs as Jacques slid the coffin closed. Darkness enveloped them. A flash went through Evanangela's mind, frightening her. All at once, she was back in the carriage with the lid closing over her. But then, Àmichemin rubbed her nose in Evanangela's hair, inhaling her scent. The hot air fluffing her hair. Evanangela sighed, allowing the sudden fear to slip away. The journey was over, and she was with Àmichemin and Verseau once more. All was well.

The nights passed slowly at La Maison de Printemps. Life at the château became a faded fantasy world for Evanangela. She perched herself in a window seat of the library. The moonlight spilled over her as she flipped through a book. The title read "Du Contract Social Ou Du Droit Politique."[1] It was all suppositions and contradictions. Evanangela found it rather boring and was about to put it away, when Verseau dipped his head over her shoulder.

"What are you reading, ma chère coeur?" He lifted the book from her hands and inspected the cover, then made a face. "Ugh! Rousseau, a repugnant mortal."

He tossed the book onto a nearby chair. Evanangela regarded the tome with mild curiosity. "Do you know him, Seigneur?"

"I have not met him, and if I did, I would suck him dry so he could no longer speak! But don't worry about him, ma chère. N'important."[2] Verseau shook his head.

He sat down next to her in the window seat and drew her in. She rested her head against his shoulder.

"Où est Àmichemin?" She peered up at him from under her lashes.

Verseau kissed her forehead. "Ah, I am sure she is wandering about somewhere. I know you had mentioned the garden, would you like to see it?"

1 The Social Contract
2 It's not important.

Evanangela squeezed his arm. "Oui, Seigneur!"

"Well then, ma fleur. Shall we?" He chuckled and drew her up as he stood.

They walked together out one of the side doors. The fresh night air tickled Evanangela and rustled her hair. She realized she had not truly spent any time outside in the world since the night of her fall. The new sensations excited her. She squeezed Verseau's hand.

He looked down at her as they walked toward the ancient apple tree. "Qu'est-ce que c'est,[3] ma chère?"

Evanangela became shy. She huddled against his side as they walked. "I have not been outside, Seigneur. It is refreshing."

He nodded, and gestured for her to sit. They curled up against the tree trunk. The gnarled roots seemed to embrace them. Withered apples lay scattered about in the grass. Evanangela picked one up and sniffed it.

"Careful, ma chère," Verseau warned, "we cannot eat food. It would be most *uncomfortable* for you."

She let the apple slip from her hands. It rolled away to join its fellows. Evanangela looked up into the canopy of the tree. The leaves were dark and glossy. It would be quite some time before the apple blossoms burst their buds. She recalled the magnolias and apple blossoms at the château.

"Verseau," she contemplated, "how is it that there are blossoms in full bloom at the château, and it is only a few days past the spring frost?"

He slid his hand into her auburn curls. "That is simple, ma choupinette[4], they are enchanted."

Evanangela recalled the enchanted candles. She wondered at what else was magicked at the château. It was such an odd place, and even after living there for some time, she felt she hardly understood it. Time itself seemed to unfold differently at the château as well. Had it been weeks? Months? She was unsure how long exactly it had been since she had fallen. It was becoming a faded, forgotten memory.

Verseau ran his hand through her hair, teasing her scalp. Evanangela shivered with pleasure. He smiled. "The château is a living space, so

3 What is it
4 My pet

to speak. It is freed from the constraints of such realities as weather, seasons, and other such nonsense."

The breeze was chilly, but Verseau had fed recently, and his warmth kept Evanangela comfortable. She snuggled closer to him. "Is Le Village du Sang enchanted as well?"

He nodded. "Oui, the whole of the estate is enchanted. Once we cross the gate into the peasant village, we are subject to the rules of nature once more."

Evanangela pondered this. "Then why not make it forever night, Seigneur?"

"Ah! Ma chère, you are such fun!" Verseau laughed. "If such a feat were possible, I am sure the court would never sleep. And I would have my hands full with trying to organize endless entertainment for my bored vassals. But alas, we cannot enchant away the sun."

Àmichemin appeared from the side door. She bobbed her head when she spotted them under the tree, gathered up her dress and picked her way toward them; kicking apples out of her way as she went.

"Quelle surprise![5] The two of you are out dans cette jardin misérable."[6]

Verseau waved at her. "How could I disappoint ma petite? Come and sit, the grass won't bite."

Evanangela smiled up at her as Àmichemin made a big show of dusting off a place to sit, and then flopped down onto the ground. She groaned and sprawled across both their laps.

"Alors! How can you possibly be comfortable on such hard ground?" Àmichemin whined.

"Ah, ma chère douleur, a few moments. Just a few." Verseau wove his fingers through her starry tresses.

She petted Àmichemin's hand. "Pour moi? S'il vous plait?"

"Oh, all right!" Àmichemin huffed. Then she smiled at Evanangela. "It is hard to say no to you, ma chère."

---

5 What a surprise!
6 In this wretched garden.

Verseau kissed Àmichemin's forehead. "And what have you been up to this evening, ma fleur noire?"

Àmichemin took Evanangela's hand in both of hers, and rested them upon her chest. "I was feeling a bit *suscités.*[7] So, I played with my food before I ate it."

"Alors! Vraiment?" Verseau teased.

Evanangela cocked her head. Verseau petted her hair, and chuckled at her puzzled expression.

"Oh, ma chère coeur! Don't tell me you didn't have any mortal relations before your turning."

She shook her head, a blush blossoming across her cheeks. "Non, Seigneur."

Verseau seemed delighted, but Àmichemin had a thoughtful, faraway look in her eyes. Evanangela swallowed her embarrassment. She darted her eyes about.

"S-seigneur, we haven't made time to discuss-"

He bent down and kissed her on the lips, silencing her. "Discuss? What would there be to discuss other than how sweet and naïve you are?"

"But the court, and the blood shortage-" Evanangela tried again, but Àmichemin sat up and took Evanangela into her arms. She slipped her hand behind Evanangela's head, and drew her into a long, fiery kiss. Evanangela gasped for air when Àmichemin released her.

"Never you mind," Àmichemin purred, "Verseau and I have been wracking our brains over such worrisome things. Enjoy your jardin. There will be little time for such pleasantries when we return to the château."

Verseau drew his arm around Àmichemin's shoulders and kissed her tenderly. Then he looked into Evanangela's eyes. "She is right, ma petite. This is meant to be a holiday for you. Worry not over such distressing matters-"

---

7 aroused

147

Evanangela balled her hands into fists, her annoyance rekindling. "But, mon Seigneur! You included me on the Council! Surely, I too should be searching for solutions to such issues alongside both of you?"

Àmichemin shook her head and petted Evanangela's hair. "Oui, vous bête mignon[8]. However, we are just beginning to train you in the ways of leadership in the court. We do not expect you to handle such weighty decisions. You have just begun your education on the inner workings of the château."

Verseau slid his hand up Evanangela's leg to her thigh, his eyes teasing. "Besides, it seems we have *far more* to teach you about the world at present."

The chilly spring air did little to deter their heated romp in the garden. Àmichemin cradled Evanangela in her lap, showering her with kisses as Verseau kissed under her skirts. Their moans echoed off the crumbling stone walls of the garden, and Evanangela was sure the neighboring peasants would hear them. But soon, her mind melted away and there was only the sensations of Àmichemin and Verseau's hands and mouths. It was just as needy and insistent as blood sharing, and yet there was a deeper, more primal depth to the pleasures she experienced.

Evanangela quivered as she caught her breath. Her head was in Àmichemin's lap, and she was stroking her hair. Verseau continued to tease her with feather soft strokes of his fingertips up and down one of her thighs. The sky was turning the first faint flush of grey, prompting Verseau to sigh and get to his feet.

"The sun never waits, even for magnificent creatures like you, mes dames."[9] He held out his hand.

Àmichemin gave Evanangela a gentle push, and she took Verseau's hand, letting him help pull her upright. Her legs were still quivering from his attentions. Once she was standing, Verseau offered Àmichemin his hand, and she took it; rising with far more grace. Evanangela leaned into Verseau's side as they entered the maison. The dusty library was musty and cramped compared to the airy garden. Evanangela sighed as they wound their way through the narrow halls toward their apartments.

The attendants hustled about, helping to prepare the court for the sunrise. Gabriel was waiting in the sitting room. He bowed as the trio

---

8 You cute creature
9 my ladies

148

walked past. Jacques was standing at attention in the bedroom. He also bowed, and began scooping up the garments as they shed their clothes.

Verseau untied the stays of Àmichemin's corset while Evanangela kicked off her shoes. Gabriel peeked around the corner, and Jacques sent him a scathing glare. Evanangela giggled as she let her skirts pool about her feet. He looked away, blushing. Verseau darted his eyes from Gabriel to Evanangela, then smirked. He grabbed her chin and roughly kissed her, nipping her bottom lip with his teeth. Evanangela gasped when he pulled away.

"My, my, it seems we'll have to *entertain* you again tomorrow." Verseau purred.

Àmichemin rolled her eyes and scoffed as she flopped into the enormous coffin. "Yes, well *I* am simply exhausted!"

Verseau chuckled as Àmichemin beckoned for the both of them to join her. Evanangela crawled in after her, nestling herself into the crook of Àmichemin's arm. He groaned as he lowered himself into the plush cushioning. Àmichemin pressed her forehead against his.

Jacques slid the lid of the coffin shut, blotting out the first streaks of grey-orange. The curtains were drawn tight, and the trio drifted off into their death sleep; their bodies growing cold and stiff in their tangled embrace.

Chapter Seventeen

Evanangela rose from the coffin. Àmichemin was perched on the edge of the bed in an open robe, and Verseau was fully dressed in one of the chairs, reading something. Verseau did not look up as Evanangela crept out of the coffin and pulled a robe about her naked body. Àmichemin patted the bed, prompting her to sit.

"Qu'est-ce que-?"

Àmichemin silenced her with a finger to her lips. The soft pressure sent a jolt through Evanangela. She shivered as Àmichemin drew away and resumed her vigil, staring at Verseau.

After a few moments, Verseau set the paper face down on the side table. It looked to be a letter with a broken official wax seal. The only sounds were the crackling of the fire in the grate, and the gay laughter of a pair of vampires running past the window, playing on the lawn. He sighed, rubbed his face, then finally, regarded them.

"Je regrettes, mes Mademoiselles," Verseau shook his head, "it seems our holiday is cut short."

Àmichemin took Evanangela's hands and squeezed them, keeping her gaze fixed on Verseau. Evanangela swallowed the gasp in her throat, the hairs on the back of her neck stood on end.

"It seems we were right in escaping the château when we did – the villagers rose up and attacked. The estate is in shambles. Le Village du Sang is safe. The attendants barred the gates and did not allow the peasants entry. Our guards did what they could to drive the attackers from the château, but many perished in the process."

Alarm rang through Evanangela's mind. Àmichemin squeezed her hands tighter. They remained silent as Verseau continued.

"I have received a report that this attack was in revenge for the death of Henri, that miserable peasant that was secreted into the château. They are determined to put us to death 'for our crimes' so they claim."

151

A low growl emanated from Àmichemin. "I am at the ready, mon Seigneur."

Verseau raised his hand. Àmichemin fell quiet, but Evanangela could feel the rage and shock vibrating through Àmichemin's body.

"Oui, il faut necessaire que nous retournerons à le château.[1] La Maison de Printemps can act as a fortress of sorts, we simply do not have the supplies to survive such a siege. While the blood shortage is still very real, there are *meals* to be had at the château. Here, they must be brought from the neighboring towns by our attendants. And there is much risk in that. Here also, we would be utterly trapped with no means for escape."

The news was a blow to Evanangela. It seemed that the layers of gilded varnish had been scraped away since her first days with the court. What was once a glittering world of joy and beauty was crumbling into a nightmare with scrambling scavengers. She shivered.

Àmichemin spoke, her voice low. "Mon Seigneur, the court has faced such perils in the past. We shall overcome."

Verseau nodded. He turned and gazed out the window. "Oui, ma chère. But at what cost?"

The maison was buzzing as attendants dashed to and fro, and the sounds of bumping and scraping filled the halls as trunks were hastily packed. Evanangela shivered as she looked down at the wineskin Jacques had brought her. Verseau and Àmichemin had already downed their own. Their pinched faces revealing their disgust. It was bull's blood, hastily acquired from a local butcher. The court had been provided with similar wineskins of sheep or bull's blood. It was revolting as it was both dead and not human. Evanangela struggled to swallow each mouthful.

"Drink, ma choupinette. You will feel sick, but it is better than starving when we are about to travel with only boire à petites gorgées du sang." Verseau nodded.

Evanangela sighed and forced herself to drink the last of the blood. It tasted musky and stale. She gagged as she set aside the empty wineskin.

Àmichemin stood before the fire, her gaze faraway as the glow of the flames illuminated her like a bright star in the night sky. Evanangela

---

1 Yes, it is of the utmost importance we return to the castle.

joined her, unsure of what to do with herself as Verseau scribbled orders to be sent ahead to the château.

Jacques knocked on the doorframe and bowed. "Mon Seigneur, mes Mademoiselles, a crowd of peasants bearing torches and weapons have been spotted in Riquewihr and are advancing a day's ride from the maison."

Verseau set aside his pen and nodded. "We are to leave tonight. No exceptions."

"Bien, mon Seigneur." Jacques bowed and turned heel to inform the other attendants.

The pen scraped across the paper as Verseau hastily finished his orders. He folded the letter and dripped wax from the nearby candle.

"Garçon!" Verseau bellowed, making Evanangela flinch.

Gabriel trotted into the room, then bowed at the doorway. "Oui, mon Seigneur?"

Verseau extended the letter. "Take this to the messenger. Tell her it is of the utmost importance that it reaches the château quick as a bat's breath."

He bowed again and took the letter. "Absolument, mon Seigneur."

Evanangela watched as Gabriel sprinted away. The click of the door signaled his departure. Verseau rubbed his face with his hand, then leaned back in his chair and gazed out the window.

"Nous avons fait un beau rêve et c'est tout."[2]

She slid off the bed and sat herself at Verseau's feet and placed her head in his lap. Verseau petted her hair, his fingers twining through her short auburn locks. He heaved a great sigh and looked down at her.

"Ma petite, I fear history shall repeat itself. And you shall have your innocence stripped from you."

Evanangela tilted her head so she could look up at him. "I am knowledgeable of the ways of the court, mon Seigneur."

He shook his head. "Non, I mean that you too shall become hardened, like Àmichemin and myself."

---

2 We had a beautiful dream and that was all.

153

"I shall try not to be, for both your sakes." Evanangela whispered.

Àmichemin turned away from the fire. She sat down on the bed, hugging herself tight. "It's not something you can pretend away, ma chère. A great fall scars you."

Evanangela flinched at her words. The pain and screams of her unholy fall flashed through her mind. Verseau lifted her into his lap, and embraced her.

"It is the way of things. We shall endure."

The cool spring air tickled Evanangela with one last breath of apple blossoms as the court was escorted to the line of waiting coaches. Verseau was already packed into his carriage, and Gabriel led Evanangela to her own.

Anxiety stole her voice as she settled herself into the plush cushioned seat. She pulled her cloak tighter about her. The handkerchief was tucked into her corset, next to her dead heart.

"Forgive me, princesse, but the trip will be longer this time, as we must take an indirect route to the château to avoid the rabble rousers from catching up to us."

She balked at the news. Her hands trembled. "H-how much longer?"

"Longer by four days." Gabriel bowed his head, his face pained. "We shall have to perform boire à petites gorgées du sang the first three days, as we did before. Then, on the fourth, le Seigneur has ordered the caravan to stop at a small village where...where-"

He grimaced and turned away. Evanangela understood. The court was going to slaughter the village. Her heart fell and her breath caught in her throat.

Mon Dieu! Nous sommes des monstres![3]

The carriage lurched forward. Evanangela steadied herself, then pulled out her handkerchief and held it to her nose. The sky was lightening by degrees, signaling the beginning of her captivity in the carriage.

---

3 My God, we are monsters!

"Ç'est l'heure, princesse,"[4] He lifted the trap door.

Evanangela nodded. "Merci, Gabriel." She folded herself into the coffin, and held her breath as he closed the lid.

She pushed aside her discomfort the following nightfall and she took Gabriel's arm without a word. Her heart screamed in protest of the small mouthful of blood, but the wailing of her mind was louder.

"Gabriel, I simply must find a solution before we reach the château. Amichemin and Verseau have protected me from the worries of the court for too long. Now with the château under attack, they have more worries than ever!"

He reached out his hand, then recoiled remembering how his touch had pained her in their previous travels. "Princesse, it is not your responsibility to worry over such matters. Seigneur and Mademoiselle are doing all they can to address this crisis. Even with the Council, they were unable to find a solution. Such a matter cannot be resolved by you alone."

Evanangela nodded. She remembered the summit; how dull and useless it had been. They were no closer to a solution than when they had started. She rubbed her knuckles against her forehead, a poor attempt to soothe her growing headache.

"I must try." She shook her head. "There must be a better way. The list of suitable mortals is dwindling, and Verseau has stressed that attacking the peasants is far too dangerous."

Gabriel glanced out the window at the dark expanse of trees. "And yet, Seigneur is ordering for you to *visit* one of these villages." He turned his sad gaze back to Evanangela. "Surely, you can see how desperate the court must be to do such a perilous thing."

"How is attacking this village different than simply preying on the villagers every night?" Her annoyance was growing. "Surely such an act will only fuel the villagers' desire to attack the château again?"

He nodded; his face pinched with discomfort. "That is why Seigneur has commanded the court to ensure every last villager is slaughtered. There are to be no survivors. We are then instructed to burn the bodies and the buildings so it appears the village was attacked by raiders."

---

4 It is time, princess,

Evanangela's hands flew up to her mouth as horror spiked her heart and her mind. "Even," her voice wobbled, "even the *children*?"

"They will meet merciful ends, ma princesse." Gabriel whispered. "To leave them alive would endanger the court. They would also meet dismal fates such as starvation, slavery, or being attacked by wolves. Children cannot survive on their own. To leave an entire village of children to fend for themselves would be far crueler."

Her mind whirred as she processed Gabriel's words. It was true, there was no way to reasonably save the children without endangering the court. There was no way the Village du Sang would be able to support such a large population increase, especially with them unable to properly work. Evanangela struggled to swallow her tears, to protect her precious blood.

"Je suis un monstre." She whispered and hugged her arms about herself. "Perhaps the court does deserve justice at the hands of the peasants."

Gabriel shook his head. "Non, ma princesse, do not say such a thing! A proper solution may yet be found. The Seigneur has lived through many disasters, and Mademoiselle has been alive for hundreds of years, have seen the court flourish and wane and flourish again. There are several answers they are considering. It is because of their desire to maintain balance with the villagers that they have not yet decided. Many of the solutions used in the past call for the extermination of the surrounding villages; something they want to avoid if possible."

The thought heartened Evanangela. Knowing that Verseau valued the lives of the neighboring peasants restored her faith in the court. She leaned her head against the cool glass of the carriage window. Her breath did not make little clouds on the glass as Gabriel's did. She pulled away, discomforted at the reminder that her veins were empty.

Darkness enveloped the carriage as the vast forest blotted out the starlit sky. The lanterns did little to illuminate the endless gloom. Evanangela tore her gaze away from the window. She wondered how Àmichemin and Verseau were faring. Jacques was traveling with Verseau, but Evanangela had never seen Àmichemin's attendant. The thought of her dear companion traveling alone squeezed her heart.

"Gabriel, does Àmichemin have an attendant?"

He perked up at the sound of her voice. "Non, ma princesse. The Mademoiselle only cares for the company of the Seigneur and you. She prefers to be alone otherwise."

Evanangela flinched at this. "Àmichemin is traveling alone! Why can we not travel together? It must be unbearable!"

Gabriel took her hand and squeezed it. "Your heart is so big, princesse." His smile was warm. "Unlike you, Àmichemin is a hardened, ancient, creature. She does not seek comfort and companionship as you do. Her solitary nature means she is happier to travel alone. Though I'm sure your company would bring her joy and amusement. She will be fine. As well as, the carriages would be too cramped with the both of you and both of your coffins. It would make the journey even more of a misery."

Her gaze drifted down to the floor at the latch for her coffin. There was no way two coffins would fit, and they would be far too cramped bedding in a coffin together. Only Verseau's coffin was large enough to comfortably hold multiple bodies. She wondered at how large Verseau's carriage must be to hold such cargo.

"Is it odd that I have you as my attendant?" Evanangela fidgeted her hands. It made sense to her that Verseau had Jacques. As the Seigneur, he required a personal attendant to see to helping him run the court. But Jacques did not provide any sort of companionship for Verseau. She bit her lip, wondering if her desire for company was considered odd in the court.

Gabriel petted her hand. "Many of the others at court have personal attendants." He caught her gaze and gave her a reassuring smile. "Just as mortals are, some vampires prefer to be solitary, while others seek out companionship. You are not the only one, princesse. And even so, your rank entitles you to a personal attendant. It is not out of the ordinary."

She nodded, relieved at his words. Her thoughts drifted to the couple who had been turned from attendants to vampires after a court member had attacked them. She returned Gabriel's gaze.

"Do the attendants wish to be members of the court? Do they desire to become vampires?"

His eyes widened. "That is certainly an odd question. One I have not considered." He darted his eyes away. "I have never heard such grumblings from the other attendants. However, I am sure there are some who wish it. There are always those who wish for more than what they have. But the Village du Sang is largely content. They are free to live their lives from dawn to dusk. The demands of a human court are far greater than that of the vampires. There are no feasts to prepare, visitors outside of the nightly feeds are few and far between. Much of the attendants' daily lives are their own. An unheard-of luxury for most mortals."

Evanangela nodded. It was true. In her time in heaven, she had looked down upon the gilded courts of mortal kings and seen the suffering of overworked and underfed attendants. Of the grueling days of cleaning, cooking, sewing, fetching, they appeared to be franticly working at all hours with scarcely a moment to sleep.

Gabriel gave her hand one last pat before releasing it. "There is no court or village that exists without sacrifice; human or otherwise. Trust in their judgement. I am certain the Seigneur and Mademoiselle will find the right choice."

Chapter Eighteen

The familiar knock vibrated through Evanangela. Her eyes opened wide, attempting in vain to adjust to the darkness. She pressed against the lid, and Gabriel helped pull it open, his hand extended. She took it, his strength easily pulling her up and out. Evanangela smoothed her skirts and sat down on the carriage seat. Her mouth and throat were dry; she strained to speak.

"Gah...bri-el?" She wheezed.

He nodded and closed the floor latch. "Bonsoire, princesse. I know you are in pain. But we have arrived. Once Seigneur gives his signal, the feed will begin."

Evanangela looked out the carriage window; they were not moving. She strained her ears and heard the sound of impatient horses fidgeting. The last threads of the sunset were being snuffed out by the horizon. She reached for the door latch, but Gabriel took her wrist, his grip firm but gentle.

"I must insist you stay in the carriage, princesse." He released, but kept his hand by the door. "If you exit the carriage too soon, it could trigger a chase, and you could be gravely wounded."

"Vill-agers?" Evanangela licked her lips and coughed.

Gabriel shook his head. "No. The lesser members of court do not possess the mercy and self-control that you do. And this journey is already pushing everyone to their limits."

A shrill whistle cut through the air. It seemed to scream inside of Evanangela's skull. She clamped her hands over her ears, the pain scraping at her mind.

"That is the signal, princesse," Gabriel moved away from the door, "the feed has begun!"

The door swung open. Evanangela removed her hands from her ears. The whistling had stopped. She could hear the creaking of carriage doors and a great many footsteps advancing. She stepped down from the carriage, aided by her footman. Once she was on the ground, the footmen and driver climbed into the carriage to join Gabriel, and shut the door.

Dozens of vampires and vixens marched toward her, but their eyes looked on past her. Evanangela turned and saw the village at last. Smoke curled from the chimneys. The warm glow of fires in the grate illuminated the windows. A few stragglers wandered about in the gloom.

Evanangela marched alongside the court. Her eyes darted, desperately trying to find Àmichemin and Verseau. The mortals that were out walking froze, the whites of their eyes gleaming in the darkness as they beheld the horror at last. Hisses and low growls rippled through the crowd. All at once, the mortals fled, screams tearing through the air. Then, the church bells began to ring. Evanangela stopped, clapping her hands over her ears again. The confusion and terror of the night she fell flashed through her mind. Vampires bumped and jostled her as they strode past. Then, a cold hand settled onto her shoulder.

"N'aie pas peur."[1]

The whispering voice was soothing and familiar. Evangela opened her eyes and lowered her hands. She saw Verseau smiling at her and threw herself at him, winding her arms about his neck.

He embraced her, his cold body enveloping hers. As he drew away, another cold hand pressed on Evanangela's back. She whirled about and came face to face with Àmichemin.

"It is time."

Her voice was hoarse. Evanangela nodded. Together, they walked into the village. Once at the entrance, they split off, running faster than a hunted deer. She recoiled once more, this time, at the guttural sound of dying screams. The heady scent of living blood filled the air. Frightened animals bellowed and mewled. A cacophony of fear and pain.

Evanangela clenched her teeth. *We truly are monsters! They should have killed me in the churchyard. So many innocent lives-!*

The miasma of blood seeped into her mind, quieting her frantic thoughts. Her body trembled as her dead heart tightened in her chest;

---

1 Be not afraid.

her empty veins burned. She screamed, the pain clouding her mind, the blood making her feet move.

Feed! Must feed! Feed!

A mortal burst from a nearby cottage, their limbs flailing as they tripped and fell into the street. Evanangela felt her mind go blank. Her body stooped; her muscles coiled. It was only a blink, and she was on top of the mortal, her body having lunged out of reflex at the frightened prey. Her jaws opened, revealing her fangs.

"Dieu sauve-moi!" The mortal screeched.

Evanangela brought down the full force of her bite. Blood spurted from the neck wound, rushing into her mouth and down her throat. At last, her body relaxed. Her mind hummed with pleasure as she lapped at the blood. She held the peasant tight, despite the heartbeat slowing and weakening. Evanangela pulled the body against her, cradling it tighter, her lips sucking the last of the living blood as the heart stopped.

She let the drained corpse fall back. The head hitting the dirt street with a metallic thud. Evanangela swallowed her last mouthful, her senses returning as her heart thundered in her chest, the blood filling her veins and warming her body at last. The corpse was a young man, his eyes still wide with terror, though they were now glassy and clouded with death.

The scent of blood was thick in the air. Evanangela tried to follow the scent, but it was everywhere. Overwhelmed, she barreled into a nearby cottage. The door was in splinters. A hiss stopped her in her tracks. It was Àmichemin. She was holding a villager. He reached out for Evanangela, blood burbling from his mouth. Amichemin turned back to the villager and bit down again. His eyes widened from the impact, then his body went slack. Death glazing over his eyes.

Evanangela backed out of the cottage. Her mind continued to scream, *Feed! Feed! Feed!*

A pair of vampires were working to wrench the door off one of the cottages. The wood groaned and cracked as they pulled against the iron bolt. With a mighty boom, the door fractured and the iron bolt smashed the cobble entryway. They tossed the broken door into the road and burst into the house. Screams erupted as they made quick work of the mortals inside.

She kept running, her mind egging her on. The scent of blood taunted her, intoxicating her senses. At last, she found a store room. All seemed quiet and dark, but she could smell the frightened mortals that were hiding within. An excited growl rumbled in her throat as she sunk her fingers into the seam of the doorway, bending and breaking the door. The bolt was made of wood, not iron, and after a few moments of pulling with all her might, Evanangela wrenched the door off its frame. She let go as it swung open. It hung on by the bent metal hinges, like a loose tooth in a crone's mouth.

A muffled gasp pricked her ears. There were shelves of pickling jars, barrels, and sacks of grain. Evanangela scanned the gloom, then spotted a seam in the floor. Her feet were silent as she approached. It was a trap door leading down to a cellar. She lifted the heavy iron ring, pulling open the panel as quiet as a whisper and descended, pulling the door closed behind her to prevent her quarry from escaping.

The scent was overwhelming. A pack of mortals were hiding in the depths of the root cellar. Evanangela hissed, eliciting screams of sheer terror. She lunged as the mortals began to scatter, breaking wooden crates and scrambling to get past her toward the ladder. A large man faltered and she tackled him. His calloused hands flailed, then attempted to punch Evanangela in the face. She laughed as her hand flew out, blocking his attack. He appeared to be a laborer; a farmer most likely. His tanned skin smelled of sunshine, sweat, and earth. But the tantalizing overtones of fear and blood were what made her heart race.

"Papa!" A small child squealed.

Evanangela threw open her jaws, latching onto the vein in his neck. It was gloriously ropy and thick. The blood sprayed into her mouth from the force of the bite. He struggled against her; his screams silenced by the pressure of her suckling. His blood was rich and earthy, unlike the delicate quality of the merchants and vassals that were paraded at La Valse Noire. She moaned into his neck, relishing in the syrupy quality of his blood.

Mortals escaped as the trap door was thrown open, but Evanangela did not care. The heart was still beating, which meant there was still blood to be had. She sucked harder, gorging herself. Her veins swelled and her heart fluttered as it pumped harder. Never had she felt so full; so *alive*. At the feeds, she had only ever been allowed one mortal. If she felt this good with two mortals, what kind of ecstasy could be reached with three, or four?

She swallowed the last mouthful. Her ears pricked, listening for her escaped mortals. There was still one in the storeroom; frightened footsteps pacing above. She dashed up the ladder, and found a young lass pacing about. Her eyes darted out the window and toward the doorway. She had not yet seen Evanangela.

"Maman! Maman!" She called, her plump body shivering.

Evanangela found that the scent of fear was far more intoxicating than the rich stench of blood. She crept toward the trembling lass. Her eyes followed the line of the veins in her exposed neck and bosom. She locked eyes with Evanangela, and screamed. It echoed in the storeroom, sending Evanangela into a frenzy.

Her hands shot out as she grabbed the lass by the hair and threw her down to the floor in one swift motion. Evanangela slammed herself down on top of the body, straddling the poor girl's homespun skirts. She lowered herself down, her nose snuffling at her neck. The lass was scared stiff and silent. Evanangela dragged her fangs along the vein, feeling the pliant skin dimple. She drew back, then plunged them deep. The girl's body lurched against Evanangela, her limbs flailing for some means of escape.

The peasant girl's blood was not as rich and syrupy. Instead, it had a sweeter quality, but it was just as rustic and full. Evanangela's eyes rolled into her head as she drank. The voice still urged her, *Feed! Feed! Feed!* It became more insistent with every mouthful. Evanangela's heart struggled against the glut of blood. Her limbs grew heavy. Stupor settled into her mind and a haze dulled her senses. There was only the delicious taste of blood and the mouth-watering scent of fear.

Choked gasps escaped the lass' throat as the heart slowed until it stopped, and the blood ran sour on her tongue. Evanangela sat back on her heels, her awareness expanding. Endless screams surrounded her as the vampires fed. She stumbled out of the storeroom and back onto the street. More humans were tackled, caught escaping out into the road.

A mule trampled a discarded corpse, its halter caked in blood. The wailing shrieks of a small child cut through the air. Evanangela followed the sound, and found a babe clutching their deceased mother. She knelt by the body, extending her hand to the frightened child. A new feeling curled up from her swollen heart and into her mind. Her stupor began to clear, and a gnawing sorrow took hold.

"There, there," she crooned as the grubby little hand settled into hers, "it will be over soon."

Evanangela hugged the child, rocking them. The scent of blood tempted her, but she pushed the desire away.

"Dieu, hear my prayer, though my heart be damned and my soul burned away. Take this child up to your kingdom."

The child leaned against Evanangela, trusting as only a babe can in the face of true fear. She carefully pulled down the collar of the child's tunic, revealing the back of their neck. She found the delicate space at the base of the skull and let her fangs rest there. All at once, she wrenched her jaws across the child's spine; severing it and giving the blessing of a swift death.

A small gasp was the only sound as the child went limp, like a ragdoll in her arms. Evanangela settled the babe against the dead mother. She stood and licked the blood off her lips. It was sweeter, but not as satisfying. Evanangela wrapped her arms about her, dread settling like cold lead in her stomach. The taste deepened her sorrow. She spit the blood onto the dirt road. The wail of many, many more babes rang out into the night. She put her head down, and moved back toward the carriages, careful not to run and trigger the vampires that swarmed about.

Evanangela found her carriage. She knocked on the door, and Gabriel's face appeared in the window. The latch clicked, and the door swung open revealing the two footmen and the driver that were crowded in the carriage with him. Evanangela climbed inside, seating herself next to the driver; the two footmen on either side of Gabriel.

The driver bowed his head. "Pardonnez-nous, princesse. It is not safe to be outside until the frenzy is over."

She nodded. "C'est d'accord. I would not want for you to be mistaken for a feed."

Gabriel nodded to the driver. The attendants relaxed. They shuffled about, switching places so he could sit next to Evanangela. Grief hit her like a fist to the chest as he wrapped his arms about her.

"Ne pleure pas, princesse," Gabriel crooned, "don't waste your blood on tears."

She bit her lip, holding back the urge to cry. She wondered how many of the screaming children would meet awful deaths, or if any of the vampires had the compassion to end their lives quickly as she had. Her body shook as she remembered his chilling explanation that the village would need to be utterly exterminated in order to protect the court from blame.

"Oh Gabriel!" Evanangela choked down her sobs, "Je suis un monstre! Je suis un monstre! I will never again drink the blood of mortals! I deserve to suffer the foulness of dead bull's blood! I must atone-!"

He rocked her, his hands petting her hair, "Non, ma princesse, tu n'es pas une monstre. I know you did not cause them to suffer. You never do."

This new thought shocked Evanangela, quieting her self-flagellation. It was true; she took down all her victims swiftly. Draining them within moments, the body growing cold before the musicians could strike up the next waltz.

"It never occurred to me," Evanangela took a deep breath, "I do not wish them to suffer."

Gabriel nodded, giving her one last squeeze before releasing her, "I know."

The acrid smell of smoke began to fill the air. She sneezed. Gabriel offered her one of his plain linen handkerchiefs.

"The feed is over. They are now burning the village and the bodies." He whispered.

Evanangela clutched the handkerchief, taking deep breaths to stifle her new bout of grief. The sky began to lighten, but not from the dawn. She watched as the air grew foggy from the smoke, the orange glow of the flames brightening the empty road. The horses began to stamp and snort.

"Pardonnez-moi, princesse," the driver bowed his head again and exited the carriage to soothe the horses.

She could hear other drivers doing the same for the carriages around them. The sound of footsteps grew, and then figures cut through the smoke. It was the court walking back to their carriages, their clothing stained and torn; their faces were ruddy and streaked with soot. The ghoulish parade reminded Evanangela of the terrors she had witnessed as an angel, wishing she could interfere when humans attacked villages in war or in raids. Though this was neither, it was just as destructive and heartbreaking. Evanangela pulled out Verseau's handkerchief and took deep breaths of the scented fabric to calm her frayed nerves.

A knock at the door startled Evanangela. She hissed, but her threat died in her throat when she saw Verseau's face in the window.

"Mon Seigneur!" She squealed as the footman opened the door.

The footmen stepped out of the carriage, bowing and allowing Verseau access. He hoisted himself inside, and the door closed behind him. Evanangela threw her arms about his neck, her heart racing with joy.

"Ah, ma petite, it is good to see you happy and well-fed." He squeezed her and sat down.

Gabriel retreated to his rear-facing seat; his eyes downcast. Verseau petted Evanangela's face. He smelled of smoke and blood. She inhaled his scent anyway, comforted by his presence.

"Àmichemin is safe and satiated. She is waiting for me in her carriage." Verseau pressed his forehead against hers. "I came to see you first. I was worried when I did not see you with the rest of the court in the village."

Evanangela kissed him, her body pressing against his. "I am glad you are both safe. You are both my heart."

Verseau nodded. He kissed her neck just below her ear. His warm breath tickling as he whispered, "As are the both of you, you are both my heart as well."

They sat together, the singing of their bodies filling the silence as they embraced. At long last, Verseau pulled away.

"I must lead the progress. We must be away from this place before dawn. It is only a matter of time before the ruins are discovered and accusations are made."

She nodded clenching her hands in her lap to prevent herself from reaching out to make him stay. "Oui, mon Seigneur."

He exited the carriage, but gave her one last smile. "I will see you soon, ma choupinette."

Evanangela curled up against the wall of the carriage, her body shivering. Gabriel stood, and opened his seat, pulling out the fur-lined blanket.

"Ici, ma princesse," he draped it over her body.

She snuggled into the blanket, comforted by the warmth, though she was not shivering from the cold. The screams of the villagers and the clashing of the church bells flashed through her mind once more. Evanangela flinched, drawing a long shaking breath to steel her nerves.

"It must be difficult for you." Gabriel kept his eyes downcast as he seated himself. "It is difficult to say whether it is because of your youth or you simply possess compassion that the rest of the court does not."

Evanangela nodded, settling her gaze out the window. She flinched as the driver knocked on the roof of the carriage, and then the vehicle lurched forward. The smoke blotted out the windows. She brought her handkerchief up to her nose as the fumes burned her throat. Gabriel held another of his handkerchiefs to his own nose.

As the caravan of carriages made a wide loop around the ruined village, the smoke cleared enough upwind that Evanangela could see the glow of the flames leaping toward the sky. The buildings were reduced to black crumbling wreckage. The sound of crackling fire and the groan of splintering wooden supports punctuated the silence.

Gabriel tore his gaze away from the window, and lifted the floor latch. "The dawn will soon be upon us. It is time."

She conceded, slipping off her shoes and leaving them on the seat. Gabriel offered his hand to help her into the coffin. She considered bringing the blanket with her, but there was hardly room for such a large item. The extreme heat of the burning village had made the carriage quite warm as she slid from the blanket. She lowered herself down, allowing her body to sink into the cushioned coffin.

Gabriel lowered the lid. "À demain,[2] princesse."

---

2 See you tomorrow

Chapter Nineteen

Evanangela fidgeted in her seat as she gazed out the carriage window. The screams of the peasants were still fresh in her mind. After two nights of monotony with only Gabriel to distract her thoughts from the fire and the rampage, it was all she could do not to run screaming into the darkness. She shivered as the village came into view; the churchyard she had been born in gleamed in the moonlight.

"Princesse, we are almost home," Gabriel's voice was soft and measured, "we must prepare ourselves for what we may find."

She nodded, leaning back in the carriage seat. "Verseau said the peasants attacked the château. He did not reveal the extent of the damage."

He glanced out the window and his face blanched. "Ne regardez pas!"[1]

Evanangela froze as he tugged the curtain pulls, covering the carriage windows. Gabriel took a deep breath, his eyes wide.

"Pardonnez-moi, princesse, these are horrors you should not witness!"

She bit back the urge to draw the curtain. "Gabriel, what could possibly-?"

He wiped his face with a handkerchief. She wrinkled her nose at the stench of fear rolling off him. "The villagers have slaughtered the guards-"

The carriage lurched as it stopped short. Evanangela slid from her seat, tumbling onto the floor. He helped her back up, her legs tangled in her skirts. The driver knocked on the carriage door. Gabriel opened it.

"Pardonnez-moi, Mademoiselle, Seigneur has ordered for all the carriages to wait outside the gates. We are unsure if the château is secure. Please stay inside the carriage."

---

1 Do not look!

Gabriel closed the door, and the driver climbed back up onto his perch. Evanangela pulled back the curtain on the opposite side of the carriage. Le Village du Sang was still in one piece. There appeared to be no damage. She let the curtain drop once more and leaned back in her seat.

They waited in silence. The only sounds were the snorts and stamps of the horses and the creak of carriages as their passengers fidgeted. Evanangela closed her eyes, trying to block out the burning emptiness of her dead heart and withered veins. The boire à petites gorgées du sang at nightfall had not been enough. It was never enough. The fear and pain gnawed at her mind as memories of screaming villagers grew louder.

He patted her hand, ripping her from the chaotic thoughts. "I will protect you."

Evanangela squeezed his hand. It was warm; she could feel his pulse alive under his skin. She swallowed and released him. "Merci beaucoup, Gabriel."

At long last, there were footsteps outside the carriage. He opened the door, revealing Verseau standing in the road.

"Come to me, ma petite." His voice was strained, his face lined with worry.

She stepped down from her carriage but she did not find comfort taking Verseau's hand. It was as if his worries were directly transmitted from his grip. Àmichemin stood a few paces away, her eyes wide; transfixed on the château gate.

"It seems my fears have come to pass." Verseau held her face in his hands, preventing her from turning her gaze. "Prepare yourself."

Evanangela closed her eyes and took a deep breath. When she opened them again, Verseau let go and nodded. Evanangela turned. Twelve bodies were hanging from the château gates. They were beaten and bloodied; their clothing torn to shreds. A soiled fleur de lis adorned one of the bodies. They were part of the court guard left behind to protect the château.

She sank to her knees, her knuckles pressed against her mouth, her fangs cutting into her skin. Each guard had their throat slit; the ropes tied around their chests, leaving their heads flopping as they swayed in the wind. Verseau turned, ensnaring first Àmichemin's gaze, then Evanangela's, his face stony with controlled rage.

"Attendez ici."[2]

Verseau headed toward the middle of the caravan where the mid-section guards were posted. Evanangela tore her gaze from the wretched scene, following his movements. He spoke a few words with the guards, then pointed at the gates. The guards blew their horns, and rode straight for the château. Two of the guards posted at the front of the caravan opened the gates wide, allowing them passage. The bodies swung, their weight banging a cacophony against the metal.

"Retournez dans votre calèche, vite!"[3] Verseau ordered.

Àmichemin snapped out of her reverie and dashed into her carriage. Evanangela gathered herself up, the footman helping her scramble inside. Gabriel took her elbow and helped her flop onto the seat. The door swung shut, and he bolted it from the inside. They counted the moments, waiting for the guards to return bearing news.

"There is a possibility we have come home to a trap." Gabriel whispered. "I want you to prepare yourself, princesse. We may need to escape."

She took a deep breath, her hand on her chest; her dead heart was like a stone in her ribs as her fear forced it to beat. The shuddering pain put her mind in a haze.

"Escape? What about Verseau? And Àmichemin? And the court?"

Gabriel shook his head. "It would be safer to escape separately. We cannot afford for the three of you to escape together and risk capture. The court would be doomed."

Each new thought bathed Evanangela in fear. The acrid scent of her unbridled terror soured her mouth. Her mind screamed for her to flee, but her body was frozen, pressed hard against the cushions. The guards' horn blared. Evanangela shrieked. Bright spots danced before her eyes as she swooned.

"Princesse!"

His face swam in her blurred vision. He patted her forehead and cheeks with a damp handkerchief. After a few moments, her mind cleared and her vision righted itself. She sat up, clutching her head. The carriage jolted. They were moving.

2 Wait here.
3 Return to your carriage, hurry!

"Verseau!" She screeched, trying to reach the door.

"Arrêtez-vous!"[4] Gabriel grabbed her hand, "The château is safe! Everything is all right, princesse."

Evanangela gulped air into her lungs, trying to process his words. She pulled back the curtain; the courtyard came into view. The grounds were trampled, the beautiful flowers and trees hacked and burned. Piles of dead bodies littered the lawn. Scraps of their uniforms were visible through the dirt and blood. They were the retinue of guards that had been left behind. She let the curtain fall again.

"But what about the guards?" Evanangela trembled, her mind straining to understand.

Gabriel took her hands in his and squeezed. "The peasants are gone. The château is empty."

Her breath caught. "What about the attendants? Le Village du Sang?"

"I don't know," he shook his head. "The signal only indicates the grounds are clear and that it's safe to enter."

He released her hands, allowing her to fall back into the cushions. She was exhausted. Her body cried out, begging for the sweet release of blood. She licked her dry lips. Thoughts of the ransacked village flashed through her mind.

Is that what happened here? While we were destroying that village and snuffing out lives, were the peasants doing the same here at the château?

The carriages stopped, lined up just as they had been the night the court had fled to La Maison de Primtemps. Gabriel unlocked the door, allowing the footmen to open it and escort Evanangela out. He followed close behind. Evanangela trembled as she swiveled her gaze, taking stock of the ravaged grounds. Gabriel took her shaking hand and led her inside.

Verseau and Àmichemin were already in the receiving room. Shards of glass littered the floor. Curtains were shredded into rough ribbons. Evanangela gasped when she looked up and saw that the portraits lining the great hall had been slashed.

---

4 Stop!

Together, they toured the château; surveying the damage. Personal apartments were destroyed with burnt furniture and ransacked wardrobes and cabinets. Trampled clothing and other belongings were scattered about in the halls. Members of the court broke away from the procession as they examined their personal rooms and wept.

The grim tour ended at Verseau's apartments. Jacques appeared at their side and unlocked the doors. They were cracked, as if by a battering ram of sorts, but they stood strong. Inside, his apartments were untouched. Jacques got to work lighting the fire in the grate.

"How could this have happened?" Evanangela's words hung in the air.

Verseau sank into his chair. Àmichemin remained standing, her hands balled into fists at her sides. He shook his head, refusing to look up. Jacques bowed and exited back into the hallway taking Gabriel with him; leaving the trio alone.

"This cannot stand!" Àmichemin thundered at last. "We have pandered to those villagers for *decades* and this is how they repay us?!"

"We knew this day would come. Peace is not an eternal thing-" Verseau massaged his forehead, his face pinched.

"It can be if we *kill* all those wretched vermin!" Àmichemin hissed.

He groaned and leaned back in his chair. "As satisfying as that would be ma chérie, we both know that would attract more attention to the court and endanger our neighbors as well."

Jacques knocked on the door and bowed, "Excusez-moi, Seigneur, the court has assembled in the ballroom."

Verseau sighed as he rose from the chair, dusting himself off. He took Àmichemin's hand and kissed it. Then took Evanangela's hand and did the same.

"We must put away our personal thoughts for now. It is time to address the court. There is much to do."

Jacques led the way to the ballroom; Gabriel walked a few paces behind them as added security. They threw open the doors, revealing the nervous vampires and vixens shuffling on the cleanest sections of the floor. Most of the windows were shattered. Splintered furniture littered the corners of the room. The attendants stood at attention near the back wall. Evanangela felt the air rush from her lungs as relief washed over her.

At least they are alive!

Verseau let go of their hands and cleared his throat. "Tonight, we recognize the true threat of our peasant neighbors. They trespassed into our home, destroyed our belongings, and killed our guards."

Jacques motioned for one of the attendants to approach. An elderly mortal bowed to Verseau, then addressed the court.

"Le Village du Sang was spared, but not for lack of trying. We were able to bar the gates. Some of us were injured holding the doors against their attack. We mourn the loss of our family and friends who worked in the royal guard."

They stepped back, bowed again to Verseau, then to Àmichemin and Evanangela in turn, and returned to the back wall with the other attendants. Verseau nodded and continued.

"We are fortunate that our loyal attendants survived the attack. But we are vulnerable without our guards and with our stronghold broken. Necessary repairs must be made immediately. Luxuries such as finery and idle time must be set aside in the face of this disaster. Together, we will help to rebuild alongside our attendants in order to ensure the safety of the château."

Groans and hisses erupted from the court. Verseau held up a hand to silence them. He continued on, despite a few grumbles and muttered insults.

"We shall work alongside you, Mademoiselle Evanangela, Mademoiselle Àmichemin, and myself, your Seigneur. Aside from our elderly attendants who have retired from active service, *all* will be required to work. The Nacre Court has survived for over nine hundred years. We shall not be beaten in less than a fortnight due to slovenly behavior. We shall endure!"

His words were met with tense silence and resentful bows and curtsies. Verseau waved his hand, allowing the court to exit the ballroom. The trio followed them out into the hall soon after.

Evanangela bit her lip as some of the vampires turned and shot them seething glares. Doors slammed and the sound of whispered arguing floated about. She sank onto the couch in Verseau's apartments.

At long last, Verseau leaned against the mantle, the air escaping from his lungs. His face crumpled with grief.

Àmichemin grabbed a footstool and screamed, hurling it against the wall where it shattered and put a hole in the wallpaper. She took a deep breath and flopped onto the couch next to Evanangela. Rage radiated from her. Evanangela leaned against the arm rest of the couch, giving her space.

"How *dare* those spoiled wretches put themselves before the château! I will paint, hammer nails, whatever it is those attendants do to fix things in order to turn this palace into the fortress we need. We are at *war!*"

Evanangela darted her gaze between the two, at a loss for words as fear swallowed her voice.

Verseau stared into the fire. "Mes chéries, let us hope history does not repeat itself."

Àmichemin's anger cooled. She crossed her arms and leaned into the couch; her face arranged in a scowl. Evanangela straightened up, her mind whirring trying to find an appropriate response.

"They only care for their lost trinkets and the temporary ban on La Valse Noire. There will be no history to repeat or future if we do not act now!" Àmichemin growled.

Verseau shook his head. "An attack on the château is a direct attack on the court and the Seigneur. It shows weakness. That is how coups started in the past – the Seigneur could no longer be trusted after a direct attack on the château and the court."

Evanangela darted her eyes between them. "But the court is safe. You took everyone out of harm's way."

"Yes, but the château was not safe. If our home is not safe, then neither is the court. And they will not stand for a life in exile or on the run." Verseau clenched his fist.

Àmichemin scoffed. "They have become spoiled and have forgotten the tyrants of old. We must crush even the faintest whisper of uprising within the court. Otherwise, they will tear themselves apart."

Verseau turned to look at them. The exhaustion clear in his eyes. "This is how it started. This is how the former Seigneur fell and the beginning of my rise to power. We cannot allow the court to fall apart as it did before."

"We will survive this. The court is resilient. *We* are resilient. Do not let their selfishness soften you." Àmichemin's face fell. The sharpness disappeared from her tone.

"Regardless, security is the issue at hand," Verseau rubbed his eyes, "our royal guard is gone and there are not enough attendants left to replace them. We will have to request reinforcements from the Council."

"No!" She jumped up from the couch, "That will show our weakness! We are already at a disadvantage with the blood crisis. We cannot make another request!"

He leaned against the mantle. "Then what do you propose we do? We cannot protect ourselves without a retinue of guards."

Àmichemin dropped her gaze to the floor, her shoulders slumped. "There must be another way."

They jumped at a knock at the door. Jacques peered his head in, then bowed. "The sunrise shall be upon us, Seigneur, Mademoiselles."

Verseau nodded. Jacques closed the door again. He sighed and held out his hands.

"A good day's rest will help us think of a better plan, mes chéries. To bed."

Evanangela took his hand, allowing him to help lift her from the couch. Àmichemin stared at his other hand, then took it. She leaned her head on his shoulder, her back trembling.

He nuzzled against her hair. "It has been a long night, ma chère douleur. Come now. No more worries."

Together, they shuffled toward Verseau's great bed. His coffin had been placed atop it. Evanangela and Àmichemin's coffins were stacked by the far wall. Verseau climbed inside.

"Allons-y!" His cheer was half-hearted.

Evanangela climbed in after him, snuggling onto his chest. Àmichemin lowered herself into the coffin. Her eyes were clouded with far-away thoughts. Footsteps approached, and Jacques' shadow crossed over the coffin as he lowered the lid. The darkness enveloped them, bringing peace and comfort at long last.

Chapter Twenty

Evanangela climbed out of the coffin. Àmichemin lay inside, still asleep; though her chest did not rise and fall. Her body was rigid and cold. Verseau looked up from his papers, quill in hand. She waited on the bed until he beckoned her over.

"Bonsoire," Verseau slipped his arm around Evanangela's waist. She bent down to kiss him.

"Bonsoire, mon Seigneur," Evanangela leaned against him, gazing down at the papers, "What are you working on?"

Verseau sighed, withdrawing from her and picked up the letter he had been writing. "An official plea to our neighbor, the Mors Ivoire Court, to send a temporary guard until we can replace them with our own royal guard."

Evanangela nodded, her eyes glossing over the flowery script, "They are our neighbors, surely they will send aid?"

"That is the hope," Verseau set the letter aside, "However, this also reveals that we are vulnerable. In darker times, such a plea for help would be a death sentence. They would send their warriors to our court and annex us. Taking our lands for their own."

She gasped. "B-but they're our *neighbors!* Neighbors are meant to help one another."

He gave a cheerless laugh and leaned his head against her. "Ah ma petite, such a sweet, naïve creature you are. Never lose that."

A groan indicated that Àmichemin was awake. Evanangela turned and saw her sitting up in the coffin, stretching and yawning. Her long tresses covered her naked body. She ran her fingers through her starry locks, her eyes hazy with sleep.

"Up before me? Well, now I know you're serious." Àmichemin slipped out of the coffin and padded over to them. "Don't tell me you have her writing official letters now."

177

Verseau shook his head. He signed the letter with a flourish, then sprinkled sand to help the ink dry. "Evanangela is reminding us of her sweetness. And I am swallowing my pride and sending word to the Mors."

Àmichemin scowled. "Are we truly backed into such a corner?"

He took her hand and patted it. "I'm afraid so, ma chérie."

Evanangela watched as he pulled out the official court seal. He took one of the enchanted candles that was sitting on his writing desk, and poured it into the mold. No wax spilled, instead, flames burned the mark of the house seal onto the paper. The edges were sealed by the heat. He then tied the letter with a black ribbon, weaving it into an elaborate knot and finished it with a gold coin that had a hole drilled through the middle.

"Jacques!" Verseau called.

The door flew open at once. He bowed in the doorway, then approached the writing desk. "Oui, mon Seigneur?"

Verseau held out the letter. "Have Manette deliver this to the Mors. Vite! Vite!"

Jacques took the letter and bowed. "Tout de suite, mon Seigneur."[1]

Once he was gone, Àmichemin dug into the wardrobe and pulled out one of Verseau's dressing robes. She wrapped it about her body. "Where are our traveling trunks?"

Verseau gave her a confused look, then snapped back to his senses. "Ah! They are in the sitting room. There was not enough space here with all the coffins."

Àmichemin strode off to get dressed. Verseau went back to organizing the papers on his desk.

"Verseau, why are all our things in your apartments?" Evanangela sat on the edge of the bed. "Were our apartments destroyed in the attack?"

He did not look up. His voice was low when he spoke. "Your apartments were also barred. Apart from the small damage to the doors, they are pristine."

Evanangela fidgeted her hands. "Then why-"

_____
1 Right away, my Lord.

"Please," Verseau took her hand but would not meet her gaze, "I need you here with me. Both of you."

She squeezed his hand, then brought it to her lips. "I am forever at your side, mon Seigneur."

Verseau looked up at her and smiled. "Thank you."

Àmichemin returned, dressed in a sultry burgundy gown, her bosom barely covered by the delicate embroidered edging. "Come now, the court is expecting us."

He rose from his desk, took her hand in his and kissed it. Then turned to his wardrobe. Àmichemin smirked, then settled her gaze on Evanangela's rumpled appearance.

"Be sure to wear something suitable. We are 'rallying the troops' so to speak."

Evanangela nodded and trotted into the sitting room. Àmichemin's trunks were opened, discarded garments and shoes spilling out onto the floor. She kicked a stray stocking aside, and knelt before her own traveling trunks. As she sifted through the garments, she realized how much she had relied on Gabriel to help dress her prior to their travels. At long last, she found a striking crimson gown and all the necessary accoutrement.

Àmichemin swept into the room, and arranged herself on the couch to watch Evanangela dress. Verseau followed close behind, struggling to clasp his cuff links while navigating toward the chair.

"I fear I have become slothful," Evanangela muttered as she pulled on her stockings, "this was so much easier when Gabriel did all the dressing for me."

Àmichemin nodded, sitting up to help lace Evanangela into her corset. "Of course, the court used to have bevies of attendants to wait on us. We gave up our grooms and valets when the great shortage first began."

Evanangela flinched as Àmichemin tightened the stays. "I thought the Village du Sang was self-sufficient. Why would you need to dismiss your attendants?"

She tied off the corset and gave Evanangela a pat on the back. "The plague killed hundreds of mortals. This meant there was a food

179

shortage, as there were not enough humans alive to till the fields. We sent many of our attendants away to neighboring courts to prevent the Village du Sang from starving."

Verseau nodded. "That is why I wrote the letter. It is my hope that the Mors remember our generosity and will return the favor."

Evanangela dragged her gown over her head, tugging it into place. "So, we may have our attendants returned to the court?"

Àmichemin burst out laughing. "Goodness, no! That was decades ago! Those mortals are most likely too elderly to work or are long dead. And there is no guarantee we would receive their descendants." She waved her hand. "Not that it matters."

"In any case, we must act now with the resources we have at hand." He stood from his chair and took Evanangela's arm in his, then offered his elbow to Àmichemin.

Together, they exited into the hall. Two of the remaining guards stood at attention outside Verseau's apartments. They bowed upon seeing the trio. Verseau nodded, then escorted Evanangela and Àmichemin into the ballroom.

The doors were wide open, though the hall was silent and the band was nowhere to be seen. Attendants were posted at the windows. The court stood at attention, murmuring amongst themselves until they caught sight of Verseau. They bowed as he entered the room.

Evanangela swept her gaze over the crowd. Their stares were sharp and the air was thick. She fought not to dart her eyes away. Instead, she straightened her back and rolled her shoulders, cooling her gaze to haughty indifference.

"As your Seigneur, it is my duty to protect the members of this court and our interests. So long as we stand strong, these attacks will dissolve into nothing more than the annoying buzz of inconsequential vermin. We must strengthen our walls and strengthen our bonds. Today, we shall do both by working together to repair the château."

Grumbles rippled through the crowd. They were quickly silenced by Àmichemin's sharp glare. Verseau cleared his throat and continued.

"Show your strength and your loyalty for the Nacre Court by lending your hands to rebuild the château into the foreboding fortress it once was. We shall make those *peasants* tremble like the frightened sheep they are!"

He spat the word "peasants" and a few cheers sounded from the court. The attendants moved forward, passing out tools and handing out official assignments. Verseau nodded to Àmichemin. She strode toward the large writing desk that had been laid out near one of the windows, and seated herself. Verseau turned to Evanangela.

"We must play to our strengths, ma chère choupinette. I am assigning you as Overseer, to ensure that the attendants are treated properly. Remember, the court is only as strong as the loyal attendants who protect us from the damning sun."

She nodded and curtsied. "Merci beaucoup, mon Seigneur. I will see to it that our attendants are treated with respect."

Verseau squeezed her hand, then strode off toward a knot of attendants. They handed him several papers, each of which he looked over with care. Evanangela turned back to the clusters of vampires and attendants. One such vixen dangled a hammer from her hand, rolling her eyes as an attendant pointed at a paper. Evanangela approached them.

"Mademoiselle." The vixen bobbed a shallow curtsy.

Evanangela nodded. "What plans have you been assigned?"

"How should I know?" She waved the hammer, "It's all just pomp and show. Seigneur does not *actually* expect us to work with the attendants."

Anger bubbled up inside Evanangela. She narrowed her eyes and hissed. "Every member of this court is expected to work. Any attempts to shirk will be seen as suspected treason."

The vixen flinched and the attendant's eyes grew wide. Evanangela continued.

"Our walls have been breached. *Everyone* is expected to do their part to protect this court. Any hindrance or lack of effort toward rebuilding this château will be seen as aiding the treacherous peasants. Is that *clear?*"

"Oui, Mademoiselle!" The vixen trembled, the hammer clattering to the floor.

181

Evanangela bent down to retrieve the hammer. She stuffed it back into the vixen's hand, her face inches away from hers. "*Good.*"

The nearby vampires and attendants broke out into a frenzy of whispers. Evanangela scanned the room, dozens of frightened eyes met hers. She softened her face, then clapped her hands. "Allons-y! Let's begin!"

A wave of "Oui, Mademoiselle!" swept through the hall, bows and curtsies meeting Evanangela's command. She nodded. Her eyes met Verseau's for a brief moment. He smiled, then went back to his work. She relished the silent praise. Gabriel motioned for her to join him and another attendant. They were holding many official papers.

"Mademoiselle," the attendant gave a shallow bow, "Seigneur has ordered for the windows to be replaced; however, the current peasant revolts will prevent the Venetian traders from delivering the new panels of glass. We need a temporary solution to barricade the windows against attack, but we cannot spare the necessary resources. What shall we do?"

Evanangela glanced over at Verseau. He was absorbed with another group of attendants, his fingers pointing from the official papers to different walls and doors. She turned her gaze to Amichemin, who was busy writing papers and handing them off to waiting messengers. Images of the beautiful fountain she had seen the night they had left for Maison de Primtemps paraded through her mind. She turned back to the attendant.

"Seigneur Verseau said that the gardens were destroyed by the rioting. What is the extent of the damage?"

The attendant nodded, flustered by the change of subject. "Much of the garden was burned, Mademoiselle. The storage buildings and nursery were greatly damaged-"

"Then we shall use the rubble from the garden buildings to reinforce the windows." Evanangela ordered. Her heart pained at the thought of sacrificing the beautiful garden. She took a deep breath, "We cannot protect the court with beautiful flowers and trees. Sacrifices must be made."

"Oui, Mademoiselle. I will send a team out to salvage the rubble at once." The attendant bowed again and scurried off.

Gabriel nodded and gave Evanangela a sad smile, "Princesse, that was a decisive motion. Well done."

"Merci, Gabriel," she whispered, "though it pains me to know such beauty will be lost."

He took her hand and squeezed it. "Unfortunately, Mademoiselle, the beauty was already lost. The peasant revolt destroyed most of the gardens. You are simply utilizing the bones left in the ashes."

Evanangela took another deep breath. "You are right. There will be time again for gardens."

Chapter Twenty-One

Each night, the court drained their feeds in their apartments, then were shooed out to work alongside the attendants. At first, their grumbles were loud and their glares sharp. As the château transformed into a ramshackle fortress, they quieted. The tension in the air was thick; the eerie calm that snuffs out all else before a storm.

Verseau climbed out of his coffin, then turned and helped Àmichemin clamber out onto the bed. Evanangela sat, leaning against the lip of the coffin, watching as they hurried to dress.

"The Venetian glass should be arriving today," Àmichemin muttered, "I'll see to the delivery and ensure the rubble is moved to reinforce the outer gate."

He nodded, lacing up his breeches. "Oui, excellent. A representative from the Mors Ivoire Court is scheduled to meet with me tonight. I will be here, discussing the terms of our agreement for the new guards."

Evanangela froze as they turned their gaze her way. She darted her eyes about. "Things have been going well as Overseer. I have only had to quash minor complaints. All is well."

They both nodded, then continued dressing. Evanangela climbed out of the coffin and began to dress. Just as she was pulling on her stockings, a knock rapped upon the door.

"Entre!" Verseau barked as he slipped his jacket on.

Jacques appeared in the doorway. He bowed, then motioned for a disheveled messenger to enter the room. They smelled strongly of horse and sweat. Evanangela wrinkled her nose.

"Pardonnez-moi, Seigneur et Mademoiselles," they bowed low, "I bring grave news. Several members of the court have fled the château."

Verseau jerked upright, staring at the messenger. Jacques cleared his throat, urging them to continue.

"They are headed toward the village to the south, our closest peasant territory."

Àmichemin growled, causing the messenger to flinch. Verseau put a hand on her shoulder, but it shook as he seethed with rage. Evanangela sat, frozen in place holding her stockings.

"The risk you took to inform us of this news is great. You shall be rewarded thusly." Verseau nodded. "Jacques!"

He stepped forward. "Oui, mon Seigneur?"

Verseau gestured to the bewildered messenger. "See to it they receive distinguishment for their bravery. Inform the official receiving committee that Master Étienne, diplomat of the Mors Ivoire Court will be arriving tonight. I am to receive him in my chambers and must not be disturbed. I am sending Àmichemin to the peasant village to deal with these defectors. Hopefully, we can quell their mischief before they provoke another revolt."

Àmichemin nodded to Verseau, her face cracked into a smirk that gave Evanangela gooseflesh. "Ah, merci mon cher for assigning me to a most *delicious* task."

Evanangela's eyes widened as her mind filled in all sorts of implications. Àmichemin was known for her cruelty, but she had only ever shown it when playing with her feeds. She shivered at the thought of the horrors a vengeful Àmichemin could wreak.

He turned and settled his gaze on Evanangela, his eyes softening. "Evanangela shall stay here and continue her duties as Overseer. We must ensure the remaining members of the court are rewarded for their good behavior and hard work."

"Oui, mon Seigneur," she bowed her head, "I shall see to it."

Verseau clapped his hands, and Jacques bowed again, as he turned to leave, Verseau cleared his throat.

"Be sure to keep me informed. The attendants and Le Village du Sang must be protected at all costs."

Jacques bowed, a smile hinting at the corners of his mouth, "Oui, Seigneur. Merci."

The messenger followed Jacques out of the apartments. The moment the door was closed, Verseau dropped his face into his hand, rubbing his eyes, a growl bubbling in his throat.

Àmichemin swiveled her mad gaze onto him. Her fangs were on full display. The flesh on her lips they rested on were turning purple, ice coating them as her excitement grew. "Do I have your permission?"

He nodded. "Oui. Do what you must."

She gleefully bounded out the door, screeching as she ran down the hall. Evanangela swallowed, her insides chilled with fear.

"That is the *true* Àmichemin." Verseau whispered as he tore his eyes away from the door. "She is a merciless beast. I love her for it and despite it."

Evanangela twisted her stocking between her fingers. "Surely, we are all beasts." She swallowed, remembering her animalistic behavior while glutting on the peasants in the now destroyed village.

He shook his head. "Àmichemin is a vampire-slayer. Before I came to power, members of the court were punished by her; she *ate* them."

She gaped at him as he straightened his cravat. Evanangela's mind reeled. *She ate them?!*

"It is not something I or anyone else in the court is capable of," his voice was low, "Àmichemin is one of the ancients. She has abilities beyond our wildest reckonings. Keeping her happy and loyal is one of my important responsibilities as Seigneur. She was originally a true noble princess, set to be married to a neighboring lord. But a clan of vampires took over the castle, slaughtered her family, and turned her into the beast she is now. That was nearly one thousand years ago. She was one of the original ancients that established the Nacre Court. This château was her original home."

Evanangela froze as she tried to process Verseau's words. Àmichemin had spoken of "ancients" and how they were the only ones left in the court. The implication of that title had not occurred to her until now.

"But how is that any different than you turning the attendants into vampires, mon Seigneur? Why does Àmichemin have such

187

extraordinary abilities?" Evanangela took a deep breath to soothe her churning thoughts.

He wrinkled his nose. "She was turned by originals. Vile things," He spat, glaring, "fallen angels."

Alarm bells rang in Evanangela's mind, blotting out all else. She flinched when Verseau petted her head.

"Vite, ma choupinette. You must dress quickly and keep an eye on the others. We don't need more of the court slipping away to their doom."

Verseau exited out into the hall, shutting the door behind him. Evanangela hurried to dress. She found Gabriel waiting for her just outside the door.

"Bonsoire, princesse," he bowed and followed her down the hall, "You seem troubled, may I be of assistance?"

She shook her head, Verseau's words echoing through her mind. "I am distressed. But I must see to my duties. Verseau is depending on me."

Gabriel nodded and handed her some papers. "In that case, the attendants that can be spared are working alongside members of the court to repair and polish the armor of the deceased royal guard. These will be used by the guards we hope to receive from the Mors Ivoire Court after tonight's negotiations."

Evanangela glanced over the papers, then handed them back to Gabriel. "And I suppose I am to watch and ensure the job is done?"

"Oui, princesse," he led her down into the armory, "the remaining attendants are seeing to the arrival of the diplomat for the Mors Ivoire Court and supplying the feeds to all the court's personal apartments; including yours."

He cleared his throat and darted his eyes away, a blush appearing on his cheeks, "The Seigneur wants to keep you in good spirits and has arranged for a *special* feed for you in your personal apartments. Do you have a preference for this evening?"

She stopped in her tracks in the dim underground hallway and blinked at him. "What's so special about it? Why does it matter?"

Gabriel kept his gaze to the floor, his face turning red, "Your feed will be of the understanding they are to erm…*service* you before you feed."

A cool sapphire blush flooded Evanangela's cheeks. "Oh! I-I see!" She stammered. "Well, in that case, I would prefer a man this evening for my feed, s'il vous plaît."

He nodded, then glanced at the papers again to get his bearings, "I will inform the attendants. This way, princesse, the armory is just through here."

Gabriel opened the door to a cavernous room. It was sweltering hot and there was a cacoughany of metallic banging. A few heads turned as Evanangela entered the room, then went back to their work. She cleared her throat and held up her hand.

"Bonsoire, we thank you for your hard work. The safety of the château and the court are paramount. I shall inspect the finished armor. Please, see me for any needs or concerns you may have."

Murmurs rippled about the room, and then they continued with their work. Gabriel bowed and trotted back down the hall to make the arrangements for her feed. Evanangela took a deep breath and settled herself near the rows of armor that stood upon wooden dummies. She lifted each piece and inspected them, seeking any signs of dents or cracks.

As she scanned each suit of armor, she strained her ears against the grating noise. There seemed to be no derisive discussions or snide comments. All seemed focused on their tasks, only complaining of the heat or pains in their hands. More dummies were soon suited with armor, keeping Evanangela busy. Her thoughts drifted again to her chilling revelation about Àmichemin.

How does one even 'eat' a vampire? What did Verseau mean? I knew Àmichemin was cold and dangerous, but such an accusation is madness!

An attendant approached, breaking her thoughts. She nodded, allowing them to speak.

"Mademoiselle," she bobbed a curtsy, "there is a member of your court who is whispering dissonance amongst the others. He speaks of 'breaking free from tyranny' and 'getting revenge on the villagers'. I fear he will convince others to leave."

189

Evanangela set aside the wrist guard she had been inspecting and straightened up. "Show me."

The attendant led her over to a vampire that was bent over a leg section of plate armor. His tools lay on the table, his hands gesturing as he whispered to the vixen next to him. Indignation spiked in Evanangela, and she slapped both her palms on the table, startling the vampire to attention.

"And what are you so *busy* discussing?" She bared her fangs, "There is work to be done!"

The vampire flinched as Evanangela hissed. "Mademoiselle!" He bowed his head, "My apologies! My thoughts seem to have run away with me."

She grabbed the vampire by the throat and hauled him to his feet. His shoes squeaked as they slid on the floor. "Your *thoughts* have run away with you? Or are you trying to have *my court* run away with you?"

Her growl silenced the work in the room. The vampires and attendants stared up at Evanangela as she squeezed the vampire's neck. "Answer me, vermin!"

He glared at her, his fear forgotten, "I shall see to it your ashes are spat upon as they boil under the damn sun!"

A screech pierced the air as Evanangela threw him to the ground, a sickening thud sounded as his head hit the hard-packed earth floor. He scrambled about, trying to get to his feet while clutching his head. Evanangela's eyes burned into him, her anger boiling over.

"Gabriel!" She barked.

He appeared at her side at once, his face pale as he beheld the scene.

"See to it this *traitor* is escorted to the dungeon. I will inform Verseau myself after his meeting."

Gabriel bowed. "Right away, Mademoiselle!" He turned back toward the hallway, "Guards! Seize him!"

A trio of guards rushed in bearing silver shackles. The vampire screamed as they tightened them around his wrists, the serrated cuffs biting into his dead skin. They dragged him away, Gabriel following close behind. Evanangela scanned the room. Heads bowed as her eyes fell on each attendant and member of the court.

"Let this be a lesson to all of you. Anyone spreading such dissonance will be punished for *treason*. Is that clear?"

A chorus of "Oui, Mademoiselle!" echoed through the room.

"We are the Nacre Court. Le Château d'Astucieux is our home. And in this time of crisis, we must do all we can to protect it and one another. Running off to wreak havoc in the village is *not* protecting anyone or anything. I am working alongside you. Your Seigneur, even as I speak, is doing all he can to protect you. Do not allow the poisonous tongues of traitors to lead you and the court to destruction."

Evanangela nodded, releasing them to their work. The din of banging and metal-working returned. She let the air rush from her lungs, her anger cooling as she took up her post again; inspecting the armor.

The evening passed without further incident. Gabriel returned to the armory and approached Evanangela. He bowed.

"It is time, princesse. The evening is waning." He whispered.

She nodded and strode to the center of the room. "Your work is completed for tonight. Retire to your quarters for the feed. The château is safer because of your hard work. We thank you."

Groans and muttering replaced the hammering as vampires and attendants alike stood and stretched. Gabriel followed her out into the hall.

"Seigneur sends his regards and wishes to inform you that the dealings with the Mors Ivoire Court went smoothly. He knows how you worry."

Evanangela relaxed a fraction, "That is good news. I look forward to hearing from him when the guards arrive. In the meantime, I'll inform him of our new traitor and discuss what we shall do with him."

He slowed his walk. "Seigneur was clear that you are to focus on your feed tonight and to forget your worries. I shall inform Seigneur of the prisoner."

"How can I forget my cares when the safety of the château hangs by a thread? I must-"

Gabriel took her hands in his and squeezed them. "Princesse, you have done marvelous work as Overseer. Seigneur is proud of you. But you must take time to care for yourself. I can feel how cold your hands are. You are starving."

Evanangela sighed and squeezed his hands back. "I suppose. These past few nights have been grueling. I can feel the exhaustion down to my bones."

"All the more reason to accept the Seigneur's gift. Your feed awaits, princesse. Seigneur has requested you enjoy yourself fully and forget your worries." He darted his eyes away. "Seigneur did specify to *finish your feed* and that you are not to have any more *pets*."

She nodded. While she had overcome her misgivings about feeding on mortals, this was her first time "playing with her food" as Àmichemin had put it. Blood sharing and physical relations with Verseau and Àmichemin had strengthened their bonds tremendously. She wondered if she would be able to overcome such feelings with her mortal entertainment.

Evanangela smiled for the first time in several nights, as Gabriel opened the door to her apartments. She had not set foot in them since they had departed for La Maison de Primtemps. They were as beautiful as ever. Her coffin had been moved to her sitting room; the overstuffed couch moved aside to make room for it. She stroked the lid, sighing.

"Merci, Gabriel," she whispered.

"I will be back before sunrise to move your coffin and bid you goodnight." He bowed and shut the door behind him, leaving Evanangela alone.

She strode into her bedroom and saw a young man perched on her bed. His unfashionable clothing suggested a low-ranking noble; most likely a house of dwindling wealth. He perked up at her approach, slid off the bed, and bowed.

"Bonsoire, Mademoiselle!" His voice was low and rich. It sent pleasant shivers through her. He straightened up. "It is an honor to meet you at last."

Evanangela held out her hand, allowing him to kiss it. "Merci, monsieur," she giggled, "tell me, what is your name?"

"Nicolas Aubert, Mademoiselle," he hesitated, "I do not wish to presume, but I have been informed by your attendants that I am here for *private negotiations*."

She unlaced the bodice of her gown, allowing it to drop to the floor. His eyes followed the garment. She then reached for him, snaking her arms about him in an embrace.

"Oui, that is what I wish."

His mortal scent hit her nose, awakening her hunger. She licked his neck, tasting his skin. Excitement rippled through her body. She fought to maintain her sanity, wanting to see what pleasures Verseau had sent for her to enjoy.

Nicolas began unlacing her gown, and helped tug it over Evanangela's head. His hands explored her body, the heat of them warming her cool skin.

"Mademoiselle, you are working yourself to death." He whispered, rubbing her shoulders. "You're ice cold!"

She turned and gave a coy look over her shoulder. "Would you be so kind as to warm me up, Nicolas?"

"Of course, Mademoiselle. Your wish is my command."

He peppered her neck with kisses as he unlaced her corset. The stiff fabric gave way and dropped to the floor. She slipped off her chemise, allowing the air to hit her skin. Her body leaned back against him, giving in to a flurry of kisses.

"Please," she begged as she tugged at his tunic, "Je vous veux."

He chuckled and shed his clothes. Evanangela watched, her eyes hungry as they raked over his form. She had only ever taken her feeds while they were fully dressed. In fact, she had only ever seen Verseau and Àmichemin in the nude. And often, their nudity was a simple comfort, lying together, dressing together. His figure enticed her nearly as much as his blood.

"Pardonnez-moi, Mademoiselle," he crooned as he swept her into his arms, then tossed her onto the bed.

Evanangela giggled as she felt her body rush through the air. She wriggled on the soft bedcovers as he crawled onto the bed. He pressed his body against hers, allowing her to feel him between her legs.

"I am yours, Mademoiselle," he kissed her neck again, then lower onto her chest, "what are your orders?"

She tittered and let her legs drop open. The growl in her throat turning into a purr, "Ravish me!"

His hands and his mouth played Evanangela like a beautiful harp, plucking her strings, winding her tighter until she came to a crescendo over and over. He speared her, filling her inside and quenching a hunger that blood could not. She moved against him, her body wild and her thoughts blurred. As he ripped another scream from her, stars erupting before her eyes, Evanangela pulled his body against hers, hard. Deep moans spilled from his lips as something warm rushed into Evanangela as they were joined. She sunk her fangs into his throat and drank, sucking hard. He did not fight her, his body and mind lost to the magnified pleasure. His hands dug into her skin, pulling her harder against him.

Her legs pulled him deeper, her hips bucking against him as his body grew limp in her arms. The warm rush of blood quenched her throat. Her mind went blank as she was overwhelmed and her body sang as the pleasures combined. At long last, his body began to cool and his blood soured at his last heartbeat. She released her hold and rolled his body away from her. It flopped onto the opposite side of the bed, face up. His eyes were glazed over with death, but his expression was one of bliss, not terror or confusion as all her previous feeds had worn.

The bedsheets were damp under her body and she moved away onto the cool dry side of the bed. Her chest heaved as she fought to catch her breath. She smiled up at the ceiling. Her vision cleared and the pleasure dissipated.

This must be what Verseau and Àmichemin had wanted me to learn. Oh, what a sweet lesson this has been!

Her body was warm and her skin was rosy, both from the blood and the love-making. She giggled as she sat up on one elbow, and kissed his cheek, leaving a smear of blood.

"Merci," she crooned, "I'm sorry I couldn't keep you."

Chapter Twenty-Two

Evanangela roused as the lid of her coffin slid open. Gabriel peered over the edge.

"Réveillez-vous, princesse."

She stretched and yawned. Her feed had been disposed of, leaving behind only a few stains on the sheets. Gabriel stepped back as Evanangela slid out of her coffin, her feet finding the floor. She shivered as she plucked her folded dressing gown from the nearby chair and swathed it about her body.

"Seigneur is expecting you. I will bring your clothes." He gathered up a bundle of garments from her dressing table and led the way to Verseau's apartments.

Evanangela gazed about her sitting room as she shuffled after him. She had forgotten how beautiful her rooms were, and was disappointed to leave them so soon. Gabriel led her down the hall. When he knocked on the black and gold door, Jacques answered and bowed.

Gabriel settled her clothes onto an empty chair, bowed, and followed Jacques back out into the hall. Verseau turned, his face brightening when he saw Evanangela. He stood and embraced her, his body cool and familiar.

"Ah, ma petite! I hope your feed was to your liking." He kissed her forehead and looked her over. "You seem bright and happy this moonrise."

She inhaled his faint scent. "Merci beaucoup, Verseau," she wound her arms around his neck and nuzzled the side of his face, "that was a lovely gift."

Verseau chuckled; it rumbled against her, soothing her. "I'm glad you found it so." He released her and gave her a mock-serious look. "You did not keep another pet, did you?"

Evanangela smiled and shook her head. "Non, mon Seigneur. I followed your orders to the letter."

He grinned, revealing his fangs. "Ma chère choupinette, wonderful! Go on, get dressed. We have much to discuss."

She looked about, realizing they were alone. "Where is Àmichemin?"

Verseau sighed and sat back down. "She glutted herself. She will need to hibernate for a few nights."

She recalled his horrifying words and shivered. His face dropped with concern. "Please, get dressed. I don't wish for you to be chilled."

"Merci," she whispered as she shed her dressing gown and began pulling on her stockings.

Verseau leaned back in his chair, watching her dress. "I was informed by one of our messengers that Àmichemin disposed of the traitors, but not before they started a rampage in the village. The foolish actions of the court have once again put the château at risk. Many peasants were slaughtered. Thankfully, Àmichemin was contained and brought back here before she could rampage as well."

Evanangela froze, her mind filling in the blanks of his implications. She fought not to shiver again, and focused on pulling her silk underthings onto her body.

"The Mors Ivoire Court agreed to send us reinforcements for our royal guard. Unfortunately, they will not arrive for another three days' time." Verseau gazed out the window into the ruined gardens. Small flecks of green dotted the charred trees, showing signs of new life. "We are in danger until then, ma chérie. Without Àmichemin or the royal guard to protect us, we are vulnerable to attacks from the court."

"What?" Evanangela spluttered, dropping her corset, "Surely the court would not think to harm us. Not after such punishments have been served."

Verseau shook his head. "The court is selfish and opportunistic. They do not think beyond the moment. They desire power, but haven't the slightest idea of how to wield it. There was much chaos as I learned the ways of ruling as Seigneur. You are the first vampire with any sense that has joined the court in over a century. The Nacre Court will implode if I am usurped."

196

Her legs wobbled as she struggled to seat herself onto the couch. Verseau sat beside her and took her hands in his.

"I do not mean to frighten you, ma choupinette," he whispered, "I only want to protect you. We must be cautious."

Thoughts of her heated romp flashed through her mind. "If our situation is so dire, then why did you send for such a celebratory feed for me?"

Verseau gave her a sad smile. "We must take what comforts and joy we can, ma chérie. It is a heavy burden we must shoulder these next few days."

Evanangela was silent as she laced up her corset. Her mind abuzz with all her suppositions.

Surely, Verseau cannot mean that Àmichemin is actually the true ruler of this court? And yet, he speaks as though we shall fall to pieces without her.

The only sound was the scratching of the quill as Verseau wrote more letters and orders. Once dressed, Evanangela sat on the couch, closest to his writing desk. The moments ticked by until she found the tension that silenced her was at last loosened by her growing panic.

"Surely you would like me to see to my duties as Overseer? What have we tasked the court with today?"

Verseau looked up, a puzzled expression across his face, then recognition flickered in his eyes, and he shook his head. "Non, ma choupinette. The château has been rebuilt to the best of our abilities and all physical preparations to protect the court have been completed. The court are creatures of luxury. If we work them too hard and too long, more shall surely defect. I am giving them the night to rest and enjoy themselves."

Evanangela fidgeted her hands. "You do not fear in their idleness that they will defect?"

"No," he went back to his writing, "they will be too busy catching up on lost time. I am also allowing them two hours to socialize in the ballroom after they have fed in their apartments. Even if whispers of dissonance begin to surface, I have my eyes and ears posted about the château."

197

She did her best to sit quietly as Verseau continued to write, making a neat stack of parchment, the official ribbons hanging off the desk like a waterfall of rainbows. The scuffing and clicking of her shoes grated on Verseau's nerves. She fidgeted on the couch, trying to get comfortable. At last, he set his quill down and sat back in his chair.

"Forgive me, ma chérie. I know this is dull work and you haven't anyone to play with. Perhaps you can find something to amuse yourself with in the library?"

Evanangela sat up. "The château has a library?"

"Yes, it is maintained despite the lack of use. I shall have your garçon escort you." Verseau tilted his head toward the door, "Garçon!"

The door opened, revealing Gabriel. Jacques stood off to the side, maintaining his post in the hallway. Gabriel bowed.

"Oui, Seigneur?"

Verseau waved his hand. "Please escort Mademoiselle Evanangela to the library. She is bored and in need of entertainment."

He bowed again and held out his hand. "Of course. Right this way, Mademoiselle."

She took his hand and allowed him to help lift her from the couch. Verseau returned to his work. Jacques closed the door behind them. Voices floated about in the hall, as some of the court were taking their feeds in their apartments. Others were meandering toward the ballroom.

Their footsteps echoed as they turned down one of the disused halls. The portraits looked as if they required a good dusting, the frames in need of polish. Gabriel opened a large oak door, revealing a dingy room filled with bookshelves.

Evanangela's heart sank. "*This* is the library?"

The library at La Maison de Primtemps had been cheery and cozy with plush sitting chairs and low couches. This library was cold and hard with severe wooden benches and lecterns. The space was lit with red enchanted candles and the drapes were drawn shut over the windows.

His face was pained. "Oui, princesse. I have been told by the older attendants that the library has not seen regular use in over two-hundred years. Many of the books are far older. Is there anything in particular you were searching for?"

She shook her head. "Non, Verseau sent me here to keep me busy while he works."

"I am sure he meant well by it." Gabriel began searching the shelves. "What do you enjoy reading, princesse?"

Evanangela plopped herself down on one of the cold wooden benches in a huff. She looked up at the massive bookshelves. The top shelves were covered in dust and gathering cobwebs. She dropped her gaze lower and saw titles in a variety of languages and she pointed at a thick tome.

"Beowulf. I have heard mortals speak about the grand stories written in that book."

Gabriel nodded and plucked the book from the shelf. "Anything else, princesse? I suspect le Seigneur wishes for you to be *entertained*. Especially considering this siege may take time."

She looked down at her shoes and the floor, disappointment tightening her heart. "It seems Verseau does not find *me* entertaining anymore, does he?"

He flinched and turned; his eyes wide. "Why would you think that, princesse?"

"He sent for my feed to pleasure me last night, he has sent me away to this library. He is distraught without Àmichemin by his side. I am simply a passing fancy it seems." Her voice was low with her arms huddled about her.

Gabriel sat down on the bench beside her and took her hands in his. "Princesse, le Seigneur is doing all this to protect you. Not just physically. He wants to protect your heart, your innocence. We are entering dark times and there is no hiding from the dangers that have yet to befall the court."

"What are you saying?" Evanangela met his gaze. "What dangers? We rebuilt the château, Àmichemin killed the defectors, the Mors Ivoire Court is sending us more guards, what else could possibly threaten the court?"

He turned away. "It is not my place to tell you, princesse, but there are whisperings in Le Village du Sang that this is only the beginning. The attendant elders have passed down tales from generations before of when the previous Seigneur fell and Seigneur Verseau came to power. We must be prepared for any outcome."

Gabriel squeezed her hands, then tilted his head to the bookshelf. "In any case, there is no need for you to be bored, princesse. Come, show me the books you would like."

They left the library with a stack of books, many featuring fanciful tales to distract Evanangela from the ominous warning Gabriel had given. She followed him through the maze of halls, back to Verseau's apartments. When they arrived, a pair of mortals were waiting in the sitting room. They perked up when they saw Evanangela.

"Good evening, Mademoiselle," they both bowed, "we have been waiting for you."

He settled Evanangela's new books onto one of the receiving tables, bowed, and exited into the hall. Verseau appeared from the bedroom, and the mortals bowed to him.

"Bonsoire, Seigneur Verseau. It is an honor to be summoned to discuss trade with you."

The older mortal extended a scroll of parchment. Verseau took it and unrolled it. His eyes did not move and his jaw was tense. He rolled the parchment back up and set it on his writing desk.

"Excellent, we are always looking for more trade opportunities."

Verseau nodded to Evanangela, then turned back to the mortals. He leaned in, as if to whisper something in the mortal's ear, then sunk his fangs into his neck.

His companion blanched; his eyes wide as fear rooted him to the spot. Visions of the terrified peasants paraded through Evanangela's mind. She hesitated. As Verseau sucked at the vein, the faint scent of fresh blood wafted through the air. The mortal bolted for the door.

Instinct took over and Evanangela dashed after him. She grabbed the collar of his jacket, her nails sinking into the soft fabric. The force snapped him backward into her, and she dove into his neck, piercing the skin with her serrated fangs. Her mouth flooded with blood, quenching the buzzing in her mind. It was not as earthy and rich as the villagers' blood had been. Instead, it was sweet and delicate. Her eyes rolled into her head as she drank. She could feel her veins swelling with new blood, her heart beating life back into her body.

As the last heartbeat whispered through the mortal's veins, she let it drop to the floor. Evanangela sighed, allowing herself to relax. She leaned against the couch; her elbow propped up on the cushions as she sat on the floor. Verseau was sitting at his writing desk, staring into the fire.

"Ça va?" Evanangela rolled her languid gaze over his face. It was pinched, his eyes intent on the fire.

Verseau sighed through his nose and leaned back into his chair. He saw the parchment scroll, plucked it from his desk, and tossed it into the fire. Evanangela cringed as she watched the edges blacken and curl. An ominous pall settled over her, making her fear that she was staring into her own future.

Chapter Twenty-Three

Evanangela followed Verseau down the hall. The moon had just risen, and she was still in her dressing gown. Jacques and Gabriel followed close behind. The halls were quiet, as most of the court was either still asleep or just waking up. Verseau pulled a key from his pocket and unlocked Àmichemin's apartments. The door swung wide, revealing her luxurious sitting room. The violet flames crackled merrily in the grate. He marched straight to her bedchambers. Evanangela hurried to follow.

Àmichemin was still in her coffin. She sat, gazing about the room; her eyes glazed over. Verseau's shoulders rolled, his jaw relaxing into a smile. He took her into his arms, holding her tight.

"Ma chérie!" He gasped, then kissed her with such passion that Àmichemin giggled when he released her. "You have returned to us!"

She took a deep breath, the sapphire blush bright on her cheeks. Her legs wobbled as she sat down on the violet bed quilt. Verseau took her hands in his and kissed them. Then, he extended his hand to Evanangela, coaxing her.

"Come here, ma choupinette," he crooned.

Evanangela stepped forward, allowing Verseau to squeeze her hand and kiss it. He smiled at each of them in turn.

"I am whole again. My heart has returned to me."

Àmichemin bopped him on the shoulder then leaned back into the bed. Verseau released their hands and straightened up. The smile hung on his lips as he turned to the attendants.

"Bring the feeds into my apartments. We are not to be disturbed tonight."

Àmichemin turned to Evanangela, then spread her arms wide. "Ici, ma chère," she purred.

Evanangela threw her arms about Àmichemin's neck. Her body relaxed as Àmichemin's arms squeezed her tight. She had not realized she had been so tense, but now she felt her worries melt away as she inhaled Àmichemin's faint scent. Her starry locks fell about Evanangela, shielding them from the world.

Verseau held up Àmichemin's dressing gown. She released Evanangela, but not before she pecked her on the cheek. Her body swayed with her typical sashay as she allowed Verseau to slip the dressing gown about her. He dragged his fangs over her neck, his eyes teasing. She laughed and pushed his face away, her eyes alight with mischief.

Evanangela sighed. She finally understood. Neither Verseau nor Àmichemin ruled the court. They ruled it together. Without one of them, the other was left empty. They breathed life into one another in a way that living blood could not.

He held out his hand, beckoning her. Evanangela slid off the bed, and joined them. Together, they trotted down the hall; back to Verseau's apartments. The court was noisy, feeds being taken, conversations floating about the halls. Evanangela soaked it all in, relishing the feeling of Verseau's arm about her. For the first time in weeks, she felt truly alive.

After a quick feed, Àmichemin lounged on the couch, her dressing gown open, revealing the blood stains down her chin, neck, and dotted on her chest. She idly petted Evanangela's hair; her head in Àmichemin's lap. Verseau handed Àmichemin a handkerchief, and she used her free hand to mop up the blood.

"There is no way around it," Verseau's whisper was low, sending shivers through Evanangela, "we shall have to hibernate."

Àmichemin sat up straight, forcing Evanangela to sit up as well. "I should say I have struck fear in the court once again."

He nodded. "That is true. Their grumblings have been silenced, but there is still the matter of the blood shortage."

"You have spoken with the Council?" Àmichemin handed him back his handkerchief.

Verseau tossed it onto his writing desk for Jacques to launder later. "Oui, they suggested the same. The Mors have sent replacements for our guard. They just arrived this morning. We will be well protected."

Evanangela fidgeted with the lace on her chemise. "What happens when we go into hibernation?"

Àmichemin took Evanangela's hand and patted it. Her face softened. "Fear not, it is just like our death sleep. You shall wake up completely unaware that any time has passed. And this whole mess will be behind us."

"Oui, absolument." He nodded. "The Council has agreed that there is simply not enough to go around. We have also received word that there is another plague making its way through Europe. If we continue as we are, we shall starve."

Evanangela remembered the lonely frantic dawns whilst they were traveling. The heavy silence of her coffin. She shivered and Àmichemin put her arms around Evanangela.

"What troubles you, ma chérie?" Àmichemin kissed the top of her hair.

She dropped her gaze to her lap, shame blossoming a blush into her cheeks. "I am fearful of being alone for so long."

Àmichemin squeezed her in an embrace. "Not to worry. You won't be alone. We shall all be together."

"Actually, that is part of what I need to discuss with the two of you." Verseau stood. "Come."

She released Evanangela, then tied her dressing gown shut. Evanangela pulled her dressing gown on, shivering as her bare feet slid into her silk slippers. Jacques bowed as they entered the hall.

"To the west stables." Verseau tilted his head.

Jacques nodded. "Allons-y."

"The western stables?" Evanangela murmured. "But why there?"

"Shhh!" Verseau hissed.

They walked in silence. Jacques led them through a maze of doors and staircases. He held a candelabra aloft, the crimson candles illuminating the cramped space. Evanangela shivered, trying not to chatter her teeth. The air was becoming colder as they traveled further into the bowels of the château.

At long last, Jacques opened a large vault with a series of keys. Inside was a large rug and three stone pedestals. The walls had sconces with black candles. Their ever-burning flames a bright vermillion. On the wall opposite the door were three stylized portraits in relation to the pedestals. Evanangela then recognized that they were portraits of her, Àmichemin, and Verseau.

"This is where we shall hibernate." Verseau's voice was a low whisper. "The rest of the court will be housed in the main hibernation cell of the catacombs."

Evanangela gazed about the room. It was cheery compared to the gloomy caverns they had trekked through. But the thought of the door being so heavily locked spiked her fears of becoming a trapped animal. She looked from Jacques to Verseau.

"Why must we be separated from the court?"

Àmichemin traced her fingers along the edge of her pedestal. "They cannot be trusted. Many past Seigneurs have been assassinated whilst hibernating."

Shivers ran up Evanangela's spine as she imagined members of the court throwing their coffins open and stabbing stakes through their hearts. She swallowed hard as her heart raced, pumping the living blood through her trembling body.

"We will be safe here." Verseau turned and nodded to Jacques. "My attendants are a direct bloodline. They can be trusted to keep us safe. The keys will be held in a location only known to their family."

He turned his gaze to Gabriel. "Your pet, unfortunately, will not live to see you again, ma choupinette. You must enjoy him now. The life span of mortals is finite and short."

Fresh alarm struck Evanangela. She turned and saw Gabriel's sad smile. He took her hands and squeezed them.

"It is all right, ma princesse, there is still time." He kissed her hands. "Your safety matters most. I will guard you while you sleep."

Àmichemin leaned against one of the walls, an annoyed scowl puckering her lips. "How long?"

Verseau sighed and shook his head. "That is uncertain. We will have to wait several generations for the mortals to repopulate, more if this plague enters France. I have instructed Jacques to wait until the population has reached the numbers of old. The court will not tolerate another reign of restriction when they awaken."

The silence pressed down on them, the decades ticking through their minds. Evanangela leaned against Gabriel, reassuring herself of his presence. At long last, Verseau ushered them out of the vault. Jacques pulled the heavy door closed and locked it with the combination of keys again.

Their muffled footsteps sounded monstrous as blood pounded in Evanangela's ears. The three pedestals meant she would have to hibernate in her own coffin; alone. There would be no comfortable tangle of cooling limbs, no scent of Àmichemin's hair, no reassuring squeeze of Verseau's hands. As it was in the carriage, there would only be the cold darkness and the bitter silence.

Evanangela was silent as she pulled on her clothes in Verseau's apartments. Àmichemin was in a foul mood, muttering as she yanked on her skirts. Verseau sat at his writing desk, already dressed. He stared into the fire; his jaw tensed.

"The court is ready for you." Jacques bowed in the doorway.

Verseau nodded and stood up, straightening his jacket. Àmichemin flicked her hair behind her shoulder. Evanangela slipped on her shoes and stood with the help of Verseau. Together, they marched down the hall into the ballroom.

Again, the court was waiting for them. There were no indignant sneers or heated whispers. Instead, they shuffled, darting their eyes about. Verseau cleared his throat.

"We have gathered you all here for an important announcement." He scanned the room. Their eyes dropped as his gaze fell on each of theirs. "We have been working closely with the Council these past weeks. And it seems, there is only one sound solution for the survival of our court, and of our neighbors. In five days' time, the court will be ordered to hibernate in the catacombs."

The court burst into nervous chatter. Verseau cleared his throat again, silencing them. The acrid scent of their fear stunk in Evanangela's nostrils.

"Use this time to settle your affairs and prepare for the long sleep. We do not have an exact resurrection date. Instead, our attendants have been instructed to wait for the local populations to reach a certain number before waking us. We may be asleep for decades; possibly even a century. If we do not allow the mortals to recover, we will starve or they will destroy the court in retaliation."

"Coward!"

All heads whipped toward a vampire dressed all in burgundy. Verseau stalked through the crowd. When he came upon the grinning vampire, he glared down his nose at him.

"What did you say?" Verseau's voice was low. The other vampires and vixens scuttled away, creating a ring around the two.

The vampire laughed. "You are a *coward!* Telling us to hole ourselves up like rats. Seigneur Félix would have stood and fought these vermin!"

Verseau's hand was quick. The struggling vampire dangled in the air, his legs kicking as Verseau lifted him by the neck. His fingers squeezed the idiot's throat.

"Seigneur Félix was a *fool.*" Verseau spat. "Our territory was a wasteland under his control. Our attendants died defending us from attackers night after night. We spent every day in our coffins *trapped* in fear."

He dropped the vampire who landed with a thud and scrambled to find his feet. Before he could stand, Verseau stomped his foot onto the vampire's chest; pinning him to the floor.

"Seigneur Félix would have doomed this court if not for *me*. I know what is best. Know that if I order you all to sleep for one and one-hundred years that it is the best course of action for this court to not only survive but to *thrive.*"

Verseau lifted his foot. The vampire wheezed as he clutched his crushed chest. Àmichemin's eyes gleamed as Verseau locked onto her gaze. He nodded.

"Kill him."

The vampire tried to scream as Àmichemin ran toward him, but his voice only came out as a squeaking wheeze. He tried to back away on the floor, but his body was too slow and broken. A deep laugh bubbled up in Àmichemin's throat as she stalked him as a cat does a wounded bird. Ice crystals were forming on her lips as she exposed her fangs, licking them with glee.

"Mercy! I beg mercy! Please! Have me burned! Anything but this!" The vampire screamed, his chest heaving with each syllable. He sputtered blood as he spoke, clutching his cracked sternum.

Àmichemin screeched. All the vampires fled to the farthest corners of the room; their hands clamped over their ears. Evanangela fell to her knees, the sound blotting out all rational thought. She managed to keep her eyes open, despite the pain. Verseau stood, watching; completely unbothered.

The vampire flailed his arms, trying to fend Àmichemin off. She giggled at his pathetic attempts, and pinned him to the floor. Her jaws opened wide, allowing her fangs to slide forward to their true length. They were long and curved, like those of a snake. Evanangela licked her own fangs, pointed stubs in comparison. Àmichemin dove into the vampire's neck. Instead of puncturing it for blood, she ripped out his windpipe, leaving a bloody tangle of mangled flesh and ribbons of skin.

Evanangela found she could not tear her eyes away. Horror held her captive, as if encased in stone. Àmichemin tore hunks of flesh from the vampire's body, mauling him into a pile of crooked bones and pulpy flesh and organs. Once it was clear he was completely destroyed, Verseau stepped forward. Evanangela found her voice did not work; strangled by fear. He strode up to Àmichemin; his movements slow and methodical. When she noticed his presence, she hissed at him. Verseau did not flinch. Instead, he reached out his hand, as one would for a wild animal to sniff. Àmichemin stared at his hand. He then knelt down beside her, and lowered his face slowly toward hers. She was transfixed, sitting still until he placed a tender kiss on her forehead. Àmichemin drew back. Her whole demeanor was changed.

"You did well." Verseau whispered, helping her to her feet.

Àmichemin dusted herself off. He handed her a handkerchief, which she began dabbing onto her face and neck. Her gown was completely soaked with blood, but she seemed unbothered by it. She flexed her jaw, and the terrifying fangs that hung down to her chin retracted back to their usual length. The court began to crawl out of their hiding spots around the room. They gathered again, leaving a large gap around the mutilated body.

"The time for death decorum has passed." His voice was firm. "Defectors will be dealt with as you have seen. This is not about petty squabbles. It is about the very survival of this court. Anyone seeking to undermine that will suffer the most ruthless penalty. Is that clear?"

Murmurs rippled through the crowd. "Oui, Seigneur!"

Verseau nodded. "Bien. To bed. It is nearly sunrise."

Evanangela flinched as Àmichemin knelt down and held out her hand. She took it, hesitant. Àmichemin's eyes were kind and warm once more. Their violet hue was bright and beautiful, sucking her in. She stood, allowing Àmichemin to fuss over her.

"I'm sorry you had to see that." She held Evanangela close.

Verseau placed his hand on Àmichemin's shoulder, coaxing them along. Àmichemin released Evanangela. They walked together side by side behind him. Jacques opened the doors to the apartments, and bowed. He followed them into the sitting room, then waited as they undressed.

"We shall speak on this no more." The edge in his voice was softened by exhaustion. "Rest now, and prepare your minds for joy. I have made plans for us tomorrow."

Chapter Twenty-Four

Àmichemin was busy fiddling with her stockings while Evanangela pulled on her gown. Verseau was at his writing desk, scribbling away.

"Should we be going off on a holiday this close to hibernation?" Evanangela fidgeted with her sleeves, her anxiety growing.

Verseau set aside his quill and began folding the letter. "This is a crucial excursion. One you will enjoy, I promise."

She nodded, settling into the overstuffed couch to wait while Àmichemin tugged her skirts into place.

"We deserve it," Àmichemin huffed, "Those ungrateful twits have been coddled for far too long."

"Jacques!" Verseau called.

The door opened, and Jacques bowed before taking the letter from Verseau, then bowed again and exited into the hall. He sighed and leaned back in his chair, finally turning his attention to their dressing.

"Ah, mes fleurs! You look magnifique!" He gathered up Àmichemin and held her tight, released her, then bent down to kiss the crown of Evanangela's hair. "It is a shame I will only see you for a few moments before we depart."

Evanangela flinched. "What do you mean?"

He sat down on the couch, watching as Àmichemin tied a few ribbons into place. "Not to worry, it's a short trip, only a day's journey from here."

"All this pomp and bother," Àmichemin teased, "Are you sure you aren't sneaking us away from the hibernation all together."

Verseau shook his head. "I wish that were so, but the hibernation shall come to pass. Until then, we have wonders to enjoy. Vite! The carriages are waiting."

Evanangela took Verseau's hand as he helped her stand. Àmichemin smoothed her skirts and together they exited out into the halls. The court was just rousing itself, sounds of activity floating about. Jacques appeared, escorting them to the entryway.

"Everything is prepared, mon Seigneur." He bowed at the threshold of the great doors.

"Where is Gabriel?" Evanangela craned her neck about, trying to see down the adjacent halls.

Verseau whispered something to Jacques, then turned to her. "We are not taking our attendants for this trip, ma chérie. They are needed here for the preparations."

She bit her lip, the worry gnawing her insides. Verseau ushered them outside, and the doors groaned as they closed behind them. Three black carriages were waiting. They were nondescript, not the elegant carriages with gilding and the gemstone monograms. The horses stamped and tossed their heads.

"I want to keep a low profile while traveling," He gestured to the carriages. "We will have a small guard, but I want to be sure the main guard stay at the château to prevent any *mishaps* while we're gone."

Evanangela nodded. She took his hand and allowed him to steer her toward the carriages. The footman opened the door and bowed. She climbed inside, situating herself. Verseau took her hand and kissed it.

"Soon, you shall be in the most wonderful place, ma choupinette," Verseau whispered. "Rest now, we shall be there before you know it."

He stepped back down, and the door closed. She watched out the window as Verseau led Àmichemin to her own carriage. They disappeared from view, and Evanangela sank into the cushions; which were not as soft as the ones in her personal carriage. Her eyes fell on the empty seat in front of her. She sighed and looked out the window again. Tension knotted her stomach. No one would be there to distract or comfort her. She was truly alone.

The carriage lurched forward, and Evanangela grabbed onto the curtains to prevent herself from falling. She huffed and smoothed her skirts, rearranging herself as the carriage bumped along the road. The metallic squeal of the gates opening made the hairs on the back of her neck stand on end. She fidgeted, watching the empty, desolate lawns fade away.

Moonlight poured in as the lid to Evanangela's coffin was opened. Verseau leaned over the side and lifted her out. She blinked, trying to grasp her surroundings. They were in a carriage, but it had stopped moving, and the door was open. The chilly air filtered in, bringing the scent of water and fresh leaves up into her nose. Evanangela stretched, gathering her wits as Verseau kissed her forehead.

"Welcome ma chérie, to the most beautiful place sous la lune."[1] He set her on the carriage seat and stroked her hair.

Verseau had changed out of his traveling clothes and into something truly spectacular. A cool sapphire blush appeared on her cheeks. His charcoal grey frock coat was accented by his red handkerchief. A ruby ascot pin sparkled in the low-light as he moved. Evanangela touched the cool gold buttons on his coat, each bearing the stag and briars seal. He took her hand and escorted her out of the carriage.

Evanangela gathered her cobalt velour skirts and allowed Verseau to guide her as she descended from the carriage. Her bare feet became slick with dew from the cool grass and the hem of her gown soon became soaked through. An enchanted tree swayed in the cool evening breeze. It was a deep hue of dusty purple with magenta toned leaves. A raven called from high in the tree's branches, chilling Evanangela in a pleasing sort of way.

She was startled by the crunch of boots behind her, but they were only Verseau's footsteps. Evanangela turned and saw Àmichemin on his arm. She was wearing a voluminous violet velvet gown with lilac petticoats peeking out at her ankles. Amethyst pins glittered in her hair. Evanangela smiled, but shivered as a chill breeze struck her. Verseau drew her close to him, and Àmichemin pulled away. He led them to a lake that was clear as glass.

Àmichemin was carrying a thick bearskin blanket. Verseau took this from her and spread it at the edge of the lake. Grass did not grow at the water's edge and on closer inspection the water did not stir. No fish swam in the lake, and crows' skulls gleamed from below the surface.

"This is a damned place." Evanangela whispered to herself, barely audible over the rush of the waterfall that fed the enchanted lake. To her, the skulls were like fragments of the grim reaper's scythe.

A squirrel scurried by in the distance, chirping and growling in response to the raven's cackling. Evanangela shivered again, and Verseau

1 Under the moon.

drew her close as the three sat together. "There, there, ma chérie. Il n'y a rien à craindre ici au Lac des Morts."[2]

She nodded but Verseau caught her chin in his gentle grasp. His face moved toward hers. She closed her eyes and moved toward him in response. Their lips met, and Evanangela felt the fire in her heart was in danger of consuming her. Shrieks from the horses cut through the haze of her mind. Her body lurched away from Verseau; her eyes wide as terror swept through her mind.

"Que Dieu te damné!"[3]

The trio turned and gaped at the horde of villagers bearing down on them. Àmichemin jumped to her feet and ran toward the mob.

"No!" Verseau screamed.

The retinue of guards was unable to hold them back. Evanangela watched in horror as the peasants overtook them. Their sheer numbers swallowed them up. The sounds of rent flesh, the crack of bone, and inhuman cries filled the air. Fresh blood wafted into Evanangela's nostrils. Her brain ignited. She jumped to her feet, but Verseau grabbed her arm, holding her back.

Àmichemin grabbed a peasant by the throat and tossed him several feet, knocking the wind out of him. She turned and seized another by the face, gouging her eyes out. More kept pouring toward her, weapons bearing down; forcing her to retreat.

"How did they know we were here?" Àmichemin scanned the mob, "Something is not right."

Villagers swarmed the carriages. The footmen and drivers tried to fight them off, but they pounded on the wood, overturning them. Their pitchforks and torches seemed to scrape the sky as their belligerent shouts cut through the air. The horses reared and bucked as their harnesses took them down with the vehicles. The wood groaned and split as one of the carriages was crushed as it toppled over. They began bashing the side door in with pitchforks and other farming tools. The yoke of the carriage splintered and speared one of the proud black geldings in the belly. Blood and intestines dropped as its stomach ripped, spattering the other horses. Their wide rolling eyes and jets of hot breath in the chilly air made them appear as hellish beasts.

---

2 There is nothing to fear here at the Lake of the Dead.
3 God damn you!

214

Evanangela watched in horror, rooted to the spot. Then something caught her eye. One of the villagers looked familiar. His dark hair and dark eyes belied his stormy demeanor as he brandished a boar-hunting spear. All at once, she recognized him.

How can that be? Why would Michael resort to this carnage?

He locked eyes with her, sending a fresh wave of terror through her body and mind. She shook her head. *Non! Arretez-vous, s'il vous plaît!*

A deep bellow cut through her thoughts. She gasped and clamped her hands over her ears. The deep rumble of the familiar and frightening voice filled her mind.

Oui, petite plume[4]! It is I, Michael! This is your penance! There is no joy in retribution for sins, or have you forgotten?

Evanangela's knees wobbled, her body faltering as the pressure weighed her down. *There is grace in finding joy even in the darkness. Please, end this madness! You are harming innocents!*

His cold laugh pounded in her skull. *There are no innocents here! Only sin!*

The attendants attempted to flee, but one of the peasant archers shot them cleanly in the back, through the heart. As the arrows hit their marks and sunk deep, the blood poured out, staining the coarse grey wool jackets and white cotton shirts. They crumpled forward, their knees buckled, and they fell face first into the dirt. Two villager women produced fish-gutting knives, and used them to cut the fleur de lis off the grey jackets of the attendants' corpses. The sharp knives sliced through the fabrics, and down into the corpses' backs. They peeled off the bloody fleur de lis squares and waved them like war flags. Their chanting whipped the other villagers into a frenzy.

"Vive le Seigneur Dieu![5] Vive le Seigneur Dieu! Vive le Seigneur Dieu!"

Àmichemin grabbed Evanangela, and Verseau followed. Together they ran toward the waterfall.

"Vite, Verseau! Vite!" Àmichemin gasped as the villagers advanced; her heavy velvet skirts gathered in her free hand. Verseau

4 little feather
5 Long live the Lord God!

215

grappled with the steep bluff. His shoes sent down small rocks and debris raining down on the two below. He clawed at the grass, his hands digging into the soft earth at the crest of the cliff. He hauled himself up onto the flat surface, almost kissing the ground in gratitude that he had made it. Verseau spun around, reaching as far as he could over the precarious edge, and thrust his hand over for Evanangela to grasp. She scrambled to find footholds as Àmichemin shoved Evanangela up the bluff. Àmichemin spit and flicked her silvery blond hair as dirt sprinkled onto her face.

"Vite mes fleurs! Vite! You are almost to the top!" Verseau called.

Evanangela's shoes were slick heels with opal inlay and made climbing the cliff like climbing ice. She gripped a nearby tree root and stretched her hand until Verseau grabbed her wrist and hauled her onto solid ground. Once Evanangela was safely over the cliff, Verseau reached down again for Àmichemin's hand. She glanced behind her. The mob had made quick work of the carriages and was advancing toward the bluff.

A peasant woman stretched her arm straight out at the cliff. Her gnarled fingers were knobby and twisted from years of weaving at the loom. She shrieked; her eyes were wide as she pointed at Àmichemin. One of her eyes was covered by a milky film. Her snarling teeth were yellowed, and some were missing. Grey hair waved about her head as if it had taken on a life of its own.

"Mon garçon, Henri, est mort! Il est mort parce que toi, salope d'enfer!"[6]

The woman grabbed a bow from one of the archers. She drew the bowstring as Àmichemin struggled to climb the cliff.

"Vite, Àmichemin! Vite!" Evanangela begged as Verseau pushed her away from the edge.

Stray arrows flew from the woman's bow. They whistled through the air. One struck the bluff harmlessly and plunked into the lake. The villagers ran past the woman with the bow, intent on capturing at least one of the vampires.

Verseau leaned over the edge, but Àmichemin was just out of reach. The villagers were closing in as she tripped over the hem of her dress. Àmichemin squealed as her heels slipped on a rock, dislodging

6 My son is dead! He is dead because of you, you bitch from hell!

216

it. For the first time, Evanangela saw fear in her eyes. Her right hand slipped from a crevice and the whole right side of her body swung freely as she managed to hold on.

"Àmichemin!" Evanangela screamed once more as Verseau strained to reach for her.

Michael took the bow from the old crone and notched an arrow. Evanangela felt the air rush from her lungs as he took aim. Wild gee stamped across his face as he loosed the arrow. A snap resonated, and a whirr pierced the air with a solid thud, resulting in Àmichemin screaming and slipping.

"Voici! Le chienne cris comme une bête!"[7] One of the peasants cried as they swarmed beneath her.

"No!" Verseau bellowed as the villagers started climbing the rough wall and grabbed hold of Àmichemin's skirts.

They dragged her down the face of the bluff before Verseau could grab her hand. Evanangela made to throw herself over the cliff, but he restrained her.

"Àmichemin! Ma chérie Àmichemin!" She screamed as she reached in vain.

This is your penance, petite plume! Michael growled. Repent, lest I take more of what you hold dear!

Her wailing reverberated through the oasis, the raven adding his own lament to hers. Evanangela watched, tears blurring her eyes as the villagers held Àmichemin down and Michael plunged the boar-hunting spear through her chest. Thick black dead blood seeped from the wound. A putrid scent cut through the air. The villagers dropped her, covering their faces as they scrambled away. Michael was gone, disappeared back to the eternal kingdom. Àmichemin's limbs were akimbo, and her spray of starry hair dulled.

"I'm sorry." Verseau whispered as he consoled Evanangela, but there were tears in his eyes as well and his voice was choked with bitterness.

He pulled Evanangela down the path to a small cave and stooped to crawl inside. She followed, tears streaming down her face. Verseau cradled Evanangela in his arms, her skirts spilling over his lap, her hair

7 Here! The bitch screams like a beast!

tangling in the gold buttons of his jacket. Evanangela wept on Verseau's chest, her fists beating on the lapels of his coat.

"Oh, ma petite, there is no use in your bitterness." But Verseau had a distant look in his eyes that suggested he did not believe himself.

The first rays of the sunrise began to creep up the bluff, and Verseau covered them both in his overcoat, deep inside the cave, protecting them until night fell once more.

Chapter Twenty-Five

Verseau unwrapped his overcoat from Evanangela. He kissed her auburn bangs and watched as her eyelashes fluttered.

"Àmichemin-?" Evanangela yawned and rubbed her eyes.

"Non, ç'est moi." His eyes were empty, even the twinkle of mischief was gone. There was a twinge of remorse in his words.

Evanangela stood up, not quite remembering the previous evening just yet. He put his arm about her waist to steady her and then led Evanangela down a winding path following the river that fed the waterfall. Near the bottom of the sloping path, one the of carriages was waiting for them. Three attendants stood near the horses. They waved when they saw the vampires. The other two carriages lay in ruins, the dead gelding rotting as swarms of flies devoured him. The flesh had rotted in the sun, and now in the cool night air, it stunk. She drew her handkerchief from her corset and held it over her nose as they made a wide circle around it. Only three of the horses remained, stamping and tossing their heads. The attendants did their best to comfort the beasts but their ears swiveled to and fro. Plumes of steam erupted from their nostrils and mouths as they rolled their eyes.

The driver nodded and the footman opened the door. Verseau took Evanangela's hand and helped her climb inside before he alighted into the carriage. The footman shut the door, and then with a crack of the reins they were speeding away from Le Lac des Morts.

"Oh, my love!" Verseau cried as he clasped Evanangela close to him. His voice was barely a whisper as he wept.

She hugged him close, not knowing what else to do. "Mon Seigneur."

"Please do not speak. I cannot bear that I have lost another one." He leaned forward with his head in his hands. His hair grazed the edge of Àmichemin's coffin. It was perched on the seating opposite them. Verseau's enormous coffin was chained to the back of the carriage on a sled. It weighed them down, and the horses panted from the effort of pulling.

There were deep gouges in the inlay of Àmichemin's coffin. Evanangela ran her fingers over the cuts that warped the beautiful carvings of twined roses and briars.

"Àmichemin," she whispered. Her chest was tight and her eyes burned, unable to cry, from the lack of blood.

Verseau remained that way, his head in his hands as his back trembled. Evanangela stroked his back, but her mind was far away, visions of Àmichemin falling to her death flashed before her eyes over and over. Her mind fought to calculate a way to save her, but it always ended the same. She squeezed her hands in her lap to prevent herself from sobbing. Her heart filled with rage as she looked up at Àmichemin's coffin again and traced the gouges in the decorative wood.

How could Michael do this? I am already serving my penance as Dieu saw fit! What need was this for this waste of life? To torture me?

Evanangela tore her gaze away. The carriage windows yielded no comfort as the forest canopy was thick, blotting out the moon and the stars, leaving only inky blackness. Evanangela sank back into the cushions, the grief building in waves. She leaned her head back and stared up at the ceiling, allowing her eyes to unfocus.

At last, Verseau took a deep shuddering breath and sat up gazing out the window away from Evanangela. His eyes were glassy, his mind far away. Evanangela heaved a deep sigh and rubbed her eyes.

The silence was suffocating as the thoughts buried Evanangela alive. She pressed her hands against her ears and shook her head, willing Àmichemin's screams to quiet in her mind. The sway of the carriage as it bumped along the path grated on her nerves. Every jostle enflamed her anger and magnified the pain of her empty veins. She gritted her teeth, trying to ignore the tightness in her chest, how heavy her heart was; filled with desolation instead of blood. Evanangela flinched when the carriage rolled to a stop. Verseau broke from his reverie and took her hand. The door was opened and Evanangela peered outside into the gloom. She could hear the chatter of creatures and the burble of a nearby stream. The footman bowed as Verseau led Evanangela out onto the forest path where the driver and one of the footmen stood at attention.

"It is yet another day's ride before we reach the château, Seigneur." The footman kept his head bowed. "Please feed. The sunrise is approaching."

Verseau nodded. One of the attendants stepped forward, offering his arm. Verseau took it, and the sharp intake of breath was punctuated with the vapor cloud from his mouth in the chilly air. He sucked for a moment, then wiped his lips on his handkerchief. The attendant stepped away.

"Merci, Seigneur." He whispered as he trotted away and clambered back onto the carriage.

The second attendant stepped toward Evanangela. She turned to Verseau. He nodded. "Go on and feed, ma chérie. But only enough to quiet the hunger. These are our faithful attendants. We do not wish them harm."

Evanangela nodded, taking the attendant's arm into her hands. The warmth of his skin was enticing. She brushed her lips against the vein, then pierced it with her fangs. The attendant gasped, but stayed still as she sucked. Blood rushed into her mouth, assuaging the aching hunger in her heart. Before she could clear the haze, a hand tugged her hair, pulling her away.

"That's enough." Verseau patted her head as Evanangela swallowed the last of the blood. "Now, get inside. The sun is upon us."

The attendant bowed, then scurried back up into the driver's seat. Verseau helped her into the carriage and the footman closed the door behind them. He lifted the floor panel, revealing Evanangela's coffin. Much of the precious inlay had been stripped by the peasants. There were burn marks on one of the corners. Evanangela gasped.

Verseau put his hand on her shoulder, urging her forward. "The sun, ma choupinette."

Were I still an angel, I would be rejoicing with the villagers. And yet, it is all too terrible to bear!

She ran her hands over her ruined coffin, shaking as she held in the sorrow that threatened; took a deep breath, and slid inside. Verseau's face was the last thing she saw before the darkness enveloped her as he closed the lid. She could hear the sound of him climbing into Àmichemin's coffin. Her heart lurched; such a thought was unbearable.

221

Before her grief could burn any more, the deathlike sleep quieted her thoughts and overtook her.

The lid of the coffin slid open, and she blinked in the darkness, moonlight spilling onto her face.

"Réveillez," Verseau whispered.

Evanangela sat up and saw Verseau crouched over her. He leaned back, allowing her to climb out into the carriage. Memories from the previous night came flooding back into her mind; sucking the air from her lungs. She collapsed into his arms and bit back the sobs that hiccupped in her chest.

He pulled her up into the carriage seat. They held one another tight, as if both were afraid the other would disappear if they let go. Verseau's chin rested atop Evanangela's head, his hands idly stroking her back as she petted the front of his jacket. Their hunger was but a whisper in their minds as they sat together. The squeak of the carriage wheels, the hollow clopping of the horses' hooves, the scrape of Verseau's coffin being dragged behind, all of it was monstrously loud as they huddled together.

Evanangela flinched when the carriage rolled to a halt. His embrace tightened out of reflex, the buttons of his jacket pressing into the side of her face. He loosened his grip when the footman opened the carriage door and bowed.

They extricated themselves and stepped out into the cool night air. Le Château d'Astucieux loomed above them. A bevy of attendants spilled from the doors, rushing to carry the coffins inside. Verseau and Evanangela walked in silence through the vast doors. Jacques bowed; his face grim as he led them to Verseau's apartments.

Despite the impending dawn, the court was quiet as they passed the various apartments. The attendants scurried about, but no vampires or vixens leaned against the walls or adorned the benches and stools. Verseau sank into his couch and Evanangela sat beside him. Her mind was groggy as she was jostled and confused from not having a proper feed.

A knock sounded at the door, and Jacques escorted a team of attendants in. They carried Verseau's massive coffin through the sitting room, and settled it onto the bed. Jacques bowed before Verseau.

"The necessary repairs will be made by Dubois while you sleep, Seigneur."

One of the attendants stayed behind, and bowed. Verseau waved his hand. Both the attendant and Jacques bowed, taking their leave out into the hall.

At long last, Verseau pushed himself up off the couch. He shed his clothes, leaving them on the floor, and walked into the bedroom. Evanangela followed suit. Her body relaxed as the soiled heavy velvet gown fell from her body with a dull thud.

The broken lid of Verseau's coffin was leaning against the side. He gestured for her to enter first, and Evanangela snuggled into the thick velvet-lined cushioning. Verseau climbed in after her. He lay with his stomach to her back and pulled her close.

Jacques' familiar footsteps approached. He lifted the lid and slid it onto the coffin. Verseau's hands squeezed her and she could hear a sob catch in his throat. Then he relaxed, and his body began to stiffen as the death-sleep spared him from his grief.

The next evening was worse than the last. Evanangela stared up at the ceiling as she lay in Verseau's coffin. He had already risen, and she could hear him shuffling about. Her empty veins urged her to get moving and find a feed, but her heart was a weighted stone in her chest, knotted with anguish. Her limbs were heavy and refused to move.

Verseau leaned over the lip of the coffin. He was a comforting sight, easing the pain by a degree. Evanangela reached up, and he took her hand, helping to lift her to a sitting position. He smoothed her bangs and stroked her cheek. She reached up and placed her hand over his, soaking up the familiar feel of his cool skin on hers. At long last, she released him, and he withdrew and sat at his writing desk.

Evanangela climbed out of the coffin. Her limbs were awkward as they were numbed with sorrow and guilt. She sat on the bed; the effort of moving had exhausted her. Verseau toyed with a quill on his desk, his eyes unfocused. Evanangela wrapped her arms about herself, staring down at her stocking-clad feet and the floor. She closed her eyes, willing the thoughts to leave her; Amichemin's terrified face burned into her mind.

It is my fault she was killed. Michael acted only to punish me. Were it not for me, Amichemin would be alive.

Sounds of life filtered in from the halls; the court had risen and were socializing and getting on with their feeds. The hunger was but a dull ache compared to the pain of her bereavement; her body weighted as if with lead and her mind struggling to find a distraction.

She shuffled over to the couch and collapsed upon it, her body sinking into the cushions and pillows. One of them smelled of Àmichemin. Evanangela hugged the pillow close, inhaling her scent. Her eyes pricked, but no tears fell.

A thought bubbled up in her mind. She loosened her grip on the pillow and sat up to face Verseau. His crumpled form was still at his writing desk, his face clouded with anguish.

"What did you mean by 'I have lost another'?"

Verseau turned away. "Please, let me be."

An attendant knocked and Verseau covered his face with his hands as Evanangela opened the door. "Here is Monsieur Jean-Claude, just as Seigneur Verseau requested." The attendant motioned for the slim man to come forward.

Evanangela did not think Verseau had wanted to receive anyone, but when she smelled his mortal blood, her empty veins tightened. "Ah yes, Monsieur Jean-Claude. Entrez, s'il vous plaît."

She closed the door behind the man, and Verseau looked up. He composed himself and engaged in mock conversation. Then he struck with a swiftness that startled her. There was a spray of blood as the man screamed. Verseau lapped at the man's throat, then offered Evanangela his kill. She took it, grateful to ease the tension in her chest and fill her veins. Once she had drained the body, her mind cleared and the full weight of Àmichemin's death smacked her in the heart and took her breath away.

"Oh, Verseau, whatever shall we do without her?" She trembled, smearing her bloody hands on her face.

Verseau drew her away from the dead body and back onto the bed. There he kissed her and whispered in her ear. "Ne gaspille pas ces larmes, ma chérie. Je ne veux pas te voir pleurer."[1]

Evanangela's hands shook and Verseau steadied them with his own. She shook her head. "But…Oh, Àmichemin!"

1 Don't waste those tears, darling. I don't want to see you cry.

He stroked Evanangela's hair. She held her breath to quiet her sobs. Once she had tired herself out, she let her head lean on his shoulder with her eyes closed. They sat together; the hours ticking by as their minds raced. Laughter skuttled in from the hall every now and again, fueling Evanangela's annoyance.

How can anyone laugh? Àmichemin is dead!

She shivered as Verseau bent down to kiss her temple. The blood had warmed his body and made his scent come alive. His presence soothed her anger, but her grief remained.

They stayed there on the floor, staring in silence at the fire, until a knock at the door startled them both. Jacques appeared, and bowed to him once he reached the bedroom. Verseau and Evanangela straightened up.

"The sun is due, mon Seigneur et Mademoiselle."

Chapter Twenty-Six

Evanangela moped on the couch as Verseau sat at his writing desk. The corpses from their feed were cooling on the floor before the fire grate. Their peace was shattered when the familiar knock sounded, and Jacques entered the sitting room.

"Mademoiselle Àmichemin's ashes have been recovered. The attendants have finished repairs on Mademoiselle's coffin. She will be placed in the ballroom for the viewing before she is put to rest, mon Seigneur."

They stared at Jacques, the news thundering through their minds. He bowed; his face pained.

"Do you have any instructions for Mademoiselle's final resting place, mon Seigneur?"

Verseau nodded. "She is to be interred with La Petite Mademoiselle Violette."

Jacques flinched at the name, then bowed again; his eyes on the floor. "I will make the necessary arrangements, Seigneur."

Once the door was closed, the silence broke, and tears streamed down Evanangela's face; wasting her feed. Verseau hid his face as red tears made their way down his cheeks. He took a deep breath, choking down his sobs, then mopped his face with his handkerchief.

"Get dressed, ma chérie. It is time I told you the truth of my reign."

The hall was empty and Evanangela's heels echoed off the stone floor and pillars. Verseau walked a pace behind her, his glassy eyes trained on the path ahead. Tears ran down Evanangela's cheeks, the bloody trails dripping onto her gown. She stopped at the stairs, unable to proceed. The sound of vampires and vixens giggling and talking together rumbled through her, making her cry more.

Verseau put his hand on the banister next to Evanangela and handed her a bloodstained handkerchief. His own tears were beginning to darken into stains in the silk. A hiccup knocked her chest and she swallowed before dabbing the scarlet off her cheeks and from her eyes. She sniffed before returning the soiled cloth. He turned the handkerchief over in his hand, and then let it drop to the floor for an attendant to gather up and wash later.

She turned to face the stair railing and dug her fingernails into the wood. The château seemed an old ruin, empty and full of echoes without Àmichemin's gay laughter. Evanangela's legs trembled and she allowed her body to fold into itself, her legs buckling until she sat upon the floor with her arms around of the wooden poles in the railing. She bared her fangs as her heart burned. Evanangela clenched her teeth so hard that her head began to ache.

Verseau did not look down at her as she made an undignified mess of herself. He stared straight ahead at the tapestry on the wall. It was of the woman on the stag. The one Evanangela had wondered over her first evening at court. He glared at the wall, clenching his fists at his sides. She looked up, took Verseau's hand into hers, brought his knuckles to her lips and kissed them. At this, Verseau looked down at her, his eyes soft, and sighed.

"Come, ma petite, she would not have us idle."

Evanangela nodded and allowed Verseau to help her to her feet, and escort her down the stairs, walking toward the giant tapestry. He pushed it aside. There behind the fabric was a door with a solid opal doorknob. Verseau stroked the stone, rubbing the dust between his fingers.

"Long ago, I loved a young vampiress such as yourself. She was newly born and the most beautiful vampire the court had seen for many years. Her eyes were the most startling. Never have I seen a vampire with crimson eyes like she had. The brightest I have ever seen. Originally, she was brought to the court for the Seigneur who used to preside here. He was a cruel vampire and she did not love him. He tried so hard to make her his own, but she had a wild spirit."

Verseau produced a key from his pocket and unlocked the heavy door. Inside, many white candles were burning with golden flames. Like the rest of the candles in the château, these were enchanted and did not drip wax or lower, simply burned on. There against the center of the back wall was a wooden coffin with a portrait of a lovely lass hanging over it. It looked like a younger version of the woman in the tapestry. Her black curls held back with a black ribbon. And yet, those startling red eyes seemed almost alive. What gave away that this was a painting

228

of no ordinary lass were the tiny cruel points that hung over her lips, slightly open in a smile. Her dress had an embroidered white rose on the bust. Evanangela remembered the night she had worn the same dress, and the alarm in Àmichemin's eyes. Now she understood.

He looked up at the painting and cleared his throat. "This is Mademoiselle Violette."

Evanangela looked up at the portrait again. Before she could ask, Verseau continued.

"Instead of growing to love the Seigneur, she had fallen in love with me, and we stole many a night hiding in the north tower making sweet love. Back then, I was merely a mortal attendant."

Evanangela gasped. "*You* were an attendant?"

Verseau nodded. "Yes, Jacques' family is my family. His forefather was my brother. That is why their line shall always recognize me as their true Seigneur and will protect me."

She drew up Jacques in her mind's eye and began to see the resemblance – the curly hair, the dimple in the right cheek when they smiled, the dark complexion. Her mind buzzed with a dozen questions, but Verseau continued.

"It has been several generations since my brother died," he patted her hand, "Since then, I have seen to it that the attendants be treated with the respect they deserve. They protect us. We are nothing without them."

Evanangela looked up at the portrait again. "What happened to her?"

His face was pained. He took a deep breath. "She loved me as if I were her own kind. She longed to leave the control of the Seigneur and to live a simple life with me. Though of course, such a thing was impossible. But fate smiled upon us. One night when we were making love, I let her feed on me because she had missed the feed just to be with me. I was so taken with the feeling of connection between us when she drank from my veins that no such love making could compare. It was that night I allowed her to take my humanity. She made me into a vampire so I might never be separated from her by time. Once I was a vampire, we engaged in blood-sharing nearly every night for the thrill of that bond. I truly loved her."

229

She recalled Verseau's disdain for her taking Gabriel as a companion. She darted her eyes away. "Wasn't the Seigneur angry that she turned you?"

He shook his head and grimaced. "No, he hardly noticed. In those times, the court was thrice the size. They glutted themselves on so many mortals each night that the bodies were often left rotting in the halls because the attendants could not keep up with the mess. The Seigneur was preoccupied with his harem of vixens and oft ignored La Petite Mademoiselle for nights at a time."

Evanangela cringed. The current court seemed a monastery of godliness compared to such a bordello of gluttony. "What a terrible fate."

Verseau nodded and took Evanangela by the hand and led her up to the coffin. The lid was painted with a single white rose. He stroked the petals. His eyes softened, filled with love, his smile pained.

"When she came to the château, I painted this for her. We fell in love because I was her personal attendant. I built this coffin to keep her safe with my own hands. It's made of the finest teak."

He kissed the coffin, his gaze far away in thought. "I took her to the most magnificent place in all of France, Le Lac des Morts. They say a bond forged in that enchanted place will last eternity. I could think of no better place to seal my love with ma petite princesse."

Evanangela's heart caught in her throat. *So, Verseau had meant to seal his love with me there. Then why did he bring Àmichemin along as well?*

Verseau pulled his hands away from the coffin and held them in clenched fists near his chest.

"But those damn peasants found us there! Whenever they can catch a vampire, they make a holiday of it. They caught us right in the middle of making love in the lake. We made to escape up that same cliff, since there was no other way out, but fate was against us. As we ran toward the cliff a strong archer shot his arrows at us. The first one hit her in the leg, rendering it useless. I carried her, but the archer hit his mark once again, my leg. I fell under her, and yet I still scrambled with her in my arms. I nearly made it high enough up the cliff with her, when the villagers closed in."

Evanangela drew close to Verseau, his arms shaking. She pulled his hands into her hands, and held them, looking at them, not at his face. He too stared at their hands, his voice shook and he cleared his throat again.

"Then, my lovely little princess looked right at me with those beautiful red eyes and said 'I'm too heavy. Let me go, mon cher coeur. Let me fall so you may live.' And even though I told her I could not possibly live without her, she let go of me and dropped right into the mob. They shoved a stake through her heart and later I heard that they left her body there to turn to dust in the sun. I narrowly escaped."

Her eyes were wide. *To think that this vampiress had sacrificed herself so that her love would live. If presented with the opportunity, would I be able to do the same?*

Verseau took a deep breath. His back shuddered as he held back a sob. Evanangela stood, debating whether to comfort him or not. Finally, he spoke again.

"We had broken hibernation to seal our love. It was the only way for us to finally be together. And upon hearing the news that she was dead, the Seigneur destroyed himself and I became the new Seigneur because I had been her lover. The court accepted me, as by that time, the Seigneur had driven the court to famine and destruction. The story was retold that I had been the one to drive the stake through his heart, as no one had witnessed his death. That is the true story of my coup."

Verseau turned back to the painting. "This is how she truly looked and it is haunting to think that such a young lass became damned so early in her life."

Evanangela slid her hand into the crook of Verseau's arm. "How old was she when she was turned?"

"Fifteen."

"How did that happen?"

"The Seigneur found her playing in a garden one night and could not bear the thought of losing her. He made her a vampiress on the spot and discovered his grave mistake in taking her so early after bringing her back to the court."

"Why was it such a terrible mistake?"

"Her face haunted the court. At first, they believed her to be an abomination, a demon child, even to their kind. To have such a young creature flitting about and still discovering the world was eerie to them. That is why the tapestry was made with her looking older, while this true portrait is tucked away."

Evanangela nodded as she stared at the portrait of the smiling girl and shuddered.

"My attendants eventually found her ashes and brought them to me. They are safe in this coffin so that she can find shelter from those monsters in the afterlife."

Verseau led her out of the room. As he locked the door, he uttered a startling comment. "I plan on placing Àmichemin here after the mourning ceremony."

She felt a stab of jealousy and had to stop herself from recoiling as she recalled his earlier command to Jacques. He was to have Àmichemin buried with his true love? Then what did that make her? Evanangela felt a hot blush rush to her cheeks.

"Is that why you brought her with us to Le Lac des Morts?" Her voice sounded fierce, even to herself. And once the words tumbled out of her mouth, she regretted uttering them.

But Verseau only kissed the crown of her hair as they walked. "Oh, ma choupinette, there is no need to be so envious. I loved you both, and I still love you both now. I took you so Àmichemin and I could seal our love with you. We had already sealed our love many, many decades ago. I had wanted us to take that sweet memory into hibernation."

Evanangela dropped her gaze to the floor. Àmichemin's death weighed heavily on her heart once more. She placed her hand over her chest and took a deep breath to ease the wave of grief. It was mixed with the bittersweet joy that Verseau truly loved her at last. She looked up at the tapestry and smiled; glad Àmichemin would not be alone in death.

Together, they walked to the ballroom where an attendant stood before the blood-stained vampires. Verseau hurried Evanangela up to where the attendant was standing and then the attendant began to speak.

"Our dear Mademoiselle Àmichemin was recently killed by those horrible villagers. They drove a stake through her heart, and left her body to burn in the sun."

The court gasped in horror at this. Evanangela felt her heart race as she relived the gruesome death.

"It is due to this tragedy that the hibernation has been delayed as we mourn her loss and honor her dark spirit."

Murmurs rippled through the crowd. The attendant bowed, and allowed Verseau to announce that the night's festivities were over. The vampires dispersed, talking amongst themselves as they headed back to their apartments. A heavy pall of sorrow was drawn over the court; their merriment snuffed out. Evanangela followed Verseau back to his apartments, the newfound secrets whirring in her mind and weighing her body down. With the hibernation delayed, there would be no release from her grief; only the brief respite of their daily death-sleep. Evanangela stared up at the ceiling while draped on the couch until the threat of the sun chased her back into Verseau's coffin. She considered staying, allowing the morning light to burn her to ash so she might join Amichemin. But the thought of leaving Verseau behind with such staggering grief to bear alone pushed her up from the couch and motivated her to shuffle into the safety of the death-sleep.

Chapter Twenty-Seven

Evanangela's body moved on its own as she pulled on a heavy velvet gown. All the sounds around her were muffled; her eyes unseeing as her mind's eye played the gruesome memory over and over. She was aware that Verseau was nearby; buttoning his jacket and straightening his cuffs.

A wave of grief overtook her; her knees buckled and she sunk onto the couch. Her fingernails dug into the soft fabric as her chest tightened and prevented her from breathing. They had not yet fed, so her burning eyes yielded no tears; even as her body lurched with suppressed sobs. After only a few moments, but felt an eternity, a rush of air sucked into her lungs, the grief released its hold, and Evanangela stood up.

"It is time, ma chérie," Verseau whispered as he held out his elbow.

She took it, and together, they glided out into the hall. Only murmurs and breathy whispers punctuated the air as they marched to the ballroom. The vampires and vixens kept their eyes lowered, bowing and curtsying as they passed.

Jacques gestured to the raised stage opposite a grand altar that had been erected where dozens of orchid and violet candles blazed. Their flames were silver, and crackled on their blackened wicks. Amichemin's coffin had been repaired, the beautiful amethyst inlay sparkled as the candlelight flickered.

Verseau's body tensed as his gaze fell on the coffin. Evanangela tried to catch his eye to reassure him, but he looked on. He cleared his throat and let go of her hand.

"We gather this night to mourn and honor our beloved Mademoiselle Amichemin. She ruled by my side for one-hundred and seventy-two years. A true consort and a fearless warrior. I owe her my life, as do all of you. She protected this court again and again. Her loyalty and love are what caused her to lay down her life to save her Seigneur and her dear Mademoiselle Evanangela. For this, we celebrate her life and lay her to rest with the highest of honors."

Polite claps and a few broken sobs punctuated the air. Verseau continued, his fist clenched at his side.

"Àmichemin fought rebellious villagers and defectors of the court with equal vigor and vengeance. It is a great burden that we will enter the long slumber with such a bright star snuffed out. But it is because of this it is all the more important that the court stand united. We cannot stand against this insurgence alone. It is only together that we shall survive."

The court clapped, but without gusto. Evanangela gazed out into the crowd. Amongst the crumpled, crying faces of those lamenting, she also saw stony indifferent faces. Her breath hitched as panic inflamed her heart. Without Àmichemin to protect them, it was clear that some of the court may attempt to assassinate them during the hibernation. Evanangela swallowed her growing dread and stared back at them.

"Now, we feed, and tomorrow the preparations for hibernation resume. You have two nights to see to your affairs."

Verseau nodded, then stepped down from the platform. Evanangela followed him. The doors to the ballroom opened, and a pack of mortal guests streamed in. Excitement rocketed through the air as the court celebrated a modified Valse Noire. The doors were quickly locked, as the vampires could not contain themselves and began slaughtering the mortals at once. There was no dance or play, just brutal ripping of flesh and screams.

Evanangela followed Verseau into the frenzy. He grabbed one of the mortal ladies by the back of her neck, spun her around, and sunk his fangs deep into her vein. Her shocked expression slacked as death crept in. Evanangela allowed her instincts to bubble up through the thick sludge of her sorrow. She slid through the crowd, her eyes darting about, until she found an untouched young man. Her hands were quick as she grabbed him by his jacket, hissing in his face.

"Mon Dieu!" He squealed as she wrenched his head aside by gripping his hair, exposing his neck.

His body thrashed under her, trying to punch and kick her away. She held fast and dove her fangs in for the kill. His blood burst forth and nearly went up her nose from the force as it gushed into her mouth. Evanangela took deep, impatient swallows. Heavy breaths escaped her nose as she suckled, her mind lost. There was only the feed, the blood, the terror; no room for anguish. For a blissful moment, her mind was quiet.

An odd sound ripped Evanangela from her respite. She opened her eyes and allowed the corpse to fall to the floor. The ballroom doors had been unlocked. Several attendants were scrambling to close them once more, but there were no mortals left alive to escape. She stood, wiping the blood from her face with a handkerchief, and approached the frazzled attendants. They recoiled when they saw her and bowed.

"Mademoiselle, our deepest apologies! Three members of your court forced the doors open and ran back into the hall. Such a thing has never happened! We could not stop them-!"

Evanangela put her hand on his shoulder, he quaked under her. "Fear not, you did the right thing. We would not want you to risk your lives dealing with a pack of fools. See to it they are evicted from the château and unable to return. Be sure you have the guards at your side. Let the traitors leave. They can see what life is truly like beyond these walls without the might of the court to protect them."

"At once, Mademoiselle!" He bowed again, relief spreading on his face, and the other attendants followed suit. They scurried off.

Evanangela turned heel and searched for Verseau. He was lounging on the floor, the corpse facedown with limbs askew. She bent down, her voice a tight whisper.

"More have escaped!" She hissed.

His eyes widened and the stupor on his face drained into fear. "More mortals have escaped?" He whispered through his teeth.

She shook her head. "Non, mon Seigneur, more traitors of the court. I ordered the attendants to have the guards banish them and bar them from the château. It all happened so fast, pardonnez-moi."

Verseau got to his feet and dusted himself off. He approached the attendants that were left to guard the doors and nodded to each of them.

"See to it the remaining members of the court are escorted to their apartments. No one besides Mademoiselle and myself will be allowed to roam the halls unattended."

The attendants bowed. "Oui, mon Seigneur!"

He nodded again and the doors opened. Evanangela jumped when they slammed shut behind her with the heavy grind of the locks being set back in place. The click of his shoes echoed in the empty hall. An attendant scurried past, their demeanor frightened and agitated. Evanangela trotted alongside to keep up with his hurried gait.

"Mon Seigneur, the traitors have been spotted leaving the château toward the village." Jacques bowed and hurried alongside Verseau.

"Bien," he did not slow his stride, "they have chosen banishment. They shall be killed on sight should they be foolish enough to return."

"Bien sûr." Jacques bowed again, then opened the apartment doors for them. He locked the doors once they were inside.

Evanangela balked as Verseau turned on her, grabbing her face between both his hands. A startled squeak escaped her throat.

"Be on your guard *every moment.*" His voice was low and his hands were shaking. "I fear history is repeating itself ma chère coeur."

Words escaped Evanangela's mind, her mouth would not move and her voice was lost. She stared into his eyes, her body trembling as he released his grip.

"We may need to hibernate outside the château entirely." He ran his hand through his hair, his eyes darting about. "There is a chance they could find the vaults, harm Jacques and his family. We are sleeping for *one hundred years.* That's plenty of time for them to find us! The risk is so great…so great-"

He trailed off as he sat down at his writing desk, his head in his hands. Evanangela was frozen, unsure if comforting him would help or make him more frantic. Jacques stood at her side.

Verseau sprang up again, his eyes wild. "We shall leave! We shall leave tomorrow once the last ray of light has extinguished-"

"But what about Àmichemin?" Evanangela cried, her voice bursting forth at last.

"Àmichemin?" Verseau was bewildered, as if she had struck him. He dropped his gaze to the floor, his voice cracking with sorrow, "We shall have to leave her."

Evanangela felt a strange rage grip her as she screamed. "She has yet to be interred! We cannot leave her!"

Verseau grabbed her face again, covering her wailing mouth with his hand. "Quiet! We cannot let anyone hear this!" He hissed in her ear. "Control yourself!"

She nodded as tears slid down her cheeks. He released his hand and she gasped for breath. Jacques caught her before she crumpled to the floor and helped guide her onto the couch where she dissolved into hysterical sobbing.

He stared at her; his eyes glazed over with far-away thoughts. Jacques cleared his throat, bringing him back to the present.

"Seigneur, what are your orders?"

Verseau nodded, his reason returning. "Oui, oui. I cannot risk the court harming your family or holding you hostage in order to discover and open the vault. We shall have to wait until the court has fallen into hibernation, lest they suspect our absence. Your daughter is a swift rider. Send her to request an official summons with Master Étienne. Express to them our dire situation and request sanctuary for myself, Mademoiselle, you, and your family."

Jacques bowed low. "At once, mon Seigneur."

Evanangela sat up, a new wave of panic ripping through her mind. "But we have already asked so much of them! And you said they will see our weakness as an opportunity to take our lands!"

Verseau sat down on the couch. His shoulders slumped as he took her hands in his and kissed them. "Ma chérie, are you prepared to give up being a princess in order to safeguard your life?"

She stared at him in horror as she put the pieces together. "You are going to give them the Nacre Court? Le Château d'Astucieux? La Maison de Printemps?"

He nodded. Evanangela pulled her hands away. "How can you not fight for your title and your lands? This is our home!"

A long gust of breath escaped his lips. He did not meet her gaze. "I have already lost so much. I cannot lose you, ma chère coeur. We have already killed nearly half the court. Those that are left are still defecting. And now, we no longer have Àmichemin to protect us. We have lost."

The room spun as she absorbed his words. Evanangela could hear the muffled sounds of the court being escorted to their apartments. Some were cheery as they chatted, others sounded indignant. She shivered as she recalled the stoic faces that stared up at her in the ballroom. How many of them wanted her dead?

"The previous Seigneur died because he foolishly held onto the court when it was clear the court was no longer his. It would only have been a matter of time before a defector killed him, had he not done it himself. Now, the court has decided that I am no longer their Seigneur. It is unclear if they have chosen a new leader or not. Either way, with the blood shortage and the looming hibernation, the court will fall into chaos and likely eat itself whether we are dead or in exile."

His words chilled her. She met his gaze; his eyes were forlorn and brimming with red tears. He opened his arms, and she curled up into his lap, resting her head on his shoulder. Verseau embraced her. She could feel his living heart beating as she leaned against his chest. It was soothing. But even as the frantic thoughts dripped away, the looming danger still hung over her like a sword about to drop.

"Àmichemin would not have us lay down our lives in vain," he whispered, kissing her hair. "We must live. That is her greatest wish."

They sat together in silence, absorbing strength from one another as they embraced. After what seemed hours, Verseau gave her head one last kiss, then settled her back onto the couch and sat down at his writing desk.

She watched as he wrote an official statement, their plea to the Mors Ivoire Court. As the words were inked onto the page, she felt the gravity of Verseau's words come to roost in her heart.

I shall no longer be a princess. I shall be a common vampiress in their court. I shall have to bow to their Seigneur, simpering and skulking about hallways. Verseau and I shall have to live together in a cramped room. Will we bicker as they oft do?

Evanangela looked about the room, seeing the luxury and beauty of the space around her that she lounged in night after night. All this would be gone; likely pillaged by the remaining members of the court, or destroyed by the peasants. She dropped her face into her hands. Had her heart not been so swallowed by grief and fear, she would have laughed.

A fitting prison. I have fallen from Heaven for my vanity, and now I shall fall further. I do not deserve the grand airs that have been bestowed upon me.

"Jacques!" Verseau called.

Evanangela jumped at the sound of his voice. Jacques strode in at once, having waited in the sitting room. He bowed, his eyes falling on the parchment held out to him.

"Have your son take this to Master Étienne. He must explain the dire need to send word before the official written request and our humble apologies in our need for haste."

Jacques took the letter and bowed again. "At once, mon Seigneur."

Once the door shut, Verseau slumped in his chair and heaved a great sigh. He leaned his head back against the chair and looked up at the ceiling.

"I fear I must retire early, ma chère fleur," he mumbled, "I cannot stand another minute of this night."

Evanangela stood from the couch as he heaved himself to his feet. He kissed her on the forehead, gave her one last sad look, kicked off his shoes, then climbed into the coffin, fully-clothed. She sat back down on the couch. The room felt as if it were pressing down on her, as if the weight of the entire château was upon her back. She curled up against the armrest, allowing her body to sink into the cushions and pillows.

The moon was high in the sky; another hour yet to pass before sunrise, at least. Her thoughts returned to Àmichemin. The thought of escaping into exile while her remains sat in the ballroom, at risk of desecration made Evanangela's heart drop. She made up her mind; she would take Àmichemin with her; no matter the cost.

Chapter Twenty-Eight

Evanangela crept through the massive doors to the ballroom, her bare feet silent on the marble floor. The court was locked in their apartments, leaving the halls empty; save for the few attendants scurrying about. The pine boughs that had once adorned the ballroom had been replaced with holly leaves, the red berries dripping like tiny bleeding hearts. It seemed odd to her that with the château barricaded for a siege that such details were still carried out. She scoffed as she ran down the stretch of dance floor to the altar.

As she approached, her throat tightened and her heart trembled. The finality that Àmichemin was truly dead struck her. Red tears dripped down Evanangela's cheeks like tiny bloody rivers as she threw herself before the stone pedestal. The lacy hem of her gown fluttered about her knees and settled over her calves in ripples as she knelt.

She wailed, open mouthed, and gasped in a raspy whisper, "M'Àmichemin! Ma chère Àmichemin!"

Evanangela beat her fists upon the stone step, her teeth clenched tight. Her fangs cut into her bottom lip until blood trickled down her chin. "Pourquoi?" She demanded with every bash of her fist. "Pourquoi?!"

Her cries echoed in the grand empty ballroom. She choked on her sobs and wiped her face with the back of her hand. Evanangela drew herself up and stared into the coffin. The sight she beheld made her gasp and retch. It was not Àmichemin's body at rest, but a disheveled pile of ash and charred bones. Her lovely star-filled hair was gone; only a bald skull with empty eye sockets remained. The sun had burned away all her loveliness and the skeleton had been hastily arranged into the coffin, adding to the grotesque farce.

"Those monsters!" Desperation and rage howled in her heart as she recalled her shreds of decency, giving quick dispatch to the peasants while the court was returning from the maison. "Foul monsters leaving you like this!"

"Princesse-?" A familiar voice echoed through the ballroom.

Startled, Evanangela whirled about, her back pressed against the side of the coffin. Her shoulders slumped when saw Gabriel.

"Non! Non!" Evanangela wailed as she covered her smeared face with her bloody hands. "Ne me regarde pas!"

He kneeled and tried to put his arms around her, clumsy with protocol. But Evanangela writhed away. He grabbed her wrist, but she thrashed like a wild animal.

"Non! Non! Àmichemin!" Evanangela screamed as she flailed. Her attempts were useless under Gabriel's strong grip. She fell as her unshod foot slipped on the lacey hem of her dress, knocking her head on the stone step with a metallic thud. Her jaw snapped her teeth and a shriek of pain pierced the air.

Gabriel gasped and scooped Evanangela up off the floor into his arms. She clutched her head. Protocol momentarily forgotten; he rocked her like a small child.

"Ç'est d'accord, ç'est d'accord." Gabriel whispered. He ran his fingers through her hair, and Evanangela buried her face in his jacket. Soon, the two of them were smattered in blood from her tears, but he continued to soothe her. After a length, Evanangela pushed him away and glanced about at the remaining glass windows.

"Le soliel!" She gasped, but Gabriel ensnared her once more and forced her to face the window.

She tried to bite Gabriel, but he kept her jaws at bay with his arm locked under her chin. "Princesse! Quietez-vous s'il vous plaît! Voici! Ç'est la lune! La lune, princesse!"

Evanangela froze and opened one eye. Sure enough, there was the moon beaming innocently through the windows. "Quoi-?"

"You have been so swallowed with grief that you have lost track of time. There are still two hours before the sunrise," he loosened his grip as she was overcome with confusion, "Princesse, I have something wonderful to tell you."

"Quoi?" She stood blinking at him.

"Le Dieu sent me to watch over your punishment, Evanangela."

Hot terror shot through her. She gripped the edge of the coffin to keep herself from swooning as she had not fully recovered from fearing the rising sun. "How did you know about that?!"

"I am the archangel, Gabriel, sent here by Seigneur Dieu to watch over you. You have learned so many things, petite plume. Since you have been here, you have put aside your obscene sin. Mended your wings so to speak."

Evanangela wrapped her arms about herself. Being forgiven had never crossed her mind since she had fallen. Had she been presented with that option the night in the churchyard she would have taken it in an instant. But now, the thought of abandoning Verseau and Àmichemin was even more frightening than the looming threat of her exile to the Mors Ivoire Court.

"But Michael came to punish me further. *He* is the one who killed Àmichemin." She took a deep breath. "Her death is on my hands."

She looked up again at the window. Only Gabriel's reflection was visible. She stepped forward and traced her fingers on the glass, creating the outline of her reflection from memory; lingering where her wings had once been.

"Dieu gives gifts, and to you he gave the lovely gift of the most beautiful silver wings any angel had ever seen." Gabriel traced the faint scars on Evanangela's shoulders from under the lace of her gown.

Evanangela flinched and moved away from his hands. "That was a long time ago." She darted her eyes away from the window to the floor.

"You were so very vain, petite plume. So very vain. You thought those wings of yours made you higher than even the archangels. Michael still holds such resentment in his heart that you choose me over him. He saw our bond as an extension of your vanity – of your bond with Àmichemin as an extension of your vanity."

Gabriel moved closer behind Evanangela, his eyes on the moon. "And even when Dieu damned you to the most painful existence – eternity without being able to gaze upon your own beauty; you found a way to truly live."

She spun around, her hair spraying with a ghost of how Àmichemin's hair used to. "I am not vain! I don't even think of that life anymore!"

Gabriel removed his jacket, and enormous white wings unraveled from his shoulders. The crystal chandelier above tinkled as his flight feathers brushed it. "Because you learned how to care about something other than yourself. You were willing to burn in the impending sunrise for the love you bear this creature. You care for the attendants and for Verseau. You even cared for me and safeguarded my life."

"Àmichemin." Evanangela turned back to the coffin. She slid her hands over the lip, gazing down at the gruesome remains, her mind filling in Àmichemin's features.

Gabriel placed his hands on her shoulders. "Because you have attained grace, even while living as a damned creature, Dieu is willing to forgive you."

She shook her head. "There is no forgiveness for the things I have done. I have killed so many. And I took pleasure in it! I am a damned creature."

"All creatures do what they must to survive. That is what you did, *survived*. You did not glut yourself as these other vile creatures did. You did not cause unnecessary suffering when given the choice. You showed mercy in the face of everything. I have been able to stay by your side through the grace of your mercy."

"What does that mean?"

"It means that you can come home." A light emanated from Gabriel.

Evanangela backed away from him until she felt the chill of the window panes against her skin. "No! I cannot leave Verseau."

The light around Gabriel dimmed. "But you can become an angel again. Isn't that wonderful to you?"

"No!" Evanangela shifted uncomfortably. "I can't leave Verseau," she looked over at the coffin, "or Àmichemin."

She squared her shoulders and nodded. "You can tell le Seigneur Dieu that heaven is no longer my home. I am a damned creature of the night."

Gabriel sighed, exasperated. "I don't understand. Isn't there anything? Even to just have your wings back?"

Evanangela cracked a weak smile. "I don't need those anymore. But I do need her." She gestured at the coffin.

"But, Evanangela, she is a truly damned creature. Though Michael's vengeance was born of selfishness and ill-intent, the atrocities she has wrought-!"

"Elle est ma meilleur amie! Ne parlez-vous malade elle jamais!"[1] Evanangela bared her fangs. "Àmichemin showed me grace the night I fell from heaven. She saved me and brought me here. She raised me up to have status where my mercy *mattered*. I owe her *everything!*"

He did not flinch at this furious display, instead, he turned and strode up to the coffin.

"What are you doing?" Evanangela hissed as she leaned over the coffin, shielding the remains.

"I am giving you the only reward you will allow me to grant. I am giving you back the thing that has given you grace among the damned."

Gabriel flared his wings and held his hands over Àmichemin's ashes. Slowly, the grey dust began to melt together, smoothing and lightening, until it became supple skin. Her hair grew from the naked skull until it nearly clothed her in its radiant locks. At long last, her eyelashes grew black and full, and fluttered to reveal her vibrant violet eyes. Evanangela could scarcely breathe as Àmichemin sat up in her coffin and scanned her surroundings.

"Evanangela, what-?"

"Oh, Àmichemin!" She threw her arms around Àmichemin's neck and wept until her tears fell onto Àmichemin's smooth back.

"What is all this about? And what am I doing sleeping in the middle of the ballroom?" She trembled and patted her body with her hands. "Didn't the villagers put a stake through my heart? I thought I was dead!"

Àmichemin untangled herself from Evanangela's grip and climbed out onto the marble steps. "We must tell Verseau-"

"You were killed, Àmichemin." Gabriel folded his wings behind him. "You became ash and bone at the hands of the mortal peasants."

---

1 She is my dearest friend! Never speak poorly of her!

She screamed when she saw Gabriel's angelic form and pushed Evanangela behind her. "Stay back!" She hissed and bared her fangs. "I *knew* there was something wrong with you! I always thought it was odd she insisted on keeping you!"

"Pardonnez-moi, Mademoiselle." Gabriel gave a deep bow. "Je suis Gabriel, l'ange d'élevé de Dieu."[2]

"What are you doing here?" Àmichemin growled.

Evanangela's voice was low. "He was sent here to bring me back home."

Àmichemin spat her words with vehement disgust. "What?! You're leaving? You're going to leave? Just like that?"

"No. She has refused to return to the heavens. Instead, I resurrected you as reward for her grace. She insisted." Gabriel smiled.

She stood, mouth agape. "You gave up returning to heaven for me?"

Evanangela nodded, a fierce blush burning on her cheeks. "Tu es ma meilleur amie, Àmichemin. I cannot live without you."

More tears escaped down Evanangela's cheeks, and Àmichemin brushed them away with the tip of her finger. Evanangela threw her arms about her waist in a tight embrace. Àmichemin made a small noise of discomfort, then rested her head on Evanangela's shoulder. "Tu es vraiment ma meilleur amie, Evanangela."

They separated, and Àmichemin gave a wry smile. "Honestly, how could you refuse *heaven* for me?"

"You were the first to show me grace," Evanangela took Àmichemin's hands into her own, "you saved me in that churchyard when the priest sought to kill me. Were it not for you, I would not have learned true mercy and love."

Gabriel nodded. "Yes, the true hallmarks of piety. You are an odd one, you cursed creature."

Her eyes unfocused as she heard Dieu's voice for the first time since she had fallen.

---

2 I am Gabriel, the exalted angel of God.

Child of Darkness, I cannot forgive you, but I can love you.

Evanangela brought her hands to her chest while still holding Àmichemin's hands. She heaved a shaking sigh as the spirit moved her. "I once was a child of the light, but then you banished me to desolation in the darkness. But in the darkness, I found the light of friendship and love. Are we not but the two sides of the same coin? One cannot exist without the other and together they birth the mortal creature, keeper of powers from both worlds, keepers of the ultimate power: the power to choose. The choice to be one or the other, and yet be ultimately both. There is no evil and no purity, only the light and the darkness."

"Ah, you have discovered the divine Truth, petite plume." He smiled.

His face dropped, and he whispered to the both of them. "I give you this gift, petite plume, for a reckoning is coming. One that I cannot protect you from. I'm sorry."

Gabriel folded his great wings about him and disappeared. Only a single feather remained on the cold marble floor. Evanangela bent down and plucked it. She straightened up and held it before her, admiring the luminescent sheen.

"Thank you," she whispered before tucking it into a pocket in her gown alongside Verseau's handkerchief.

Chapter Twenty-Nine

Àmichemin snapped to attention. "We must tell Verseau! It's impossible to keep your secret now that you've had me resurrected of all things!"

"What?" Evanangela flinched. "But he'll have me killed!"

"Why would he do such a thing?" Àmichemin wrinkled her nose, "You *saved* me!"

Evanangela darted her eyes away. "So much has changed since your death. The court is turning against us. Verseau has sent word for us to escape to the Mors Ivoire Court."

"The Mors Ivoire?" Àmichemin grabbed Evanangela's hand and dragged her toward the doors. "We must speak to him, immediately."

They strode down the hall toward Verseau's apartments. Evangela felt the panic rising in her chest with every step. The attendants froze at the sight of Àmichemin, their faces paled. Jacques flinched; his shoulder banged against the door as he beheld her form.

"Mademoiselle Àmichemin!" He squeaked, "You're *alive?*"

She nodded. "Oui, there is much to discuss."

He fumbled to unlock the door and his body shook as he bowed to grant them entry. Àmichemin strode past, unbothered. She flung open one of the wardrobes and pulled one of her dressing robes on.

"There, that's better." She muttered. "So, your angel friend said we still have an hour of night?"

Evanangela nodded. She tried to find her voice, but her nerves silenced her.

"Good." Àmichemin flicked her hair over her shoulder in her familiar haughty way. "We'll need all the time we can get if everything truly has gone to hell without me."

251

She knocked on the coffin, then pried it open. Verseau's form was stiff, though his body was not yet cold. Àmichemin poked him in the chest, causing his eyes to snap open.

He drew in a shaky breath and struggled to move his limbs as the death-sleep was only just melting away. "Àmichemin?"

"Yes, it is I. Apparently, neither of you bumbling fools can live without me, so here I am." She grinned.

"Àmichemin!" Verseau cheered. "How is this possible?!"

She took his hands and helped pull him from the coffin and he threw his arms about her. "You're real!"

"Oui, very real," she embraced him.

Jacques cleared his throat, startling the trio. "Forgive me, Seigneur et Mademoiselles, I must insist, *how* is this possible?"

Àmichemin released Verseau and gestured to Evanangela. "Care to explain?"

She squeezed her hands to keep them from trembling. She dropped her gaze, unable to meet Verseau's eye. "J'étais une ange." Her voice was low, nearly a whisper.

"You were an *angel?*" Verseau spat the word. "That's…that's impossible! What do you mean by saying such an atrocious thing?"

Àmichemin patted Verseau's hand. "C'est vrais, Evanangela, *Evan-angel-a*, was an angel before she was turned."

Verseau's eyes widened. *"How?"*

Evanangela took a deep breath, her limbs shaking. "I was banished from heaven by Dieu for my vanity. I was more concerned with my appearance than my duties. My vanity grew into pride, thinking myself above even the highest of angels and comporting myself with selfishness. My shame still burns bright for my gross behavior. Dieu cast me from heaven to be reborn as a vampire, damning me to an eternity of never gazing upon my own reflection again."

He struggled to form words. Àmichemin released his hands.

"I knew."

He cringed. "You knew? How dare you keep such a thing from me!"

Àmichemin's voice raised an octave. "I did it to protect all of us! Can you imagine what would happen if the court knew of such a thing?"

"Non! Non, non, non!" Verseau shook his head and marched toward his writing desk. He collapsed into his chair, holding his head in his hands. "I am dreaming. I am somehow dreaming. This is not real. *You* are not real."

She put her arms around Evanangela. "I'm sorry we could not tell you. But now you know the truth. And I am here. We can save the court."

Verseau waved his hand. "It is too late. I have already sent the missive to the Mors."

"You're giving up?" Àmichemin spat, releasing Evanangela, "How *dare* you! After all I've done to keep that crown on your head!"

"The court is utterly poisoned. More traitors have defected. Your death pushed them over the edge. There is no going back now. We cannot survive a hibernation and a coup. The previous Seigneur showed us the impossibility of such a thing."

Àmichemin pressed her lips together until they were a harsh line. She balled her hands into fists, then blew out a long breath, allowing the rage to escape her body. "You are right. This is why you are the Seigneur. Damn your level-headedness."

"I still don't understand how you are alive," Verseau's voice was tired.

Evanangela met his gaze at last. "It was Gabriel's doing. He was not a mortal at all, but the archangel Gabriel. I was unaware until he revealed himself to me tonight. It was he who resurrected Àmichemin, as a gift for my grace since I refused to reenter heaven."

Verseau stared at her, his eyelids peeled back. "Quoi?"

"My personal attendant," she repeated, "he was also an angel."

He jumped to his feet and threw his hands in the air. "Is *everyone* un ange?"

Àmichemin rolled her eyes, "Now you're just being ridiculous."

"*I'm* being ridiculous?" He hissed, then threw his hands at Evanangela, "*this* is ridiculous!"

Àmichemin softened her gaze and took Verseau's hands in hers to help calm him. "It is overwhelming to say the least. Gabriel has gone back without Evanangela. She chose to stay with us, as a vampire. She chose to save me instead of reclaim her grace. We can trust her."

Verseau stood, and Àmichemin moved aside. His bewildered eyes scanned Evanangela's face. She trembled; afraid he might strike her. At long last, he stroked her cheek.

"All this time," he shook his head, "your naïveté, your odd little suppositions, all of it was because you were never mortal to begin with. But why would you choose to continue your punishment? Why not escape eternal damnation?"

Evanangela smiled as she held her hand against his as he cupped her cheek. "Because it was only a punishment at first. I will miss Gabriel, dearly. He was my favorite companion in the eternal kingdom. But I have grown to love you and Àmichemin. This has become my home. And if existing as a child of darkness is the price, I happily pay it."

Verseau embraced her. "Ma chère, chère choupinette. I cannot thank you enough. Thank you for bringing ma chère fleur noire back to me."

She wrapped her arms around him, relief washing over her, relaxing for the first time that night. Evanangela drew in the comfort of his familiar faint scent. When he pulled away, he took a deep breath and smiled at her.

"We cannot change what has already been set into motion, but now the three of us can escape together."

Jacques cleared his throat and gave Verseau a cheeky smile. He laughed and clapped him on the shoulder.

"And you and your family, my old friend. Of course."

Verseau sat back down at his writing desk. Evanangela sank onto the couch, allowing the cushions to envelope her. Àmichemin leaned against the wall, her familiar bored expression restored.

"We cannot allow the court to discover our true plans," Verseau fiddled with a quill, "we must keep it a secret that we are escaping the château. After the court has been laid to rest in hibernation, we will make our move. No doubt, they will begin searching for the vault the following night. We will only have an hour before sunrise to get into the carriages and away from the château."

Àmichemin nodded, then gestured to Jacques, "I'm sure that's where you come in."

He nodded and bowed.

"Bien, bien," Verseau waved his hand, "now, Àmichemin, did anyone see you?"

"Oui, some of the attendants saw me in the hall, but none of the court." She shrugged.

Verseau shook his head. "There is no way we can lie about your resurrection. There will be rumors flying wild. Best to give them a piece of truth to protect our more important lie."

She scoffed. "And how exactly are we going to explain that?"

"That I did it," Evanangela piped up, "the court has no idea what I'm capable of. Let's make them fear me."

"Oh, ma chérie, becoming bold at last?" Àmichemin grinned, a playful glint sparked in her eyes.

He shot Àmichemin a look. "We must stay focused. Evanangela, that is an excellent idea. The court *doesn't* know what you are capable of. It will be an easy lie. Now then, that makes our plan easier as we will have an excuse to set the hibernation in motion, rather than delaying it to mourn Àmichemin. The sooner we leave, the safer we will be."

Àmichemin shifted away from the wall and draped herself onto the couch. "Then it is agreed. Tomorrow night, we shall put on a grand play detailing my incredible resurrection, and Evanangela will dazzle them with her touching story of love and devotion to me."

Evanangela giggled. Her heart felt at ease hearing Àmichemin's sarcastic tone and seeing her mischievous smile. She leaned against Àmichemin and sighed.

"I missed you."

Àmichemin wrapped her arms about her and kissed her hair. "I missed you too."

Verseau cleared his throat, then flicked his gaze to Jacques. "I trust you with the necessary arrangements for our coffins and the carriages. Be sure the swiftest horses are yoked, but be sure not to arouse suspicion. Pack as light as your family can, there will not be much room for us in the new court."

"Of course, mon Seigneur," Jacques bowed low.

He departed, locking the door behind him. Verseau sighed and leaned back in his chair, his face weary. He rubbed his eyes.

"Ah ma chérie douleur, what am I to do with you?" Verseau grumbled.

Àmichemin lounged on the couch, allowing the dressing gown to fall open. "Ah yes, how dare I rise from the dead without consulting your schedule?" She snarked, then laughed as she tossed a pillow at him.

He caught it, grinning. "Now you're just asking for trouble."

"When am I not?" She slid further down on the couch into an unflattering position, her voice cheeky and low.

Verseau sprung from his chair and tackled Àmichemin, showering her with kisses. The two of them giggled and laughed, hitting one another with pillows. Evanangela leaned against the couch armrest. There would be little time for mirth once the court found out about the resurrection. She held her hand over her chest, willing the moment to last.

He wrestled the pillow away from Àmichemin and kissed her deep. She slid her arms around his neck, pulling him against her body. He released her, then dragged his fangs over her jugular vein.

"As sweet as blood-sharing would be, the sun is nearly upon us."

Verseau took Àmichemin's hand and kissed it, his gaze locked onto hers. He tilted his head and smiled at Evanangela, holding his hand out to her.

"Merci, ma petite, for making my heart whole again."

The following nightfall, they Jacques slid the coffin lid back, letting the firelight coax them to wake. Evanangela yawned and sat up; first to awaken. Verseau stretched, his arm bumping Àmichemin. He gasped, the previous night flooding back, and squeezed Àmichemin in a tight embrace.

256

"Ma chère coeur, it was not a dream! You are truly here!"

Àmichemin batted him away as she yawned. "C'est vrai."

After a few moments, Verseau released her. "There isn't a moment to waste."

Evanangela clambered out of the coffin and began sorting through her clothing. "Oui, Seigneur. There are many preparations we must make with the new plan-"

She glanced back and saw Verseau and Àmichemin kissing, their arms wound about each other, their fingers gripping flesh tight as if they could not bear to let go. Evanangela's voice died in her throat.

"We must celebrate your return," Verseau's voice was low as he nipped at her neck, eliciting a fresh gasp from Àmichemin, "but we must save our strength for the dangers that lie ahead."

Àmichemin leaned back into the coffin and wound her legs around his waist. "Well then, we shall find another way to celebrate."

Verseau's chuckle sent shivers through Evanangela as he dipped his head to kiss Àmichemin's neck, making his way down. All at once, she felt lonely. She had never seen them make love together without her. Evanangela dropped her stockings and walked into the sitting room. She huddled on one of the footstools, trying to ignore the sounds of their pleasure.

This must be why the court bickers and sends envious side glances and snide comments to one another. This jealousy could eat anyone alive. Can I overcome it for our cramped life at the Mors Ivoire Court?

Evanangela wound her arms around herself leaning her head against the wall. The hallway was quiet, and at first, she found it eerie, then she remembered that the court was likely sleeping as it was only the first hour of nightfall. She traced the pattern on the tile with her toe as she waited for their moaning to die down.

"Are you all right?" Àmichemin put her hand on Evanangela's shoulder.

She flinched; her thoughts had taken her far away. "Oui! Ça va."

Àmichemin held out her hand and pulled Evanangela to her feet. "Why are you pouting? Did you think we had forgotten you?"

She kept her gaze lowered, knowing she was acting childish. "A little."

Verseau leaned down and kissed her hair. "Ma petite, you should have said so."

"Besides," Àmichemin gathered her up in her arms and hugged her tight, "it's always so much more fun with you!"

Evanangela laughed as Àmichemin set her back down, then led her back to the coffin. Àmichemin untied Evanangela's dressing gown and pushed until it slid to the floor. Verseau sat down behind her, and kissed her neck, dusting his fingertips over her back. His touch flared her heart, making her skin ripple with pleasure.

"We may not do everything together when we leave for the new court," Àmichemin whispered, "but we will always make sure we all feel included when it matters most."

She squeezed Àmichemin's hand, grateful for the reassurance. His hands explored her body, teasing her most delicate places while Àmichemin guided Evanangela. The château melted away as Evanangela joined in. The moon glimmered through the windows against the inky black sky. With the court asleep, the only sounds were the faint scurrying of attendants in the hall bustling to and fro on their daytime chores, and the guttural sounds of the trio's love-making. They reveled in one another, seeking comfort for the challenges that loomed before them until the clouds dispersed and the stars sparkled in all their glory.

Chapter Thirty

Verseau slid from the tangle of limbs on the couch. He stretched and looked down at his consorts. "Ah, mes fleurs, the time has come. The court will be waking soon."

Àmichemin grumbled as she pushed herself up off the pillows. She gave him a naughty look as she sauntered over to the wardrobe. He laughed and shook his head.

"Come now, we must reveal your resurrection to the court."

She stuck her tongue out at him, then began sifting through the gowns. Her hands caressed the fabrics until she plucked a dainty lilac gown and threw it at Evanangela. "Wear this."

Evanangela gathered up the lacy garment into her arms. "Shouldn't we wear something more practical for our *departure*?"

Àmichemin shook her head and pulled out a deep violet gown with a daring neckline. "Non, we need to impress the court with our power. We may not be able to regain the allegiance of the court, but we can strike fear into their hearts to deter their desire to strike against us."

She stood up from the couch and set aside the dress. Àmichemin began tossing undergarments, and Evanangela gathered them up. Verseau was deep in his own wardrobe, futzing over which jacket to wear.

"The red one," Àmichemin called over her shoulder, "we are celebrating. The black was for my mourning."

He nodded and slid the jacket back into the wardrobe. They settled into silence as they dressed, each lost in their own thoughts. At long last, Àmichemin tossed her hair back and looked both of them over.

"This will certainly have the court in an uproar. I can't wait to see their faces!"

Verseau laughed as she trotted to the door. Together, the three of them alighted into the hall. Most of the court were still in their apartments, as it was only just past the hour of the newly fallen night. Those that entered the hall to be first to the feed froze when they saw Àmichemin stride past.

The whispers grew as the trio marched toward the ballroom, the rumors flying quick as lightning; and soon, the entire court was spilling out into the hall to catch a glimpse. The vixens hid behind their fans their faces ranging from awe, to fear, to scathing rage. Evanangela held her head high, keeping her gaze straight ahead. She would not give them the satisfaction of revealing her masked fear.

"Presenting, Seigneur Verseau, et Mademoiselle Àmichemin, et Mademoiselle Evanangela!"

Several courtiers flinched at Àmichemin's name as the attendant's voice rang out. The doors to the ballroom opened and the trio stepped over the threshold. Their chatter echoed as the court spilled into the ballroom. They huddled together on the dance floor. Evanangela saw the slight twitch in Àmichemin's face as she beheld how small the court was, how many were missing. Her fearsome icy glare softened, replaced with her cheeky grin as she stepped forward, spread her arms wide, and called out to the court.

"Bonsoire, mes charmants! I have returned!"

Her cheer was met with silence. Àmichemin gestured to Evanangela, urging her to step forward.

"My unprecedented revival was carried out by Mademoiselle Evanangela." She allowed her gaze to fall on a few of the court members, cementing the power of her decree. "Though I take away life, Evanangela has revealed she has the power to give life."

Àmichemin took Verseau's hand. "A perfect combination for our Seigneur."

Evanangela looked out at the court. She took a deep breath to still her nerves. "It is true. I resurrected Àmichemin. My love for her was so great, I willed her ash to become soft flesh once more. I risked the burning sunrise to perform this act, as without Àmichemin, my heart would have forever been incomplete."

Verseau stepped forward with Àmichemin draped on his arm. He held out his hand to Evanangela and she took it. The trio was a formidable monolith against the court. As whispers flicked about, the tension in the room rose.

"With Àmichemin once more at my side, we can finally move the court forward into the new era. Together, we shall sleep in love, not loss. Take this night to celebrate Àmichemin's return and for the coming hibernation. Tomorrow night, the court will be moved down to the catacombs."

Outrage erupted in the ballroom as the vampires protested. Evanangela knew they would not take the news well, but she never thought they would be so forward with their feelings. She held her hand over her heart.

They truly do hate us. There is no going back.

"Silence!"

Verseau's voice boomed over the wave of unrest. All at once, the ballroom was silent again. But the tension buzzed so loud Evanangela could hear ringing in her ears. Àmichemin's face was that of stone, unyielding and unfeeling. He cleared his throat.

"Enjoy the night. Tomorrow, we sleep."

The finality of his words cut through the court. Evanangela saw some of them shiver and others flinch. Verseau led them off the stage, allowing the music to fill the room, cutting through the stifling pressure. The trio kept their distance as the court formed little knots and clusters about the room. Verseau had Evanangela and Àmichemin keep their backs to the wall with a clear sightline to the doors.

"I suppose that could have gone worse," Àmichemin whispered as her eyes darted about the chatting vampires.

He titled his head, his eyes still on the crowd. "Your death emboldened them. And so, it seems your resurrection cannot return that discord to its box."

The doors to the ballroom opened again, and the royal guard spilled in. Gasps bounced about the room as the vampires became frantic, looking from them to Verseau. But the guards did not approach the court. Instead, they took positions in front of the windows, and on either side of the doors. The nervous chatter rose to frightened whispering and outraged defamations.

All ceased once the powerful scent of mortal flesh wafted into the room. The attendants announced various merchants and even lowly tradesmen as the mortals entered. Members of the court broke off, pairing up with the new arrivals. On the surface, it seemed as if they had fallen back into complacency with La Valse Noire.

Evanangela took a tentative step toward the dance, but Verseau ensnared her wrist. She flinched, looking up at him.

"Ne vas pas,"[1] he shook his head, "It is not safe for us to separate."

One of the attendants approached the trio and bowed. He had three mortals in tow behind him.

"Seigneur Verseau, might I introduce Monsieur Thomas Renard and his associates?"

Verseau released Evanangela's hand and nodded. "Oui, bonsoire gentlemen. I hope the night finds you well."

The merchants bowed low. "Mon Seigneur et mes Mademoiselles, it is an honor to be in your presence!"

"Oui, it is a pleasure to have you in my court. There is much to discuss. However, let us enjoy the offerings of the night before we fill our heads with negotiations and our coffers with gold." Verseau's smile seemed genuine, his charming gaze disarming the men further.

Evanangela watched as the attendants left the ballroom, the doors booming shut behind them. The guards remained. Their gazes followed the mortals and the members of the court. Àmichemin stood a pace away from them, her gaze also following the members of the court as their waltz brought them closer to the trio, like the ebb and flow of the tide. She swallowed her alarm and focused her attention on her prey.

Verseau was chatting with two of the merchant men, but the third stood apart from them. He appeared younger. An apprentice perhaps. Evanangela allowed her instincts to take over, the haze of the hunt pushing her voice to purr and her hands to delicately invade his personal space in the guise of simpering conversation.

"Is this your first time at court? I have not seen you before." Evanangela allowed her eyes to rake over his form. The mortal shivered and his face went red.

"Ah! Oui, Mademoiselle, oui! Papa has granted me the privilege of attending tonight."

---

1 Do not go,

She giggled and brushed her hand over his shoulder. "Such conversations of stuffy old trade bore me. I'm sure you have far more *engaging* things to tell me about your visit."

His eyes went wide and he struggled to speak. Evanangela sighed, feigning boredom and leaned against him. His body was warm. She could feel his pulse thundering as his nerves mixed with his masculine excitement. The scent of his arousal amused her.

"Tell me, is this what you envisioned for your first trade negotiation?" She caressed his cheek, sliding her hand down until it sat idle on his shoulder.

He was so red in the face and far too flustered to speak. The music swelled, rising to the crescendo and the first sprays of blood and screams of the victims urged the other vampires to strike. She held his gaze, his oblivion shielding him from the gruesome deaths.

"Jean-Claude!" The older merchant screamed. "Jean-Claude! Run!"

Evanangela hissed and barred her fangs at him. All the color drained from his face as his body froze, rooting him to the spot. The older merchant's cries were muffled as Verseau tore into his neck. Blood burbling from his lips. His eyes trained on the apprentice.

"Papa!" He squealed as Evanangela lunged.

His body was taut, the fear tensing his muscles and made the blood spray as Evanangela broke the skin. She lapped up the blood and latched onto the vein. Her mind was aflame. So long she had been denied the pleasure of the hunt and now all the treasures of the world paled in comparison. She moaned as she suckled, the living blood filling her dead veins and making her heart plump.

Once the heart ceased to beat, Evanangela let the body drop to the floor. She looked from the apprentice to Verseau's kill, also discarded. Their eyes were still wide open, locked on one another. She felt a twinge of guilt, killing a son in front of his father. A terrible way to die. The blood in her mouth soured as she turned away. She wiped her face with a handkerchief, then flinched when she saw Amichemin.

"Go on, ma chérie. It is your turn," Verseau crooned.

Àmichemin nodded. Her hands were around the mortal's neck. His eyes bulging and his lips taking on a blue tint. Verseau motioned for Evanangela, and she stood at his side.

"Àmichemin stood guard while we feasted. Now, we must guard her." He whispered.

Evanangela stood fast, gazing out over the court. The cold reality splashed upon her, washing away the haze of the hunt. There were a pair of vampires that looked up from their kills, gazing at the trio, then darting their eyes away again. Fresh apprehension spiked her mind.

They were waiting to attack us when we were vulnerable while feeding! How can we stay in such a dangerous place for another night?

Àmichemin drained her kill with speed and brutal efficiency. After a few moments, she was standing next to them, scanning the court again. Verseau offered her a handkerchief. She took it and dabbed her mouth.

"Merci," she muttered.

The music softened, like a lullaby. In past feeds, the court often fell into a stupor, lounging about the halls, or into giggling fools romping in their apartments. But their hard glares contrasted with the soothing melody. One of the vampires straightened up, his eyes burning with hate.

"You keep us locked here like a menagerie of animals, and even resurrected your attack dog to keep us fenced in!" He shouted. "No more! There is no need for the hibernation when food lives just outside our doors! I say we take the village and our vengeance!"

Other members of the court began to cheer. A vixen stepped forward, standing beside the bold dissenter.

"You kill members of your own court to protect those vermin! We are above them. It's time we take back our power!"

More cheers erupted as the court began to mob together. Evanangela balked at the sudden change of mood. The guards began to shift, their gaze on Verseau, waiting for his signal. He stepped forward and held up his hand.

"You are short-sighted in your desire for revenge." His voice was calm, but his eyes revealed his disdain. "I do not protect those peasants. I am protecting us *from* them just as one does not disturb the bees' nest in order to avoid being stung. You think they will be content to sit in their village while you sleep? How many moonrises do you think you will survive before they storm the château and take your lives?"

The vampires and vixens looked at one another, whispering. Their faces drawn in concern. Evanangela could feel their shift from outrage to fear. Verseau was right, they desired power, but did not have the foresight to know what to do once they had it. He continued speaking, his voice firm and cold.

"Even if you were to avoid an attack, you might go and feast on those bastard villagers. And they shall satiate you for what? A month? Maybe two? What shall you do once the last woman and child of that wretched village is drained?"

The court was stunned into silence. They blinked at him, then glanced about at each other. Verseau lowered his hand. The guards regained their ease.

"The blood shortage is not a rouse or a means of control," he tilted his head, "I myself have adhered to the same rules. The plagues have decimated the mortal populations. Our food source is dwindling and slaughtering what's left of it will leave us to truly starve. The decision to hibernate was not easily made. It is indeed our last resort."

Murmurs rippled through the crowd. The tension slackened. Evanangela kept her gaze fixed on the window; her eyes on the moon to keep herself from shaking. Though the court was, for the moment, placated. She was sure it was only for the moment. Amichemin stood cold and distant at her side. Her arms crossed as she stared out over the court.

"The feed has concluded. Go now to your apartments for your final preparations. For tomorrow, we sleep. Bonne nuit."

The doors to the ballroom creaked open again and the attendants filed in and began disposing of the bodies. Vampires and vixens picked their way out into the hall. Some still sent nervous glances at the trio. Others seemed to seethe with cooled anger. Evanangela waited until the last of them had disappeared out the doors, then let out her breath all at once. She gulped the air, not realizing she had been holding her breath.

Amichemin put her hand on Evanangela's shoulder, but her eyes were glassy and far away. "It is not over yet, I'm afraid."

Verseau nodded and took their hands, kissing each in turn. "Be brave, mes fleurs. We shall live through this day. I swear it."

Chapter Thirty-One

When they arrived, Jacques was waiting outside Verseau's apartments. He bowed when he saw the trio.

"All has been made ready, Seigneur." Jacques whispered as they marched into the sitting room.

Verseau nodded. The door was locked, then Jacques led them into the bedroom. He produced a key from a chain round his neck and slipped it into a crack in the wall. The whine of rusty gears grinding jolted Evanangela from her morose thoughts. She gasped when Jacques pushed the wall and it revealed a doorway.

Jacques took one of the enchanted candles from the sconces and settled it into an old iron candleholder. He held it aloft and led them down the dank stone stairs.

"Mademoiselle Àmichemin and Mademoiselle Evanangela's coffins have already been loaded into the carriages. One trunk each of your belongings have also been packed away. We shall load Seigneur Verseau's coffin tomorrow night while you are performing the hibernation ceremony in the catacombs." He explained as they walked deeper into the château.

"What is this place?" Evanangela wondered aloud as she looked about into the gloom.

Verseau batted away an old cobweb. "We are in one of the secret passageways. The previous Seigneur was too proud to use it."

Àmichemin nodded. "This particular room is an underground vault used to temporarily hide the Seigneur. None of the court knows of its existence."

Evanangela ducked to avoid a jagged stalactite hanging from the ceiling. "Then how did you know of it?"

"*She* told me." Verseau whispered.

Memories of the young vampiress in the tapestries played through Evanangela's mind. She wondered at what the court was like when she was alive. Her thoughts were quashed when Jacques unlocked a wooden door bloated from water damage. The musty smell of mold made Evanangela sneeze. Àmichemin covered her nose with a handkerchief. Jacques lit the grey candles in the room with the enchanted candle. They too were enchanted with white flames.

"I will collect you once the last of the sun's rays have darkened past the horizon." Jacques bowed. "Bonne nuit."

Verseau nodded and Jacques locked the door behind him. Evanangela listened to his fading footsteps, then turned to the small, dingy room. He lifted the lid of a heavy coffin large enough to fit several vampires. She did not recognize the wood. It was dark and seemed to be lacquered with something to protect it from rot. Other than a few shelves carved into the stone walls and the candles, there was nothing else in the room.

"This reminds me of my first days." Àmichemin muttered as she cast off her dress.

He unbuttoned his jacket. "It is the first of many sacrifices that lie ahead I'm afraid."

Àmichemin shrugged. "We do what we must."

Evanangela unlaced the stays of her dress while listening to their disjointed conversation. The many conflicting thoughts and the rise and ebb of her anxiety had exhausted her. She could barely keep her eyes open. Verseau climbed into the coffin first. A cloud of dust puffed up from the old cushions. He waved them away with his hands.

"I can only hope our accommodations at the Mors will be better." Àmichemin scowled as she climbed in and settled into the crook of his arm.

Verseau kissed her forehead. "Not to worry, ma chère douleur, I have sent more letters to Master Étienne, and in exchange for our lands, and the villages and strongholds built upon them, we will be given our own wing at the Mors Ivoire's favorite stronghold, Le Palais des Loups."[1]

---

1 The Palace of Wolves.

Evanangela climbed into the coffin. He held out his free arm, ushering her inside. She snuggled against his chest as he rested his arm over her. It was larger than Verseau's coffin, but not nearly as comfortable. She yawned and closed her eyes.

Àmichemin stifled a yawn of her own. "How are we to be sure they will keep their promise once they have taken our lands?"

"We have always been strong allies in the past," Verseau's voice was low as the death-sleep was creeping over him. "And the Council will see to it the exchange is upheld."

Their words drifted away as the black void crept over Evanangela. The world blotted out as the sleep overtook her.

Booming knocks startled Evanangela awake. The lid of the coffin was drawn back. Jacques' face was set in a grim line, panic blazed in his eyes.

"Réveillez-vous!" His voice was strained.

Verseau sat up in the coffin, rubbing his face. "Is the court attempting the coup at last?"

Jacques shook his head. "Non, Seigneur, it is the peasants!"

"Quoi?" He flinched.

"There is an army of peasants advancing on the château. More than just the nearby village – hundreds of peasants! Perhaps even a thousand!" Jacques stepped back as Verseau climbed out of the coffin.

"Will the battlements hold?" Verseau began pulling on his breeches. "Do they have any weaponry?"

Jacques darted his eyes about, as if trying to remember. "They were still far off in the distance. The guards spotted them with their spyglasses. I am unsure."

Verseau nodded and began buttoning up his tunic. "It is time then. The siege will be a perfect distraction. We leave for the Mors Ivoire Court *now!*"

Evanangela gasped. "We are to leave the court to die?"

Àmichemin scoffed. "The guards were going to slaughter them once the Mors took control anyway. What does it matter if they die at the hands of unruly peasants instead?"

She reeled, "Can we not save them? I'm sure there are vampires still loyal to you!"

Verseau shook his head. "This is the way it must be. There is no way to know who is truly innocent, and who shall lie in wait. It is our lives or theirs."

They dressed quickly while Evanangela sat in the coffin, still in shock. Àmichemin tossed the stained lilac gown at her.

"Get dressed!" She barked, shaking her from her fearful thoughts. "Unless you would like to stay here and starve."

Evanangela pulled on the dress, her fingers fumbling with the stays. Verseau brushed her shaking hands away and helped her with the ties.

"It is all right, ma petite. Take a deep breath."

She took long deep breaths, her mind clearing as she did so. He kissed her on the forehead.

"You must keep your head, ma fleur. Our battle has begun."

Jacques led them back up the stone stairs. Verseau caught Àmichemin when she slipped on a patch of mildew. Together, they climbed back up to the stone door, which Jacques unlocked and pushed open. Verseau's enormous coffin was gone.

Evanangela clutched his arm. "Seigneur! Your coffin-!"

"Not to worry, Mademoiselle," Jacques whispered, "it has been loaded into the carriage."

She nodded and took another breath. They marched through to the sitting room where Jacques knocked three times on the door. Another three knocks answered on the other side. He opened the door, revealing one of the royal guards who poked his head in.

"Seigneur et Mademoiselles, the situation is dire," his voice was gruff, "the peasants have a makeshift catapult. They will be at the gate at any moment. What are your orders?"

Verseau nodded. "We shall surrender the château. Do not waste your lives on this lost cause. The guard shall escort us to the nearest Mors Ivoire outpost, Le Pavillon de Chasse au Sanglier.[2] See to it that the attendants are locked in Le Village du Sang. They will be protected there from the revolt until the Mors arrive to collect them."

The guard nodded. "As you wish, Seigneur."

He bowed his head, then galloped down the hall with his orders. Jacques motioned for them to follow. He locked the apartments, then led the way toward the stables.

"Ma famille is ready and waiting with the carriages," Jacques explained over his shoulder as they dashed through the halls, "All is ready."

A thunderous boom shattered the air. Evanangela tripped and fell as the entire château shook. Àmichemin was on her knees, her hands clamped over her ears, her eyes wild with terror. Verseau regained his footing, whipping his head about trying to find the source of the noise.

"Vite! Vite!" Jacques shouted over the din. "The siege has begun!"

Evanangela scrambled to her feet. She pulled on Àmichemin's arm. "Allons-y Àmichemin!"

Àmichemin writhed, trying to jerk her arm out of her grasp. "Non! Papa! Aidez-moi, Papa!"

Verseau pushed Evanangela aside and gathered up Àmichemin into his arms. He turned to Evanangela. "Don't stop running!"

She nodded and gathered up her skirts. Another boom shook the château. Àmichemin's screams echoed in the hall as she sobbed in Verseau's arms, her head bouncing as he ran. Evanangela tripped again, the force of the attack knocking her feet out from under her. She pushed against the wall, propelling herself forward to prevent her fall.

Screams filled the halls as vampires burst from their apartments. The cacoughany made Evanangela's ears ring until all she could hear was solid noise. Her eyes were trained on Verseau's back. He and Jacques pushed the stunned court members out of the way as they barreled down the hall. There was another boom, and this time, the smell of smoke curled into the château. Guttural roars blared over the screams of the court. A chant echoed from the ballroom, muffled by the west corridors.

2 The Boar Hunting Lodge

"Vive le Seigneur Dieu! Vive le Seigneur Dieu! Vive le Seigneur Dieu!"

Evanangela fought her body, willing it to keep moving as her mind screamed. It was the same peasants that had attacked them at Le Lac des Morts. Her chest heaved as she struggled to keep up and push aside her fear.

At last, a pack of three royal guards burst in from the adjacent hall. They ran ahead of Jacques, shoving courtiers out of the way. Some were knocked into the wall, others fell, scrambling to find their feet.

"Make way! Make way for the Seigneur!" They barked as they cleared the path ahead.

Evanangela's dead heart burned in her chest as her lungs sucked in air. The guards threw open the heavy wooden door that led out into the side courtyard. Two kept running, while one stood at the base of the stairs, ensuring they made it down unscathed. Before she could reach the guard, something grabbed the sash of her gown.

"Le Seigneur et ses chiennes s'enfuient!"[3]

A voice screeched in her ear as one of the vampires jerked her back into the doorway. The guard charged up the stairs and punched the vampire in the face. He grabbed Evanangela and pulled her down the stairs, her feet tripping as she tried to regain her footing.

Verseau was still up ahead, Àmichemin clutched tight in his arms. Evanangela was able to find the pace once more, keeping up with the guard as he held her hand tight. She could see the archway to the stables. The two guards were pulling up the gate.

Evanangela turned her head and looked back at the château. Vampires and vixens were chasing after them. Their hands outstretched like claws; their eyes wide with rage. Smoke billowed overhead. Another boom sounded along with the tinkling of broken glass.

The guard pulled her arm, nearly tearing it out of its socket. He gathered her up into his arms and sped forward. Verseau crossed the threshold of the gate, the top spikes of the bar just grazing his hair. They began to lower it as the guard approached.

She screamed as the guard ducked, rushing them through as the guards pulled themselves round the pillars, letting the gate crash down

3 The Lord and his bitches are escaping!

272

behind them. They had broken the mechanisms used for raising the gate. The vampires crashed into the metal bars. It clanked as they rattled it, their hisses and screams spurring them on.

Her ears perked at the sound of horses stamping and snorting. A tiny flame of hope ignited in her chest. Her body hurt from how tight the guard was holding her, her head bouncing as he raced forward. There were several attendants Evanangela did not recognize. They were standing at attention near several carriages along with a retinue of the royal guards. The drivers were already on the carriages, and the footmen scrambled to open the doors as they saw the group approach.

"Vite! Vite!" Verseau bellowed as he alighted into one of the carriages.

Screams erupted behind them. Evanangela contorted herself in the guard's arms, looking over his shoulder. A wave of peasants was spilling out of the château into the side courtyard. They slaughtered the vampires against the gate, driving stakes through their hearts, decapitating them with farming sickles, and riddling their faces and bodies with holes with their knives and pitchforks. One of the peasants held a head aloft, screeching in triumph.

"Ici la princesse!" The guard shouted.

Suddenly, Evanangela was flying through the air, as the guard had tossed her. Verseau caught Evanangela, pulling her into the carriage. Àmichemin was already inside, curled against the cushions, her eyes wide and her arms wrapped tight around her body as she rocked back and forth while muttering.

The carriage door slammed shut and the horses neighed as the drivers urged them to gallop. Evanangela tumbled to the floor of the carriage as it lurched forward. The thundering hooves of the horses drowned out the shouts and screams. She pulled herself upright onto one of the seats and peered out the window. The stables disappeared behind them and opened up into the grey skies above the west lawn.

Panic flooded her as she beheld the bright first rays of the sunrise. Before she could scramble to find the coffin in the floor, the carriage turned down the lane, and she saw it was still night, but the light was from the blazing orange flames towering atop the château. Evanangela gasped, covering her mouth as she watched her home burn. As the carriage turned further, she could see the line of four carriages hurrying behind theirs. A retinue of guards on horseback surrounded the carriages, twelve that Evanangela could see. Dark figures raced after the carriages, but they could not keep up on foot.

"Ne regardez pas." Verseau's voice was quiet, "Come, sit with me."

Evanangela tore her gaze away from the window. Her body was numb as she curled against his side. He drew her into his lap, his arms around her, shaking with silent sobs.

She did not know what to say and her voice was gone. Her mind was on a loop of the roaring flames and the vampires being slaughtered at the gate. Evanangela turned her gaze on Àmichemin who was still rocking in her seat, her eyes unblinking.

"What about Àmichemin?" She whispered.

Verseau shook his head. "She is lost to her old life. She was turned during a vampire raid not unlike this and watched her entire family die. We must wait for her mind to return."

Evanangela's heart sank as she watched the most powerful being she knew babble like an invalid. She turned away, burying her face in Verseau's tunic. Her eyes burned as her veins were empty and afforded her no tears. His heart was still, no heartbeat to soothe her. She breathed deep, sucking in his faint scent. As her breathing slowed, she realized the screams had stopped. The only sounds were the thunder of horses' hooves and the rumble of the carriage wheels on the road. She looked out the window again and saw guards on horseback riding alongside the carriage.

Jacques had kept his word. All had been ready, and not a moment to spare. Evanangela relived the jarring nightfall over and over again, her mind trying to make sense of the chaos. Her exhausted body soon gave way to her first real slumber since her turning. She relaxed in Verseau's arms, her eyes closing and her mind drifting off to nothingness.

Chapter Thirty-Two

"Wake up, ma petite."

Evanangela stirred as a gentle voice broke through her disjointed dreams. She opened her eyes and saw she was still in Verseau's arms.

"We are safe," Verseau kissed her forehead, "but we must get into the coffin before the sunrise."

She turned and looked out the window at the greying sky. They were on an open road, dotted only by trees and the low stone walls of rugged farmland. Their pace had slowed, causing the carriage to sway, rather than jostle and bump.

It was then that she realized they were in Verseau's personal carriage. It was much bigger than her personal carriage and took a team of eight horses to pull, rather than the standard four. The cushions were burgundy and embroidered with the Nacre Court crest. She traced it with her fingertip, melancholy spreading in her heart as she realized that crest was now meaningless.

Her body was stiff and sore as she unfolded herself to crouch on the floor. She looked up at Àmichemin. Her eyes were downcast, and her body limp and leaning against the wall.

"Àmichemin-?"

Verseau lifted the trapdoor in the floor, revealing his coffin. "She will be fine."

Evanangela climbed down into the coffin, a sigh curling up from her lips as the plush cushions embraced her body. Verseau disappeared from sight, but she could hear his voice coaxing Àmichemin.

"Come now, ma chérie, I'm here." He crooned.

He reappeared with Àmichemin and helped lower her into the coffin next to Evanangela. Verseau then clambered in after them. Àmichemin latched onto his arm as he closed the coffin lid. Evanangela stared up into the darkness, her body feeling too rested for the death-sleep to take over just yet. She could hear them rustling beside her. In all the excitement, she had forgotten about her hunger. Her heart burned in her chest, but the pain was a pinprick compared to the booms of the catapult and the heat of the inferno.

She understood what Àmichemin had meant, about becoming hardened by the court. She had begged Verseau to somehow save the innocent vampires amidst the defectors. And yet, when she found herself on the other side of the gate, all she had felt was relief that it was them instead of her trapped with the horde of peasants. She squeezed her eyes shut, the guilt boiling in her stomach.

That could have been me. Had Àmichemin not plucked me from that churchyard, I would have been a common vixen. That could have been me.

Her thoughts went round and round, until the void took her at last, ceasing her tirade. When she woke again, she could see Verseau sitting up in the coffin, the lid open. She pulled herself up, sitting next to him.

"Verseau, ça va?"

He shook his head, but said nothing. Àmichemin was still asleep, her body rigid. Evanangela hauled herself out of the coffin and onto the seat. Her dress felt tight and itchy. It was stained with blood and sweat. She peered about the carriage, but did not see anything resembling a traveling trunk and resigned herself to the soiled clothing.

Àmichemin stirred, stretching and sitting up. Her eyes were still glassy with sleep.

"Où sommes-nous?[1]"

Verseau turned to her. Evanangela could see the pain radiating from his eyes.

"We are safe, ma chère. We are on our way to Le Pavillon de Chasse au Sanglier."

She rubbed her head as she gathered her bearings. "Et le château?"

He shook his head and turned away. Àmichemin sighed and gathered up her skirts, climbing up onto the carriage seat. Verseau sat for a few moments before leaving the coffin and shutting the lid and

---

1 Where are we?

trapdoor. His shoulders slumped and his hands dropped into his lap. Àmichemin looked out the window.

"The Nacre Court is no more." She whispered to no one.

Her words cut Evanangela. Though it had been her home for less than a year's time, she found the loss devastating.

"I lived through *nine* coups and this one finally shatters the court." Àmichemin growled as she glared out the window. "Ungrateful bastards."

They huddled together as the carriage slowed, then came to a halt. Evanangela perked up as the door swung open, revealing the footman and a pair of guards.

"We have arrived at Le Pavillon de Chasse au Sanglier, Seigneur et Mademoiselles." One of the guards bowed and gestured to the building in the gloom.

The footman helped them down from the carriage. Evanangela wobbled as she found her footing. One of the guards took her elbow to help steady her.

"Bonsoire mes amis!" A cheerful voice called.

A short vampire strode toward them. He bowed once he was a pace away from Verseau.

"It is wonderful to meet at last, Monsieur," he grinned.

Verseau flinched at the demoted title, then bowed his head to show respect. "We thank you, Master Étienne, for coming to our aid. It has been a tumultuous journey."

He nodded, his face grave with sympathy. "It has been three-hundred years since a province was lost. I suspect more will go the same way as the blood shortage worsens."

Master Étienne gestured for them to follow and led them inside the hunting lodge. The guards remained outside. Evanangela shivered. Jacques and his family were still waiting in their carriage. She looked around at the unfamiliar guards that stood at attention in the entryway. In that moment, she yearned for Gabriel as her attendant once more. She felt alone, despite Verseau and Àmichemin walking beside her.

"Le Seigneur Tristan is a noble and generous lord," Master Étienne tilted his head, "it pains us that you had to forsake your court and your lands, and to seek sanctuary in our court. I can assure you, le Seigneur is happy to accommodate you, so long as you understand your place as new fixtures in his court."

Verseau bowed his head. "We understand. We have no ill will against Seigneur Tristan and only seek to live our nights together. The banality of ruling a new court does not interest me. I am tired and simply wish for the comfort of my consorts."

"Bien, bien!" Master Étienne's face relaxed and his smile became more genuine. "Anyone would understand such feelings. And as such, the Nacre Court has always been very loyal in their alliance with the Mors Ivoire Court. And the gift of the whole of the Nacre Province certainly seals your fealty."

"I am at Seigneur Tristan's command," Verseau bowed his head again, "On the single condition that he does not interfere with my consorts."

Master Étienne gave a solemn nod. "Of course. Seigneur Tristan has consorts aplenty. No reason to lure one of yours away. Though, fresh flowers do cause a stir about court. I am sure you will enjoy the attention while it lasts."

Verseau did not respond, and Master Étienne did not hesitate to fill the empty space.

"Le Palais des Loups is two weeks travel from here. We have sent for provisions to be provided along the way. It is lucky I have been posted here for the time being in our ongoing negotiations with your court." He glanced about the lodge and wrinkled his nose. "I'm glad to leave. Such a stuffy place."

He glanced out the window. "The night is still deep. We will set out immediately. Unless you require time to rest?"

Verseau shook his head. "No, we are eager to put as much distance between us and those loathsome villagers as possible."

Master Étienne signaled the guards. "Then we shall be off. Le Seigneur is eager to meet with you."

"As am I." Verseau bowed his head.

The guards led them out of the hunting lodge, and locked it behind them, settling large stone pillars in front of the doors. Evanangela hurried back to the carriage. The footman opened the door, and the trio clambered back inside. Master Étienne and his guards circled to the back of the hunting lodge, to the stables.

Evanangela fidgeted as they waited for their progress to begin anew. She glanced over at Amichemin. Her eyes lacked their mischievous spark, and her mouth was set in a hard line. The madness was gone, and all that was left was dour emptiness. Evanangela turned away and gazed out the window. The path led along the edge of a dense forest. She could see the glinting eyes of woodland creatures staring back at her.

The silent stillness pressed on Evanangela until her ears were ringing. She tore away from the window and leaned back against the cushions, staring up at the ceiling. Her heart squeezed in her chest as her empty veins contracted in vain. At long last, the carriage jerked forward and began to move. The pace was that of when they had gone on progress to La Maison de Printemps, rather than the breakneck speed they had gone to escape the château.

Their first stop was at a small outpost, nothing more than a barracks and a training ground. A small group of guards were doing drills. They stopped and stood at attention when the vampires exited their carriages. Master Étienne called out for a man named Bastien, who then appeared from the barracks with three other men in tow, all were carrying crates, which were loaded into the carriages.

"What are these?" Verseau gestured at the crates.

Master Étienne's face soured. "Bull's blood, I'm afraid. It's standard for travel in the court."

Evanangela grimaced at the memory of choking down the bull's blood at the maison. Verseau smoothed her hair and gave her a reassuring smile.

"We are alive, ma petite, we can survive a bit of discomfort."

They had already been traveling for three days' time, and Evanangela's empty veins were burning. Jacques had prepared them with bladders filled with mortal blood, but those had been drained after the second day. She settled back into the carriage as Master Étienne gave Verseau instructions.

"We still have nine days' time until we reach le palais. You each are rationed two bladders per night. We shall be making a stop tomorrow night to change the horses at one of the outpost stables, and once again in four days' time. Seigneur Tristan is very strict on travel regulations. There is absolutely no mortal blood consumed outside of le palais or any of the lodges or maisons."

Verseau nodded. "Bien. Understood."

The trio suffered through the remainder of the journey. Only their hunger and empty hearts pushing them to drink the foul swill. One such night, Àmichemin cursed as she tossed her empty bladder back into the crate.

"Ugh! I suspect *Seigneur* Tristan is trying to weaken us so he can destroy us on his doorstep."

Verseau shook his head. "He would not go to all this effort. He would have left us to die at the château. Though I do agree, this might be a bit of fun at our expense."

Evanangela nodded, grimacing as she drained her share of bull's blood. The silence was not as tense as it had been when they were locked in Verseau's apartments at the château. Evanangela's worries of turning into a bickering vixen began to melt away as Verseau teased Àmichemin, goading her into a mock fight to lift her spirits. Their company had been a comfort, rather than a burden. Her thoughts drifted to the lonely nights she had spent on progress with Gabriel. She looked up at the stars that floated above the dark trees.

Can you see me now, Gabriel? Do you regret granting my wish?

On the twelfth nightfall, Evanangela peered out the window. Out of the gloom, a great fence with severe spikes grew up from the horizon. As they drew closer, she could see the western wing of the palais. It was three floors, while Le Château d'Astucieux had only two floors. She marveled at the sprawling estate and sumptuous lawns dotted with lush trees and flowers.

"Lovely, isn't it?" Verseau whispered in her ear.

She nodded, a twinge of sadness striking her heart. "It shan't be home though, not like the château."

He tilted her chin, forcing her to turn away from the window and look at him. "It will be, ma choupinette. This is our new home. So long as the three of us are together, we shall always be at home."

The carriages pulled into the large circular avenue that led up to the palais. A herd of attendants spilled out and stood at attention as the footmen began opening the carriage doors. The younger attendants led the horses away, while the older attendants began unpacking the luggage from the carriages. Evanangela spotted Jacques and his family. They were chatting with an elder attendant, nodding and gesturing with smiles on their faces. The guards filed away to the palais barracks. In all the flurry of activity, Evanangela felt as if she were frozen, looking on at herself. She snapped to attention when she heard Master Étienne's voice.

"Allons-y! Seigneur Tristan is waiting!"

A series of groans further startled Evanangela. She turned and saw a team of attendants following them with a coffin. It was Verseau's first love. Evanangela gasped.

He did manage to save her! I am happy for him; but then why does it make me sad?

Master Étienne led them through the grand doorway of the palais. It was much taller than the château and the ceiling had mosaics of the different seasons painted on them. On the walls were large portraits of various vampires, similar to the ones at the château. As they walked further in, she could hear hushed murmurs.

Once they reached the first doorway in the hall, Master Étienne stopped and gestured to an attendant standing just outside. He nodded and cleared his throat.

"Presenting Master Étienne, Monsieur Verseau, Mademoiselle Àmichemin, Mademoiselle Evanangela, et La Petite Mademoiselle Violette!"

His voice echoed into the massive receiving room. Evanangela flinched upon hearing Violette's name. They entered, the coffin still trailing behind them. A sea of faces lined the walkway up to Seigneur Tristan's dais. He sat upon a throne, as if he were a king. Evanangela began to wonder if the Nacre Court had been a lesser province in comparison.

Seigneur Tristan stood and held out his arms wide. "Ah! Mes amis, I'm grateful to see you made the journey here."

Verseau bowed before the dais. Evanangela and Àmichemin curtsied deep. As they rose, Seigneur Tristan gave them a playful smirk.

"You are now without a court and seek sanctuary in my palais. How do I know you shall not defect and seek to usurp me?"

A hush fell over the room. Verseau draped his arms around Evanangela and Àmichemin's waists, pulling them close. He then gave a warm look to Violette's coffin as the attendants settled it to the far left of the seats.

"This is all the court I require, Seigneur Tristan. I am glad to be rid of the crown and all its weight and worries."

Seigneur Tristan laughed and gestured toward a row of seats to the left of his throne. Several vampiresses sat in seats to the right. They raked their eyes up and down each of them while hiding their faces behind black and gold fans.

"Sit, sit, s'il vous plaît!"

The trio stood in front of their seats, waiting until Seigneur Tristan sat back down. They seated themselves and he began to clap. The court met him with a thunderous applause.

"Regardez ma famille!" He cheered, laughing as the court continued to applaud him. He turned and winked at Verseau. The trio follow suit and clapped as well.

Evanangela took the opportunity to whisper to Àmichemin through the clapping. "Is that all? We're safe now as a part of his inner court?"

Àmichemin laughed, then whispered without moving her lips. "Oh non, ma chère petite. Look out at their jealous faces. Prepare yourself. We shall never be safe again."

The End.

Printed in Great Britain
by Amazon

23503066R00159